ECHOES

IN THE GREY

Book 2 in the Ross 128 First Contact Trilogy

DAVID ALLAN HAMILTON

DeeBee

ECHOES IN THE GREY
Copyright © 2019 by David Allan Hamilton.

For information contact :
davidallanhamilton00@gmail.com
http://www.davidallanhamilton.com

ISBN: 9781896794228

First Edition: March 2019

10 9 8 7 6 5 4 3 2 1

For my Dad

"The first envoy to a world always comes alone. One alien is a curiosity. Two are an invasion."
   Ursula Le Guin

"Beauty is unbearable, drives us to despair, offering us for a minute the glimpse of an eternity that we should like to stretch out over the whole of time."
   Albert Camus

ONE

Saturday, June 7, 2092

Titanius Space Resources Lunar Geophysical Lab

Mare Crisium, Luna

Kate

THE TIP OF HER POCKET KNIFE scraped over ancient scars and recent cuts, carving a mesh of trails across her chest where her breasts would have been, leaving dark tracks and pimples of deep red blood in their wake. Kate inhaled, closing her eyes, sensing the only thing left she could feel: intense, personal relief. Approaching 30 years old. There were no prizes.

Mary Atteberry, 17 going on 30, stirred on the upper bunk where she dozed. The lab engineers created this geek's dream habi-tat to house six scientists and technicians at a time, but in reality, only a few ever stayed more than a few days. The isolation, danger, and nature of the work—lunar geophysical surveys—chased away most worthy and sane people.

Except for Kate Braddock.

The rhythm of Mary's breathing stuttered as she woke up from her snooze, knocking one of her treasured books on the floor. Kate brushed the coagulating drops of blood from her chest and lowered her form-fitting shirtskin over the mess. Then she sat up, hid the knife, and pulled on her jacket before rising and padding over to the bank of powerful computers.

"What's it look like, Kate?" Mary yawned and swept the golden hair from her face.

Kate hovered over two large monitors in front of the work-table. "Still running data from the last survey. It's weird, though."

"How come?"

"Should've finished a while ago. This array wasn't massive. Just a routine shallow-crust tomographic study."

Mary inhaled a deep breath and swung her legs over the edge of the bunk. Then she hopped down, bouncing lightly in the low-g of the Moon, picked up her Ray Bradbury book, and drew a couple gels of water from the biofeeder. She padded over beside Kate in her socks, handed her one of the packs, and squeezed a gulp of her own.

After inspecting the filtered data on-screen for a moment, Mary said, "There's jammage in this area." She pointed to the surface coordinates of the survey at the top of the monitor. Kate grim-aced. The problem with these surveys near the *Mare Marginis* on the eastern limb was that if anything went wrong, it's a

2

hell of a hike on the LunaScootas to get back out there and fix whatever needs fixing, then running it all again.

"Let's wait and see what the filtering algorithm comes up with," Kate said. "It may be nothing, just some data glitch or anomalous readings from the strong magnetic fields there."

"Still," Mary said, "it doesn't seem to be anything systematic with the survey itself. See, Kate? The comp power focuses on that one spot, like there's something in that location the program can't resolve, so it keeps going."

Kate turned to her and smiled. "You sure learned the fundamentals of this work quickly." She chuckled and squeezed Mary's forearm. "Come on, let's have a look at tomorrow's survey lines." She pulled up a lunar topographic map on another set of monitors, and they reviewed the coordinates and variables of the next series of near-surface seismic arrays. Luna was a desolate, curious place, but it was also strategically important for its minerals, especially the extent of Helium-3, water, and metals. Fortunately, international treaties limiting the amount of strip mining and ore extraction had been established for decades. Now, resource operations on the Moon were all automated, and highly-regulated, and all out of sight on the far side.

The Titanius Space Resources Corporation was the only official outfit with a science lab on the Moon's surface. It won the contract to perform routine geophysical surveys in the quest to locate and map new deposits and potential future mining sites. Data from the studies Kate performed were critical to Titanius's clients, which included national and continental governments, private sector interests, and military units.

As they revisited their next lines, a soft chime indicated the data analysis was complete.

Kate nodded to the large monitors. "Shall we check what that hiccup was about?" She pulled up various layers of information on the screen, showing surface coordinates, the survey lines, and the shallow-crust tomographic image. The data covered a depth of only a few hundred meters, but there was something clear just underneath the dusty surface causing an odd-shaped anomaly. *We couldn't have missed an object that close, Kate thought, so why didn't we see it out there?*

"The resolution sucks with this setup," Mary said. "We can't resolve anything less than 10 meters wide or deep, at least not with any confidence." Kate leaned closer to the monitor, zeroing in on the green and blue seismic wave patterns and the anomaly that grew more defined as the dregs of data ran to their completion.

"Doesn't seem natural, does it." A statement, not a question. Kate's heart pounded louder in her chest.

"Come on, suit up. Let's have a look at this . . . whatever the hell it is."

They exited the lab through the main airlock, unplugged the heavy charging cables from the LunaScootas, and tore off toward the *Mare Marginis*—a boundary between the light and dark sides of the Moon on the eastern limb where they'd established the seismic array. The lunar day had barely dawned, so virtually all of the 600 km journey would be in darkness. At top speed, the single-person workhorse haulers would reach the zone in just over an hour. As they hurtled closer to the target coordinates, Kate reflected on what this anomaly could be. She had seen nothing as well-defined as this in her five solitary years on Luna. Sure, there were odd readings from time to time, but these typically resolved themselves as random outliers or some malfunction or noise and dust in the geo-phones.

But this one was different.

Larger.

Artificial.

The two said little as their scooters flew on, kicking up surface spray as they screamed across the moonscape. Sunlight greeted them as they approached the site, and everything appeared in order. The array, now quiet since the automated thumper had timed out, looked normal. They checked the lines, looking for objects that might have caused the data anomaly, but found nothing.

"Let's head to that volcanic slope." Kate pointed to a rough incline about a hundred meters away. "I want to get a better view."

They whirred up the short hill and Kate eased her scooter down on its two nacelles in a smooth patch of dust. She dismounted and surveyed the entire area. The cause of the anomaly, assuming it wasn't a malfunction in the software, did not appear anywhere on the surface.

"Infrared spectrum lock," Kate said, and the images on her helmet visor shifted as her viewer panned through the ultraviolet EM band. Nothing. The whole field was exactly as it should be, precisely as—

"Are you seeing this?" Mary's audio crackled as she waved to their right at an area near the edge of the array grid. "Something in the infrared range. That shadowy patch over there."

Kate turned and followed Mary's arm where she pointed to the surface below. A dark blue image emerged from the dust, and as she adjusted the visual filter embedded in her visor, the object resolved into a perfect geometric shape. A small, oval, charcoal grey body appeared, twenty meters long, she guessed, five meters wide, and expanding another few meters near its center.

"What is that ... *thing*?" Mary now looked straight into Kate's eyes through the helmet.

And Kate knew.

She understood Mary was thinking the same: that this was no random occurrence, no outlier. A little over six years ago, she and Jim had both observed the blip on a screen; confusing data scrolling by at the Mount Sutro transmitter site in San Francisco, suggesting a vessel en route to Earth traveling faster than the speed of light.

"Kate?"

Fear suddenly cut deep into her bones . . . a steadying horror that rooted itself in the fibers of her soul as she realized the frightening *thought* had become the terrifying *thing*.

"Come on, let's get the hell out of here."

"But—"

"Now!"

Kate climbed the LunaScoota, swung her leg across the flight seat, and buckled herself in. Mary scrambled back to hers, and within seconds they tore off, blowing past the seismic array at full throttle toward the lab. Kate grimaced and bit the inside of her lip hard until the comforting ferric sting of blood hit her tongue.

This could mean only one thing.

Only one.

They had come.

TWO

Kate

WHORLS OF MOON DUST KICKED UP FROM the racing scooters and floated momentarily, suspended in the lunar vacuum like dandelion seeds in dark flight. Half the trip passed before her heart resumed its normal rhythm. Fear of the alien ship gave way to panic, and Kate realized how fortunate she was that the return voyage allowed her to process the madness in her mind and keep her emotions well-hidden from Jim Atteberry's daughter. She'd learned over the years working in space that anxiety could be deadly. It sucked up oxygen reserves; caused bad decision-making. And Nature's cold equations, in their own immutable form, did not care.

Kate and Mary approached the lunar lab, down-throttled, and slowed to a rest beside the habitat's powerbanks. Kate dismounted first and plugged her machine into the recharger. Then she did the same to Mary's before the scooter engine had even powered down.

"You were pretty quiet." Mary glanced at her, eyes full of questions. "What got you so spooked out there?"

Kate ambled away from the powerbank and gazed across the desolate landscape. Perhaps this was the ship they tracked years ago at Mount Sutro. Or, it could be something else. She adjusted the audio in her helmet and, while scanning the horizon, said, "Do you remember what happened that night?"

"At the transmitter site?"

"Yeah. Your mom took you into hiding before her soldiers put an end to the only functioning subspace radio on the planet." She turned to face Mary still sitting on her scooter. "And do you recall what happened when we later reassembled at that old school house?"

Mary dismounted and joined her. "Sure. Bits and pieces, anyway. Dad talked a lot about the aliens—the *Rossians* he called them—and how they could arrive any day and we'd have no way to contact them."

"Exactly."

"Do you believe that's an alien ship in the dust?"

Kate felt a dull ache rise in her neck. "I do. It's likely the one Jim heard, and that the TSA detected from the Ross 128 star system." She faced Mary. "I also think we have to get the hell off this rock as soon as possible." She bounded toward the lab access port.

"Just like that? Without investigating that object?"

They entered the hatchway. "See, if that is the Rossian ship, it means there's concrete evidence we're not alone in the universe. Think about it. You and I are ill-equipped to deal with that." Thoughts of cautionary First Contact protocols raced through her head, along with international squabbles over who should reach out to the aliens, and who would secure their technology.

Mary hesitated before saying, "Well, before going all neural, maybe we should confirm what it is before calling headquarters. Let's get inside and check that data."

Kate considered it, then agreed. The airlock cycled through pressurizing and depressurizing to eliminate as much ambient dust as possible. When the safe light turned green, they opened the latch to the main lab and removed their helmets. Kate slipped out of her sleek envirosuit and hung it up before helping Mary remove hers. Even though these suits were lighter and more flexible than anything in history, they still required practice and experience to man-ipulate. After she stored the envirosuits, Kate plugged them in and clicked fresh oxygen canisters into their slots.

The two women sat at the main workstation. Images of the array site continued scrolling across one of the large monitors. "There," Kate said as an image of the mysterious object appeared. Mary paused the images and adjusted the focus, then tuned the filter to delineate the anomaly from the rest of the environment.

"Why there?" Kate asked, "And why now?"

Mary touched the viewscreen, optimizing the filtering parameters to improve the image resolution as much as possible. "I'd like to know if it's the ship you and Dad saw years ago, because if it isn't, then what?"

Kate stood, stretched, and paced around the lab, wandering between the computer consoles, powerbanks, and living quarters to the right. She'd seen a lot of peculiar things in her former career as a Spacer, working on orbiting satellites and in numerous toxic radiation zones surrounding automated manufacturing facilities. But alien technology, let alone an alien ship, was poles apart. A riot of emotions swept through her as she remembered Jim's great desire to share everything with the world, the Terran Science Academy's long-range search for extraterrestrial life, and her own desperate fear of the unknown. Paralysis was close, she knew, hovering like a shadow.

"Everything okay?"

Mary squeezed her arm and that brought the room back into focus. "Yeah, this is a lot to digest, you know?" Kate returned to the workstation and opened a new project folder, then accessed the security protocols in the network, and encrypted it.

"What's that for?"

"It's precautionary. Jim and I disagree somewhat on how to handle aliens. He's a *mi casa es su casa* no secrets person. I'm not. And the UN Protocol on First Contact is pretty clear about keeping these things quiet until the international community has a chance to process it all." The transferring files zipped into the hidden directory.

"Aren't we supposed to validate the findings?"

Kate's fingers danced across the viewscreen as she continued cleaning the data. "Yes, that's part of it, but the key is to keep such intelligence quiet. No need to alarm people. The more important reason for subterfuge is to be unnoticed by extra-terrestrials." Kate looked into Mary's eyes. "Just in case they don't come in peace."

The computer chimed when the last of the raw data files had transferred. At this point, no official record of the seismic array findings or the discovery of an alien ship existed. Kate stored all the information on an external memory tube.

Mary smiled. "You are a super cautious type, aren't you?"

She looked up from her screen. "Doesn't hurt to keep things to ourselves while we sort this out a bit."

"What do you mean? I thought you wanted to leave the Moon?"

Kate swung around on her stool until she faced Mary head on and folded her hands in her lap. "I do. This is the last place I want to be right now." She sighed. "But, there are lots of questions surrounding that object. Like, is it the ship we detected from Ross 128 back in 2085? If so, why land on Luna? Is it manned? What are their intentions? How long has it been here? And on and on." The computer churned, processing data in the background. "I'm scared to death about what that thing is, but we can't evac without providing Titanius a damn good reason." She scratched her chest. "Doing that could be worse in terms of the Protocol."

"We should tell someone about it," Mary said. "Like my Dad."

Kate chuckled. "Yeah, old Jim would love that! Perhaps someday, but not yet." Her voice grew darker, more serious. "Look, if we speak to anyone about what we've seen, all space-faring nations and corporations would surround this place, each one of them either trying to blow it up, or take its technology, or both. Anything FTL, whether subspace comms or travel, is the new gold. The first to claim it, owns us. All of us."

"It sounds so creepy, like, surely not everyone is in space for their own profit."

Kate smiled and leaned back. "No, not everybody I suppose." She paused. "I'm not."

"Me neither. My dad wouldn't be."

Kate frowned and pulled up a library of survey methods on the other monitor and searched through the titles until she stumbled across one she never dreamt would be any use on the Moon: *Methodologies for the Detection of Organic Life in Anaerobic Environments.* She downloaded it to Mary's tablet.

"This is more for microbes, isn't it?" Mary scanned the abstract.

"Well, we'll have to adapt it for the ship, but I think it might be useful."

Kate set the article aside and scanned the titles for other ideas. Establishing the ground penetrating radar parameters for higher resolution mapping was a priority, along with conducting VLF and magnetometer surveys to see if there was anything in the Moon's crust that could have attracted the ship there. After additional searching, she found an essay on increasing the sensitivity of the Titanius geophones.

"Are you going to use those as hearing aids?" Mary quipped.

"Sure am. We need to gather some fundamental information on this vessel before we tell anyone about it. Make sense?"

"I guess."

Kate sighed, more a release of her own internal fear and tension than frustration. "What humans should the Rossians contact first? Greedy terran leaders, corporate exploiters, mercenaries . . . or us?"

Mary remained silent, then looked up. "Sounds right when you put it that way. We can trust ourselves."

Relief spread over Kate's face. She reached over and squeezed Mary's shoulder. "Yes, we can. Now come on, let's grab a bite to eat before we design the next surveys."

Mary pulled herself up. "Promise me something, Kate?" She looked at her with wide eyes.

"What is it?"

"If we find out they're hostile and a real danger to Earth, promise me you'll tell my Dad right away?"

Kate smiled. Mary's love for her father reminded her of the times she and Jim took long walks together across the City College campus, not talking much, but comfortable in each other's company, nonetheless. A sudden twinge of deep shame stabbed at her gut.

"I promise. You have my word."

THREE

Kate

TEN HOURS LATER, KATE AWOKE TO THE annoying incoming message alarm on the comms system from the Titanius engineering team in New York. She scratched her eyes, crawled out of the bunk, and crept over to the main panel. She pressed the audio only channel and cleared her throat.

"New York, this is the Lunar Geophysical Lab. Good morning." She paused. In a couple of seconds, the science and engineering bay at Titanius's headquarters responded. Kate listened as she poured herself a tea from the biofeeder and popped her daily anti-rad pills.

"Ah, hello Kate . . . Stan here . . . I guess it is morning for you. Listen, sorry to rattle your cage like this, but we were expecting the data download from that seismic survey you ran a couple days ago and, well, God's eyes you know how it is here. Everyone wants everything yesterday." The satellite's repeater relay clicked, indicating the terran transmission had stopped. She let the radio carrier drop. *Ka-chunk.*

Kate sipped her tea. "I do, Stan, but here's the thing. We had a ton of noise in the array and it corrupted the data. Nothing serious, but extensive. So most of what we got was garbage, despite filtering the crap out of it, and bottom line, we'll have to run the survey again."

She held the cup under her nose and closed her eyes. She liked Stan. He was the friendlier of the two techs she spoke with. Talked about his family a lot. Cracked jokes. The other one, Dana, was a hag.

"Sorry to hear that, but I understand. Were you able to track down the problem?"

"Mary and I are heading back out there in a couple hours. I'll have a better idea for you then, but it must be a glitch in the seismic router, given how extensive the noise is."

"Okay, sounds good. And we're here to help you any way we can. I could tie our computers into your system and boost processing power, if you like. Just say the word."

Kate turned her head and saw Mary sitting on the upper bunk in her underwear and tee-shirt, swinging her legs back and forth. "Thanks Stan, but we got this under control. I'll check in again once we've solved the issue. Lunar Geophysical Lab out." She ended the transmission.

Mary yawned and hopped down. She stumbled to the biofeeder, grabbed a water gel and snorted. "They're an anxious lot."

"They are," Kate said matter-of-factly, "but their contract requires almost real-time, simultaneous delivery of results to client subscribers. It's why Clayton Carter and his precious Titanius are as rich as they are and can afford to build a resource company here in space." She pulled up the lab's monitoring program and reviewed the habitat's environmental parameters.

"Everything look okay?"

"Yeah. The engineers built this to last a hundred years. It's more solid than a nuclear waste site." Kate had grown accustomed to the lab functioning properly. In her time there, she had had no issues with the operational systems, the integrity of the habitat itself, or any of the computer equipment. Still, she treated Nature here with deep respect. Humans require oxygen, and you can't just open a window to get it.

"The only problems I've ever had involved a couple of geophones affected by dust, and one of the scooter batteries needed replacing." Kate drew a protein package from the biofeeder and unwrapped it. "Still, we take no chances here. Everything's backed up. There are redundant life support systems everywhere."

"Yeah, I remember Esther Tyrone briefing me on all that before I came here." Mary pulled on her blue form-fitting lab skins. "I had to memorize every safety protocol ever written in the history of the universe. No exaggeration." She smiled.

"She was after me too about keeping you safe from harm. I think she likes you. In fact, I figured she and your dad would, you know . . ."

Mary smirked and busied herself by pulling out their envirosuits from the rollers in the storage bin. Esther had a thing for Jim and vice versa a few years back, and Kate expected them to get together. But they never did, and the topic wasn't open for discussion.

"Let's suit up and hoof it to the site, shall we?"

16

THEY LOADED UP ONE SCOOTER WITH VARIOUS pieces of equipment, including two handheld VLF units, paired magnetometers, and a portable Langdon GPR imaging machine on bubble wheels. They lashed these to the box-like storage compartment behind the pilot's seat, then packed extra oxygen canisters in case they needed more time at the site.

Kate clamped a secondary tool kit onto Mary's scooter and told her to lead the way out. She'd follow closely and watch for anything rattling loose and falling off. It was one of those things you did on the Moon because if she lost gear out here, it could disappear forever, despite precautionary radio-tagging everything and following established routes. Taking chances wasn't in her DNA.

Mary fired up her LunaScoota, buckled the safety harness, and whirred away from the lab's machine shed. Seconds later Kate joined her, maintaining an easy distance behind. They kept their suit-to-suit radio comms open for the duration of the trip, and she listened to Mary's soft rhythmic breathing through her helmet speaker.

When they arrived at the alien vessel site, they first undertook a quick visual inspection of the area. Nothing had changed since yesterday. Mary landed her scooter off the edge of the shadowy grey zone—about 20 meters away from the ship's presumed location. She dismounted and loosened the equipment ties from the storage container.

Kate sensed her growing uneasiness. She had said little during the trip and concern in her voice replaced her normal cheerfulness. Perhaps the Esther thing with Jim was a more sensitive matter than she realized. She pulled up beside her and landed. "Everything okay?"

"I guess so," Mary's voice sounded tired and jittery with tension, "but I'll feel better once we understand what we're dealing with here."

"Me too, so let's get to it."

They had five hours of oxygen in their tanks, and another six in the spare canisters. More than enough to finish the surveys and return to the lab, even if they needed more time.

She scanned the surrounding area with her on-suit heat signature detector. If the ship was active, or if organic life was aboard, the sniffer would find it. So far, there was no visual evidence of any activity in the craft, and this helped Kate relax. After sampling for several minutes, the sensor showed no abnormal readings. The object appeared dead.

Then, she mapped out her survey lines for the GPR. She'd be taking real-time, continuous readings at one meter row separation. She turned on the GPR, calibrated the sensors, and walked the first line. Mary flew her scooter to the far edge of the seismic array and collected the geophones.

When Kate reached the tenth line, she sensed this was the location where the shadow began, although the exact position was impossible to tell at this proximity. Before she started, she checked that the instrument still functioned well. As she set her pace, pulling the Langdon GPR unit, she peered up at the Earth peaking above the horizon due to a favorable lunar libration.

Beautiful.

She maintained a steady gait across the shadowy area and continued surveying far beyond it. The GPR was a useful tool for near surface anomalies, like graves or archaeological structures, but lost resolution at depth. So, when Mary returned with the geophones, Kate got her to help out with the magnetometer survey, and the VLF. These would reveal more information about the ship's z-axis and, she hoped, about the crustal material beneath it.

There must be a strategic reason for this ship to land here, she thought, unless it crash-landed. But no evidence of a catastrophic impact was evident. *No, this is intentional. They touched down, then buried themselves in the dust.*

With her survey work completed, Kate bounded up an incline and sat on a plagioclase outcrop, waiting for Mary to finish up the mag lines. Twenty minutes later, she radioed, and they met at the scooter where she now lashed the coils to the machine's cargo bin for the trip home.

"See anything weird out there?"

"It's all neural to me. I have to get the raw data cleaned up before speculating. How about you?"

Kate helped secure the gear. She sensed there was something here, but with no heat signatures and little in the way of obvious physical anomalies, the shadow remained a mystery. "The GPR mapped out the same kind of structure we found in the tomographic image, but even with the higher resolution, it's unclear."

"Filtering should help, right?"

"Yes." Then Kate asked, "How's your tank? Still good?"

Mary flashed a thumbs up.

"Let's get back to the habitat. You lead."

Mary stepped up on her scooter, secured herself on the flight seat, and pushed hard on the power button. She lifted the machine a couple meters off the ground, hovered a moment, engaged the nacelles, and pulled around in a steep turn burning toward the lab.

Kate radioed, "I'll take one more sweep. Standard comms procedures: channel open." She maneuvered the scooter across the shadowy area and paused. No life. No heat. No nothing.

Who, or what, are you?

"DO YOU EVER GET THE FEELING WE'RE BEING WATCHED?" Mary peered up from her number crunching with an inquisitive look on her young face and a hint of a mischievous smile. They sat beside each other at the main computer console, entering raw data from the surveys and initiating the filtering processes. Kate wondered what precipitated the question. In the short time they'd worked together in the lunar lab, she'd discovered that Mary always thought a few steps ahead, like a chess player. Reminded her of a kid she knew, Martin something, from her early Spacer days at the Training Center.

"Well yes. Part of my paranoia. But seriously, the lab's monitored for safety reasons by New York. They don't watch everything we do—we have some personal privacy—but the techs perform random visual inspections whenever they want, and if there's a glitch in any of the systems." She cocked her head to one side. "Why do you ask?"

Mary swung her body around. "I wasn't talking about Titanius."

"Ah, yes. The mystery ship, then."

Her face lit up. "Think about it. Maybe there aren't any life signs or other bio-markers because this isn't a vessel at all."

Kate loved the excitement in her voice, the unfettered scientific enquiry at work. The isolation of the lab posting, by her own choice, had dampened her curiosity toward the universe. Mary's presence contrasted that with a fascinating perspective and intelligent questions that only a passionate, hungry mind could conceive. Was it possible she'd been self-isolated too long? Had she missed a beat? In her quest to be left alone, to disappear, perhaps she'd lost more than just social interaction.

Kate pulled away from her own data cleaning routine and gave Mary her full attention. "Tell me what's rattling around in that head."

Mary rose and paced in front of the console, working the problem out as she moved, rubbing her fingers together in her right hand. "I wonder, like, if there's already bias in the data."

"What do you mean?"

"Suppose we're treating this thing not as it *is,* but what we *think* it is?"

Kate tightened her mouth.

"Remember your first reaction to it?"

"Yes, I figured it was the Rossian ship Jim and I saw on the computer at the Mount Sutro site. I still do."

"Okay, but perhaps that's because you *expected* to see it someday. You reasoned they were on their way to Earth. You assumed that what you heard with Dad on that tracking computer was real, and then when this shadow appeared, your mind joined the dots."

Kate's face flushed, and she lowered her gaze. "So, what you're saying is that because I predicted to find—or at least detect—an alien ship from Ross 128, I automatically concluded this was it when a more rigorous approach could have opened up other possibilities." She raised her head again and sighed.

Mary sat back down. "Does that make sense? It's not my intention to question our work, but we don't want to miss or forget anything either."

"No . . . no, I suppose we don't."

Katie

"KATIE, DID YOU REMEMBER YOUR ID MARKER?"

"Yes, Daddy, it's right . . ." she patted down her pockets. "Where is . . ." Panic set in and she looked at Harve Braddock,

overwhelmed with guilt. He sat across from her in the hovercar with a warm smile and pulled the marker from his jacket.

"It was on the kitchen table."

Katie sighed. "I guess I'm a little nervous about the Aptitudes." The vehicle slid into the drop-off zone at the Testing Center and came to rest. An odd assortment of other ten-year-olds, and their parents, milled about the concrete entranceway. She recognized a few from her school.

"You'll do fine, sweetie. Remember, if you don't know an answer just move on to the next question. There's no pass or fail."

"Yeah."

His hand brushed over her long, brown hair. Despite what her dad said, Katie understood these initial Aptitude Tests predicted what future school she'd go to, and the career she'd have. Some well-meaning teachers kept telling her class that the results were only indicators, not predictors, but she knew better.

All grown-ups were untrustworthy. Except her mom and dad.

Outside the testing hall, a friendly woman asked for her marker, and Katie handed it over. She scanned it and said without looking up, "Welcome to the Aptitudes, Kate."

"I prefer Katie."

She eyed her and looked at her dad. He shrugged.

"Okay, Katie, it says here your father is a nanotronics engineer and your mother is a mathematician." Her smile widened. "You should have fun today."

Katie scrunched up her face. "She's not a mathematician."

"Hm?"

"She's a logician who does math for government. There's a difference."

The woman leaned back in her chair. "Well, now . . . my mistake." She punched some keys on the screen. Katie noted the brand of computer, a Smithworks, visualized its on-screen keyboard, and tried decoding the woman's writing based on her finger movements. All she read was a Spacer Aptitude *but didn't know what that meant.*

Katie relaxed and peeked into the massive hall. Black work stations peppered the white-tiled floor and seemed to go on forever in a checkerboard pattern, but unlike the great room at school, this one had no echoes. Baffles killed every sound in the place. Emily from her class sat in the third row and waved.

"Here's your tablet, Katie. You can sit anywhere you like. The Aptitudes will begin shortly."

She grabbed the device and was about to run off and join Emily when her dad stopped her, bent down, and held her shoulders. "I'll pick you up when you're finished, okay? Ping me when you're done." She pulled away. "Oh, one more thing . . . no, two more things."

"What, Daddy?"

"Have fun with the tests."

"And?"

"And your mother and I love you so much. We'll be thinking of you all day."

Katie kissed him on the cheek and strangle-hugged him around his neck.

"Bye!"

She never saw her father again.

Kate

"Lunar Gee Whiz Lab calling Kate Braddock . . . come in . . . over."

"Hm? Oh, sorry. Just thinking about what you said. Perhaps my experience has colored what I'm seeing."

"Like the speed of light being a constant."

"How's that?"

Mary explained. "Einstein fixed a limit on the speed of light to make special relativity work. So, no surprise when the velocity actually was a constant. They assumed it was and their bias confirmed it."

Kate considered her comment. Under certain conditions, neutrinos had broken past the limit, leading to several mind-bending puzzles in her understanding of time and space, but nothing on a practical level. Still, as a thought experiment, Mary was correct. "Because I felt a ship was on its way, I assumed what we found was *the* ship from Ross 128. It could be something other from somewhere else, too."

Mary smiled. "Perhaps this object is a piece of junky old space garbage from a passing cargo ship. Or if it is alien, it could be a surveillance probe designed to watch us, learn stuff, gather intelligence." She leaned closer to Kate. "Maybe it's not the Rossians you're expecting at all."

Somewhere between leaving the Spacer Program and rotting away on Luna, she'd missed a beat.

What's happened to you? Where'd this lack of discipline and focus come from? Mary's right: this thing isn't necessarily a ship at all.

She vowed not to make that mistake again, and never to underestimate Jim's daughter, despite her age. There's a reason the TSA chose her for this summer internship.

"Thanks, Mares, that's brilliant. I've let my bias creep in to the survey, and I've jumped to conclusions way too early. Keep checking on me, will you?"

"Sure."

"Now then, do we agree that whatever is out there *could* be a vessel, but not necessarily the Rossian one?"

"Yes, it's a definite possibility. But it could also be space debris or a probe. That would explain the lack of a heat signature, right?"

24

"True, true." Kate's attention shifted back to the monitor as the filtering algorithm for the GPR data chimed. She pressed the button on the screen and streams of numbers raced by.

"So, if it's not an alien ship and carries no detectable organic life on it, then perhaps we need to consider different tests, other surveys."

"Exactly. We'll see what the processed images reveal, then adjust our approach to the anomaly. Meanwhile, I'd better fire a note off to Stan and the others in New York telling them about the ruined survey data and that we'll return to this area later this season for a re-do."

Mary looked at her, puzzled. "Should we send them the images from today?"

"No, not yet. Let's transfer all the data to the memory tube again. I want to keep this as quiet as possible, just in case. That's why I'll tell him we're moving on to another survey target."

The pair began data cleaning protocols and scheduled the image processing to run over the next few hours. After a quick dinner, they retired to their bunks. Kate fought the urge to reach for her knife that overwhelmed her after being schooled by Mary, and instead closed her eyes and cat-napped.

"Can I ask you something, Kate?"

Mary's voice startled her and killed the mental drift. She inhaled and whispered, "Sure, anything."

Several moments passed before Mary spoke, her voice soft and distant like an echo from Kate's childhood.

"Why do you cut yourself?"

FOUR

Kate

KATE HAD NOT SLEPT WELL. Normally, the comforting white hum of the lab's oxygenator, scrubbers and recyclers would lull her to sleep in minutes, but yesterday's events replayed continuously in her mind. Before retiring for the evening, she reviewed the initial imaging results and followed a more objective approach in its analysis. The anomaly was clearly artificial; they confirmed its dimensions, approximately twenty by ten meters, resembling a small shuttle craft or scout ship, streamlined for efficient movement through atmospheres. However, the lack of heat signatures or evidence of an ambient power drive raised a doubt that this was, indeed, a space craft—let alone the anticipated Rossian ship. It required further investigation.

And Mary's question, which she avoided answering completely, remained hanging in the air like an unanswered question.

She pulled herself out of her bunk and grabbed a water gel from the biofeeder, then downed a couple of gulps. It wasn't close to the water back on Earth, and Kate still hadn't grown accustomed to it. This recycled mix of waste and H_2O teased from the Moon's crust tasted flat and tin-like. The unit also dispensed her anti-rad pills, and she popped them down too, an artifact of her Spacer days to prevent more cancer cells from blooming.

An amber light flashing on the comms panel showed a message had arrived over night from Titanius headquarters, audio only. Kate glanced at Mary who was still asleep in her bunk and squeezed the remote receiver into her ear. Dana Goran's stern, perpetually angry voice greeted her.

"LGL this is Titanius HQ. I trust all is well." Static crashed across the transmission from sunspot activity, or possibly magnetic flare-ups from the *Mare Marginis*. "... the latest seismic data. Stan tells me you ran into some problems with line noise... (garbled)... to check in and offer help. There's considerable interest in the magnetism out there at the limb, as you know." More garbled audio appeared. Kate adjusted the filters with little effect. "... return to the area and re-do the seismics once you've isolated and fixed the equipment problem. Please confirm... receipt. Titanius out."

Kate replayed the message, tweaking the audio filter to capture the garbled bits lost in static without success. Still, Dana's tone was clear and if there had been any doubt before, her serious tone with an edge of *what was it, sarcasm?* compelled her to re-think the day's activities. The plan she hatched the previous night focused on conducting a few more surveys over the anomaly, including taking soil samples to search for any known radioactive tracers, indicative of space flight as they understood it. She also wanted to run a tight micro-seismic tomography array to image the interior of the object. Mary could be right: it may simply be some ship's garbage or a chunk of one of the cargo ships on a water run. Or she could be wrong. The need to conduct the original survey line again was problematic. *They'd expect results this time and when New York sees the anomaly, who knows what might happen?* Kate felt like running away and hiding. She left Earth to escape the uproar over the Ross 128 signal, and now the damn business had parked itself on her doorstep.

She drew a coffee from the biofeeder and sipped, scalding the tip of her tongue. Mary stirred and came to life, joining her at the comms panel.

"What they'd have to say?" She yawned and nodded at the Titanius message header on the comms screen.

"They want us to re-do the initial survey of the *Mare Marginis*. Apparently, there's more interest in those magnetic fields than any-one guessed... more than I thought, anyway." Kate leaned against the panel and threw her legs on an equipment crate she and Mary prepared the day before. "Change of plans, Mares."

Mary played the message back twice and pulled up a map of the *Mare Marginis*, an area right on the eastern limb of the Moon, and a primary investigation target for Titanius. "What'll we do?"

"We must comply, of course," Kate sighed. "Mind you, we could burn some other surveys while we're there." She stared at Mary and folded her fingers together behind her head. "The high-resolution GPR will take the longest to perform, and I will ditch the planned micro-seismic tomography lines if we have to configure the original survey again."

"I can collect soil samples while you drive the GPR. Then we could set the automatic thumper before leaving. Let it run. The new numbers should be in before we're back at the lab." Mary chewed a protein tab and began her morning stretching routine.

Kate remained concerned. "It's not just that. Look, as soon as that data comes in, it'll show Titanius exactly what we found the other day: a large anomaly, maybe a ship or a probe or someone's garbage, partially protruding out of the dust around the *Mare Marginis* magnetic fields. Do you know what'll happen then?" She sat up, leaned forward. "They're gonna send a crew to investigate. Worse, so will every other interested party and signatory to the surveys contract. The Chinese for sure, the Prussian Alliance. . . possibly the Indians, NDU and Confederate States. Plus, there are the other major resource companies operating out here: Intersol Geospace, and Polaris Mining Corp."

Mary's eyebrows furrowed, and she took a deep breath. "I don't get it."

"The only thing keeping us safe and alone at the moment, running mind-numbing surveys on this rock, is the international agreement to limit mining and exploration on Luna. But if others even remotely suspect there's a ship up here—no matter it's origin—they'll figure someone else has broken the treaty and the game will be on."

Mary swallowed the last of her tab and finished her water. Her face relaxed before concern spread across it again. "Are you saying this could lead to conflict, Kate? Aren't we past all that now?" She drew her legs up underneath her on the stool.

"You saw what happened when the TSA took over your dad's discovery of the Ross 128 signal five years ago. And they covered up that news tight as a drum. This wouldn't be." She sat up straight again, nodding to the comms panel. "Titanius isn't the only one with eyes on us. You can bet all the other major space players and military organizations are watching what we do, too."

Geopolitical tensions on Earth had never been worse. In Kate's lifetime alone, she'd witnessed the breakdown of America along north-south lines, with a few independent entities emerging like the California Congressional Republic and the former Washington and Oregon states. The American cold war continued. Europe seethed with alliances forming and disappearing in rapid succession, slaughtering each other as they'd been doing since the last ice age. The Russians had well-established business partnerships with global corporations and were the first to establish a mining colony on Mars. But these days, the Chinese posed the greatest threat to security. Kate figured it was a matter of time before they expanded control over all southeast Asia. The Moon, despite its inherently dangerous environment, was infinitely safer than the terran powder keg.

Mary broke the silence. "So, if and when we send the seismic data to Titanius like they're expecting, and as soon as their clients see the anomaly, they'll all be scrambling over each other to get here."

"Yes."

"And if they figure out this object isn't an Earth ship but some other vessel or probe, then that'll make it worse?"

Kate felt a cold shiver run up her spine. "It will. Think about it, Mary. If it is the Rossian ship we detected a few years ago, then no doubt it got here with faster than light technology, and what your dad and I saw wasn't some glitch. Whoever gets that tech first rules the solar system for generations. I need to get them off the eastern limb and thinking about something else."

The lab whirred to life as the automated environmental controls suggested it was *daytime*. Ambient light grew brighter, the power units hummed, and a series of monitoring reports flashed on the console.

Mary squinted as her eyes adjusted to the brightness. "We're gonna be caught in the middle of a new war."

FIVE

Mary

"READY?"

Kate glanced over her shoulder from the LunaScoota. Mary climbed over the machine and powered up. "Want me to go first again?"

"Yes."

Mary pulled on the hover lever and the scooter lifted off the ground. Then, easing the thruster stick forward, the paired nacelles engaged and the vehicle shot from the lab on a course toward the *Mare Marginis*. She threw a cursory glance back to confirm the stability of the equipment and noticed Kate trailing her.

"Throttle up, Mary."

The machine performed well underneath her, attaining its cruising velocity of 300 km/h, splashing up moon dust in its wake. The smooth, basaltic lava flows in the *Mare Crisium* reminded her of the interior deserts back home, beautiful and endless, and the time she and her dad spent a summer exploring the west coast with side trips into the continental safe zones wherever possible. Burning through Nevada in a topless hovercar was the highlight for her.

"I've been considering this problem, and I got a couple ideas." Kate's voice crackled through her helmet speaker, and Mary felt the excitement.

"What are they?"

Kate and her machine pulled even with her as they approached the eastern impact crater zone. The Earth shone above like a deep blue, agate sun against the dark sky. She looked over the separation distance and said, "I want to run the micro-seismic tomography survey and find out what's inside that thing before we send any data home."

Her words rattled around Mary's brain as the distance to the crater edges ticked down on her dash. *This isn't what I signed up for*, she mused, but the part of her that took after her mother jumped to life, a combination of adventure and defiance, danger and discovery. She hadn't seen Janet—couldn't accept her as *mom*—since Mount Sutro, but understood she was a mercenary with the Northern Democratic Union, and responsible for destroying Earth's only subspace transmitter. She imagined the thrill Janet experienced in dangerous situations was the same rush running through Mary's veins: the reason she wanted to work off-planet; why she loved being here with Kate so much.

"I suppose we could always send those results from the original survey, right?"

"That's what I'm thinking. We'll know later today exactly what we're seeing, so we can get out in front of the message. If it's space crap, no big deal and we'll carry on. If not, we'll cross that bridge if it comes."

Mary scanned over to starboard. Kate had flown her machine in a wide arc as they approached the mare's edge and the apron of the impact crater zone. "We should tell my dad."

Silence enveloped them as they maneuvered the scooters over the craters, around ancient volcanic cones—some smashed by impacts—and on toward the *Mare Marginis* now bathed in light, and the shadowy anomaly.

GEOPHONES FOR THE SEISMIC ARRAY were separated at one-meter intervals. It took considerable time to set up and run because the wave source—the thumper—had to be moved to each data point along both sides to get the image Kate wanted. After Mary finished helping her with the initial configuration, she collected soil samples at various grid points around the anomaly, just below the surface, and again at about 25 centimeters deep. Kate wasn't concerned about the depth. She said if this object had been running nuclear power, they would easily see the tracer isotopes.

A couple strands of Mary's hair had come loose from her cap and floated into her line of vision. At one point during the sampling, she paused and gazed around her. Being the only two humans on the Moon left her with a strange, intoxicating fire. She smiled.

"How's the O_2?"

Mary blinked twice, and her suit's environmental monitoring data scrolled across her inner visor. "I've got two-and-a-half hours." Kate hauled the GPR sled over a survey line a couple hundred meters away, her body appearing small and fragile at this distance.

"We've got extra canisters in the scooter bin, right?"

"Yes, I got visuals on them."

"Good. I'll wrap up after the next station. Pull out the geophones and the seismic hub, and let's roll. The place gives me the creeps."

Mary sensed something wasn't right from that slight tremor in Kate's voice. She scrutinized the surrounding area, but everything appeared as it had the last two times they'd been out here. Perhaps the magnetic fields were messing with her brain chemistry. No matter, the relief brought on by packing up was palpable.

"On my way."

THE PAIR CRUISED AROUND THE IMPACT craters and outcrops, retracing their route to the lab. The screen on Mary's scooter console showed Kate slipping farther behind. She eased up on her throttle.

"You good, Kate?"

"Yeah," she said, in a voice that was anything but convincing. "Yeah, I was wondering what to do next. I would like to talk to your dad about what we found, but I don't want to do it through regular comms channels. Those are all constantly monitored."

Mary piloted her scooter onto the *Mare Crisium*. "I'm betting encryption isn't an option either?"

"Too suspicious," Kate's voice crackled.

The scooter's icon picked up speed on the screen.

"Could we bypass the normal comms frequencies?"

"I wish."

Mary followed the exact path she took earlier that day, tracking the scooter's earlier burn scars on the Moon's surface like a monorail. "What if you used your indie-comm through a frequency multiplier and transmitted an RF signal?"

Kate's voice grew louder. "Can you rig that up?"

"Sure. My dad's a ham radio nut, remember? I've helped him build circuits and antennas and all sorts of things." The adrenaline surged again with the idea of circumventing normal comms. Operators enjoyed bouncing signals off the Moon and satellites—even ships—and she figured if Kate threw her own signal into the mix, no one would notice or care. It would be just another odd-sounding transmission. Not foolproof, but the encryption would deter any listeners.

"Tell you what, then. While I get the new data filtered, you work your magic and we'll give Jim a call as soon as we have the imaging results. Sound good to you?"

Mary smiled. She noticed her oxygen level had fallen into the deep amber range, but with less than half an hour to travel, she wasn't worried about running out or having to change tanks. And she realized that everything about the last 48 hours sealed it. Her dad's radio astronomy hobby sparked her interest in science at an early age, and she kept getting drawn in to a career as an explorer with every book she read about the old terran missions and the latest Martian colony news. The internship with Titanius and Kate was more than she had hoped it would be. She felt her soul shine like a band of light.

"Kate, you said this morning you had a couple of ideas. The first was to run the surveys like we planned, and we've done that." The beacon strobe from the lab flashed into view across the grey and white moonscape. "But what's the other thing?"

Silence.

"Kate?"

"Yeah, you're right. The anomaly is my priority, but I've got another one too that's hard to explain. Came to me last night after you fell asleep."

"What is it?"

"Well. . ."

A long emptiness filled Mary's helmet. Soon, the outline of the lunar lab would appear even though the outpost was still a fair distance away. But this time, her normal sense of relief in seeing the habitat remained elusive.

"Kate, what's up?"

"I guess there's no easy way to put this. After we speak to your dad, I want you to return to Earth on the closest ship. The sooner, the better."

Katie

KATIE SAT ON THE FLOOR AT THE TESTING CENTER, back against the wall, waiting. Neither her dad nor mom had responded to her indie-comm messages. Emily, and the others, had left an hour ago. Only Katie, another girl she didn't recognize, and a boy named Martin remained. The girl slumped at one of the work stations near her and sniffled.

The woman she'd seen earlier in the day entered the hall from a side door, followed by a man wearing a grey suit. They approached Martin, who stood close to the doorway. After speaking to him in low voices, they led him to the exit.

A few minutes later, the grown-ups returned and marched up to Katie. She rose as they arrived.

The woman said, "You scored really well on your Aptitudes. You're going right away to the Spacer Program."

Katie looked at her suspiciously.

The man continued. "Do you know what Spacers do?"

There was something about his black, lifeless eyes that frightened her.

"You'll be at a special training center with other kids like you, learning all about science, engineering, and how to work in space. Only a handful of young people get chosen for it. You're one of the special ones."

"I want to go home. Where's my dad?"

The woman gave her a sorrowful, judgmental look. "That's something else to talk about, sweetheart. Your dad said he couldn't come, but he wants you to join us right away."

"Now? But I've got a project I'm working on and my plants need feeding and—"

The man spoke again. "Katie, where you're going, you'll love the projects even more, but we've got to get started immediately." He picked a crumb from his teeth with his tongue. "They only select the best for this program, and you're very important. You don't want to disappoint your parents, do you?"

Before she answered, the woman grabbed her hand and marched toward the exit. She squeezed it a little too hard.

Kate

"IT'S BECAUSE I'M BROKEN," SHE WHISPERED, then paused. "That's why."

They took a break from number-crunching and rested on the stuffed, utilitarian chairs in the habitat's "library", eating supper off thick cardboard trays. She hadn't forgotten Mary's question: she hadn't bothered to answer it because she didn't understand how. Still didn't. Everything she practiced in her head sounded hollow and ridiculous.

"Hm?" Mary looked up from her tofu hash, circles under her eyes. She had said little since Kate told her she'd be on the next shuttle out of here.

"You asked me the other day why I cut myself, remember?"

Mary swallowed. "Oh, yeah, listen, none of my business. I was like so out of line."

"It's okay," she smiled, "I should've explained it from the start. No room for secrets up here." She leaned back on the soft chair and placed her hands on the hem of her shirtskin. "Do you want to have a look?"

Mary's mouth tightened, and her eyes fell to Kate's torso. She dragged the covering up to her chin. Mary gasped.

"This scar here . . ." She fingered a long white line that ran from the bottom of her scrawny rib cage down and around her belly button toward her groin. "It's a remnant from one of the Spacer operations when they hacked out my womb, my tubes, whatever else."

"Jesus, Kate. . ."

"That's how it started. I traced it with my thumbnail like this, when the wound was still fresh." She ran her nail up and down the scar, back and forth. "When I was about thirteen and working on a satellite orbiting Mars, I smashed my hand up there. Didn't notice until I was back at the colony but when I removed my glove, something broke my thumbnail. By then I was scar-tracing daily and the jagged nail drew blood."

A swell of curiosity and fear swept across Mary's face. "But why? I don't get it."

Ignoring the question, she said, "See here? This is where my . . . my breasts would have been." She pointed to a patchwork of lines resembling a net or a Dali-inspired quilt spread over the middle of her chest. "I'm not cutting all the time. Some days are better than others." She lowered her shirtskin again and watched Mary swallow hard then at last look up.

"What the hell did they *do* to you?"

"The whack-jobs in the Spacer Program?" Kate leaned forward and sipped her tea. "I don't like talking about that, but, yeah . . . I'm broken. For the longest time I'd forgotten if I was supposed to be a girl or a boy, or just a freak. They robbed me of my child-hood, my teenage years. Hell, I have no idea what falling in love even means, or how to trust someone, to kiss a girl or a boy that way. Oh, I can follow the steps, go through the motions, but I don't *feel* anything." She patted her chest and nodded. "Except this."

Mary sat in rigid silence, shaking her head occasionally as Kate cleared their trays, tossing them in the recycler. She'd told no one about the cutting before; wasn't even sure why she confided in Mary other than they shared a common history in San Fran and she hung out a lot with the Atteberrys before that damned signal appeared.

"Kate?" Mary's voice was tender, full of fear. "Can I do anything? To help, I mean?"

Kate flopped down on the chair and exhaled. She ran her fingers through her straight-cropped hair, stared at the tattoos running up and down her arms, and recalled the countless times doctors and nurses and colleagues from that program had asked her the same thing. When the answer came to her, she wondered if Mary could handle it.

"Short answer is no, other than don't tell your dad if that's okay."

"Yeah, sure."

"It's an addiction . . . a compulsion. When the skin breaks, and the pain creeps over, the relief is visceral. Pretty sick, eh?"

Mary didn't answer.

"When it's done and I'm staring at this ugly mess, the shame and self-judgment are so heavy that I have to cut again, and the cycle never stops. Never stops. Intellectually, I get why I do it. Emotionally and physically, I can't stop."

The environmental lights dimmed, indicating *night* was falling in the habitat. Kate stood and faced Mary. "You wanna know the sickest, strangest thing about cutting?"

Mary's gaze fixated on a spot on the floor. She didn't look up when she answered, "What?"

"I like it."

SIX

Wednesday, June 11, 2092
Titanius Space Resources Headquarters
New York City, New York
Northern Democratic Union

Carter

THE VIEW FROM THE 43RD FLOOR OF THE TITANIUS building in downtown Manhattan consistently impressed him. Sure, other glass and metal buildings surrounded his in the skyscraper forest, but he looked past all those to the East River and beyond. Clayton

Carter, jacket off, sleeves rolled up, put his hands on his thin hips and smiled. *Not bad for an orphan from the Heights. Not bad, but not finished yet.* His gaze shifted to the deep blue of a cloudless sky as he considered the latest technical report on his new prototype corvette class ship and what it meant to humanity's future.

A soft knocking brought him back to the room. He turned and checked his indie-comm: One-thirteen. Almost time. "Enter."

Ed Mitchell rushed into the office, carrying his notebook. He still wore glasses, unlike most others who underwent corrective eye procedures, and they slid down his aquiline nose. Mitchell's tie hung off to the side, and his rumpled suit screamed of being twenty years old, but Carter didn't care: the man was a brilliant scientist and a formidable negotiator. His lack of cultivated appearance masked a calculating, forward-thinking mind, always working several moves ahead of the rest including him.

"Ready for the call with the TSA, Ed?"

"Oh yes, Clay, but I want to go over a few things with you before we hit the negotiating table again."

Carter motioned for him to sit down. He brushed the technical report on the *Echo* off to the side and gave Mitchell his full attention.

"Esther Tyrone's digging her heels in on the mineral rights issue. It will be tough to finesse those out of her."

"Doesn't she realize what we're giving up? Dammit, Ed, we've been over this ground how many times now?" He leaned back in his chair and rubbed his temples.

Mitchell grinned. It could be the middle of a hurricane or a family Thanksgiving dinner, and you wouldn't be able to tell from Mitchell's face. "It's all part of the negotiating process, Clay, you understand that. Let's make this work for our mutual benefit. The TSA covets a larger role in space exploration and we want exclusive mineral rights coming out of those programs. They need our financial resources and access to our fleet, and we need their research and innovation capability."

Carter stared at the man, then resigned. "Okay, so what's up for today's round?"

Mitchell placed his closed notebook on Carter's desk and grinned. "More of the same. We won't reach any conclusions on anything today, maybe not even the rest of the week. Look, it's frustrating, but there aren't any shortcuts here. We're still building trust, and you need to get to know Esther better . . . develop the, er, working relationship."

"How important is it, Ed?"

Mitchell inhaled and raised his chin. "Critical. She's been running the SETI program and Space Ops for the last five or six years, took the TSA from a curious post-war academic institution to a leader in space technology innovations."

"I know who she is, but I don't have the inclination to go all smarmy on her. From what I've gleaned in our meetings so far, she'll see through that."

"Yes, just be yourself."

Carter stood and paced around the office, mulling over the never-ending discussions with the TSA and unbelievable strides the Chinese were making in the space mining sector. He worked his jaw, pursing his lips, wondering how much longer he needed the niceties before they all got down to business.

"These negotiations task me, Ed. They truly task me."

Mitchell rose from his chair and stood beside him, admiring the view. "There is one thing you could try to speed up the talks. Interested?"

Carter narrowed his eyes at the frumpy man. At six-foot-three and built like an athlete, he was a full eight or nine inches taller than Mitchell, yet still feared him . . . not for lack of courage; rather, in a fear of God way. Carter never felt he could trust him even though they'd worked together for years.

"Yes, tell me how."

Mitchell removed his glasses, folded them and dropped them in his jacket pocket. "One of our sources in the TSA came across a bunch of deleted files from six years ago. He was compiling historical data on their operations when he uncovered several erased files, scrubbed of all information."

"So? We scrub data all the time."

"So . . . he decoded the file headers. They were all related to an apparent alien signal they'd been tracking in 2085. Do you remember the story?"

Carter stroked his chin and thought back to the fall of that year. He'd signed the new lunar lab contract and his engineers were running controlled simulations on the habitat when a crazy astronomy nut in California detected a tap code from . . . *where was it?*

As if reading his mind, Mitchell spoke. "The signal originated from the Ross 128 star system, remember? No one validated it, but there's enough anecdotal evidence and whispers to suggest they heard something."

Carter turned to face him again. "Right, and that business of the transmitter tower in Frisco being destroyed . . . gossip claimed the aliens caused that too. How does this help me?"

"Oh, the event itself is irrelevant. I mean, sooner or later, we're bound to run into other creatures like us. No, the important thing here is the belief that the alien ship had faster than light capability." Mitchell awaited a response that didn't come. "And Esther Tyrone knows this to be true. Why else would she order a complete cover up of the data?"

"Indeed. Still, I—"

"If I may," Mitchell interrupted. "One rumor floating around is the Ross 128 ship was on its way here to Earth. Clayton," he whispered, "it might already *be* here."

Carter's heart jumped. Imagine if he somehow got hold of that FTL technology for his exclusive use. He'd dominate the space resources sector overnight. *Did the TSA have this tech in its possession?* Something didn't sit right.

"If the TSA has this alien tech, or knows where it is, why wouldn't they keep it for themselves? Why do they need us?"

Mitchell put his hands in his pockets and rocked back and forth on his heels. "You're right. They don't need us for exploration if they have FTL tech. What they need us for is protection. It's what the negotiations are about. Esther Tyrone is looking for a partnership with someone who would fight to safeguard the aliens and whatever they bring to the galactic mix. She wins by presenting a diplomatic, open dialogue with new life forms. We win by accessing FTL to mine the richest planets in the galaxy in a blink of an eye compared to current processing times." He wandered to Carter's desk and picked up his notebook. "That's the end game, Clayton. You need to get Esther on side and help her achieve the TSA's exploration and humanitarian goals." He glanced at his indie-comm then back at Carter with cold, expectant eyes.

"I'll consider this." Then, picking up his jacket from the coatrack, he swung the office door open and Mitchell stepped forward. "There's one other thing. Did you see the latest report on the *Echo*?"

Mitchell nodded. "Yes, it's very impressive. The orbital tests show a 23% gain in thrust efficiency over the most powerful engines in space. That'll translate to massive strides in conventional spacecraft velocities."

"Without question the *Echo* is ready for interplanetary testing. And you're sure our own tech is secure?"

"Positive."

Carter smirked, then added, "Let's hope. Either way, whether it's ours or Rossian, we must be ready to take the next giant leap and dominate the space resources sector, not the Prussian Alliance, the Chinese, or anyone else. Think of the possibilities that unlimited exploration will give us . . . and by extension, all humankind."

"Oh, I have." Mitchell's indie-comm pinged.

"Showtime."

Kate

Even with the fume hood growling over the electronics bench, the acrid smell of burning solder permeated the living quarters of the lunar lab. Mary hunched over a half-constructed UHF beam antenna for the indie-comm's transmitter. A few paces away, Kate pored over the latest survey data.

Tension hung heavy as the growing silence between the two increased. Kate couldn't tell if Mary remained creeped out by the scar talk, or still resented going back to Earth. Didn't matter. The situation was untenable.

Another reason she preferred working alone.

Mary snapped one of the aluminum directors off the Yagi and groaned in frustration. "These damn things won't stay."

"Hey, let's take a break and grab a coffee." Kate stood up and stretched cat-like over the workbench. "What do you say?"

She turned the soldering gun off and killed the switch to the fume hood, then rubbed her eyes and wandered over to the biofeeder. "Two coffees."

They retired to the sitting area, and after a moment, Mary asked, "Did you learn anything more about the anomaly?"

"I did, but we need to talk it through . . . this thing between us. It can't go on."

"I don't know what you mean."

"Bullshit. Spit it out. We've got to work and live together, and you can't escape your crap here."

Mary's eyes flashed, and a sardonic smile flickered over her face. Kate knew the irony hadn't been lost at all on her intern, and her cheeks reddened.

Kate attempted eye contact, but her gaze returned to the floor. She said, "Okay. The cutting thing, like I can handle that . . . even understand it to a degree. But telling me I gotta go back home like I'm some fragile, neural kid? That sucks. And you won't listen to what I want and what I'm willing to do." She looked up, scowling.

"Good!" Kate slapped her thigh. "We're getting somewhere now. Tell me more."

Mary vented for the next few minutes, releasing her pent-up frustration and resentment until she had nothing more to say. Then Kate reached over and touched her shoulder.

"Thank you. I was too quick on the decision to send you home without discussing it first. But you understand it's my call, right? You're my responsibility up here, Mares, and I couldn't live with myself if something happened to you on my watch."

Mary slowly nodded her head, the resentment she'd held whiffing away.

"Still, you make a good point. You're not some dopey kid requiring ongoing supervision. You're as smart as any Spacer I ever met, probably smarter, and I enjoy your company." Kate's mouth pursed, and her eyes narrowed.

"But . . . ?"

"Look, I'm struggling. I suppose my default is to protect you by sending you home before anything blows up. I've no idea if that's the best decision, whether I'm overreacting or being cautious, but I feel it in my gut."

Mary wasn't skilled at hiding her emotions. Her face grew dark as sadness washed over her. "I'm 17 but not like other teenagers. I can make my own decisions. Besides, if you send me home now, won't that raise flags with Dad and Esther and the people at Titanius?"

An incoming message alert chimed, but Kate ignored it while she considered Mary's point. Then, nodding over at the comms panel, she said, "They'll want an update on the survey data."

"Yeah, you gonna tell them anything?"

The chime persisted, so Kate pulled herself up and hit the video feed button. Stan's grey face appeared. "How are things?"

He sounded different, under stress.

Kate put on her professional voice. "Hey Stan, it's getting there. We're looking over the new data now and I hope to get you results from other surveys we're doing tomorrow. Can you wait that long?"

There was an odd echo on the comms link. She heard her voice reflecting back to her. *Kerchunk.*

Stan typed and peered into another monitor before returning his attention to her. "Well, okay, I suppose there isn't much choice. But you will have something for us tomorrow, correct?"

"Sure, day after at the latest."

He stopped typing and leaned in closer to the screen. "God's teeth, Kate, you've got to figure this out fast. The pressure's on, and the lunarsat's gonna be checking out your survey area. Folks are skittish as hell 'cause this has never happened to you before. They think Titanius is deliberately hiding something."

"I'll do my best." A pause. "Stan, there's one more thing I'd like to ask." She looked over the comms panel at Mary, sitting wide-eyed, mouth agape, across from her. "Are there any friendly transports nearby?"

He checked another screen and replied, "The *Aristobulus* is about ten hours away. Why, you need something?"

Mary shook her head once, her eyes pleading.

Kerchunk.

49

Kate bit her lower lip and closed her eyes. "No, just curious about the traffic. We're good. I'll send you data as soon as I can. Promise. Lunar Lab out." The feed disconnected.

THE TOMOGRAPHIC IMAGE OF THE ANOMALY refreshed on the monitor and she saw what Mary had been talking about. The resolution still sucked, in Mary's words, but compared to the previous survey, it was high definition. After her comms with Stan, Kate realized there would be even more attention on them unless she threw them a bone of some sort.

But this wasn't it.

"See it now?" Mary circled the area on the screen with her pinky finger. "It's not a huge object, but the density there is different, much less than the outer shell."

Kate closed her eyes. "There is a way to determine material composition if we ran another survey even tighter. But I doubt we'd have time." She looked down at her notes on her indie-comm. "Still, I'm convinced this thing is hollow. At least in this section. Almost like a living area for some oxygen breathing creature, wouldn't you say?"

Mary scratched her head. "Well, the VLF charts show other anomalies in the vicinity, but they're much deeper than this, and naturally-occurring. There's likely mineral potential, but I don't understand enough about that. Still, I believe this little area is hollow."

The image flickered and refreshed again as more data became available. The change in density remained in a semi-circular shape, although the lack of resolution affected Kate's confidence in what they were actually seeing. This was not space trash. The anomaly dimensions suggested that whoever built this thing—this *craft*—they made it for space travel in vacuum and through atmospheric conditions. Whatever it was, and wherever it came from, the small ship in the *Mare Marginis* had landed and, for now, lay dormant.

"The heat sig data shows nothing," Mary said, pulling up a second screen. The craft's perimeter was a monochromatic deep grey. No EM or radiation of any kind.

Shit.

Kate rubbed her eyes and glanced over at her. "What are you smiling about?"

Mary laughed. "Just that no one back home will believe this!"

"Yeah, well, we've got bigger problems like how the hell we'll keep this info from Titanius or the TSA or anyone else. That's a ship out there, Mares. An alien ship. And the only aliens encountered so far were the Rossians."

She stood up and waved an arm at the electronics bench. "Is your antenna functional yet?"

"I have to finish installing the feedline connector."

Kate sat at the comms panel and pulled up the master screen, the one with the key commands. The radio button with A/V OVERRIDE beside it lit up when she pressed it with her thumb. Now, she'd blocked all incoming and outgoing transmissions.

Unless you operated outside Titanius's network.

She stared at a real-time image of the Earth's near side on the global monitor, showing the western hemisphere in full view. "Finish you work. Let's call your dad."

Thursday, June 12, 2092
San Francisco, California Congressional Republic

Atteberry

MUTED SUNLIGHT PIERCED THE CIRROSTRATUS cloud cover, bathing Atteberry's living room and kitchen in an ethereal glow. He sat in a shadowed corner of the breakfast nook, a steaming mug of coffee in front of him, and scratched his beard, missing his daughter in a way that no thought could ever come close to capturing. He smiled at the notion of the English professor at a loss for words.

The modest urban house was too large and too empty with Mary gone. Atteberry understood she'd leave soon enough for university or one of the private training schools, and her internship on Luna this summer forced him to realize how close that day was. His little girl, now 17 . . . where did the time go?

He recalled the morning last March when Esther pinged to discuss the posting with Titanius. At first, he fought it and would never give Mary permission to leave. But after talking it through with her—and no small pressure from Esther—he saw how much she wanted the experience and could not hold her back. Plus, having his good friend Kate there allowed him to sleep better at night.

He picked up his coffee and a book and padded out to the living room. Sunlight streamed in, and Atteberry fell into the safety of his sofa. He opened the book to where he left off, but after reading the same sentence a few times, he knew his mind was elsewhere.

Then he realized why. The soft light melted the edges off the corners in the room, hanging like a veil . . . the same glow he remembered the morning after the Mount Sutro Tower collapsed when he, Esther, Mary and Kate returned to the house.

It was the last time he'd seen Kate Braddock.

After a short breakfast, Mary had gone to bed, leaving Kate, Esther and Atteberry alone at the kitchen table, not saying a word to each other. He and Kate had believed the Rossian ship was on its way to Earth at faster than light velocities. Esther wrestled with the shock of losing a colleague and the inevitable aftermath of her own actions in the affair. She fussed about interviews coming, and disciplinary action being taken. Coverups ordered, no doubt.

But that was then.

He regretted the early romance they shared never developed because of what now seemed a ridiculous reason: a disagreement over the Ross 128 signal and the subsequent events. He believed that everyone's responsibility was to share all information with the world, and Esther felt the TSA should purge everything connected with the ship from all databases. It became a hell of an ongoing argument. In fact, they'd avoided each other during the investigation until neither called the other, and the relationship withered from opposing views and pride, and at last, neglect. Atteberry felt as if he'd missed an opportunity but hiding the truth about Ross 128 was impossible. Yet, he still had Mary and her health to worry about, and Kate's support was solid. Or so he thought.

She'd left for her apartment that morning, exhausted, saying something off-hand like *I need to go . . .* he couldn't quite recall. And then she disappeared: no note, no letter of resignation at the college, no forwarding address. Nothing.

Atteberry sipped his coffee, picked up the book again, and read. Before he finished the first paragraph, his indie-comm pinged from the kitchen. Initially, he ignored it, but the signal continued. He closed his book and wandered into the room. The device sat there blinking on his countertop.

"Hello?"

The noise on the comms link was unlike anything he'd heard before on conventional phone networks. Static crashes, the kind produced by solar flares, crackled in the background and the binary tones of teletype sang at some weird offset frequency. It was as if he was listening in on the ham radio HF bands.

"Hello?" he said again. *Local interference, perhaps?* He hadn't noticed it before.

Then a weak, distant voice floated in over the noise. It sounded ghost-like and hollow, and he couldn't tell if the speaker was male or female, or whether the link was for him. He adjusted the signal input.

"Jim . . .? Jim, do you read?"

He strolled back into the living room. "Yes, it's Atteberry. Who's calling?"

Static noise.

"This is Atteberry. Is anyone there?"

The indie-comm pinged again. The device had detected a request for encryption mode. *Odd, how could . . .?*

Then he realized.

The only person he knew who could piggyback a security code on a call outside the normal phone networks was Kate. Something must be wrong. He pushed the ACCEPT button on the indie-comm's screen.

"Kate is that you?"

"Yes, yes, Jim! Me and Mary."

The signal strengthened as the static died down under heavy filtering.

"Where are you?"

There was a two second delay before Kate replied, "We're on the . . . lab . . . there's a . . . not sure of the origin . . ."

"Kate, you're in and out. Say again."

"Jim, can you . . ."

The interference was back, and the noise crashed in Atteberry's ear. It was impossible to hear anything. After another thirty seconds of static, he picked up an utterance sounding like Mary's voice.

"A-one . . . A-one . . ."

Atteberry frowned. The only *A-one* he knew was the transmission mode signifying the old Morse code, or more to the point, the deliberate on-off keying of a continuous wave. The indie-comm had a push-to-talk button on it used for remote applications. He engaged it and tapped out *dah-di-dah* several times, the letter K signifying "go ahead".

When radio band conditions were poor, often the only signals to get through were codes because it was possible to miss letters yet understand the gist of a message. Mary knew the Morse code, that ancient, original digital mode of communicating, because he'd taught it to her. They sometimes sat at the dinner table tapping out conversations to each other over salad and spaghetti. She must have realized the difficulty with the voice transmission and taken over from Kate.

He grabbed a pencil and a small notebook he used for grocery lists and waited for Mary to return the signal.

He didn't have to wait long.

Mary and Kate on Luna. All fb—found something—Kate says a ship—ross 128—ross 128—ross 128—K

Atteberry's mind raced as he read Mary's message again. FB meant "fine business", ham speak for "everything's good". That's a relief. The question bothering him was why the Russian vessel went to Luna instead of Earth? Why?

He tapped back:

R R—ok Mary—r u sure abt ross ship? in danger? K

Seconds dripped by like minutes as he awaited Mary's response. His heart raced and beads of cold sweat bloomed on his forehead. Then:

R—fb dad—no danger—no danger—Kate says they r hr—they r hr—on Luna—

Without warning, the signal ended. Atteberry waited several seconds, but there was nothing more, not even static. He tapped back *di-di-dah-dah-di-dit*, the code for "question mark" but in this context, he was asking if they were still there.

Nothing.

Di-di-dah-dah-di-dit

Pause. Then again.

Di-di-dah-dah-di-dit

The comms link died in a jumble of static.

SEVEN

Katie

KATIE SAT ON THE ROCK-HARD BED IN HER dorm snarling at Gwen, one of the overseers, perched on the chair on the other side of the room. "I don't care about this program or anyone else. I just want to go home."

The young red-haired woman maintained her smile, but Katie saw the tightness creep around the corners of her lips.

"Katie, this is the most important training school in the country, if not the entire world, and you were picked out of millions of others to attend. Your parents understand how serious this is, and that's why you're here. They're doing this for your future."

She folded her arms and stuck out a belligerent lip. "Let me call my dad."

Gwen sighed and leaned forward. "Sorry, honey." Then she shook her head slowly. "I hate being the one to say this, Katie, but you've left me no choice."

"What is it?"

She hesitated as if searching for the right words. Something about the quiet expression on her face was odd. "When your dad dropped you off for the Aptitudes in September, he made it very clear on the information sheet that he didn't want you home. Too much trouble, apparently. We even double-checked." Katie's eyes widened. "I'll show you the sheet."

Katie reeled, like someone kicked her in the stomach. Tears welled up, but she choked them back in an act of defiance. "That can't be true. You're a liar."

"Happens more often than you think. The Center is full of kids whose parents have abandoned them for whatever reason. That's why we're a family, why we care after each other and stick together." She bowed her head. "I'm sorry you had to find out this way, Katie, but your parents won't ever be coming back for you. Your mom and dad simply don't want you."

Kate

"THE ANTENNA CONNECTION MUST BE SHOT," MARY SAID. "I'll go check." She still wore her envirosuit from the Yagi beam installation on the lunar communications tower. On the equipment shelf, her helmet aired out.

"Never mind, contacting your dad was a mistake." Video of the *Mare Marginis* recorded by the orbiting lunarsat played on the computer console. The images were several years old but still comprised the most recent high-resolution shots of that limb area. "Ditch the suit, if you wish."

Mary hesitated, confusion spreading on her face.

Kate grunted. "Let's check the connector in the morning."

"Sure."

She struggled out of the envirosuit, racked and slid it back to the power bar, then joined Kate at the console. She disconnected the indie-comm from the remote cable and shoved it in the recharger.

"Why do you say it was a mistake to tell Dad about the alien ship?"

Kate fidgeted; concern shadowed her face. "Didn't think it through." The *Mare Marginis* video looped around again. "He'll need to talk to someone, won't he?"

Mary ran a hand through her hair. "Well, yeah, you know what he's like. Couldn't keep a secret if his life depended on it."

Kate raised an eyebrow.

Mary laughed. "Okay, that may be an exaggeration, but he shares everything he learns, everything he finds. When it comes to information, he's an open book."

"That's what frightens me."

Mary glanced over at the comms panel. "Should we unblock it again?"

Kate sighed and scratched her fingernails over her flat chest, her mind wandering off to the time Jim first heard the alien signal and immediately shared it with the astronomical society. Most laughed him down, but not everyone.

"Kate?"

"Yeah, sorry. Bring 'em online."

The screen to disengage the A/V OVERRIDE flicked on and Mary hit the switch. "No need to spook Stan, right?"

Kate sat up and paused the video loop. She fussed again about Mary's well-being and doubted the decision not to send her back on the *Aristobulus*. It wasn't too late. But Mary would have none of that, and more importantly, a whole lot of questions would arise about the object on the eastern limb. She reckoned her ops skills were damn solid, but strategically, the question of what to do remained unanswered.

"What'll he do now that he knows about the Rossians?"

Mary smiled and shrugged. "Not sure. After that night when Janet blew up the tower, he was pretty quiet. Well, more than quiet. Went into some kind of neural depression, but looking back now, it's clear one of the big reasons he moped around was you taking off."

"I warned him I'd look after myself first."

"Doesn't matter. He said you betrayed him."

Kate squirmed.

Mary continued. "Yeah, he was in a strange place, trying to have a relationship with Esther but still in love with my mother."

"I remember."

She hesitated and looked away. "And then there was you."

Kate's heart leapt into her throat and her cheeks flushed. "What are you on about?"

"It's no secret how well you two got along, is all I'm saying."

Kate recalled those days on campus at the City College. She and Jim hung around a lot, going for lunch or coffee at the cafeteria, taking extended walks through the grounds . . . but Mary raised something other, something more.

"We're good friends, that's all."

Mary scrutinized her with a disbelieving smile. "I'm no expert on this, but I'd swear Dad was really in love with you, not Esther. Only he didn't see it." She smiled. "Neither did I at the time. Oh, you and I talked together about boys, remember? Esther and I did too."

A wave of panic washed over Kate, and her mouth dried up and stuck closed. Her tongue suddenly felt clumsy, and way too

ECHOES IN THE GREY

big. She stared at the console without seeing anything, her mind drifting back years ago to that time when Jim worried himself sick over whether he could raise Mary on his own.

"But those talks weren't about me. Sure, I had a crush on Tommy Wallace . . . a boy in the next grade, shy, cute, and totally nova."

"I remember you chatting about Tommy and being quite taken with him."

"Yeah, well, I used him as an excuse to understand you better. Esther too."

Kate's stomach flipped. Mary was remarkably bright, kicked ass at everything she put her mind to, and no one got into the Space Internship Program without serious ability and high scores on the Aptitudes. But this was peculiar. Only now did she realize the depth of Mary's latent intelligence and photographic memory.

That's why Marshall Whitt pursued her for his new Spacer program back then.

When she spoke, it was barely a whisper. "So, all this time when you asked about boys and dating and such, you wanted to *test* me, and Esther too?"

"That's about right."

"Shit."

Mary shook her head. "It's nothing, really. I learned years ago how to find answers to every question I had: the Calnet, of course, and my dad knows a lot of stuff too even though he's old. So, yeah." She leaned over and patted her arm. "That's why I'm pretty sure Dad like felt something for you, but Janet's ghost kept getting in the way. Esther was a diversion of sorts."

The sides of the habitat closed in on her. The panic that began as a distant shadow had become one of those compactors that squeezes in closer and closer until, at some point, it crushes the life out of you. She was an old piece of machinery waiting to be ground into a cube.

"Can we get back on track, Mary? I can't process this talk and honestly, I hate where it's heading. So, putting that aside, what will Jim do next?"

The smile never left Mary's face. "My guess is he'll tell Esther. For a few reasons. First, she's responsible for getting me the internship here, and he worries way too much about me. Second, he'll need to talk to someone, and he trusts her. Third, he'll want to figure out what she knows."

"I don't think she has a clue about this ship."

"But he doesn't know that."

Kate clenched her teeth. "Yeah, telling him was a huge mistake."

"No, not a mistake, Kate. He'll overreact, then chat with Esther, and she'll calm him down. I'm not worried about Dad at all." She lowered her gaze, and Kate studied her.

"Who are you worried about then?"

Mary considered the question for a moment and leaned in, lowering her voice. "Our biggest concern should be Titanius. They're already pissing themselves because we haven't sent any data yet, right? If they find out about the ship, they'll go neural and crap all over everyone and everything."

Kate frowned. "True, and that'll be the end of my work on Luna."

"And they'll send me home, too."

EIGHT

Terran Science Academy
San Francisco
California Congressional Republic

Esther

THE SPACIOUS, WINDOWLESS CONFERENCE ROOM on the third floor of the TSA, down the open hallway from Esther Tyrone's office, buzzed with activity more so than usual. Representatives from the TSA's Corporate and Policy, Space Operations, and Search for Extra-terrestrial Life divisions—the latter two under Esther's leadership—prattled, laughed, and waited for her to bring New York online. A massive screen descended at the far end of the board table, and the lights dimmed as the color bars blinked, followed by an image of a smaller boardroom at Titanius Headquarters. When CEO Clayton Carter appeared on the monitor with his sidekick Ed Mitchell and a scribe, she called the meeting to order.

"Good morning, Clayton, how is the link today?"

Carter gazed up at the camera, showed off his perfect teeth in a wide smile, and boomed in baritone, "Much better, Esther, thanks again for looking into that. Your team is first-rate there. Everything's crystal clear."

"Glad to hear it." She sipped on her coffee. The problem with these cross-continent meetings revolved around food. The East Coasters were awake and sharp at 10:00 their time. Her crew had just arrived and looked half asleep. Advantage Titanius. That's why she'd been at the office a couple hours already to prepare.

"Clayton, let's get down to it, shall we? We've paid great homage to the protocols of effective negotiations by dancing politely around the maypole defining the scope of what's on the table." She stared right into the camera, ignoring the scientists and various corporate bodies in the room. "So . . . can we cut through the niceties and boil this down?"

Carter glanced at his colleague Mitchell, the one with the annoying grin that never disappeared. "I'm listening. How do you wish to proceed?"

Esther twirled her pen in her fingers. She peeked at her notebook and the three key issues she'd sketched out. When negotiations began a few months ago, she understood the impossibility of out-foxing Clayton Carter. He had more experience putting trans-national, private-public agreements together than she had, and his success running a major space resources company proved he knew what he was doing. So, finesse and layering wouldn't work with him. She preferred an upfront, honest approach anyway, one that emphasized in broad terms what the

TSA needed and what they were willing to give up or share in return. If they could not reach an agreement, so be it.

"Sorry, Esther, are we still connected?"

She peered up at the screen and smiled. "Yes, but stand by for a second." Time to make her play. She punched the mute button on the microphone and looked around the conference room at the mix of confused and sleepy faces. Mark Jefferson's eyes met hers and held them. He sat straight up, alert, and loyal. He also knew the history first hand when the former head of Space Ops, Marshall Whitt, died at Mount Sutro and she took over the division. Mark had been there as a grad student, had worked on the Ross 128 signal, and most importantly, had kept his mouth shut about it all.

"Dr. Jefferson, you stay. Everyone else out." The group froze in silence, staring at her. "Now, ladies and gentlemen."

They hauled themselves up and grumbled out of the room. Lizzy from Finance, holding her notebook against her chest, said, "I don't advise doing this, Dr. Tyrone. Dr. Kapoor wants me in the negotiations."

Esther raised her eyebrows and sighed through her teeth. "I promise, I won't be giving away the farm, so the Big Boss has nothing to fear. No numbers, okay?"

Lizzy slid around the end of the table, scowling, and left.

"Mark, come sit beside me."

"Yes, ma'am." The lanky scientist climbed out of his chair at the back and took the one next to hers.

Esther adjusted the camera angle to focus in on the two of them, then opened the microphone. "That's better. If we're going to do this, it'll be me and you doing it together. Not a bunch of pointy-headed bureaucrats and underlings, agreed?"

Clayton smiled and opened his arms wide. "By all means. I'm thrilled to talk this way. Seeing all those scientists and engineers around your table is a bit intimidating."

He understood how to play the game, and it was on. "Well that's difficult to believe. No one achieves what you have without courage and confidence."

He grinned. Mitchell whispered something in his ear.

"Esther, unlike a diplomat, I have no patience and I suspect you don't either. We both want to work more intimately together, correct?"

"True."

"So, it's no surprise we'd like access to your research in space science, and share your group's innovative tech, develop it, and apply it to further our mineral resources exploration program in the solar system."

Esther mused to herself, *nothing new yet, but I smell an end game here, somewhere.* "That's the impression I got from the last two days chatting about how we might team up and to what extent we'd be in bed together, so to speak. We're not interested so much in resource exploration, but we are looking for a dance partner."

"Good, and if I may, I understand you need something from us, too. Specifically, access to our fleet to further your space objectives . . . hunting for aliens and such, correct?" Even across the continent, Carter's dark brown eyes pierced into her. He was skilled asking questions to which he already had the answers. She was glad that Mark sat beside her, scribbling notes.

"Yes, that's right. The search for alien life is part of my mandate, and we simply don't have the operational capacity to take it off-planet where we need to be." She drained the last of her coffee. "But there's more. Something I haven't talked about yet."

"Oh?" Carter leaned forward toward the camera, fingers interlaced together.

"The cold war between the NDU and the Confederate States affects us both in different ways. I'll be honest with you, Clayton, and I expect the same courtesy in return." He nodded. "I am concerned about internal security here at the TSA, and I wonder how we might initiate a space exploration program without worrying about hostile nations or corporations, or any other rogue group out there."

"Are you anxious about anyone in particular?"

Esther pursed her lips. "No, but we've had spies of all stripes in our organization over the years, and it's a real problem. The need for security around our research is paramount." She locked eyes with him. "I want to be certain I can trust you to keep our work together out of the hands of those who would harm us."

"You mean the Chinese?"

"Possibly, but there's a greater danger here at home. I just hav-en't figured out who it is yet."

Carter leaned back. "I see." He threw a cursory glance at Mitchell, almost imperceptibly, but she caught it. The game, indeed, was on.

"Esther, would this have anything to do with that Rossian signal?"

And there it was, exposed. He'd picked up the rock and peeked underneath it. She'd made the right decision kicking everyone else out. Only she and Mark understood the details of the tap code that Jim Atteberry discovered floating through the sub-space bands one night all those years ago. Mark and Marshall Whitt undertook some off-the-record early communication attempts with the ship in the Ross 128 system with limited success. After the investigation into the incident, she purged all the files associated with Ross 128 and, over time, the alien voice from beyond grew into just another rumor, one more false alarm, a dead end, a breadcrumb for the conspiracy theorists.

But Esther understood Carter was no fool, and there he beamed innocently on the other side of the continent, his dark skin and cold eyes radiating confidence.

"What have you heard about that, Clayton?" Her voice sounded stronger, louder than she had wanted.

"Nothing more than anyone else. Only the rumors, like how it was a false signal. But somewhere in there, that damn tower collapsed in a heap, wiping out the only subspace transmitter on Earth, and nothing's been built to replace it. Curious, no?"

"What are you saying?" Esther looked at him nervously.

His face grew serious, the smile disappearing. The game shifted to another level and intensified. "Only this. If the Rossian alien encounter was real, and you know where they are, I want to help you. Titanius has the fleet and the resources to provide, er, security if you ever feel compelled to share the aliens with the world. We can take you where you need to go."

"And in return? What's in it for you, hypothetically speaking."

"What I covet is access to their faster-than-light technology. Nothing more."

Mark looked over at her and pointed to his notebook. He'd written a series of giant exclamation marks over it. She nodded.

"Very interesting, Clayton, and perhaps something we could discuss further, in time. Unfortunately, there was no real alien signal."

The silence over the connection lasted several seconds, neither one saying anything, both staring hard at each other waiting for the other to blink, but Esther could hear nervous breathing over the line. Finally, she said, "Clayton, perhaps you and I should arrange a couple of private conversations. Just you and me. Would that be helpful?"

His eyes narrowed. The smile suddenly reappeared and his teeth flashed again. "Splendid idea, yes! Let's do that."

Her indie-comm vibrated, and she glanced down at it. Yet another urgent message from Jim Atteberry. She made a mental note to call him once the meeting with Titanius finished.

Atteberry

OVER 24 HOURS HAD PASSED SINCE THE off-network call. He trusted Kate more than anyone else in the world to look after Mary and keep her best interests at heart. If she said they're all fine and that there's no danger from the alien ship, then he should accept that.

Except he couldn't. Atteberry paced around his dusty office at the City College Oceanside campus, pausing once or twice to check his indie-comm. The uncertainty of Mary's situation on the Moon gnawed away at his gut to the point where he failed to get any work done on his new literary paper. Summers were cruel that way, when his English classes were over but the weather and family made it challenging to start the academic research. The call presented another complication.

Esther's lack of response to his messages was frustrating. It seemed as if the universe conspired against him, leaving him in the dark with only his prehistoric brain and imagination for company. He had to speak with her, with *someone* about that Rossian ship and what he'd heard six years ago on the amateur astronomy subspace bands.

A soft rap on his door interrupted him. Helen, the Native American Lit prof from down the hall, smiled at him over her reading glasses. "Deep in thought, Jim?"

He brushed the hair back off his forehead with the palm of his hand. "Yeah, having trouble concentrating today. Must be the nice weather."

"I understand." She leaned her thin frame against the door jamb, the cotton floral dress hugging her. "You look bagged. Want to take a break and grab a coffee?"

Jim checked the time on his indie-comm and glanced back at his computer console surrounded by file folders and a stack of worn books from the library. A part of him wanted to go with her, tell her about the Ross 128 signal and Kate's call, but he suppressed that and instead, nodded toward his desk. "I'd better not. This mess won't resolve itself on its own. Thanks anyway."

"Maybe tomorrow?"

"Sure, sure, sounds good."

Helen smiled and continued down the hall, her summer sandals clipping along the marble floor. Jim parked himself in front of his computer for a moment and stared at the screen, then got up and paced around again, the uncertainty and his own indecisiveness killing him.

When the indie-comm pinged, he almost jumped out of his skin. A message from Esther: *meet me at Grinders 3:00?* He messaged back: *see you there . . . thanks.*

ATTEBERRY COULDN'T RECALL THE LAST TIME he saw her, but it might have been over the Christmas holidays. Cool and dark days, he remembered that. When she entered Grinders Coffee Shop and peered around, his heart leapt. He waved, and she caught his eye and smiled.

An autoserver cruised by their table and they pulled their drinks. Esther took a protein bar as well, managed a bite, and said, "Remember the first time we came here, Jim? You looked like you hadn't slept in days!" She laughed.

"Yeah, because I hadn't. That alien signal consumed me." He sipped his coffee and grimaced at the bitter flavour.

"I've blocked out a lot of what happened, especially from the night at Mount Sutro. I do remember leaving the TSA with you and Kate and one of the CalRep soldiers, but it's a blur after that." She took another bite. "Just as well, I suppose."

Atteberry leaned over the small table toward her. "I remember everything." He stared at a spot of cream on the tabletop, paused, then looked up. "What happened between us, Esther? Seems like everything changed after that night."

Esther's smile disappeared, and her grey eyes bore into his. Atteberry said the wrong thing, but that was often the case with her. She was difficult to read.

"It all changed, Jim, and we both know why. Oh look, we can pretend it was the investigation, or maybe my new work responsibilities, and perhaps those were contributing factors." Esther held her coffee in both hands. "But as much as I wanted to explore something more, I just wasn't ready. Besides, your heart belonged to Janet."

"My ex-wife?"

"You were only separated, if I recall."

He struggled to find the words, and she'd rendered him tongue-tied with the ex-wife comment. No question, he'd felt something for Janet at the time and in those moments of honesty with himself, realized that in a corner of his life, he still loved her. For him, love was not binary: it was a continuum.

Esther continued. "We also both recognize that even though you divorced her, it didn't really change your heart, did it?"

Atteberry reflected on the evening he signed the divorce agreement and the overwhelming emptiness that smothered him. In truth, he hoped there'd be a sense of relief, the dawn of a new day, a new relationship with Esther. It never happened.

"You're probably right."

"Anyway," she interrupted, "let's not relive those days again. It took a lot of time and effort to recover from you and the death of Marshall Whitt, and I'm not convinced I'm fully healed." She sipped the coffee, staring at him over the cup, and smiled. "So, what's on your mind, Jim? What's with all the urgent messages?"

Atteberry glanced around the shop, trying to curtail the paranoia that was as much a part of him these days as was his shadow. Grinders was only half-full at this time of the afternoon, with a couple of tables chatting, a young man reading by the window, and an older lady doing a crossword puzzle. He leaned in closer.

"I got a message from Kate yesterday . . . well, from Mary too."

"Oh? How's everything up there on Luna? Is she having fun?"

Atteberry opened his mouth to speak, then paused, changed his mind and said, "Mary is enjoying the work, yes, and those two like each other, so they're getting along great." Atteberry's emotions rose and he suppressed a sudden urge to scream.

Esther placed her hand over his. "What's happened?"

He gazed deeply into her eyes. "They didn't call through the regular network, Es. Instead, they rigged something up with Kate's indie-comm, to avoid detection."

Concern spread across Esther's face.

"Anyway, long story short, Kate says the aliens—the Rossians—are there. On Luna."

"Sweet Jesus . . ."

"Now they say they're not in any danger, and I believe them. But still I'm going a little crazy here. I don't know what to do." He swallowed hard and bit his lip.

Esther turned away and surveyed the room. She looked at her indie-comm and sighed. "Damn it," she whispered. "I purged all those Ross 128 files, you remember."

"Yes."

"We can't just announce, 'oh, those aliens from a few years ago? Guess what, they're watching us from the Moon.'"

Atteberry had pushed the need for open information the moment he confirmed the alien signal was real. Back then he felt the more knowledge people had, the better the world would be.

But that approach carried consequences with it, actions that almost got him, Kate and Esther killed.

"And Mary's okay?"

"She says everything's good up there. Her exact words were: no danger."

"What about Titanius? Do they know?"

Atteberry shrugged. "No idea."

He remained quiet for a couple minutes, listening to the hum and murmur of the shop and the whirr of the autoserver moving from table to table, until Esther said, "Okay, well my first instinct is to get them off Luna and somewhere safe. But this has global repercussions bigger than the lives of—"

"Don't say it, please." He shook his head.

"Bigger than the lives of any individuals. Jim, understand, this is just the beginning of a new chapter in the human journey, see? We both expected this day to come, but I'd rather keep it all quiet until we get more information and are better prepared. I must figure out how to connect with the lunar lab without Titanius listening in, or whoever else is monitoring the links." She paused. "There's one scientist I trust in Space Ops here who might help, but I'm also deep in negotiations with Titanius's CEO, and that's a complication." She checked her indie-comm again. "I've got to run. Leave this with me, okay?"

Although the inkling of relief from sharing his news provided him a small measure of comfort, it couldn't completely assuage his anxiety. "Sure, I will, but I'm afraid. Mary's all I have in the world."

Esther rose from the table. "I'll get on it as soon as I can. I promise."

"Thanks." Jim stood up, and they shuffled out of the coffee shop. Esther's hovercar was already waiting for her at the curb. Before she opened the door, Atteberry asked, "Would you like to come over for dinner tonight, and talk some more? I've got lots of food, and—"

"Sorry, I'm flying to New York in a couple of hours and haven't packed, and Kapoor's on my back. Kind of a last-minute thing with the Titanius negotiations. Rain check?"

Jim tried masking his disappointment as best he could. Something about her still touched him in his core, and he missed having that intimate connection. "Oh sure, yes, whenever you can."

Esther hopped into her hovercar and waved as the vehicle rose, then purred away from the curb and disappeared into the late afternoon traffic.

NINE

Kate

"THAT'S WHAT I'M TELLING YOU FOR THE THIRD TIME: it's all the data we've been able to clean up and it'll have to do until we find the problem in our seismic gear."

Dana glanced off screen, and nodded. "Stand by, Kate."

Kerchunk.

Her harsh face, rendered even more extreme under the bright fluorescent lights of the Headquarters comms room, disappeared and was immediately replaced by a static graphic of the full moon and the block letters TITANIUS written across it in blue. Mary peered up from the data analysis computers and grinned.

"It's not funny. I'm going to catch serious shit for this."

"Since when were you a rule follower?" she snorted. "Besides, you have total operational authority up here for pretty much everything, if I read the Titanius lunar lab policies correctly."

Kate stayed silent. The seismic data she transferred to Earth comprised innocuous findings that didn't show anything significant—certainly not the alien ship—and that helped Stan a bit, but Dana paid more attention to the details than her colleague, and she pushed to have the full set transmitted, dirty and raw, for the entire survey area as soon as possible.

Shaking her head, she said, "I can handle Dana Goran without resorting to that hammer. I'd rather save it for real emergencies."

"But?"

"But what I don't understand is why we can't figure out if that thing is alive? If it is, then the occupants are keeping quiet about it. If it's dead or dormant, then the question becomes what happened to them if, in fact, there were any?" Kate rubbed her arms, then grabbed her jacket and pulled it on. "Too many questions, eh? Maybe we ought to show Dana what she wants and catch the next train out of Dodge."

Mary glanced at the comms screen. It still held the TITANIUS graphic on it. "Yeah, lots of unknowns, for sure. But this is the fun stuff. Do you know what I'd be doing on Earth right now if I didn't have this internship?"

Kate smiled. "Selling shoes?"

"Peddling crap or pestering my dad to teach me things on the radio. I'd like go totally neural, and we'd drive each other crazy. But here," she waved around the lab, "is where I want to spend the rest of my life . . . in space."

The comms screen flickered back to live images. Dana adjusted the settings at her end.

"Oh good, you're still there. Listen, I've spoken with the guys in data processing here and they suggested we link up to your system and perform the analysis ourselves, down here. Any objection to that?"

Kerchunk.

Kate raised her eyebrows and smiled. She searched deep inside for the right tone of voice, the one that said she was cooperative yet also concerned. "I suppose that's an option, good thinking." That came out as sarcasm. She frowned again and adjusted her approach. "It'll take a while for us to sync the database, but we'll get on that shortly and then send you the rest of this noisy data. Does that work for you?"

Dana pushed her bangs off her face and raised her chin. "Yes, it does." Then she leaned into the screen and moved the mic piece in front of her mouth. Her eyes spoke of personal concern and professional annoyance. "But don't screw up, understand?"

"Happy to help. Lunar lab out." She punched the button, killing the connection, and swore under her breath.

Mary's amusement remained high. She didn't appreciate the gravity of going against Titanius's need for the data in order to meet its contractual obligations. Some partners, the recipients of her findings, anxiously awaited any excuse to break the agreement and send their own ships and crews to Luna, no matter what UN treaties existed about limiting human activity here. She couldn't be the one responsible for that, especially when it was under her control to fix.

With no warning, Mary's face suddenly turned from mock enjoyment to resigned shock. She cocked her head in disbelief. "Of course!" she said. "It's so obvious."

"What is?"

"Punch up my screen and I'll show you."

Kate toggled over to the data analysis functions. Several images of the alien ship site appeared, pictures they took when they were there over the past week. As far as she could tell, nothing strange jumped out, just a lot of grey, black and white, survey equipment, long shadows and trails of dark footprints where they'd walked around.

"What am I supposed to be looking at here?"

She sat beside Kate and expanded an image on the screen taken the day they ran the GPR line when Mary spent most of her time collecting geophones.

"Here," she said, pointing to an area west of the survey lines. "At one point, you walked back from the site to get a better overall view, remember?"

"Sure. I often do that, and I recorded some pics there, too."

"Yeah, but they're not important." Mary toggled up another image from a couple days after. It was the same ship location but taken from a different angle. She zoomed in on the area where Kate had been previously. At first, the picture was grainy and blurred, but when she applied the contrast correction, the resulting high definition image was unmistakable. A deep shiver ran up Kate's spine and beads of sweat broke out on her forehead.

The footsteps leading up to her vantage point on an outcrop were clear. The ones descending were at a slight angle as she'd bounded back to the GPR survey lines.

But there, in the dust, a *second* trail of odd-shaped marks arose, their impressions dark like hers against the stable, inert surroundings. Not from boots though. These thin prints reminded her of cross-country ski tracks, as if someone on stilts dragged poles through the lunar soil.

"What are those? They're unlike anything I've ever seen from our equipment." Mary asked, tracing her finger along the second set up the outcrop, encircling the high point, then returning toward the ship's apparent location, and disappearing.

Kate gulped and counted to ten, forcing herself to breathe, controlling her anxiety and the primitive part of her brain that shrieked in her ear.

"What do you think?"

When her breath returned, and her fingers stopped shaking, she grabbed Mary's arm. "This is real, isn't it? One day, just my prints and the next, these markings too?"

"They're real."

"And you didn't walk to that outcrop at all, did you?"

"No. Never went close to it." She paused. "There's more, Kate." Mary zoomed in to a clean area showing both sets of tracks and tuned the filters. "I can't resolve this any better, but do you notice that second set?" She tweaked the picture again, the resolution varying between a blurry mess and a marginally clearer image. The best she could do was a rendering of it that reminded Kate of seeing the world through a rain-soaked window.

"It wasn't me or you."

The second set of prints where they stopped at the outcrop was unlike any human boot she'd ever seen. They appeared to be . . . *some kind of numerous stick-like footprints*, narrower than Kate's own, and much smaller than Mary's, piercing the soil.

"We're definitely not alone up here." Mary smiled with growing excitement in her wide eyes.

Kate swallowed the urge to vomit all over the comms panel. *How long had they been here? Are we safe?* She masked the sudden fear rising in her, fought the intense craving to cut herself, and turned to Mary with a detached, cold smile. "This changes everything."

TEN

Mary

LUNA'S LANDSCAPE REFLECTED THE SUNLIGHT that bathed the ancient lava flows of the *Mare Crisium* in a brilliant, mirror-like wash. Mary studied the terrain through the lunar lab's thick window with a painter's eye: ancient volcanic cones, cratered impacts, and the smooth basaltic shadows of the mare were far more interesting than she ever believed possible back on Earth. And far more beautiful.

But, she hadn't been to the Aristoteles automated strip-mining site at the *Mare Frigoris* near Luna's northern pole, or the abandoned lunar habitat there used to support the workers who built it and could only imagine the blight it caused on the lunar landscape. Oh, she'd seen the pictures, video of the place, but as she'd learned from the *Mare Crisium*, nothing compared to seeing the real thing.

"Do you think they're interested in the resources here, Kate?"

Kate looked up from her bunk where she pored over notes and calculations for additional testing of the ship site. Her face was a mosaic of hard lines and crow's feet that Mary hadn't noticed earlier, and she wondered if Kate was still taking those anti-rad pills.

"If that was the case, they'd be more interested in the active mining operations on the far side." Leaning on an elbow, she asked, "Do you remember the first signal your dad picked up?"

"Yes, a tap code . . . a 1 – 1 – 8 signal and he figured it represented the atomic numbers of hydrogen and oxygen . . . two Hs and one O . . . H_2O. He wondered if they were looking for water. That was a crazy night."

"Right," Kate said, "and that's what the consortium was mining up at the pole. Water, helium, the odd rare metal. So, if it was only water they're looking for, they should have gone there." She thought for a second. "Well, perhaps they did, and now they're looking for something more."

"Either way," Mary broke in, "they hid by the *Mare Marginis* for whatever reason and made no effort to reach out. Perhaps the magnetic field there serves as camouflage."

Kate sat up on the bunk and frowned. Mary had known her since she was maybe five or six years old and idolized her. She learned to program from Kate through a computer game and also learned how much her dad enjoyed her sharp intellectual mind and practical experience in space. Teaching English literature at the college was fun, but Mary understood his real love was space.

Why he hadn't pursued science as an occupation remained a mystery.

"Jim, if he was here, would be out at the site with an excavator, digging up the spacecraft, wouldn't he?"

"Yeah, probably."

"And then he'd be broadcasting the findings to the rest of the world, right?"

"You know him as well as I do, Kate."

She frowned again. "And then the race to claim the Moon would be on. Imagine what'll happen if news of this gets out. The war over Luna's resources would turn hot, and more than that, the quest to capture the aliens and their tech would be on."

Mary leaned back against the lab window, facing Kate, and stretched her long legs. "Exactly. Nothing good can come from sharing this with the world. Not yet, anyway."

Kate leaned forward, elbows on knees. "We've got to contact the aliens first, find out what they're doing here, before telling anyone else."

"Except for my dad," Mary added, "and Esther."

"I trust Jim with my life. Not so sure about Esther, but he seems to like and trust her, so that's good enough for me. And, yeah, your dad *already* knows."

Silence filled the habitat, other than the hum and whirr of the computers, the air exchanger and recycler, and other noises of the life-preserving infrastructure. Mary gazed up at the domed ceiling. Now that the *Mare Crisium* was in full sunlight all the time, it was impossible to see the stars, but she remembered them when the location was in shadows . . . endless, distant, supporting life on other Earth-like planets. And so many of them.

"We need to go back out there, Mary, and this time, we have to make contact. It's easy to imagine alien creatures as nasty, bug-eyed monsters bent on taking over the world. But what if they're just curious and shy?" Kate slouched forward, staring off into some other place.

"How do you plan to keep Titanius from hijacking the computers and data?"

Kate said matter-of-factly, "That's a challenge. I could keep stalling although that won't work much longer now that Dana wants to move forward with connecting into our database. So, my idea is this . . ."

Mary leaned forward.

"We run silent . . . dark."

"What?"

"Incognito. Stealth mode."

"Ah yes, like the *Nautilus* evading the Spanish armada." Mary's love for literature, especially the classics, proved incredibly useful in understanding the grown-up world.

"It'll mean the end of my career with Titanius, Mary. Do you understand that?"

"Yes." She reflected on her knowledge of Kate. Recruited into the Spacer Program as a kid, brainwashed, trained, sterilized. Sent to work in radioactive environments, then turfed out in the American cold war, winding up as a computer programming teacher at City College, and now this.

"It's too bad, really. I enjoy being up here alone, but I'm ready for something more. Listen," she stood up and dragged a stool over. "This isn't what I'm supposed to do for the rest of my life, and I never realized how much I need human contact until you arrived. Anyone else, I'd probably throw myself out the air lock."

Mary smiled, cautiously.

"That was a joke. Anyway, what I'm trying to say is it's time for me to do something else, to find the next project, to seek out a new adventure once this contract ends. Any of this make sense?"

Mary reached out and touched her bony shoulder. "It does," she said. "Kate, whatever you do about anything here, I'm in. This is the most nova place in the world—I mean, galaxy!"

Kate's eyes narrowed and her face took on a dark, serious look. "My first priority is to keep you safe, agreed?"

"Okay."

"Then, it's making sure you're not swept along into my nasty vortex. So, whatever happens with the ship out there, hiding it was all my idea, and that I pressured you to fall in line."

Mary smirked. "There's no pressure, Kate. I'll follow wherever you go."

Kate's squinting continued. When Jim did this, Mary referred to him as "pulling a Nietzsche", scrutinizing everything, looking for absolute truth statements and hypocrisy. Didn't matter. Sometimes she imagined herself as Dickens' Little Nell, following her grandfather around from adventure to adventure. Other times, she was more like Adam, Victor Frankenstein's creature. Completely misunderstood. Completely human. But this day she felt like a co-conspirator, a bit like Scout, a bit like Holden Caulfield.

Her heart pounded with excitement.

Kate said, "All right. If we're going rogue, the first thing to do is cut the comms link with Titanius."

Carter

"I'M WAITING FOR HER IN THE HOTEL lobby, sir, then we'll be on our way."

Carter thanked the driver and cut the link. Esther Tyrone wasn't kidding about getting together for one-on-one conversations, having scheduled several meetings together, some here, some in California. He found that assertiveness invigorating, and attractive.

When she arrived at his Manhattan office, he noticed how much taller she stood in person. Wearing a dark blue jacket and skirt, white blouse, and a TSA pin, she carried a thin briefcase. He'd always liked and respected her. It couldn't be easy leading both Space Ops and the SETI divisions in a bureaucratic quagmire like the TSA, but she handled the job smoothly. Perhaps she may be interested in joining Titanius one day, but for now, he needed her at the Academy.

"Welcome to New York, Esther!" They shook hands, and the warmth and strength of her grip struck him. "I trust your flight was uneventful and your hotel's in order?"

"Yes, on both counts." She inspected the office and was immediately drawn to the large window overlooking the East River. "It must be hard to get work done with that view."

"Sometimes, I admit. When we took over the building, this view sold it for me. It's very relaxing." He sidled up beside her and caught the scent of perfume. Pointing across the river, he outlined a labyrinth of non-descript low-rise dwellings in the distance. "See those structures? That's where I grew up." Esther nodded slowly but said nothing. "Come on, I'd like you to meet my team."

He escorted her around the floor of executive suites, introducing Ed Mitchell, who joined them on the tour, and numerous others until an anxious look crept over her face.

"I'll never remember everyone," she said, smiling. "And, if you don't mind, Clayton, I'd like to get to work."

"By all means. Forgive me, this isn't a social visit, and I'm sure you've got a thousand things on your plate. Please join me in my boardroom." He guided her down the thick-carpeted hall back to his office. A small, but comfortable boardroom opened off his sitting area, and he followed her in. Mitchell skulked behind him and closed the door.

Esther chose a chair on the far side of the polished table. Carter sat across from her, and Ed took up a place in between. She stared intently at his colleague with fiery grey eyes, then turned to him. "Clayton, I thought these meetings would be just you and me. No bootlicks."

Carter bellowed with laughter and slammed his broad palm on the table, rattling a collection of glasses. Ed Mitchell smiled wanly and, without saying a word, left the room.

"I don't mean to be rude, Clayton, but if these negotiating meetings are going to work, you and I have to speak openly and freely, without interference from underlings. Yes?"

A tear of laughter fell from his eye. "Forgive me again, Esther, it's just that no one has ever referred to Ed as a bootlick before, even though he is a fine one." He smiled and leaned back. "Okay, I support that. Let's talk and see where things go, just you and me." Carter looked around the room. "Would you like anything before we begin? Coffee?"

"Sorry, I'm drowning in caffeine this morning. Even with those lag pills, my body refuses to adjust to the different time zone quickly. It's still six in the morning my time."

They made small talk for a few more minutes before getting down to business. Esther pulled an agenda from her attaché along with a worn, leather notebook. Carter's assistant knocked and entered with his file folder and a jug of water.

For the next two hours, they went over the formal activities of both organizations. Esther provided updates on the TSA's long-term strategic plan, which he found fascinating because of the emphasis placed on exploration of the solar system—with no substantive craft, he noticed—and he presented his own vision of mineral exploration and exploitation for the benefit of all humans. As he wrapped up the discussion with a series of images on the boardroom's screen showing the Lunar Geophysical Lab, the new build on Mars, and a graphic illustrating various mining runs to the Kuiper belt and beyond, Esther leaned forward, eyes widening as he talked about the need for resource extraction to pave the way for humans living and working in space.

"I don't have to be in this business, Esther. I've got sufficient funds now to do whatever I please."

"So why bother, then?"

His passion bubbled up and he, too, leaned across the table. "Because I am called. Not in any kind of antiquated god-inspired, biblical way, mind you. I'm not a believer. No, I feel a duty and responsibility—an obligation—to help all humankind achieve great things."

"In space, you mean?"

"Not just in space . . . on Earth too. Think about it," he grinned. "Our wealth throughout history has always depended on digging stuff out of the ground. That's what I do, but it's not an end in itself. I've helped build educational institutions around the world, funded hospitals, supported the arts. I'm sure you know all about that."

Esther nodded.

"And now, with ongoing expansion into space, Titanius is at the forefront of building new colonies, planetary satellites, and state-of-the-art ships. All of this," he waved at the images scrolling across the wall screen, "is only to serve one purpose: to improve the lives of all people everywhere."

His words hung in the air. Esther watched the pictures for a moment, then whispered, "Clayton, I'm not sure how much the TSA can offer. You're familiar with the research we're doing in analytical methods, new propulsion systems, composite materials. But what you're talking about is already well beyond our capability."

Carter felt her hesitation, a reluctance on Esther's part to continue with the possible partnership. The next move would be critical.

"Well, I respectfully disagree. Look, we could join ranks with any number of research-based companies and, indeed, several firms work with us right now on piece-meal projects. But the TSA—and you specifically—can offer so much more. We need your expertise, and the Academy's location on the west coast is of vital strategic importance as well." He leaned back in the chair. "With your penchant for innovation and experience in deep-space exploration, we would equally benefit from this partnership."

"Seems to me," she said with a coy smile, "that you're holding something back."

His gaze narrowed. *Am I really that transparent?* "Esther, tell me more about the Ross 128 vessel. Are you holding something back, too?"

"Clayton, there's nothing there."

"Cut the bullshit. I've been upfront with you all along. Something happened five years ago, something big. Congressional troops don't just show up one night, guns blazing and taking down a century's old tower for no reason."

Her face tightened, and she exhaled deeply. He'd heard about that night when soldiers had to shoot their escape from the TSA's lab. The destruction of the Mount Sutro Tower and sub-space transmitter must have involved her, and Ed suspected a cover up. Esther struck a defiant pose with arms crossed in front of her.

"Whatever you've heard, I guarantee there is no alien vessel. There was an incident at the TSA, true, but aliens were not behind it."

"I don't believe you."

"Then we have nothing more to discuss."

Dr. Tyrone gathered her notebook and papers and stuffed them into her attaché. She pushed the chair back and stood. "I'm disappointed, but to be frank, not surprised. Now, I've got some other meetings I need to prepare for, so thank you for the hospitality." Carter protested but as she opened the boardroom door, she turned and said, "I'll see myself out. Good day, Mr. Carter."

DURING THE REST OF THE AFTERNOON, Carter busied himself with the technical reports on the *Echo*'s new engines, and video-linked with the vessel's captain, John Powell, at Titanius's northern flight pad in Nova Scotia to discuss the timing around an interplanetary test run. There had been significant interest in the *Echo* for several months. His engineers had developed powerful thrusters, and news of the latest orbital runs spread across the world overnight. This tech would significantly reduce travel times and solidify Titanius as the leader in space exploration. Imagine what he could accomplish with the TSA on side.

At 8:30 that evening, he called Esther's hotel and relaxed when the front desk put him through.

"May I see you again before you return to California?"

"It'll have to be tonight. My flight leaves first thing in the morning."

"Great! Be there soon."

He picked up a bottle of French wine and a bouquet at the gift shop around the corner from Titanius headquarters and took a hovercab to the hotel.

Esther opened the door to her suite and invited him in. She still wore her day clothes, although she'd undone the top buttons on her blouse, and Carter couldn't miss the pile of papers, notebooks, and tablet on the small work table. She studied him, waiting for him to speak.

"Look, Esther, I'm sorry about what happened today. I was out of line and should have known better."

She raised her eyebrows.

"So, I come bearing a peace offering . . . a small gift that I hope you'll accept along with my apologies." He handed her the bottle of wine and the bouquet.

Esther smiled and invited him to sit down on the sofa. She inspected the bottle—a fine Merlot—put it on the coffee table, went into the kitchenette and returned with two glasses and a corkscrew.

After sampling the wine, Esther leaned back in a chair across from him and said, "The truth is, I don't know yet how far to trust you, Clayton. But I believe we can work well together, as partners, so I'll go out on a limb here." She sipped her drink. Carter's tall frame didn't fit the small sofa, and he struggled to find a comfortable pos-ition while Esther searched for her words.

"Understand," she said, "this must stay here, in this room. No sharing with Ed Mitchell or anyone else. If you do, I'll deny it all and that'll be the end of our discussions."

"Okay."

"There's no easy way to say this so here goes. We contacted an alien vessel from Ross 128 six years ago. It was a disaster for many reasons, poorly managed, a real cock-up. Anyway, long and short of it is, the readings we took just before the tower came down suggested—and I choose that word carefully—it was headed to Earth."

"Unbelievable . . ."

"Yes, well, there's more." She savored the wine on her lips before swallowing. Carter noticed the dark circles under her eyes, the strain of jet lag and too much work taking its toll. Still, she was somewhat attractive for an older woman.

"What is it, Esther?"

"That ship, or whatever it is, or was . . . well, all our readings showed that it was traveling faster than the speed of light."

Carter put his glass on the coffee table and scratched his head. "Hang on. The Ross 128 star system is, what, about 11 light years from us?"

"More or less."

"How much faster was it going?"

"Impossible to tell without proper analysis, but the Spacer veteran, Kate Braddock, figured it could arrive in weeks or months."

Carter gulped, struggling to suppress a smile. "Where is it now?"

Esther grinned. "No idea. There's been nothing detected, no sightings, not a thing. For all we know, if the ship in fact was real, it could be anywhere in the galaxy."

He leaned back, nodding. A thousand ideas raced through his mind, not the least of which was: *how can I find it first?*

"Why are you telling me this now, Esther? You could have said something earlier."

She shrugged. "Call me paranoid, but maybe the boardroom is built to record all your meetings." His gaze dropped to the table. "I can't be talking about such things in an unknown space." After pausing a moment, she continued. "This room is clean, by the way. I swept it."

Carter drained his glass and stood up. "Thank you, Esther. I appreciate your confidence and I swear I won't repeat a word of this to anyone. I'm glad I could see you tonight, but you need sleep and I've got a big day tomorrow with one of my ships."

She walked him to the door and thought *others do this all the time without fear or consequence.* Then, pivoting, she looked up and whispered, "Clayton, stay the night."

ELEVEN

Kate

TRANSFERRING THE NEW DATA FROM THE ALIEN ship site to the external memory tube took a little longer than Kate anticipated, but it was a necessary step. She knew the techs at Titanius headquarters were more than capable of tapping into the lunar lab's database and servers, and the last thing she wanted was to cause more panic. This way, if anyone on Earth needed to see what she and Mary had been doing, they'd have to travel physically to the lab. That would not happen. The cost of a special trip was far too high, and the nearest transport, *Aristobulus*, had disappeared from the area. She'd have one more day, maybe two at the most, before all hell broke loose and Stan and Dana and whoever else back home would read her the riot act.

But that's all the time she needed.

This morning, with almost half of Luna in sunlight now, they agreed that Kate would set up the new test equipment and communicate with the alien ship to see if anyone or any*thing* was inside it. Mary assured her she could monitor the lab environment, and would stay behind to analyze the data as she received it. They'd save a lot of time doing it this way, and it would give her a chance to be on her own for a while, something her introverted self needed, and this was her opportunity.

She flew Mary's LunaScoota since it already had the equipment strapped in its cargo bay. She added new gear to it: a biodetector to map and analyze the interior organics of the vessel, and a series of remote cameras she planned to leave there in case whatever creatures were in it went for another walk on the surface. Most importantly, she wanted to communicate with it, and if this was the Ross 128 spacecraft Jim detected back in 2085, then what better way to announce herself than with the same 1-1-8 tap code and see where that would lead.

"I'll remain in contact with you, Mary, when I'm out there."

"Got it." Mary's voice crackled over Kate's helmet speaker.

The one hour, ten-minute flight out to the ship site was uneventful. Kate didn't hammer the throttle since the effort required there wouldn't take a full day, and she spent the trip thinking more about the consequences of her impending actions. The Spacer community—what remained of it after the second American civil war—was close-knit, yet mysterious. No one really wanted to talk about what they'd done, so other than helping each other cope from time to time with the professional and medical after-effects, there was nothing connecting them except that they were recruited identically: brainwashed and trained the same way, and sent out to perform dangerous tasks in toxic environments. But, once Titanius relieved her of her duties on Luna—and they would—she'd have to find somewhere safe to live for a while, and that's where the strength of the network came through. On several occasions, Kate sheltered fellow Spacers who needed to go to ground. When she left Jim after the Mount Sutro explosion, she crashed at a colleague's apartment in Oakland for two weeks before she landed her own, quiet place.

Their earlier trails out to the site guided her like a zipline, weaving through the impact zone and over volcanic cones and outcrops. When she arrived at her destination, everything appeared normal. The tracks of the previous GPR surveys remained along with other evidence of their work. No surprise since it could take thousands of years to erase a footprint on Luna. She eased the scooter toward the outcrop where Mary had seen the second set of steps. She needed to see them herself, first-hand.

The odd shapes were still there.

She radioed to the lab. "Are you picking this up?"

After a moment, Mary came on. "Got it. Your body-cam is working fine. Are those the alien foot prints I'm looking at?"

Kate eased the scooter to a stop and nestled its nacelles onto the dusty surface. "Yep, that's them. I've seen no others here." She pulled equipment out of the cargo bay. "But there's no doubt. These are real, and they don't belong to us. They remind me of poking sticks in deep snow."

A trio of cameras around the area was the first thing Kate established, all focusing in on the suggested location of the alien vessel. She and Mary tested them out beforehand to ensure everything was working and being recorded at the lab. Then, she brought the bio-detector unit out, slung it over her back, and bounded toward the grey shadow zone. When she arrived, she dropped the instrument on the surface.

"Before I set this up, I'll try your tap code with these creatures, okay?"

"Sure thing."

Kate checked her internal position locator and determined where the front edge of the ship's hull should be, based on what she knew about ship design. Then, she fell to her knees and brushed the moon dust away, digging deeper and deeper by scooping material out with her hand. *This is the most inefficient way of doing it*, she thought, but also hoped it was the least aggressive. If there were aliens inside with technology that could bring them this far, then they undoubtedly had the ability to destroy her if they saw her as a threat.

Still, after scraping and scooping for close to an hour and not finding any sign of the ship's hull, she returned to the scooter and retrieved the portable excavator from the sled. This tool balanced on her shoulder like a rocket launcher and moved considerable amounts of material in a quarter of the time it would take to do it by hand.

"Are you scanning in the infrared range?" Kate asked as she readied the tool.

"I've got it on continuous scan across all spectra . . . nothing strange yet. I still have the ship's shadow appearing. It might be about one or two meters below the surface where you are now.

"Roger that."

Kate hoisted the excavator up to her shoulder and targeted the hull's edge again. On Earth, this pig weighed in at over 200 kilograms, but in Luna's low-gravity environment, it was like picking up a bag of fertilizer for her garden.

Within a few minutes, several hundred cubic meters of dust and debris had been moved, exposing a dark, metallic hull buried in the soil. Kate hammered the machine off and set it down next to her. A surface area about the size of a large sofa glistened from the center of the grey hole. It was opaque, like nothing she'd seen before. It showed no signs of scarring or any other external damage, ruling out the possibility of a crash landing in her mind.

"Not sure what to make of this, but I'm trying the tap code now," Kate said as she knelt down in front of the smooth, black surface. She pulled a ball peen hammer from her tool belt and crept up to the ship.

"Are you recording this, Mary?"

"Affirmative. Go ahead."

She remembered the sound of the original signal when Jim first detected it on the subspace amateur radio astronomy band, like someone shoveling gravel, only heavier, if that made any sense. Reproducing that sound was impossible, and even if she could, the silence of the vacuum prevented her from hearing it. Instead, Kate raised the hammer up to her chest and brought it down on the dark surface. The thin vibration of the strike shot through her thick gloves.

Ting . . . Ting . . . Ting-Ting-Ting-Ting-Ting-Ting-Ting-Ting

She waited a moment.

Nothing.

"Try again, Kate."

She tapped it out again, maintaining the same cadence as before, trying to reproduce the timing of the signal Jim heard in 2085. She repeated this for several minutes, pausing in between each sequence to see if the environment changed. Kate knew she wouldn't be able to hear anything in the vacuum, but if someone was inside the ship and wanted to communicate, they might try a tap code through the hull too. And if that was the case, she'd sense the vibration.

However, nothing happened.

After almost twenty minutes of tapping and pausing, Kate abandoned the attempt and finished setting up the bio-detector. The scanning unit reminded her of a proton magnetometer—a two meter pole with a cylindrical head on top carrying the sensitive electronics that could map out near surface structures. The sensor instrument had proved itself useful in many applications on Earth, Mars, and Ganymede, but this was the first time she believed someone used it on Luna. Because it could detect water and helium in shallow crust, she hoped it might shed some light on whether the interior of the ship was a vacuum or not, and detect any evidence of organic life.

"Mary, I've set the scanning angle wide for this. Are you ready to receive data?"

Static crackled across Kate's audio link, then Mary came on and said, "It's ready here. Send me a couple of test sweeps to make sure everything's functioning."

Kate punched the ENGAGE button on the bio-detector and watched the amber STAND BY lamp turn green. After two minutes, she turned it off.

"It's working fine at this end, Kate. I got a stream of data and it all appears clean and ready for analysis."

"Great. I'll fire up the unit again and return to the lab. Keep monitoring the transmissions and let me know if there's any problem, okay?"

"Will do."

Kate gazed around at the desolate moonscape. Again, she asked herself the question: *why would an alien ship choose this place to land ... and hide.* The Earth shone like a beacon against the dark sky, even in night-time shadows.

It was the most beautiful sight she had ever seen.

Katie

SHE ALMOST DIDN'T RECOGNIZE MARTIN. He sat alone under a maple tree, eating a sandwich on an unusually warm, late fall day. Despite the small size of the training center's campus, it had taken several weeks for Kate to meet anyone from the Aptitudes Testing Center back home. Martin—even though he'd grown frailer—she remembered, but that other girl, the one who cried a lot in the hall, wasn't here.

Katie strolled over to the tree and waited for him to lift his head. "Hi. Remember me? We did the Aptitudes together."

Martin's face remained blank until he recognized her and invited her to sit down. She introduced herself, then they sat in silence for a few minutes, avoiding eye contact. She picked at the thin, brownish grass beside her.

"Do you know what they do to us?" His eyes widened, and a sliver of fear appeared.

"What do you mean?"

"When they take us away for surgery, they . . ." his face reddened, and he looked down. "They remove . . . you know . . ." He motioned at his lower body, then quickly added, "Girls too. Notice none of the teenage girls have any . . . er..." He waved at his chest this time.

Katie couldn't look at him. The blush boiled through her cheeks, partly from embarrassment at the subject, and partly because she felt something for this boy she hadn't experienced with others. An ancient yearning; a crush, perhaps. She fixed her eyes on a distant bench near the path.

"Supposedly, it's to protect us from radiation when we're in space and other harmful places. That's not all." He sighed and finished chewing the remains of the sandwich. "Without those . . . parts . . . we never grow up. Never reach puberty. Did they tell you any of this?"

Katie shook her head.

"You'll hear all about it soon."

A perfect silence enveloped them for the next ten minutes. Katie felt an urgent kinship with him, a smoldering desire to hold his hand like she'd seen older kids do back home. Instead, she *wedged her fingers under her thighs and concentrated on the rough tree bark scratching through her shirt.*

Finally, curiosity got the better of her. "How do you know all this, Martin?"

He brushed some crumbs off his jersey, dead grass from his pants, then stared right through her, eyes distant and helpless, lips tight. "A trainer went over it with me this morning." Tears welled up and Katie reached out to touch his shoulder, but he pulled away.

"My surgery's in two days."

Kate

KATE MOUNTED THE LUNASCOOTA AND NOTICED, as if for the first time again, the patchy blue-green-white of Earth. A fleeting thought crossed her mind that if the universe existed through some random, chaotic event, then the odds of producing such beauty were infinitesimal and we all should feel a deep sense of privilege and good fortune for evolving from it. Yet, if some deity created it, and humankind, then we're here by design, not an accident, and must be more significant than we think we are.

Mary's voice over the helmet pulled her out of the reverie. "Everything okay there? All I'm seeing is Earth in the sky."

Kate grinned wanly.

Martin would have loved this view . . .

She squeezed her eyes, pushing Martin's memory and the Training Center out of her mind. That's when the urge to cut screamed in her brain, and she swallowed hard to kill the pain of those days. "Yes, all good here," she lied. "I'm just enjoying the scenery, is all. Gotta secure the gear in the cargo bay, then I'll be on my way."

TWELVE

Esther

THE EARLY MORNING HYPERSONIC AIRCRAFT HOME to San Francisco rested on the apron, almost ready for boarding. A few keeners milled about the final security scanner cage, awaiting the call. Esther grunted, leaned back on a green, faux leather and steel chair, coffee in hand, yearning for sleep.

She was miserable.

She checked her indie-comm for a message, but nothing showed. Odd, but not unheard of in these situations. She'd try again when she got home.

The mystery and disconnect between what she *thought* would make her happy, and the reality of how her depression the morning after, loomed large and heavy, a silent burden crushing her shoulders. *It was supposed to be better than this, wasn't it, Esther?*

Clayton Carter was blameless: he was not the problem. The disturbing emptiness slithering through her was the only consistency between him and the handful of others she'd been with over the past few years. It was impossible to understand. The physical urge of release, of reptilian mating, didn't appeal to her in the moment since the after-effects were hardly rosy and fulfilling. Intellectually, she understood there was nothing to gain from giving in to her base desires but, like the alcoholic who hates drinking, she was at a loss to figure out how to stop.

Her indie-comm chimed, and she peeked at the screen. A message from Clayton, trying to be sincere and thankful and whatever. The negotiation dance . . . an investment. She deleted it and dropped the device into her jacket pocket.

Esther recalled one of her university friends—who had been married three times—talking about relationships, desire and fulfillment. Amy hadn't found an answer yet, but claimed to be close, exploring the need for some kind of *spiritual intimacy* she called it, something more than a dim-witted, reactionary lizard brain. Esther wasn't buying it, but, her random sexual encounters consistently led to a week or two of profound unhappiness and regret.

I don't know why I do what I loathe doing.

As ridiculous as it sounded, whenever she thought about physical needs, she saw Jim Atteberry and their near-miss of a relationship.

Out of habit, she checked her indie-comm again for something from the lunar lab, then scolded herself for being a slave to her personal tech. Kate Braddock had returned none of her previous messages, and yes, that was strange. However, it wasn't unusual to wait 24 hours or more for a response from Luna. Between differences in "day time", the survey requirements, and now mentoring Mary, the lack of a message could be almost normal.

"Good morning passengers, we'll be boarding shuttle flight 202 to San Francisco in a few minutes. Please have your security passes and tickets ready."

Mary was such a fun child back then, and Esther smiled at the memories of the girl time they'd spent talking about space and boys and all kinds of other things. It was the closest she'd come to any kind of urge to be a mother. The relationship with Jim evolved too, but after Mount Sutro, Esther conceded it was doomed. He still loved his estranged wife, the policy consultant turned NDU mercenary. The rumor was Janet had been a spy when they'd met too. Whatever, even though Mary's parents weren't together, he remained in love with her, and Esther refused to compete with an apparition.

Oh, she'd thought about getting back with him numerous times in the months that followed, but found it easier to immerse herself in the merger of the two TSA directorates instead. *Affairs of the heart are over-rated,* she thought. Plus, she needed to purge all the Ross 128 records and data, every one of Marshall Whitt's notes, both private and professional. No evidence of the truth surrounding the alien signal would remain. If the Rossians ever came to Earth, she wanted to be far away, and play no part in it. That was for the politicians.

Except she opened that door again by discussing it all with Clayton. *You did it now, Esther.* It was a sordid, calculated move to aid the negotiations, as was inviting him to stay the night. The TSA needed a fleet of ships and security, and Titanius had the capacity to provide that. Although California was its own independent republic, it still had much in common with the northern democratic states, so a relationship or partnership with Titanius made sense. Coming clean with him about the Ross 128 signal was inevitable, so why be coy about it? As long as he didn't broadcast it to the world—something he wouldn't do lest it tip his hand—there should be no problem. After all, the challenging work was paramount here. Only the job. At least, that's what she kept telling herself.

Her indie-comm chimed again with another message. She pulled the device from her pocket and saw it was from Jim. *He's up early, no doubt worried about Mary and this thing they'd seen on the Moon's surface.* She texted back "nothing heard yet . . . not unusual. I'm getting on the aircraft in a few minutes and will check comms again in CA."

Esther drained the last of her coffee and stood up. The flight was ready to board, and she pulled out her ticket and security pass from her purse and moved into the queue. To her right, a young man with a crew cut and athletic build peeked at her over his tablet. When she smiled at him, he averted his gaze and walked away toward the auto-server where a handful of late arrivals picked up drinks and snacks. She hadn't recognized him at all, but she'd seen the type before. Even today, she was being watched. It didn't matter which side this guy was on: the game was in play and she wanted him to know that *she knew.*

Esther's turn to be scanned at the security cage came up, and she glanced around once more. The young man had disappeared.

Mary

KATE HAD SPENT A LONG TIME STUDYING THE SITE, AND Mary struggled with the intense isolation in the lunar lab. She peered out the viewing window at the harsh, grey environment, thinking how strange and frightening it was to be one of only two humans on the entire Moon.

Travel to the *Mare Marginis* took a little over an hour, forever if she wasn't actually riding it. Mary managed her time alone if she had something to work on, a problem to keep her busy. There was music and books, and she still wanted to fix up the antenna they'd used on Kate's indie-comm when they talked with her dad, so, yeah, lots of things to occupy her mind.

The radio crackled. "I've got the bio-detector standing by, Mary. You ready to receive there?"

She scurried over to the computer panel and engaged the recording switches for primary and backup data reading. "All set here . . . go ahead any time, Kate."

"Engaging now."

Within seconds, the feed from the remote site showed up on Mary's screen. It flew by, too quickly to read. A file size counter appeared at the lower right-hand side. Once there was sufficient data buffered, she could begin preliminary cleaning and initial filtering. Kate told her she'd need about two gigabytes, but safer to wait until the counter hit three.

"I'm reading the data one hundred percent. Are you done out there now?"

"Stand by . . ."

A minute passed. Then another.

"I'm gonna give the tap code one more try before returning, okay?"

"Sure," Mary said, then switched the screen over to show the view from Kate's body cam. She watched her bound over to the shallow excavation, look around, then fall to her knees.

"Kate is there any kind of radiation coming off that ship?"

"Checking the rad monitor . . . no, nothing at all. Just normal background emissions."

Mary's eyes flashed over to the small container of anti-rad pills by the biofeeder. She'd seen Kate take these every day, but unlike hers, they must be for something more than just Luna's background radioactivity. She made a mental note to ask her about that when she returned. Kate was far from the perfect vision of health, but the extent of her illnesses—physical and mental—remained hidden.

Mary watched the hammer strike the ship's hull in the one-one-eight pattern numerous times, interspersed by Kate's own grunting as she repositioned herself on the craft. She monitored the vital signs from Kate's suit on a secondary viewscreen. After a while here, it became easy to forget that if a suit breeched and the sealant foam failed, their blood would boil in the low pressure, followed by death. She remembered a short story from the early days of space exploration, about the cold equations and the inevitable jettison of a stowaway from a small ship in deep space. A smile crept over her face as she gazed around the habitat. Despite being a million kilometers from home and bothered by the isolation, working here for the summer was about the greatest thing she'd ever imagined.

"I'm not sensing any return taps. Are you picking up anything anomalous from the detector?"

Mary flipped screens again and freeze-framed the scrolling data. "Reviewing it now, and, ah, I see nothing weird. We might have a better idea once it's cleaned and filtered."

"Roger that." Kate's breathing filled the open transmission link. "Another possibility for not hearing anything is that the ship may not be the Ross 128 vessel. I hate to think that's the case."

"I agree."

"Anyway, I'm heading back in Mary, so I'll see you shortly."

"Sounds good. Would you pick up a pizza on the way home?"

"Say again?"

Mary chuckled. "Never mind, just messing with you."

"Back soon."

Mary sighed heavily and looked around the habitat. The bio-data streamed in with no issues. The environmental controls showed everything operating normally: air scrubbers, oxygenators pumping in pure oxygen, hygiene station, backup systems, power supplies . . . all good. Over an hour to kill and no one to talk to. Repairing the indie-comm antenna sure sounded like a good idea.

"Kate, you there?"

"Yeah, I'm en route back to the lab."

"Do you mind if I suit up and retrieve the antenna from the tower? I'd like to fix it, check the connection, you know, so maybe we could contact my dad again?"

A pause filled the space between them, and it felt enormous. Mary understood if Kate refused; standard operating procedures required that all envirosuit connections be confirmed manually. However, she wasn't a neophyte anymore and besides, Kate seldom double-checked her own.

"Sure, I guess that's okay. Just be really careful, run through the suit-up checklist with me by radio, and stay in touch when you're outside."

Mary leapt up from the computer panel and fist-pumped the air. Then, leaning forward over the radio mic, she said, "I will, Kate, thanks! Let's keep the link open, and don't worry, I won't be out there long."

"Roger."

BEFORE SNAPPING HER HELMET IN PLACE, Mary cast a quick glance at the data streams on the viewscreen, and at the environmental monitor. All seemed in order, so she secured her envirosuit, went through the final checks with Kate, and entered the airlock. The internal parameters screen on her visor showed all suit systems green, so she engaged the pressure rotator and, when it had completed cycling, she opened the hatchway to the moon's surface.

The isolation overcame her again as she bounded toward the comms tower. When Kate was around, she'd never faced this fear of being abandoned, of being the only remaining soul on Luna, but now, terror bordering on outright dread enveloped her. *How did Kate last up here so long by herself?*

The tower was a poorly-named structure. In fact, it was a non-descript crank-up telescopic pole, about 20 meters in height, with a boom on which various comms dishes and antenna arrays were affixed. She had attached the Yagi for the indie-comm at the top and run a thick coaxial cable down to a junction box at the base of the crank. The connection to the junction was her first checkpoint. With all the dust kicking around on Luna's surface, the biggest surprise was how much of the delicate equipment continued working. Kate said it had all been housed in material specifically built for these extreme conditions, but Mary still found it fascinating.

The junction was the size of a shoe box. She engaged her helmet light and pried the lid off the container and inspected the noodled cables within. As she followed the antenna feedline through the terminal, she saw nothing obvious that could have caused her signal to wink out the other day. She recognized the interior of the cable itself may have been damaged, and that would be the last thing she'd check if no other problems showed up. She removed the airvac tool from her belt and blew dust out of the area before securing the cap on it again.

"Hey Kate, the terminal looks good. Nothing out of the ordinary. I'll bring the Yagi down and have a look at it."

"Roger." Kate's voice shot back, with a slight tremolo as she flew across the moonscape.

The tower crank held a lot of resistance and it took Mary several tough minutes to lower so she could work on the boom.

She inspected the Yagi, and no elements were out of place or damaged, but just as she prepared to remove it from the cylindrical pole, the connection where the cable running to the antenna from the junction box had been frayed.

"I may have found the problem. The input feedline connection to the beam needs replacing."

"Glad to hear it." Kate's voice rose. "Can you fix it?"

"Sure, I'll remove the antenna and repair the cable in the lab."

As she worked on removing the large connector lug, Mary suddenly felt a massive pulse vibrate up through her boots, through her bones, screaming in her head. When the sonic explosion came, the surface shock wave launched her airborne and sent her tumbling, spinning hard across the moonscape, blue arcs dancing through the vacuum like perverse lightning. More flashes of yellow and blue filled her visor.

"Say again, Mary, I missed that."

She bounced and rolled several times off the crust, coming to rest on all fours against a shallow dust dune that swallowed her up to the elbows. Everything whirled around her and she struggled to catch her breath, but sharp pain ripped through her elbow and shot up her arm. When she tried pulling herself up, she lost her balance and fell on her face.

"Mary, you there?"

A wave of nausea broke over her and she fought to swallow it down. Then, breathless, alarms blaring in her helmet, she tried to see how far the blast had thrown her from the lab, but couldn't find her bearings. Her envirosuit was torn but fortunately the foam sealant repaired that. Around her there was nothing but debris and a fog of dust clouds. A high-pitched squeal roared in her ears as expanding black pools emerged, until her entire world drifted into a deep darkness.

THIRTEEN

Kate

SHE'D NEVER HAD A COMMS PROBLEM WITH the helmet radio before, but figured there's a first time for everything and perhaps Mary's lack of response was because of a circuit failure and nothing more.

Perhaps.

Still, in this environment, the slightest mechanical issue had to be dealt with quickly and thoroughly, for the consequences were dire.

"Mary, are you there?"

No answer.

Not even the static of an open comms link.

She glanced at the industrial dashboard on her scooter. Her ETA at the lab was about forty-five minutes. If something had happened to Mary and her suit breeched, she'd be long dead by the time she'd arrive, no question about that. Kate shuddered.

Yeah, it's probably a radio circuit malfunction. Since Mary had been outside the lab working on the comms tower, and assuming she could receive but not transmit, it would make no sense to go back to the habitat, return the call, exchange helmets and begin again outside. No, that's inefficient, and Mary was smarter than that. She'd finish up her work, *then* go to the lab and call. *I'll bet that's what she's doing.*

She gave herself another twenty minutes to allow Mary ample time to complete her task and check in. Still, the nagging feeling of something not being right caused her to pull back on the throttle and push the scooter's drive engine until it red-lined its energy output.

"Mary . . . come in."

Her scooter followed the snaking dust trails across the volcanic zone toward the *Mare Crisium.*

"Mary . . . come in please."

Carter

THE DOTS JOINED UP SO WELL THAT AN APPARENTLY random set of incidents now made coherent sense. Carter sat in his office at 7:30 in the morning, reviewing the production numbers from various operations across the solar system. He'd left a message for Ed Mitchell to join him as soon as he arrived, to discuss the *Echo,* and then pored over the reports again.

Point 1. The TSA needed Titanius at least as much as he needed them. Esther's plans to transform space exploration depended on acquiring reliable craft and crews to run them. His company had both. In return, he'd gain access to their world class research lab, and perhaps more.

Point 2. Her hesitation to discuss the alien signal that Jim Atteberry heard in 2085 had more to do with information control and global stability than it did with the truth. After their chat last night, he now understood the Ross 128 alien ship was real; humans were not alone in the universe. More importantly, it was only a matter of time before that vessel arrived and when it did, he could secure its technology. He replayed that part of the conversation he'd recorded on his indie-comm without Esther knowing, and smiled.

Point 3. In the meantime, his new engine configuration on the *Echo* proved that even in the absence of Rossian FTL know-how, Titanius was poised to dominate the resource extraction industry in the solar system. The Chinese needed five years at least to catch up and by that time, he'd be screaming across the universe.

The previous day's briefing report from Technical Operations remained open on the same page it had been for the last twenty minutes, his eyes resting on the update from the Lunar Geophysical Lab. An *absence of complete coverage* from a shallow surface survey at the *Mare Marginis* raised a cautionary flag. Kate Braddock had failed to transmit significant amounts of data, and the tech team was concerned that, if this continued for any length of time, they could miss the reporting deadlines under the current partnership agreement.

On its own, this wouldn't have merited more than a quick e-comm from Ed to fix. But now the dots were aligning. He recognized something familiar with that name, Kate Braddock, when they hired her to run the lunar surveys, and now he understood why: it was the same Braddock that Esther mentioned last night . . . the one who provided Jim Atteberry with a subspace radio filter of her own design to detect coherent signals below the noise level that led to his discovery of intelligent life in the universe. Was it also a coincidence that Braddock's intern was none other than Atteberry's daughter? There they were, the four of them all connected to the initial Ross 128 signal pulled from the sky over five years ago. And wasn't it curious that now, lunar data happened to be missing or late?

Point 4. The lack of geophysicals from Luna's eastern edge was no unfortunate operational hiccup. This was not a case of statistical failure rates in equipment . . . not at all. Braddock must have found something she wanted to keep quiet. Something important enough that she'd jeopardize her work for it. If he was a betting man, he'd put his money on the discovery of a certain alien ship on the Moon's surface.

Carter leaned back and sipped a glass of ice cold water. The elevator down the hall chimed announcing the arrival of some of the office workers. Within a few minutes, Ed Mitchell poked his head around the corner, a wide smile across his face.

"Ed, come on in."

He entered, put his coffee cup on a sideboard table, and eased the door closed until it clicked shut. "Morning, Clayton. What's up?"

Carter motioned him over to the sitting area and told him what he learned last night when he and Esther chatted at the hotel. He also played him the recording where she talked about the discovery of the signal and the chaos that grew from it. Mitchell's expression did not change at all. He maintained a pleasant, almost ambivalent demeanor, but Carter knew his mind was busy calculating through several potential scenarios.

"Everything we talk about in here stays here, Ed. If in fact the Rossian ship is on the Moon, and Braddock has discovered and confirmed it, the future of the entire human race changes completely."

"Understood." He shifted his gaze to the floor, then looked Carter in the eye. "This has a significant impact on the negotiations, doesn't it," he said flatly. "I mean, if the ship is there and we secure its technology, do we even need the TSA?"

Carter raised his eyebrow in a symbolic shrugging gesture and inhaled slowly. "I believe so. It's one thing to secure the tech, but quite another to keep developing it over the long term. We simply don't have the horses or facilities like they do in California. But to be clear, it gives us a lot more scientific and geopolitical leverage."

"Undoubtedly." He sipped his coffee and winced. "What are the next steps, Clayton?"

Carter strode to his desk, grabbed the tech report, and handed it to Mitchell on the page he'd been studying. "You've seen this?"

"I have. Average production is up slightly from last week across the Martian operations—"

"No, not that. Look at the note from the ops chief for the lunar lab."

Mitchell read the short paragraph and shrugged. "A small delay in getting seismic data. It wouldn't be the first time our little Spacer has had to fix things or run additional surveys because of equipment issues or changing parameters." He cocked his head. "Am I missing something?"

Carter smiled. He felt a growing sense of confidence and clarity in what needed to be done next. "Sure, we've had glitches before, but Braddock's always fixed them quickly and got us the data for dissemination to the partners well within the required time. This one's different."

Mitchell looked over the report again. His eyes narrowed. "You think she's deliberately holding back information?" Then the gentle smile returned to his face. "Has she found evidence of the alien ship?"

"Undoubtedly."

"And she wants no one else to know about it, including us."

Carter leaned forward and clenched his jaw muscles. "Precisely. Now there may be many reasons she's keeping this to herself. Maybe some allegiance to Esther or that Atteberry fellow. Perhaps the bug-eyed monsters are threatening her or the intern. Or," his voice lowered to a whisper, "she plans to auction off the discovery to the highest bidder. Who knows?"

"We need to get up right away."

"Yes, yes we do. And that raises the next testing phase of the *Echo*. As far as we can tell, *Echo*'s the fastest ship in the solar system and we all agree she's ready for an interplanetary test run, correct?"

"Well, sure, but the crew just returned, and they haven't even submitted their complete report yet. It's too early to—"

"No, it's too *late*, Ed. We've got to prep her for a flight to Luna and see what's up there first-hand."

Mitchell nodded, thought about something else, then continued. "I'll contact Captain Powell once we're finished and figure out how soon he can pull the crew together. I take it you'll be on the flight?"

Carter smiled.

"Okay, leave the details with me and I'll keep you apprised."

A timid knock on the door interrupted their discussion, followed by a more forceful rap.

"Enter!" Carter's baritone thundered across the room as he looked over his shoulder toward the entrance. His assistant Marla Sullivan came in with a sheepish, worried look on her face, followed by an operational technician from the lab below . . . Stan something-or-other.

"I'm so sorry to interrupt, sir, but Stan Petrovic has some news I think you'd want to hear immediately."

Carter stood, facing Petrovic, hands on hips. "What is it?"

"Sir, Mr. Carter, I'm one of the guys who talks with Kate Braddock—with the Lunar Geophysical Lab, and there's been an incident."

"What kind of incident?" He glanced warily at Petrovic who licked his lips. "It must be serious to come see me personally, so spit it out."

"Well," he began, checking his tablet, "we monitor the lab activities, as you know, especially the operational parameters of the habitat, oxygen exchange rate, power ratios, all that kind of environmental stuff."

"Yes, I understand what you do. What happened?"

Stan gulped and drew a deep breath. He looked at Carter, eyes wide and strained, then to Mitchell, and back to Carter. "Everything appeared to be functioning normally, when, with no warning, the system flat-lined. The entire panel just died. One minute, normal readings. The next, nothing. By God's hands, sir, it's as if someone pulled the plug on the lab . . . like it was never even there. We've run all the diagnostics, rebooted the platform, but whatever happened, it's not at our end."

Carter's jaw dropped. Mitchell sprang to his feet. "I'm heading down now," he shouted and raced out the door. Other curious workers, who had been milling outside the office, scattered out of Mitchell's way.

"Have you been able to communicate with Braddock at all?" Carter asked in a low, measured voice.

"No, sir. Comms are down."

"What about the intern, the Atteberry girl?"

"Sir, *all* comms are completely non-functional. We're totally in the dark. It's as if the lab itself just disappeared off the face of the Moon."

FOURTEEN

Kate

IN THE ABSENCE OF ANY ATMOSPHERE AND, along with the desert-like flat surface of the *Mare Crisium*, the two and half kilometers to the Moon's horizon shone bright and clear in front of her. Kate adapted quickly to the *smallness* of Luna when she began work at the lab, but the sensation of overshooting her headlight never left when she pulled the LunaScoota at full throttle. That's what made the massive habitat strobe so important and welcoming: it beamed vertically into space in a dispersed pattern, and was visible over great distances even through bright sunlight, Earth shadow, and black space beyond.

Not this time.

As the scooter approached the lunar lab coordinates around the twenty kilometer mark, the massive beacon should have been shining in the sky. The part of her brain that kept telling her nothing was wrong, that Mary had a comms malfunction and would be waiting for her, poring over the new data when she arrived, was now quiet and afraid.

"Dammit, are you there?"

If anything happened to you on my watch, I swear I'll kill myself. Please answer.

She couldn't push the scooter's velocity any higher without risking a total overload and shutdown of its power drive, and the feeling of helplessness, of waiting, crushed down hard on her shoulders.

Half a dozen kilometers out from the habitat, a thin light glowed against the dark sky. The beacon, in its emergency non-strobe configuration, grimly reached into the surrounding gloom. *That means it's fallen off the mast and must be partially buried in the dust*, Kate thought. As she strained to see beyond the horizon and find the silhouette of the lab, the soft edges of what remained of the structure shimmered into view. Her heart sank. Utter panic crept up her spine.

No . . .

A guttural moan disappeared in the muted silence of her helmet.

The lunar geophysical lab lay before her in ruins.

THE MAIN UNIT HOUSING THE COMPUTERS AND living quarters had imploded. What normally resembled a solid yurt-like dome now appeared as though the palm of a giant's hand had squished it down into the Moon's surface. The top had cratered in and the sides splayed out. Blue arcs flickered across the electronic consoles and life support systems, into the vacuum of space.

Kate throttled down and before the scooter came to rest on its nacelles, she leapt off and bounded to the habitat, tears welling up in her eyes. "Link to Mary's suit," she commanded, and the *SEARCHING* icon appeared on her visor. After several seconds, the symbol changed to *UNRESPONSIVE*. Two thoughts needled their way into her head: *where's Mary,* and, *is the oxygenator operational?*

"Mary, where are you?"

Silence.

The radiation sniffer on Kate's suit shrieked in her helmet. On-visor data images jumped to the rad counter. Gamma rays fired at her from every direction but mostly from the destroyed power supplies, and she knew that staying here for any length of time was a painful death warrant. She searched through the shattered lab, kicking junk to the side, pulling away large sections of the structure to find her. They built these units with 3-D printing technology from the rock and dust on the Moon itself, and were foolproof, solid. There was no record of any catastrophic, random event like this happening. The only one she remembered was on the Martian moon Eros when she was a Spacer, but the technology had changed so much since then.

What the hell happened? The lab breech was massive, and she knew immediately the prospect of repairing it quickly was hopeless. She fought back more tears and, unable to wipe her nose, sniffed hard and swallowed. While searching for Mary, she lumbered over to quickly inspect the main life support generators. Both the primary and backup oxygenators were blown out, leaving only their footings visible in the surrounding cratered dust. The huge recyclers, water extractors, and power supplies flopped on top of each other, non-operational, leaking radioactive material everywhere. The beacon strobe light leaned awkwardly off to the side of the debris. Kate shielded her eyes while she disengaged the internal emergency power switch, turning it off.

This is it.

Two smaller outbuildings where they kept survey gear and other equipment had toppled outwards as if from a blast wave. The metallic spines used to reinforce their shape now twisted and poked through the concrete, like structural compound fractures. All the equipment lay scattered across the moonscape. She located the comms tower, folded over on itself in an inverted vee, and various dishes and antennas that hung from it crushed and mangled, couplings, cables and wire strewn about.

But Mary, or whatever remained of her, was gone.

Inside Kate's helmet, her own vital signs and suit parameters scrolled along the bottom left-hand side of her vision. Her heart rate pumped well over normal, and her VO2—measuring oxygen uptake—fluctuated wildly. The rad counter flashed in large numbers, below it, an estimate of how much longer she'd be able to withstand the radiation before serious health implications arose.

The urge to cut overwhelmed her.

Not now, dammit.

Kate focused on her breathing, deep and slow. Panicking, even though her source of life had been levelled, would interfere with finding a solution

Where the hell is she?

Mounting the LunaScoota again, she hovered and assessed the area. The blast radius appeared to be skewed toward the east, so she searched in an ever-growing cardioid pattern in that direction. With knowledge of Mary's weight, more or less, and where she probably was when the implosion occurred—near the comms tower—Kate estimated the distance the explosion might have thrown her. The mass of thick debris suggested whatever happened, the force had been formidable. She floated farther and farther away from the main lab's foundation.

Several minutes passed with no sign of Mary. Fortunately, the rad counter dropped as she distanced herself from the power supply leaks. Then, just before she gave up hope of finding her, a glint of light flashed at her about 50 meters away. Kate broke the search pattern and throttled the scooter toward the light.

Mary lay motionless on her stomach, half-buried in dust and rubble, a corner of her helmet's visor catching the sun's rays, her arm twisted at a disturbing angle.

THE FIRST THING SHE CHECKED WAS THE envirosuit's integrity. Without a remote suit-to-suit link, Mary's condition remained a complete mystery. She scraped away the powder from around her helmet, and as far as she could tell, there had been one breech, repaired with sealant. Vital signs flashed across Mary's visor, and to Kate's relief, appeared almost normal except for the elevated heart rate and shallow breathing. Alive, but unconscious.

She pulled the external data cable from its housing on her chest and hooked it into Mary's receptor near her shoulder. Immediately, the envirosuit readings and bio-signs scrolled across Kate's visor. The remaining oxygen was sufficient, several hours' worth (at which point, her gaze dropped to her own reserves and she found just under two left). The impact had knocked the radio link off-frequency, so Kate rebooted that circuit and synched up their comms again.

"First aid screen for Mary's suit."

The medical page flicked on and scrolled up, showing the connection to the envirosuit had been established.

"Pump 0.15 CCs of ammonium carbonate inhalant into Mary's helmet."

Two standard warning signs appeared on Kate's visor, reminding her of the dangers of using inhalant too often, or overloading it in the suit's bio-system if the first shot didn't work. She ignored these.

"Proceed."

Mary's vitals jumped as her head snapped back. Volume of blood rose; her breath stuttered and hung suspended for a moment.

"Come on, wake up!"

After what seemed like minutes passed, Mary coughed and inhaled, then groaned in pain. She tried drawing her legs up but failed.

"Hey, it's Kate. I'm here. We're outside the lab on the Moon's surface. Do you understand?"

She nodded her head once, then again.

"Kate?" Her voice sounded weak, reminding her of that night at Mount Sutro when a much younger Mary experienced the kind of terror that no one should have seen.

"You're okay, but listen to me carefully. You've been unconscious for a long time and it'll be awhile before you can think clearly again. Your elbow's dislocated. I'm gonna give you something for the pain, do you understand?"

The smelling salt had taken its effect and she stared out her visor. "Yes . . . it hurts bad."

"Pump 60 CCs of pseudophine inhalant into Mary's helmet."

Again, the warnings appeared, and Kate told the medical system to proceed.

"That'll take the edge off until we can get you fixed."

In a few minutes, Mary sat up with Kate's help. She then disconnected the data tether and returned to the scooter where she dug a binder strap out of its repair bin to serve as a sling.

"I need to do something with your elbow. Now listen Mary, we've got to move, and I can't leave it this way. It'll hurt like hell, but once it's back in place, you'll feel better."

"I know." Tears welled up in Mary's eyes.

"If you need more painkiller, you're in control of it now, okay?"

Kate stood in front of her. The initial panic of the situation here had passed, and she focused on whatever the next critical problem was: in this case, fixing Mary's arm so they could move. Finding oxy-gen was an issue too. So was calling for help. But she'd deal with those later.

"Is the pseudophine working?"

Mary nodded.

In an instant, Kate's left boot pressed into Mary's shoulder and, grabbing the broken elbow in one hand, she extended her arm, pulling it palm up to her chest. Mary screamed, and her body kicked and bucked in reaction to the pressure, so Kate increased the weight on her boot. Then, she folded the arm up and twisted it in front of her, all in one motion, yanking it hard toward her to overcome the natural hesitancy of the suit and forcing the elbow to pop back in. Mary's high-pitched shrieks dissipated.

The procedure, if she could call it that, was over and Kate wondered if Mary had passed out from the pain. She was still conscious, panting, almost in shock.

The elbow now hinged in its proper direction, so Kate worked it into the sling.

"How are you doing? Watching your vitals?"

"Yeah, better now. I'll need more of the painkiller, for sure."

"Do you think you can move?"

"I'll try."

Kate grabbed her by the waist and pulled her to an upright position. The lower gravity helped absorb much of the effort. Mary's balance was off, and she had to spread her legs wide to remain standing, but after a few seconds her body adjusted, and she took a couple of tentative steps.

"What are we going to do? The oxygenator's destroyed and—" Mary realized the full impact of her observation. "Oh god."

She listed to one side, favoring the slinged arm. "Is this how we die?"

Kate wouldn't lie to her. They were in a serious, catastrophic position and within hours (in Mary's case) or less (in her own), their oxygen canisters would expire and that would be that. She'd never given much thought to death, always accepted it as inevitable and ironically part of life. After several years working in dangerous and toxic environments, Kate respected death but did not fear it.

"It's possible, Mares, maybe even likely, but first, we need to find more O_2 and call for help." She looked around at the total devastation of the lunar lab site and retold herself there was nothing here to glue or patch or resurrect back to operational life. If they were to make it beyond the next hour or two, they'd have to go somewhere else, and they'd have to uncover more oxygen.

Mary staggered up beside Kate. "What about the active mining operations on the far side of Luna?"

Kate thought for a moment. "We don't have sufficient O_2 for a trip that long, but . . ."

"But what?"

"There's that old mine site at *Aristoteles* in the north. It's been left to rot but a functional habitat was there for the workers who built the place. It was never meant to be a permanent structure, and the builders abandoned it as soon as the automated strip mining operations began. Still . . ." her thoughts drifted to the possibility that the oxygenator and communications systems might still function. If they could hold out until a passing ship arrived, they may make it. "It's not as far as the active site, Mary, but still a day's trip. We'll never arrive there without more oxygen."

"So, let's look around here . . . for the emergency cylinders and anything else we might need."

Kate helped Mary get in the scooter's small cargo bay, propping her up in a spare seat, and they floated back to the main housing unit, scanning the area for the red and gold canisters. As they approached ground zero, their rad counter alarms screeched.

"Just mute it. We won't be here long."

Under what looked like the remnants of the primary console computers and databases, Kate spotted two of the extra suits. She unclipped their cylinders and placed them in the bin beside Mary.

"Check the gauges for capacity."

"One says about 12 hours ... the other is just over 11."

"Let's keep looking."

After ten more minutes of combing through the debris, she finally found the cache of emergency cylinders. Normally, several days' worth of supply was always available, but many of the canisters had cracked and emptied. Still, she retrieved a dozen full ones and put them in the bin.

"Kate?"

"Yeah."

"Any idea what caused this?"

Kate sighed. She'd run an infrared diagnostic on the debris, scanning for any kind of marker to help her trace the cause, but nothing obvious appeared."

"I've no theory. Someday, they'll root up the automated log recording box from this mess and figure it out."

Silence returned as she collected a few tools that still worked, scattered around the area. She figured Mary had dozed off with the painkiller, so her trembling voice surprised her when she whispered, "Do you think I did it?"

"Accidents happen all the time, and despite what we'd like to believe, sometimes there are no reasons for them." She secured the salvaged tools in the cargo bin next to Mary. "Oh, no doubt there are specific causes for lots of effects, and our tiny brains love it when the dots all line up. But not every accident has a knowable cause, and I'll bet this is one of those." She mounted the scooter and gazed across the horizon. "Let's get out of here."

"Do you still have your indie-comm?"

"It's connected here on the dashboard . . . why?"

"Maybe . . ." Mary struggled to find her words as the full effect of the pain meds kicked in. ". . . call my dad. The antenna . . . working?"

They returned to the mangled comms tower and Kate poked around in the dust until she retrieved the Yagi antenna, still in one piece. "I'll use a spare cable in the scooter's accessory kit, and hook it in through the comms port. But we must put some distance between us and this radiation."

Kate rode the scooter back to the remains of the power station and located the second LunaScoota tossed into the dust, not far away. Other than being on its side, it appeared to be fully operational. Good thing they built these to withstand a whole lot of abuse. "I'll tether this one to my machine in case we need it later."

What crossed Kate's mind was not whether Mary had somehow caused the implosion: she felt certain Mary wasn't responsible for that at all. In fact, short of deliberate sabotage, she could think of nothing that might have caused this amount of devastation. Instead, a darker thought had crept into her head and settled there, one that kept calling for attention.

Was our discovery of the Rossian ship somehow behind this?

FIFTEEN

Kate

LUNASCOOTAS OPERATED EITHER AS SEPARATE units or in tandem, much like old-school terran locomotives, except they could be linked side by side and one after the other. Kate latched the second scooter that Mary rode to starboard of her unit, but left it powered down to conserve its battery.

The decision to fly to the abandoned mining outpost at *Mare Frigoris* was correct, she knew, but there was no guarantee they'd find the old habitat livable. Still, one objective at a time was the internal mantra. Taskers in the Spacer Program drilled this into her, over and over until it became automatic in the face of an emergency: fix the most critical problem, then move on to the next. It didn't mean that a Spacer in a dire life or death event could always work their way through it—she'd seen too many of her colleagues perish despite the one obstacle approach. Rather, experience in space and on Earth of people facing insurmountable odds showed they sometimes survived by focusing on the closest challenge first and working the solution for it. One small accomplishment followed by another. The most powerful action, the Taskers said, was to never surrender.

Mary remained in the cargo bin, propped up on the spare seat by a rolled up tarp and bags used for rock specimens. An odd assortment of tools, crates of oxygen cylinders, and anything else Kate could salvage that may prove useful surrounded her. She located the coordinates of the *Aristoteles* mining site in the *Mare Frigoris* on the scooter's nav system and punched in the route. Then, she engaged the antigrav thrusters and as the consist lifted off the surface, it tilted starboard because of the mass of the second scooter. As soon as it was a meter off the ground, its internal compensators kicked in and the machine leveled off.

A hundred meters from the lab ruins sat a high outcrop, and they flew to it, stopping for one last look around before calling Jim on the indie-comm. Kate's rad counter had fallen into the normal background radiation range, and Mary confirmed hers had too. She attached the Yagi with its new transmission line to a five meter stake and, after a couple of attempts, planted it in a spot where it sank about a meter, more than enough to prevent it from tipping over. Once the comms port on her dash was released and opened, she plugged the other end of the cable into it and, using the commands on the dashboard, synced it to the indie-comm.

Mary groaned as she shifted her weight to get a better view of the set up.

"How are you holding up, Mares? Need any more of the painkiller?"

"Yeah, I'll take care of it."

She released another 60 CCs of pseudophine inhalant into her helmet. Kate linked the comms device to both of their radios.

"Ready?"

"Yes."

The indie-comm connected with the Yagi antenna and it turned out the problem with their previous link to Jim must have come from a bad cable connection. No such issue existed with the current configuration although whether her signal would reach Earth remained uncertain.

Kate punched up Jim's number and put the call through her encryption filter. After several attempts at establishing a link, the transmitter timed out. She played with the position of the Yagi to improve beam coherence to the west coast of North America and tried again.

Still no luck.

"The signal isn't powerful enough for reception on Earth. If Jim realized we were trying to communicate he could increase the receiver's sensitivity at his end." Kate saw the indie-comm drawing power from the scooter's electrical system and had an idea. "I'll try boosting it at this end and see if that works."

By adjusting the controls on the dashboard, she stepped up the current to the device and retransmitted her call signal. Several minutes passed with no connection.

"I'll boost it some more, but I'm worried about overloading the circuits. Still, here goes."

She raised the scooter current again and a warning light flashed on the indie-comm's screen about the power overage. She looked at Mary. "Here goes."

Atteberry

"KATE IS THAT YOU? HOW IS EVERYTHING UP THERE?" The connection crashed with static and atmospheric noise making readability tenuous.

"Jim, listen carefully. We've had... *garbled...* catastrophe here. The entire ... *garbled...* been destroyed. Mary and I are safe for... *garbled...* We'll wait there... *garbled...* but we need a ship... *garbled....* Copy?"

A pause, then Jim's voice returned. "I copied most. As soon as we're done, I'll call Esther and get help."

"Okay, sounds good... *garbled...* is serious. We may not survive."

"Is Mary there? Can I speak with her?"

In a moment, Mary's voice came through. "Dad, I'm here ... *garbled...* a bit but otherwise ... *garbled...*"

"Oh my god, I'm so sorry I let you go."

"It was my choice, remember? You wanted ... *garbled...* this summer. Anyway, we've gotta ... *garbled...* if we're gonna make it ... *garbled...* I just wanted to say that I ... *garbled...* love you, Dad, and ... *garbled...*"

The connection was deteriorating fast.

"You too, Mares, so much." Jim's voice sounded higher than usual.

Kate jumped back on the line. "Tell Esther the cause of ... *garbled...* is unknown, but my ... *garbled...* alien ship had something to do with it ... *garbled...* better be cautious. It's still here."

Atteberry waited until he was sure the transmission was over. "Yeah, I'll tell her." Then he added quickly, "You took off without leaving a note, Kate. There's so much we left unsaid."

Another long pause, full of static and frequency shifts. "I'm sorry, and in . . . *garbled*. . .happens, I . . . I wish we'd . . . "

ATTEBERRY SAT ON HIS BED IN THE EARLY MORNING darkness of his bedroom, the indie-comm still in his hands, and cried. The cruel realization that he may never see his beautiful daughter again tortured him, ripping his heart out with overwhelming guilt for allowing and encouraging her to take the internship on Luna. The pain was like nothing he'd ever experienced before, his own girl, a tangible part of him, torn away for good.

A hint of light slashed across the San Francisco skyline, shining through the parted curtains, and over the bed and wall. The Moon, reflecting the sun's rays, bled into the black sky. Atteberry wiped his eyes and took several deep breaths.

He thought Esther was still in New York and probably awake, doing whatever it was she did there, so he punched in her code to link her up. After a few seconds, her v-mail came on and Jim said, "Esther, it's me. Listen, call me as soon as you get this. It's about Mary and Kate. Something bad has happened on Luna, and I need your help. Please call."

He stumbled down the hallway to the kitchen and hit the lights, the sting of which caused his eyes to close for a second or two. He poured a glass of water from the tap, took several swallows, then paced around the breakfast nook feeling useless.

A few minutes later, his indie-comm pinged with an incoming link from Esther.

"Got your message, what's up?"

Something in his mind screamed at him to be careful. "Esther is this connection secure?"

"Stand by." Atteberry heard the double tones and ping of encryption on the link. "What's going on, Jim?"

Jim swallowed hard, pushing the fear and panic from his chest. "There's been an accident at the lunar lab. Kate says something destroyed it. She and Mary are okay for the moment and they're going to wait, so we need to get a ship there right away to rescue them."

Esther paused at the other end. Atteberry heard her breathing amid the background sounds of other people talking, laughing, something being announced over a PA system.

"Esther, you there?"

"Yes, I got all that . . . just thinking. Listen, I'm about to board my shuttle flight home but I'm wondering if I should stay here in New York instead. Titanius must be on top of the problem with their lab, and may already be diverting ships. I can speak with the CEO about it too."

"Thank you so much, Esther, really, I can't—"

"That's okay. I'll make some calls and get back to you soon. In the meantime, if they contact you again, tell me right away, okay?"

"Of course, but it's possible their comms unit malfunctioned too. Before we finished speaking, we lost the connection, and that was that."

"Understood. Talk soon."

The link terminated, and Jim surprised himself by having wandered into the living room while on the call with Esther. He flopped onto the sofa and turned on the side-table lamp. The sun would be up soon and, no matter what happened next, that thought alone gave him a small measure of comfort.

I need to tell Janet.

They'd been estranged since Mary was eight years old, divorced shortly after the Mount Sutro business, and had had no further contact since. Not a card on Mary's birthday, not an update on where she was or what she was doing . . . nothing. Of course, as a spy or NDU agent or whatever the hell she was, it made sense for her to be incommunicado. Atteberry didn't know if she was still alive although someone should have told him if she'd been killed. He felt gutted and broken when she left him and Mary all those years ago, and even though they were now apart, he missed her terribly al-though their marriage was, for all intents and purposes, a sham, a part of the NDU plan to do the things those spy agencies do.

Still, after the tower came down and the subspace transmitting station with it, Janet said she'd *know* if they were in trouble, so there was no point trying to contact her . . . she would simply *be aware.* That brought him no comfort. He needed to speak with her, to tell her that their daughter's life was in serious jeopardy.

He sighed and padded back into the kitchen to brew some coffee. While he poured water into the machine and measured out the beans, Atteberry shook his head in disbelief. Exploring space was as safe, if not safer, than air travel on Earth. The advances made in safety redundancy systems and monitoring over the past few decades were huge. This should not have happened. He understood something about the setup, about the operating protocols, life support, comms, and so on from the Astronomical Society meetings. Several speakers from the TSA and other groups spoke to them about space exploration, not only on Luna but on Mars and Eros too, and plans for the other planets and asteroids in the belt. Despite the increased activity, an incident in space like this was rare.

The machine gurgled and Atteberry poured himself a mug. He carried it over to the breakfast nook and sat down. The sky over the city was beginning to lighten in muted pinks and oranges.

Something Kate said before their link ended haunted him. She pointed out the alien ship was still there, on Luna, and he concluded she wouldn't mention that if there wasn't more going on. If that vessel was the Rossian craft they'd heard in 2085—and it seemed likely it was—then what was it doing on the Moon?

Could it have destroyed the lab and put the lives of Kate and Mary at risk?

So many questions, but first: he needed to get them home safe. Atteberry trusted Kate with Mary's life, but still, as her father, he had an obligation to help somehow, to do something. Sitting around like this drove him nuts; made him feel like he wasn't being a good dad.

He sent Esther a non-encrypted message on the indie-comm. *Would like to help. What can I do?*

He punched the device and fired the message out, then shuffled to the basement and turned on his computer. After accessing the CalNet information system, he searched for the whereabouts of Janet Chamberlain like he'd done a thousand times before, but all he found was exactly the same as every other time. The data trail on Janet ended the day she left him and Mary almost ten years ago. Home town, school, the job in Washington, policy papers on discussion boards . . . all in the public domain.

Since then, nothing.

How the hell can I tell you our daughter's life is in peril?

Katie

THE AIR IN THE ROOM CHILLED HER, LIKE A WINTER MORNING. She wondered for a brief instant whether she'd left the window open in her bedroom back home, then realized where she was and what they'd done.

"Katie . . . Katie?"

A warm hand caressed her cheek. She stirred and opened her eyes.

"Do you remember where you are?"

The sound reverberated through her head, faintly recognizable. She focused on the nurse's face, the smile and pulled-back hair, the one who dried her tears before going under.

"I'm at the hospital," she whispered, surprised by the alien nature of her own voice.

"Yes, and everything went well. You'll stay here for a day and then return to your dorm."

"Mm."

The nurse poked around with the machines by her bed, then left. The smile had disappeared. Her entire un-whole body ached, especially her abdomen. Bandages covered her tummy, and she inched her hand over them, then up to her chest where more tape and gauze hid parts no longer there. She squeezed her eyes tight.

A vision of her mother appeared in her mind, from a photograph taken in the kitchen. Katie was seven or eight years old, sitting at the table with a bowl of cereal in front of her. Sunlight caught her mother's hair just so, and made her smile even warmer. She had her arm around Katie, holding her close, as if trying to fit in the camera's frame. The open, grey cardigan hung loosely over a white blouse. She held that memory, tracing every detail of the morning her dad took the photo, and fixated on her mother's face and breasts as her hand lingered over the bandages. A lump rose in her throat; a sting in her nose.

Kate

THE LUNASCOOTA, AS A MOON-ROVING MACHINE, was built solid but not designed to fly at any significant altitude. It was rated for cruising up to 10 meters high, but rarely ever did given the work Kate used it for. The secondary scooter now strapped and latched to hers, along with Mary and other supplies in its open cargo hold, forced her to cruise even lower than she normally would, around three meters off the lunar surface.

Because of this, the course she laid in for *Aristoteles* took them east across the *Mare Crisium*, past the rocky outcrops and craters near *Proclus*, then north-east along the *Mare Tranquillitatas*, and over the 1972 Apollo 17 landing site. Then, they flew through the *Mare Serinitatas*, and due north to the *Aristoteles* crater and the *Mare Frigoris*. The entire trip would cover just over 2,500 kilometers and, at a cruising speed of 300 km/h, would take the better part of eight hours. Kate calculated they had sufficient oxygen reserves to make the trip with plenty to spare—that didn't worry her. Rather, whether the mine workers' habitat still functioned remained a mystery and if their reserves would hold out until a ship reached them underpinned everything else.

She linked her envirosuit computer to read Mary's vital signs, and within a few minutes of travel at cruising velocities, those bio-markers—and Mary's rhythmic breathing—showed that she'd fallen asleep from a combination of the painkiller, the dissipation of adrenaline, and even fatigue from the stress of wondering if this was the end of her young life.

A couple hours into the flight, Kate switched the scooter to auto-pilot and stretched her back and leg muscles. Fatigue bit hard into her too, and she managed to nap for ten minutes here, fifteen there. ETA to the mine site read 9 hours, 48 minutes, and at some point, she'd need to stop and stretch properly before continuing. Their course took them close to the Apollo landing site near *Dorsa Barlow*, just before reaching the *Mare Serinitatas.* She would stop there as long as the trip proceeded smoothly.

Not only were the scooters built to take the abuse of harsh space environments, but they also had massively efficient, battery-driven thrusters that could operate full out for about 30 hours, so Kate didn't worry about running out of juice on the way there. Besides, she had the second scooter as a backup in case anything went wrong with hers. But so far, so good. She monitored its systems on the dashboard and all lights shone green. *If I ever get off this damn rock, I'll let the designers know they built one hell of a machine here.*

Mary grunted and moaned as she pulled herself out of sleep and, in a raspy voice, asked, "Where are we?"

"Cruising through the *Mare Tranquillitatas*. I plan to stop for a stretch." Her response was met with silence. "How are you doing?"

She inhaled deeply. "Good. That sleep helped. My arm feels huge, all swelled up I suppose, but the pain isn't nearly as bad. Whatever you did, it worked."

"Glad to hear. When we get to the habitat, I'll put a medi-patch on it, too."

"Where did you learn to do that? Like, is there nothing you can't do?"

Kate's gaze rested on the horizon screaming toward her. Above her head, the Earth followed like a distant alien moon. "There's plenty I can't do, Mares, lots of things. But they drilled first aid and survival into us as Spacers. I should be thankful for that training, I suppose." Mary's vitals remained stable, scrolling across the bottom part of Kate's visor. "Your heart rate's looking good, by the way."

Mary thanked her then went silent again for several minutes.

"Kate?"

"Yeah?"

"Since this might be the end of . . . if we don't make it off safely, do you have any regrets?"

She snickered. "Sure, I do."

"Me too." A pause. "I'll tell you mine if you want to share yours. Like, if this truly is it, let's not leave anything unspoken between us, okay?"

Several more minutes passed. Kate did not want to be the first to spill her guts all over the lunar landscape. She thought about all the things she wished could have been different, starting with the loss of her parents. *Didn't want her any more*, they'd told her . . . living without an identity and still screwed up over it . . . or not saying anything to Jim Atteberry about their friendship, about whatever definition of love she struggled with . . . or agreeing to have Mary join her as an intern here, and everything that's happened. The guilt and shame overwhelmed her.

"I wish none of this alien crap showed up, and because it did, I regret that you're here and that I put your life in danger," Kate spoke in a monotone voice, like she was reading some boring training manual. "That's an easy one."

"Yeah, I regret being mean with my dad sometimes. I thought he knew all the answers. Now I see he's just another human being like the rest of us, struggling to find his way in this neural universe."

Kate recalled how attached those two had been for the longest time, and could only imagine the conversations they'd had about her coming up to the lunar lab. At, what, seventeen years old, there's Mary pulling away, about to step out on her own, taking on a risky internship, and maybe losing her life over it all.

"I should have spoken to your dad before I left. That was selfish and small of me."

"When was that?"

"After the Sutro night, remember?"

"Yeah." Another long pause. "You want to tell me about it?"

Several more minutes passed, and Kate appreciated how Mary didn't push her into saying anything she didn't want to, and she sure as hell preferred ignoring her odd relationship with Jim.

Still, she recognized it had been eating away at her, and she'd rather not die without addressing this.

"When I left the Spacer Program in . . ." she thought a moment, "the fall of 2082, I got placed as an instructor at City College. My first day there—I remember it so well—the sky was a brilliant blue, soft sunlight, the way it is in September, and I showed up on campus a week before classes began without a clue." The Apollo 17 landing site blipped on to the scooter's nav map. They'd be there shortly. Kate took a deep breath and continued. "Somehow, I found my way to the bookstore. Not sure why I thought about going there, but any- way, I wandered around the computer science section, looking at all the books and data slates piled high, found the ones for the courses I'd teach, and that's when I saw your dad." She paused.

"I remember him saying you guys met at the bookstore."

"Yeah, well, I guess I looked totally lost because he approached me to see if I needed help finding anything and we ended up spending the whole afternoon together. He got me set up with the admin people, showed me around campus. Hell, he even helped me find a place to stay." Kate took the controls of the scooter and veered off course toward the landing site for a break.

"Mary, I'll be honest. I've never had feelings of love like you've had . . . the romantic kind I keep hearing about, that you fall in to, that makes you tremble when you see that special person, or the one you daydream about all the time. I've never known that." She brought the scooter a few meters higher to cross over the *Dorsa Barlow* outcrops. "But one thing's for sure, and that is I admire Jim, your dad, an awful lot, and I respect him more than anyone else." She paused and eased up on the throttle. "Is that love? I don't think I'll ever find out. But I do regret not saying anything when I abandoned him and my job the day after Mount Sutro. I should've at the very least left him a note. He deserved as much."

Five minutes of silence passed as Kate maneuvered the scooter down to the Apollo 17 landing site. "Time for a stretch, eh? You up for that?"

"Sure."

Oddly, her mood lightened, as if keeping that to herself these past years had been much more of a burden than she imagined. Releasing it brought more optimism about finding a way home, despite the uncertainty of the mine site and the alien ship. She suddenly felt happier than she had since—

The possibility of seeing Jim again also motivated her. Years ago, she'd lost her family, and vowed not to lose the next closest thing. Perhaps she'd been looking at love incorrectly all along, that it wasn't another part removed by the surgeries. Maybe it was something she had purposefully denied herself . . . that she could change if she truly wanted to.

"Thanks for telling me that, Kate."

SIXTEEN

Esther

THE HOVERCAB ESTHER RODE IN EASED UP in front of Titanius Head-quarters in Manhattan, dropped her there, and merged back into the silent traffic on FDR Drive. She pulled her small luggage bag behind her and swung through the revolving door to the lobby. A couple hours had passed since she'd spoken with Jim Atteberry; just under that, she left a message for Clayton to contact her as quickly as possible.

He hadn't called yet.

Esther's eyes adjusted to the lighting in the bright atrium. She paused and observed the activity. Two techs dressed in white lab coats ran down a corridor off the main foyer, the shorter one carrying folders and a data tablet. The commissionaire who greeted her with a wide smile yesterday now had a grim, concerned look on his face. Another pair of management types marched across the open space, entered an awaiting elevator cab, and were swallowed up.

They must know about the lab.

Presenting herself at the Visitor's Kiosk, she dropped her luggage beside her and leaned forward. "Dr. Esther Tyrone. I'm here to see Clayton Carter."

The commissionaire, with a hint of recognition in his eye, asked, "Is he expecting you, Doctor?"

Esther gambled that he'd welcome her and replied in the affirmative.

Fingers flew over a touch keyboard and the commissionaire invited her to wait while an escort arrived to take her to the executive suites. She moved her luggage off to a bank of chairs and remained standing.

Within moments, a confused middle-aged woman stepped off the elevator and approached her. Esther recognized her as Clayton's assistant, Marla Sullivan. "Dr. Tyrone, this is a pleasant surprise, but I wasn't aware that Mr. Carter was expecting you back so soon, and this really isn't a good—"

"Listen, I know all about the accident on Luna, and I'm here to assist. The two scientists, Kate Braddock and the intern Mary Atteberry, are alive. We've heard from them. Now, I must share this information with Clayton."

Sullivan hesitated, then her mood changed from that of a gate-keeper to a colleague. "Understand, Doctor, all hell broke loose here this morning. Mr. Carter and Ed Mitchell have been working on a plan to send a ship to Luna, but I don't know where they're at with it. Still gathering intel from the comms unit and satellite imagery of the area around the lab, I think."

They entered the elevator and Sullivan touched the glass panel for the 43rd floor. The doors hissed shut, and the cab ascended.

"So, Kate and the girl contacted you?"

Esther wondered how much she should divulge, but knew the assistants to these CEOs were often more trusted than their own business partners in operational matters. In the back of her mind, she recognized this would help her build trust with Clayton and, therefore, was good for negotiations.

"Yes. Both survived the incident and are heading to the *Aristoteles* mine site."

"There's an abandoned habitat there."

"Correct, and they hope to get it operational until we can rescue them."

The elevator decelerated and the moment it stopped at Clayton's floor, the doors *whooshed* open. The two women stepped out into a chaotic scene. A young clerk brushed Esther's elbow as he raced by, carrying loose papers, his tie undone and indiecomm chiming away.

"Sorry!" he shouted over his shoulder.

"If you think this is bad," Sullivan said out of the side of her mouth, "you should see the mess downstairs in tech ops. It's madness." She motioned to her. "I'll take you to the war room."

As Esther approached Clayton's office, his deep voice boomed down the hall. Two other suits pushed by her and marched into the anteroom. Esther paused beside the entrance marked CEO.

"Please wait here, Doctor."

Sullivan wandered into the melee. A moment later, she reappeared, still looking grim, but waved Esther through.

Clayton towered over his desk and smiled with no hint of emotion when she entered. He had an earpiece and was speaking with someone.

"Okay, I understand . . . thanks. Keep me apprised." He pulled the piece from his ear and tossed it on a pile of papers and maps littering his desktop.

"Esther, I'm glad you stayed but I wish it was under better circumstances."

"Did Sullivan tell you what I know?"

"Only that you heard from our two employees up there and apparently they're still alive—which is great news, but it brings a lot more urgency to what we hope to do." He motioned for her to sit down at his small table, and joined her, ignoring the other men and women in the office, some standing, some sitting at the sofa.

"Tell me what you know."

Esther recounted the entire story from the time Jim Atteberry called her at the airport to when she arrived at Titanius, but neglected to mention that Kate said she thought the Rossian vessel may have had something to do with it. As she spoke, Clayton sat transfixed, leaning forward over the small table, hands folded together, head bowed. Twice he threw her a questioning glance, as if noting a lack of clarity in the air, then returned to his assumed position.

"The bottom line is we're now talking about human lives at stake and we've got to rescue them."

He was lost in silent thought. *What is he thinking?*

"The latest star chart showing locations of the nearest ships is here, and I'm sending a copy to your indie-comm." She punched the device, then continued. "We have diverted two—the *Englander* and the *Xing Xing*—but it'll take them at least a day or two to reach Luna." She leaned back. "Not looking good, I'm afraid."

Clayton raised his head and stared at her, the crow's feet deeply lined on his tired face, worry radiating from his dark eyes. He exhaled and motioned for her to move in closer.

"This is helpful information, Esther, and distressing," he whispered. "We've been running around this morning, as you can tell," he waved across the room, "trying to assess the damage and figure out what might have happened. We finally got some lunar-sat images of the area. It's a goddamn mess. I've never seen anything like it. Thank God the two workers weren't inside when it blew."

"And now they're waiting for us somewhere up there."

Clayton nodded and lowered his voice again. "I think we have to prepare for the worst, you understand?"

"I do, but still, we've got to try rescuing them. If they can find emergency oxygen, one of the diverted ships can pick them up."

Carter's brow furrowed, much to Esther's curiosity. In her mind, this was simple: establish comms with Kate, divert a ship and see what they can do to bring a happy ending to this misadventure. *Why is he being so coy?*

Clayton's face relaxed, and he quickly suppressed the inkling of a smile.

"I think we can do better than the *Englander*, and certainly better than that *Xing Xing* piece of trash, Esther."

"Oh?"

"Have you heard about our new prototype corvette?"

Kate

IT WAS EASY IN THE MONOCHROMATIC MONOTONY of the grey landscape for her mind to wander, given the lack of solid sleep and nourish-ment. But that's what transpired after several more hours on the scooter, en route to the *Aristoteles* mining operation.

They'd spent little time at the Apollo 17 landing site, but while resting there, Mary's interest grew in the original lunar rover tracks, still visible from over a hundred years ago, and the now-defunct stars and stripes of the US flag before the second civil war ended its use. They replaced their O_2 canisters and stretched. Eventually, after walking around for several minutes, reliving what the old astronauts must have experienced, Mary noted the enduring pain in her elbow again and returned to the scooter. After pumping a smaller dose of pseudophine into her envirosuit, she fell asleep for another few hours.

During that time, Kate's mind conjured up all kinds of madness. She fought the urge to cut, hard and deep, and fall into a heavy sleep, and she hoped to hell the habitat was salvageable. At one point, she also daydreamed she was back at work with the Spacers, heading to a so-called hostile target, ready to unleash a wicked and disruptive virus into their computer systems. She even glimpsed—or had she—a beautiful blue light following her in the sky, but after shaking her head, the manifestation had disappeared. She half-dozed, half-dreamed while the scooter remained on auto-pilot, cruising ever northward.

The chime in her helmet sounded like part of a dream, but she soon realized it was the scooter's guidance system alerting her to arrival at their destination.

"Pump ammonium carbonate inhalant, 0.5 CCs."

Her eyes fluttered awake and Kate's breathing intensified. Even the low dose of smelling salt was enough to knock the cobwebs out of her thoughts and allow her to refocus. She got her bearings.

"Do you see it, Mares?" She heard Mary struggle and twist her body around to observe the Aristoteles Mining Corporation's strip mining operation in all its grotesque glory.

"It's huge."

The scooter slowed to no-wake velocity and floated past hectares of mined surface material, deep pits, abandoned outbuildings and concrete rubble. Diggers, scrapers, draglines of various sizes, all had gouged this area years ago before the United Nations secured agreements from governments and corporations to outlaw strip mining on the near side. To the right, machines had piled high the remains of their extraction in designated dump zones, left over from when the space transports arrived on their regular schedules.

"Who ran this, Kate?"

"A consortium of companies operating under the Aristoteles Mining Corp banner. The dozers and diggers were all remote-controlled from Earth. I know they still have offices in Brazil, but I think there's a group in India involved too, on the far side operations." She looked over the scarred landscape, stripped of surface material. "It's not as if they're destroying rain forest or anything like that, but good god, this is an ugly way to pull minerals and gases out of the ground, don't you think?"

Mary ignored the question. "Kate, we should scout around and see if there's a satellite cam somewhere. They might still monitor the site."

Kate eyed the abandoned habitat coming into view in front of her, then swung hard to starboard and investigated the pits and debris. After ten minutes, she made her way to the center building and circled it.

"What do you think?"

"Too soon to tell. If they're still watching this place, it's not obvious." She paused. "Hey, check out the solar panels." She pointed to an array about twenty meters away from the main building. "We might be able to salvage them. Power will be an issue unless there's operational backup." She pulled back and floated to the primary access portal. "First things first, Mares. Let's see if we can fix this junk."

Kate nudged the scooter in to land not five meters away from the main portal. *The ugly rumors about this site are all true.* There were no lights at all on the habitat, no beacon above,

146

nothing showing anyone had ever been here in years. Some broken equipment—a couple of lunar runners and tubing—lay scattered about the entrance way. Kate heaved them up and tossed them aside, clearing a spot for them to open the external port.

The airlock had no residual power, so she found the manual lever and yanked it, exposing the internal chamber. The hatchway to the interior was already open, and bands of sunlight shone in through two small viewports, but otherwise, gloomy darkness bathed the place. She and Mary clicked on their helmet lights and proceeded in through the airlock.

They walked into the main common area that served as a control room, similar to their lunar lab setup except on a larger scale. Instead of a window facing the mining operation, workers had constructed a large viewscreen in the wall, and a massive operations table curved around in front like a horseshoe.

At one point, it would have been full of workstations for the engineers and techs of the mine site. Now, nothing remained except the built-in power ports, a few cables of various lengths strewn about, a broken chair in the corner, and moon dust everywhere.

"Check around, Mares, for any obvious containment breaches."

They split up and made a close visual inspection of the control room, using infrared frequency scans in their visors, and hands and eyes. After fifteen minutes, they met again.

"I found no breaks, Kate. You?"

"No, and that gives me hope. If we can rig up the oxygenator and scrubbers, I mean, if they're still working, we'll be good here."

"Nova!"

"How's the wing?" She nodded at Mary's arm.

"Sore as hell, but I got it managed now. More frustrating than anything else."

Kate pointed to the far end of the control room. "I bet that's the door to the living quarters. There's another over here, too. The galley, I suspect."

They stepped over fallen debris, making their way to the first access port. Kate swung it open, revealing a two meter length of airlock and a second hatchway. She pulled on that and peered into the adjoining space. Remnants of personnel quarters came into view. Something—maybe one of the mining machines—had run into the habitat, tearing a massive hole and scattering broken cots and other equipment around it.

Kate said, "We have to seal this airlock up tight as hell. I'd like to rig a backup access point here if possible, but I don't see how."

Mary wandered into what used to be a bunkhouse of sorts for the builders. Most personal effects had disappeared, but a few things remained. She lifted someone's dust-covered paper notepad from a corner beside a cot leaning at an awkward angle. A mug sat on a bedside table as if a worker had just taken a sip from it. Other odds and ends were scattered about like flotsam.

"Probably twenty or thirty guys were here building this place." Mary poked through the damaged area. "I hope this happened after everyone left."

Kate motioned to her. "Come on, let's find—"

"Hey, look!" Mary raised a scratched and dented cylindrical canister and waved it around. "This is oxygen, isn't it?" Kate lunged over a broken cot and other debris on the floor and sidled up to her for a closer inspection. It appeared to be a portable O_2 tank. It lacked a gauge or any other sign of its contents although at some point it had been labeled. Despite the scars, the connector was identical to the universal standard for terran air canisters.

"If there's one, we may find more, right?" Mary's voice radiated hope and excitement.

Kate had already performed the calculations in her mind. Assuming the Titanius operators back on Earth knew of the emergency, and if they diverted a nearby ship to *Aristoteles*, then they were looking at one or two days before rescue.

Only six hours of oxygen remained in their canisters. Tops. And if they couldn't get the oxygenator running, Kate knew a single canister between them would be nothing more than a cruel joke.

Mary

A CONSTANT DULL ACHE REPLACED THE EARLIER throbbing in her elbow that pounded a trail from her wrist up to her shoulder. Mary flexed her right hand fingers, gingerly at first, and then with more confidence as she discovered the additional movement caused no further pain. The healing had begun even without the medipatch. She had infused no more pseudophine inhalant since the stretch break at that old Apollo site, and if possible, she preferred staying off the meds.

Kate busied herself by poking around the control room and investigating the various workstation panels while Mary continued her search for additional O_2 canisters. Kate seemed less than enthusiastic with her discovery of the solitary cylinder, but there must be more somewhere in this complex, abandoned or not. It's something she read about in a camping guide once, of all things, and as with other documents, never forgot: *always leave firewood behind for the next traveler.* Perhaps it applied to the lunar workers, too.

The sleeping quarters, coated in dust from the massive wall breach, sat in streaky shadows and gloom. Mary conducted a quick walk through, starting at the far end. The module ran long and narrow, with bunks aligned, one on top of the other, down the sides with a shallow walkway between them. A grey and white bulkhead covered the length of the structure. Small, metallic bedside tables and a few orphaned storage bins were interspersed throughout the cots, each pair book-ended by built-in lockers. She checked those.

The first half-dozen lockers were empty. One of them had a checklist stuck inside the door; the workers used another as a garbage bin for construction material. She'd uncovered a variety of building bricks, tubes, steel pipe and clamps in it. They were all dust-filled but otherwise in good repair.

"Find anything back there, Mary?" Kate's voice startled her.

"No extra canisters yet, but I've just started looking." Her helmet radio crackled with static.

"Listen, as soon as you're done, come with me to inspect the solar array. I uncovered the power input node here for it, and if it's still operational, we'll be able to fire up this unit and maybe get the comms working."

"Sure, on my way."

Mary glanced over her shoulder at the sleeping quarters, hesitated for a moment, then checked her balance and stepped back over the debris to the main control room. When she pushed through the access portal, she noticed Kate over in a corner, kneeling in front a large junction box, out of which all kinds of reinforced cables ran. She held a thick, flexible feedline in her hands and appeared to be studying its interior.

"What is that?"

Kate held up the cable. "It's the main power line for this control room, and possibly for the entire habitat. I can't believe it's still in decent shape, but with all this dust I'm not sure how well it'll work." She pulled herself up to a standing position. "Of course, that's moot if we have no power source, so are you ready to check out the solar array?"

"Okay." Mary was the first to admit she didn't know much about solar arrays other than their basic configurations and parts, and she guessed the system here on the moon would have a host of environmental reinforcements to withstand the extreme temperatures.

They stepped through the external access portal onto the lunar surface and bounded toward the array. Kate remained quiet, and Mary wondered if the lack of sleep and stress was more than she could handle. In the weeks she'd spent with her at the Lunar Geophysical Lab, she recognized Kate cherished her privacy and other than on rare occasions, had kept a lot of her past and inner thoughts to herself. If there was something work-related, Kate chatted up a storm, but anything else of a more personal nature, she'd close up. But she was like that back home too.

As they stopped in front of the array, Mary understood her insignificance. The panels towered over her, angled on thick metal bases with pivoting heads—no doubt so they could always face the maximum amount of sunlight. Ten massive blocks sat there like stone sentries.

Kate paused and scrutinized the design. "Seems they've got a whack of smaller panels linked up on each base. Probably not the most secure arrangement, but the Moon is normally a quiet place. Other than cold, heat and dust, the worst thing would be a meteor hitting it, and then its configuration wouldn't matter."

"Still, a machine rammed through the habitat . . ."

"Smart ass."

Mary chuckled, and Kate snorted right back at her. "There's a ladder over here," she said, catching her breath. "Let's have a closer look."

Kate swung the long metal apparatus up against the first of the solar blocks and climbed up. Mary watched as she brushed dust off the sides before descending again. "Something crushed that one. No good for us. Let's check out the others."

Mary stayed on the ground while Kate inspected the next four groups. None of them were functional. Some had either been cracked or shattered, others broken. Kate said if she had the time and the proper tools, she could repair them, but neither were available.

They would run out of air before getting them up and running.

Five panels remained. As they leaned the ladder up against Number Six, Kate asked, "Do you want to go see?"

"Sure, but what am I looking for?"

"You'll get a sense of whether the panel could work. If the protective coating is smooth and crack-free, then we're probably fine. If not . . ."

Mary took a first careful step up the ladder and it plunged into the dusty ground beneath her until she was almost level with the dust again. Since she only had the one good arm, her balance was off.

"Jump on it to make sure it's secure, okay?"

She hopped on the rung twice and it dropped again before stabilizing, then she continued her single-handed climb. A thin layer of powder coated the massive block, but she could make out the individual sections underneath it.

"Step off the ladder, Mary, and walk over it. The panels are designed to hold weight. Brush some dust away to get a sense of its integrity."

She swung a leg on top of the angled panel, then the other, and secured her balance. Once there, she tested it, kicking here and there and inspecting the panels.

"Are you seeing this, Kate?"

"Yep, your cam's good. That section you're on now seems okay."

Mary continued, taking short baby steps toward the center of the panel. That's when her boots sank. "I think I might break through it here in the middle. It's all soft."

"Yeah, I see that. Can you tell what it's like farther up?"

She shifted her body and inched forward to the far, high side. With each step, her balance became more difficult to sustain.

"Something's not right with this one either, Kate. I'm coming down." She crept toward the ladder and a couple of meters from it, the panel solidified again under her weight.

"Take your time descending with that arm of yours, eh?"

Mary wriggled off and went down one rung at a time. The two remained silent as they investigated the last four.

When they'd finished, Kate dropped the apparatus into the dust and lowered her head.

"That bad, is it?"

"I believe so. I'm sure I could rig something up, but we don't have time to repair them. Without power, there isn't a lot we can do with the oxygenator."

Mary swallowed hard as a wave of fatigue swept over her. "How much time do we have now?"

She reached out and held Mary's good hand. "About six hours, give or take."

Mary headed back to the habitat and Kate followed. As she gazed up toward the external access portal, a blue light the size of a baseball flashed across the black sky over them, hovered, flickered, then disappeared.

SEVENTEEN

Carter

"THERE IS NO LAW IN SPACE OTHER THAN THE laws of physics. Not really, anyway." He tossed the last of his stale lunch sandwich on the desk and stared at his colleague.

Ed Mitchell gaped at Carter. They'd returned to his now empty office from a quick info meeting in the comms room with Stan Petrovic and a gaggle of other technical types where they learned the details about the disaster at the Lunar Geophysical Lab.

Carter resumed. "Oh, what's with that puss, Ed? You know as well as I do that in a space environment, or on Luna or Mars or anywhere else out there, the laws and regulations we adhere to by UN agreement or otherwise are done so out of convenience. If, for example, we're able to find that alien ship and secure its FTL technology, who would it belong to, hm?"

Ed flopped into the Queen Anne chair, leaned his head back and exhaled. "Titanius, of course."

"You say that, and I say that, but the Lunar Coalition or the UN science types would undoubtedly claim it belongs to all of us, the whole collective Earth." He loosened his tie. "I'd never hand that over to someone else. Never. But for me, the simple solution is to conceal that vessel and its capability. We keep news of that ship to ourselves until we've taken what we need from it. Oddly, this is something Braddock and I agree on."

Ed wore a face of complete exhaustion. He'd seen a lot over the years, but never anything like the destruction of the lunar lab occurring on his watch, and his eyes suggested deep guilt and remorse for the two workers marooned up there. "But how are you convinced an alien ship is on Luna? That was all rumors, wasn't it?"

Clayton smiled.

"Wasn't it?"

"Let's just say I now have insider information, and I won't reveal my source."

"Understood." Mitchell grinned. He was no dummy.

"Captain Powell is overseeing the refueling and preparations of the *Echo* as we speak. She'll be ready to fly in a few hours. The captain estimates a four and a half hour flight to the Moon, where we'll rescue the two workers, salvage everything from our lab site before the vultures swoop in, and then find this Rossian ship."

Mitchell twisted in his chair, scrutinizing him. "What else is there, Clay?"

"Ha! You know me too well, old friend." He slapped him on the shoulder and continued. "Listen, I'm thinking of ordering a security cruiser from the Martian run to Luna."

"Which one?"

"The *Malevolent*. Not built for speed, I grant you, but full out, she can reach the Moon in 12 hours and her defensive weaponry will keep the curious onlookers away. Her captain, Laura Russo, is outstanding too."

"Hence the comment about no real law in space."

Carter eyed him. For a moment, a caution flag rose with Mitchell. "Surely, nothing will come of it, but just in case, I'd rather be prepared for any possible outcome."

"Naturally. Can you give me some time to check on *Malevolent*'s supplies and capacity?"

"Certainly, then call me as soon as I've got the green light to divert their course."

Mitchell still didn't look convinced. He brushed a piece of lint off his sleeve and changed the subject. "The lunarsat images of the destroyed lab are already out there in the public domain. Other ships may be on their way to assist in a possible rescue mission, right?"

"Esther Tyrone is managing the story on that with our media team. We can't pretend the accident didn't happen, and we can't keep others away forever, but she's telling all the outlets we're launching an urgent mission to assess the damage and rescue the survivors, or else, recover their bodies."

"What if they're . . ."

"Still alive? Yes, that's a complication."

Carter understood the reality of working in space: there was no room for error. A missed seal, a broken piece of equipment, and the result was most likely instant death. Esther convinced him that the two workers were alive and awaiting rescue, but unlike her, he held out little hope they'd ever make it. At some point, their oxygen would simply run out and that would be that.

The thought of losing workers in one of his labs was unfortunate. The Spacer, Kate Braddock, wouldn't be a huge loss. Those freaks were dead men walking anyway, and he remained confident she'd be easily replaced with someone less . . . ambiguous. Something about her way irritated him. And the Atteberry girl? Yeah, that was too bad with all her smarts and potential, but he wouldn't shed a tear for the kid. She understood the risks when she accepted the internship, and Esther would likely wear it more than him.

No, the worst-case scenario here was not death. Progress throughout history was built on the bones of loss and sacrifice all the time. *Someone dies in a hovercar accident because of faulty mechanics, so we change the laws to force manufacturers to improve the safety of their cars. Food companies used to poison people with sugar in their products, until we understood the evils of sugar and banned it, but only after how many millions died of diabetes. And on it goes.*

He turned his full attention to Mitchell. "Ed, if those two are still alive, then we're seen as the heroes in a race against time and space, literally, to bring them home. Even if we fail, we win, you see?"

"I do."

"That will ensure the negotiations with the TSA are a success, and that we'll have our unfettered opportunity to develop the alien's FTL technology with full public support."

Mitchell nodded, deep in thought. He'd started moving the chess pieces well into the future and by the smile on his face, understood that he liked what he foresaw. Mitchell's eyes narrowed and that sweet, annoying grin of his returned.

"What's on your mind, Ed?"

His colleague rose from the Queen Anne, sighed, stroked his chin, and gazed out the large picture window. "I'm thinking we use this opportunity to show off what the *Echo* can do." Sullivan entered the room and took up a position beside Carter. "We need to keep this under wraps. No one believes those two are alive after the lab explosion, despite what Esther says, so there's no panic for any others to go and poke around. She tells me the media are treating this as an unfortunate accident with virtually no chance of finding any survivors. So, we approach it that way, too. Then, if Kate Braddock and the intern are still alive when we get there, Titanius will not only score a public relations win, but we'll also have at least a few days of unfettered exploration of the—"

"—Rossian vessel site!" Carter beamed, faintly amused. "Marla, do you have intel on the closest ships to Luna?"

She closed her eyes. He watched her eyelids flutter in that nervous habit of hers before she spoke. "The *Englander* is on her way, ETA two days. The *Xing-Xing* is standing by in low Earth orbit, offering to assist us. There's been increased activity noted at the Prussian Cosmodrome in Baikonur, but no launch yet."

"That's it?" Mitchell asked, his voice higher than normal.

"Yes, Mr. Mitchell."

"God bless Esther Tyrone for keeping the response so quiet."

"I doubt God, or any other voodoo is responsible for this, Ed, but Esther is proving to be talented in several ways." Carter grinned, a hint of deference in his tone. "This tells us we have a huge head start. Four and a half hours from take-off to arrival on Luna, and that's not even pushing the *Echo* to her max. Powell says we could probably make it in under four." He narrowed his eyes and smiled at the other two. "Time to see what our little ship can do."

Kate

"KATE, I THINK THE PAINKILLERS MIGHT BE messing with my head. I just saw this weird blue light zip by . . . at least, I thought it was a light. Perhaps I'm pulling a Van Gogh or something. Strange . . ."

Mary bounded toward the habitat and Kate followed, retracing their earlier footsteps in the dust as they returned from the badly damaged solar array. She stopped and did a 360, taking her time studying the black sky. No stars were visible in the sunlight, but the space still looked wrong, and only the Earth shone bright. Certainly, no mysterious blue light. That didn't mean Mary hadn't seen something, for she too had caught a wisp of blue in the sky when they'd stretched at the Apollo site on the way in. At least, she thought she had.

Whether the phenomenon was associated with the alien ship at the *Mare Marginis*, or some other cause, it was the least of her worries now.

"I might have seen it too, Mary, but I figured it was just the fatigue . . . hallucinations. But I doubt we'd experience the same thing, so whatever it is, I'm thinking it's probably real."

They passed the LunaScootas still lashed together and resting on their nacelles in the soft dust to the right of the main access portal. Kate peeked over at them while Mary wrestled with the hatchway. That's when the idea struck her.

"Let's take another look at the power feedline junction, Mary. Perhaps we can do something with the scooter batteries."

Inside the habitat, Mary sat on the control console worktop, holding her slinged arm in her good hand. Kate knelt at the junction box and examined the cabling system, following each line into the power splitter, then out again.

Mary's voice broke her concentration. "Kate, even if we hook up the scooter batteries, we still won't know if the oxygenator and filters will function, right?"

Kate grunted as she yanked a stiff cable from its connecting hose in the junction box. She paused and turned toward Mary. "That's correct, but let's work on one problem at a time, okay? The solar panels are toast, so we can't use those. Unless there's another back up system here—which I haven't seen—then the scooters are our only hope. Agreed?"

"Yes."

"So, let's try powering up this console room, and get the comms or life support systems working." She cleared out a second cable from the junction and inspected the connector. "Mares, go check the accessory bin on the scooter for a box of connecting adapters. It's about the size of a boot.

Mary slid off the console and slipped through the internal access portal.

This can work. The only question is, for how long?

The dust could be a problem too, but Kate believed the batteries and overall power systems were built to withstand this kind of environment and may not be affected. Only one way to find out.

"Got it, Kate. Heading back in."

Kate snaked a thick power cable from one of the external ports on the junction box up to the main input node on the console. This was the primary power branch for the entire habitat, including life support systems. With the correct adapter, she'd hook this right up.

"Put it on the console, Mares."

The latch holding the small box closed was frustratingly annoying to turn with thick, lunar gloves, but Mary tried it and popped the lip up. The box folded open revealing a plethora of various adaptive connectors, short connecting cables (none of which would help in the habitat) and tools.

"What kind are you looking for?"

"We need one that'll accept the five pins on the junction box and adapt to three pins on the scooter's power cable."

"Like this one?" Mary held a connector the size of a plum in her palm.

"Perfect! By running the external cable from the scooter batteries to the junction box here, then connecting this power line," she pointed to the thick cable lying across the dusty floor from the junction to the console's power port, "we could be in business."

"I'll dig up the cable." Mary hopped out of the console room with more energy, and Kate allowed herself a few seconds of hope, a moment of thinking ahead to eventual rescue and getting away from that Rossian *thing.* Then, from out of nowhere, Jim's smile appeared in her mind. She stopped her work with the connector, shook her head, and smiled. Since being kidnapped by the Spacer Program and undergoing the surgeries, Kate hadn't understood gender, sexuality, but that changed when she returned to civilian life, and she saw it changing again now.

"Kate, the external power cable is marked at twenty meters long. Is that enough?"

"More than enough. If you can drag the end to the outer wall junction access port—it'll be exactly on the other side of the habitat from where I'm working—then I'll come out and hook it up with the adapter."

Silence floated over her helmet radio. Mary's voice crackled. "I see the junction input, but it's . . . it's covered in dust, Kate. That's bad, isn't it?"

"I'm hoping it'll still work. Brush the crap off the junction ports as best you can." A bead of sweat dripped off her forehead, and she looked up at the stark grey wall in front of her. "Are the access ports sealed, Mary? If they're full of dust, we won't—"

"Yes, they're covered up, Kate! There's five ports, all sealed."

"I'll be out in a second."

She attached the power cable from the junction box to the console with a shove and a twist and noted the cable map: *external cable from the scooter enters port two . . . internal power cable goes from port two to the console's power port.*

"How's your oxygen, Mares?" Kate followed her footprints around the side wall where she saw Mary holding the cable in her good hand, looking off toward the lunar horizon.

Without turning her head, she said, "Um, another four hours on this tank."

"Same here." A pause. "You see that blue light again?"

"Oh no, I'm just thinking how beautiful it is up here, and how fortunate I am."

Kate couldn't suppress a surging laugh and snorted, "Mary, not to put too fine a point on it, but we're not out of the woods yet."

She turned to face her. "Still, this is better than anything."

Kate felt an odd mix of mocking curiosity and admiration. Was Mary overly naïve? Not likely. So, how did she see past life-threatening danger, beyond present circumstances to something *other*, something greater?

The ports were arrayed pentagonally on the external face of the junction box and clearly numbered, so she grabbed the metal ring for port two and yanked hard.

"Damn."

The port cover didn't budge. She snagged the small mallet from her belt and tapped around the seal. This time, when she pulled on the ring, the seal hinged open, exposing the clean, five pin plug. Kate wondered if they had ever used these external ports.

"Now let's get that adapter on the scooter cable."

Mary handed her the cable end and with a few twists of her hand, Kate attached the adapter. Then, she plugged the other end of the connector into the five-pin port by putting all her weight against it until it slid in. Another twist secured the connection.

"Is that it?"

"Yep, come on, let's get this shit-hole fired up."

Inside the control room, Kate checked and double-checked the cable wiring. She sealed the two access hatchways to the sleeping quarters, then ensured the main airlock was sealed.

"First let's bring power to the console. If we can, and if there's sufficient current, we might pressurize this room and get the life support systems working."

"Nova!"

"Ready?"

Mary nodded. Kate walked the length of the power cable running from the junction box to the console power port and took one last look around. She had no idea whether this main room was airtight, but she'd soon find out.

Kate reached out and squeezed Mary's good hand.

Holding her breath, she toggled the MAIN POWER switch.

Katie

AN OVERWEIGHT, MIDDLE-AGED MEDICAL assistant whose breath smelled like sour cheese pulled the last staple from her abdomen, leaned back smiling, and said, "There, good as new."

Katie grimaced and stared at the concrete wall. All these doctor types poking and prodding her got annoying in a hurry.

"I'll remove the sutures from your chest now, Katie," he said, lifting the gown. She heard the snip-snipping and felt the tug of stitches shuddering out. In a moment, he drew her gown back down and stood up. "All done."

She eased herself up and swung her legs over the examination table.

"Are you okay, Katie?"

She peered around the sterile room, unsure of what she felt.

"Well, go light on the sports and physical training for the next few days until the scars are healed. If you run into any problems, have your trainer bring you in, okay?"

Katie nodded. "Can I go now?"

He opened the door and waved her out.

Later that evening, cocooned under the thin bed sheets in her dorm, Katie examined her wounds with a flashlight and mirror. The scars across her chest had already hardened. The incisions weren't too deep, she figured. But the one down her abdomen remained sore and scabby. She ran her index finger over it lightly, tracing the incision, bumping over rough bits of dried blood and skin. When her fingertip accidently ripped one off, she flinched, then relaxed. That sensation of sharp pain followed by migrating warmth caught her attention—the same sweetness she remembered, like when she pulled out a loose baby tooth.

The next evening, again under her sheets, she picked *at another scab on her tummy. This time, with intention.*

Kate

WHORLS OF FINE, GREY DUST KICKED UP OFF the floor and danced around the console as the oxygenator struggled to pressurize the control room, wheezing life into the gloom. The console's main view panel, one of the few screens left, showed a gentle rise in oxygenated air, ambient temperature, and subsequent pressure. In addition, dim, orphaned emergency lights around the room blinked.

Mary squealed with delight. "I can't wait to get out of this suit!" She leaned toward a view port opening on the cylindrical trio of life support systems: the oxygenator, scrubber, and hydrogenator, all blinking green lights. "It worked, Kate!"

Kate scrunched up her face inside her helmet. On the main view panel, two red lights appeared next to the power levels. The current draw of the systems was massive and overwhelmed the amp capacity of the scooter battery.

"What's the matter?"

"The power isn't sustainable, Mares. This won't last, and we'll be back in a vacuum."

Mary approached and planted her arm on the console. "How much time?"

"Hard to tell. We can kill the lights and the hydrogenator, reduce the filtering . . ." She worked out the math, best-case and worst-case scenarios against the backdrop of needing to hold on for at least a couple more days. "We've got whatever's left on my scooter battery, and then we'll switch over to the other. There's a portable solar kit to recharge the one while the other's in use. That'll help, but our problem is charge time. It's about twenty hours with the solar kit, and our current rate of consumption will wipe out the first battery in six hours."

Green lights blinked over the access hatchways and on the main viewscreen. Kate scrutinized the console, and released the seal on her helmet. She inched it off her head, inhaled and smiled.

"Help me with mine, Kate," Mary said, her good arm manipulating the helmet latch where she could. Kate reached over and snapped the opposite side. The seal hissed, and she pulled the helmet over Mary's head.

"Is this safe?"

"Nothing's a hundred percent safe."

Kate unbuckled her envirosuit first and shivered. The temperature inside the control room hovered around 8 degrees

165

Celsius despite the sunlight, and combined with her sweat, rudely awakened her. After helping Mary with her suit, they stood in the dust and dim light, not quite believing what they'd accomplished; they hugged each other.

"The room's holding up well. No leaks I can see or hear, but let's stay close to our suits." She blew into her fingers. "The temperature should rise with the full sunlight."

Mary opened various storage compartments, looking for anything they might use. In one of the larger bins near the external hatchway, she found half a dozen Kevlar full-body skins, a couple more oxygen canisters, and a first aid kit. Another open box held emergency shock blankets and what appeared to be flares on the bottom. They changed out of their wet skins and into fresh clothing, Kate again helping Mary negotiate the undergarment around her slinged arm. Then, she pulled a medi-patch from the kit and tightened it on her elbow to keep the swelling down.

"How's the pain?" she asked, wrapping up the last turns of the medi-patch and pinching the end in place.

"Comes and goes now. I'm still amazed at how much better it is."

Kate surmised there was no ugly break along with the dislocation, but that didn't mean she hadn't sustained a fracture of some sort. One more item for the to-do list.

"Mares, I'm exhausted. Let's sleep for a couple hours to take the edge off."

They hung their envirosuits up and used the remaining body skins as pillows, then wriggled up on the console away from the dust and covered themselves with the shock blankets for warmth.

Kate waited until Mary's breathing became low and rhythmic before she unzipped the top of her new skin and grabbed the short screwdriver from her pocket. Turning the flat edge around in the shadows in front of her, she sighed, and carved a rough line over a healed scar. Tears welled up and for a second, sheer panic shot through her nervous system as images of the past twenty hours cascaded through her mind. When the smell of iron in the air from the oozing blood hit her nostrils, her muscles relaxed, and she breathed again, eyes closed, choking back her emotions as she lay supine on the console.

"You okay, Kate?"

Mary's voice drifted over her like a soap bubble, enveloping the grim thoughts and images that pooled in her thoughts. Not for the first time, she was a complete failure: damaged, unlovable, and frightened behind a ridiculous, public mask.

"How do you do it, Mares?" She scraped a new line across her chest, inching it from left to right.

"Do what?"

Kate sniffed and wiped her nose, staring up at the dark control room ceiling. "Stay calm in the face of death. At first, I figured it was the naivete of youth, or maybe because you picked it up from books. But I'm a mess on the inside, and you? You're ... happy?"

The only sound in the habitat for the next several minutes was the low-level thrum of the oxygenator performing the way it had been designed: generate and pump pure O_2, a small miracle. Then Kate heard soft movement. She leaned up on her elbows, chest exposed, to see Mary in a weak silhouette against one of the emergency lights, sitting on the edge of the console, her legs swinging off it, face turned toward her.

"Sorry," Kate whispered, and hurried to cover the stains on her chest with the shock blanket.

"Kate, you don't have to hide from me." She slipped off the console and walked over. Mary's hand reached out and touched her warm cheek, holding it there. She leaned into her palm.

"If there's a secret to fear and courage, I really don't know it. But I believe life is more than daily struggles. So, for me, it becomes a choice. That's what Dad taught me."

Kate fought hard to keep her shit together, but with marginal success. Her voice sounded raspy and came in starts. "How can you . . . not be afraid? Here we are, a million miles from home, and you may never see your dad again or, or . . ."

Mary exhaled. "Oh, like for sure I miss him. I do every day. But worrying about this situation won't change anything. If our time is up now then I want to live it through to the end, Kate, the beautiful end." She pulled her hand away and squeezed Kate's shoulder, then crept back to her sleeping nest.

After a few more minutes listening to the oxygenator, Kate whispered, "I wish I could see the world the way you do, Mary."

"You can. My dad says it's a choice everyone has." She paused. "But maybe no one told you this before."

"What?"

"Dad used to say this when I was really young, and I didn't understand until much later, but he'd tell me this story about an abstract painter, a guy named Karabekian. He painted one of these odd pieces that was all green except for one thin orange line running top to bottom, just off to the side. Profound art, he told the world."

"Uh-huh. That abstract stuff is too weird for me. I prefer seascapes."

"Well, the people didn't like it either, and said *oh, my five-year-old could do better than that*, and *a case of beer and a couple cans of paint is all you need to make* that *art*. Then Karabekian did what few artists do."

"What's that?"

"He explained it. He said, like, if you remove all the noise and confusion and garbage from your life, all the masks we wear, all the *things we do*, all the lies we tell ourselves and others, then what you're left with is your true essence: an unwavering band of light shining for all to see in a dark and cynical world. The only thing that really matters." After pausing a moment, she added, "I think that's what we are, too. Bands of light. Nothing more."

Kate imagined a canvas of green with a single, vertical orange stripe cutting through it for a moment, trying to envision her genuine self, her authentic being, as a brilliant band of orange light in dark green space, like a solitary star, then dismissed it as completely impractical, and smirked.

Artists.

Atteberry

"DAMN IT ALL, ESTHER, I *HAVE* TO COME WITH YOU!"

Despite vain efforts to take his mind off Mary's welfare, Atteberry remained in a morose state of unprecedented worry. The one person he loved more than anything in the world was marooned on Luna, and Esther, the one person with the power and authority to divert ships from their routes, to order corporations like Titanius to throw all their resources into saving her and Kate, now mewled on the other end of the link like a stodgy old bureaucrat.

And there was nothing he could do about it.

"This isn't a pleasure cruise, Jim. We're not going on a sightseeing trip. How are you not getting this?" She sounded tired and irritated.

Atteberry set his jaw and counted to five. He hadn't been able to sit still all morning. One minute he was in the basement reading; the next cleaning the kitchen for the third time. His calls to the TSA after lunch were politely ignored (no one could or would tell him where Esther was) and, until a few moments ago, the v-mails he left with her had also been forgotten.

He forced himself to calm down, to speak slowly, articulating every measured word so as not to alienate the only link to his daughter. "Esther, I'm sorry, you're right. Understand, I'm going snaky here, and I'm so helpless and . . . and useless. I don't mean to take it out on you."

The change in tone from one of frustrated defiance to a more open, softer approach was subtle. "I know, Jim. It's been a horrible strain and I can only imagine what you're going through. I don't take it personally."

Atteberry bit his bottom lip, pushing the fear and anger deep into his gut.

"Esther, please, you've got to let me come along to Luna."

Silence resounded over the link. He could hear her breathing and guessed her answer even before she said, "I can't, Jim."

"Please don't shut me out like this. I can't take it. I've got to do something, anything, and don't tell me that staying at home keeping my mouth shut is an enormous help. That's not going to cut it."

"Okay, look, this isn't working. You know how you are, quick to challenge, putting your interests before those of others, and—"

"What are you talking about?"

"Don't patronize me. When you first heard the Rossian signal all those years ago, you didn't want to keep it quiet, couldn't hand it over to the scientists who actually know how to approach such things. No, you wanted to share it with the world, going against the UN First Contact Protocol, my wishes, and putting the entire Earth at risk. Now those creatures are on the Moon doing God knows what. Then you tell me Kate thinks they had something to do with the Titanius lab blowing up? Jim, understand, you can't be involved in the rescue mission. You're way too close to Mary and Kate, and that makes you untrustworthy."

Atteberry dropped into a kitchen chair. Tears welled up, partly from fear and partly from pure black rage. He lowered the indie-comm device from his ear and stared off into a corner of the room. He couldn't believe she'd betray him like this.

"Listen, the best available people are on this mission. The crew of the *Echo* is top-notch, and this ship is . . . well, it's unlike anything we've ever imagined at the TSA. They tell me she's the fastest ship ever built, jump-jet capability, enhanced heat shielding, next gen artificial gravity, top of the line comms. We're leaving shortly and if everything goes well, Kate and Mary will be home within 24 hours."

Her voice sounded distant and small from the end of his arm. Atteberry understood all this: she'd already lectured him, and he didn't find it helpful to be reminded that strangers (*strangers!*) would rescue his little girl, leaving him on Earth like some frightened, emasculated weakling. *How could I live with myself if I don't do everything possible to move earth and sun and bring my Mary home.* That was something Esther didn't understand, or at least wouldn't acknowledge.

In a last-ditch attempt to bring her on-side, to persuade her that he should be on the *Echo*, he played the one card he could guarantee would get her attention. He brought the device back up to his face.

"Esther, I appreciate all you're doing and I'm grateful Titanius is sending that ship to rescue Mary. But hear me well. I have to go with you."

"No."

"Listen, god dammit! I won't get in the way, promise, and I won't touch anything I'm not supposed to touch," his voice rose, parroting her schoolmarm lilt. "And, if you don't bring me with you, I'll go to the media."

"You wouldn't dare."

"You're pushing me into a corner, Es, and leaving me with no other options. I'm a desperate man, a desperate father. There's nothing I wouldn't do for Mary . . . or Kate, truth be told." He was rolling now, living and breathing the confidence and conviction of taking a decision, of moving toward action, of doing what any father in his position would do. "Make no mistake, it won't just be the lab blowing up and the alien ship on Luna. I'll tell them everything about that original signal, too. How Marshall Whitt died at the hands of the NDU because he tried controlling comms with the Rossians, and how you betrayed the TSA with your involvement in destroying the only subspace transmitter we've ever built."

"Jim—"

"Oh, and I'll make sure all your partners and the CCR and the UN know all about the cover-up you ordered to save your ass from prosecution." A novel, sickening thought bubbled up from a dark place. It hung there like a poisonous, black fog. His heart fell, and he swallowed the bile that oozed up this throat.

"Esther, wait," he whispered, "you didn't . . ." He caught his breath.

"Didn't what?" Esther's voice was cold, hard and detached.

"You didn't purposely throw my Mary on this space program just to . . . I mean, as part of your cover-up, did you?" If she took Mary into the internship and was behind the accident on Luna, he would tear her limbs off with his bare hands.

For what seemed like minutes to Atteberry, no sound appeared on the link except for Esther's constrained breathing, remote noises of people chattering in the background, and the *beep* of the routine encryption signal. His mind rolled over the possibility of Esther's involvement on Luna and how Titanius must also be a party to it. He shuddered at the thought of her, the first woman he felt comfortable with after Janet's disappearance, being this callous and ambitious to sentence Mary and Kate to death on the Moon, and for what, a cover up? It was a crazy notion, but he'd seen enough crazy to know anything was possible in these cold war days.

"Jim," she said, adopting an overwhelming business-like tone, "I'll speak with Clayton Carter in a few minutes about bringing you on board the *Echo*. Will that keep your maw shut for a while?"

Atteberry understood the breadth of powers she had as a TSA executive. She'd imprisoned a stalker indefinitely years ago and clearly had no issue with wielding her power when needed. It was a game of chicken, sure. Would he be able to take his story to the media before she had him incarcerated?

"I only want to save my daughter, Esther. That's all."

"Fine, keep your goddamn mouth shut and I'll get back to you as soon as I can."

EIGHTEEN

Kate

THE HIGH-PITCHED *PING* STOLE INTO HER BLACK dreams like a thief and launched her back into the control room at the *Aristoteles* habitat, where the first thing she noted after the rude alarm was how tight and sore her muscles had become from sleeping on the hard console.

Kate groaned. The air smelled stale, like old laundry, only more acrid. She bolted up and checked the main viewscreen: all green except for the amber light showing the degree of filtration. *The scrubber must not be working well.*

"Mary, wake up."

Mary stirred on the other end of the console, then went quiet.

Kate threw off the shock blanket, swung her legs over the edge and stretched. Despite only napping, she was more clear-headed and awake than she had been for the past twenty hours. *Every little bit helps.*

"Come on, Mares, get up." Kate's voice sounded surreal to her in the soft hum of the control room.

"Yeah, I'm coming." Mary inhaled and pulled herself up from the console, her long body stretching. She rotated the shoulder of her injured arm and Kate noticed the improvement. "So . . . it wasn't just a dream," she mused, throwing a mischievous smile Kate's way.

"Afraid not." She gazed around the room. "You didn't happen to find any food in your travels, eh? I'm starved."

"Not yet, but I only explored the sleeping quarters. There must be a galley here somewhere." She hopped down to the floor, caught her balance, and wandered to the other access hatch-way—the one she couldn't open earlier. "Probably in here."

Kate inspected the sealed airlock. "Well, let's hope we won't be here much longer. The oxygenator's working, the scrubber's seen better days, but I've been in worse in my Spacer travels and we can always pull a blast from the canisters if needed."

"You sure this oxygenator thing is okay?"

Kate listened to the hum of the machines. Nothing struck her as suspicious, and she'd been around a lot of ships, stations, out-link hubs, and machinery in her time. Still, she recognized that danger remained close, no thicker than the 18 centimeters of doubled lunar concrete walls separating them from the harsh environment.

"Sounds okay to me, but you raise a good point. Let's not be stupid. Suit up, helmets off but at the ready. If there's a breach, or if an airlock leaks, we won't have time to get everything on again."

They pulled their suits from the hangers and climbed into them. Kate's still felt damp in places and could use an ion clean, but otherwise serviceable. Once Mary suited up, Kate helped her with the sling.

"How is it?" she asked, nodding to her arm.

"Okay. Sore, but not painful. The medi-patch helps a lot."

They carried their helmets back to the console. Kate studied the main viewscreen and smiled. "Other than the scrubber, we're in good shape if the battery power holds, but let's not take anything for granted. We've got things to do: contact Earth and make sure our O_2 supply lasts twice as long as we think we need."

"I'll count up the hours in the canisters."

"Okay. Let's check out the sleeping quarters for a radio, or any kind of emergency transmitter or beacon. Whoever was here last removed pretty much everything from the console, but you never know. We might find useful gear in one of the storage lockers. I'm going to poke through this junk for something we can use."

Mary shifted her attention to the collection of canisters near the main access hatchway, and placed her helmet beside her, aiming its light at the grouping. She counted them and then joined Kate who knelt on the floor, pulling various pieces of gear out from a cupboard under the console.

"There's a box of two inch bolts," she said, hauling a long, green metal container out. "Probably for the solar array or one of the mining machines." She placed it in the pile beside her. "Nothing that looks like a transceiver of any kind, but this thing," she handed a small black box to Mary, "is a radio measuring device, right?"

Mary turned the instrument over in her gloved hands. "It appears to be passive with no battery terminals or other power ports. Dad's used this kind of thing before for measuring standing waves."

"What's that about?"

"You use it to make sure your antenna is resonant so all the juice going into it doesn't come back down the feedline."

"That tells us something."

They continued searching through the storage cupboards under the console, pulling out all kinds of things: cables, boxes of rock samples, a few detailed maps of the *Aristoteles* crater, and other odds and ends.

"Nothing here," Mary said, "but I found a 12 volt battery. Someone clearly had a radio up here other than the official comms station, and there's still the sleeping quarters and the galley to check out."

The pressure indicator at the hatchway to the workers' area showed air in the chamber. They fixed their helmets on and Kate hauled the door open. Once inside the airlock, she secured the internal port, depressurized the cell, and opened the second hatchway to the room where Mary had found the first oxygen canister shortly after they'd arrived.

"Let's go through everything here, Mares, even the areas you covered before."

"Roger."

"Note the time on your chronometer and O_2 reserves, eh?"

They raced through the sleeping quarters, searching every locker, under every trashed cot and in the few remaining bedside tables. They stepped through the massive breach and poked about in the moon dust in case something had been dragged out, but the only useful items they found included a worker's tablet (no idea if that even worked), and a pair of gravity shoes.

"There's still the galley, Kate."

"Yeah, squeezing into that cave is the trick."

Back in the control room, they kept their helmets on and studied the access hatchway leading to the galley. It appeared to be sealed shut internally, but Kate knew these habitats often had hidden external panels from her Spacer days. After several minutes of visually inspecting the hatchway, she found a smooth cover to the right of the port, flush with the concrete wall but clearly visible once she'd brushed the dust away.

Three buttons the size of poker chips sat in a vertical line inside the panel.

A combination code.

She pressed the switches in their order, from top to bottom, after which they blinked red. When the lights reset, she tried them in reverse order with the same result. She hesitated before trying another code.

"What's the matter?"

"These things usually have a limited number of attempts before there's a permanent lock out. I guess the managers didn't want the grunts helping themselves to extra rations."

"How many tries?"

"Five is the standard, then full shut down. But that's with four or more code buttons. This only has three, so who knows?" She shrugged her shoulders in resignation. "Let's see what happens."

Kate keyed a new code and red lights came up again. When she pushed the knobs to enter another, they had frozen and would not even depress.

The hatchway had locked them out.

Esther

SHE'D ANALYZED THIS PROBLEM THROUGHOUT THE AFTERNOON in between checking on projects back at the TSA office and deflecting all manner of media inquiries about the status of the Titanius Geophysical Lab: how to finesse him without his knowledge? Logic, naturally, but what else?

You have nothing to lose, Esther.

She rode the elevator up from the communications center to Clayton Carter's office on the 43rd floor, exhausted, worried, and rehearsing her best demeanor. Marla Sullivan met her in the anteroom and ushered her through. "He'll just be a minute, Dr. Tyrone."

A black leather flight bag sat open on his desk and she registered that he was preparing to board this new ship and head to Luna. Esther lowered herself onto the sofa and leaned back, closing her eyes, allowing herself a moment of peace from the stress-filled day. Voices in the hallway drifted in and she realized most of the people here had also been running full-throttle for hours, yet no one complained. They simply went about their jobs like professionals. Clayton's manner suggested he demanded a lot as a leader, from his employees and his executive team. Apparently, they responded with energy and loyalty she only dreamed of from her group of life-long bureaucrats at the TSA.

Stay focused, Es.

The CEO's baritone in the anteroom interrupted her thoughts. She sat rigid on the sofa, listening as he barked half a dozen orders to Sullivan, then entered the office.

"Looks like you're ready to go, Clayton."

"Yes," he bellowed, in a warmer tone, "We're scheduled to leave at 0100 Greenwich time."

She smiled weakly, bearing the weight of those two lives on her shoulders. "I take it you've been to space before."

"Many times, but I've never set foot on Luna, so this will be a new adventure for me and the whole crew too. This'll be the first time the *Echo* leaves Earth's orbit." He zipped up his flight bag and sat down beside her. She breathed in his cologne, a faint reminder of last night that, now, seemed like an encounter from her deep, distant past.

"Thanks for seeing me before you leave. There's a couple things I want, and you may not appreciate what I'm about to ask of you." She widened her eyes at him.

His brow furrowed, and Esther felt genuine concern spreading across his face. *Concern for what though?*

"I know you want to explore the alien site, and honestly, if I was in your position, I'd want the same thing. But this is really problematic for me."

He hardened. "I don't understand."

"The Terran Science Academy is the *de facto* leader in the search for extra-terrestrial life. Sure, we rely on plenty of other organizations and individuals to help in that task, but at the end of the day, people come to us for our expertise, our credibility and facilities. So," she continued, "if you become the first human to contact an alien vessel or the creatures themselves, it would not only undermine the TSA's efforts, but it could also cause considerable damage to our world governments, our economy, security, you name it."

Clayton sighed and stroked his chin. Then he stood and strolled to the picture window. "Yes, I see your point, Esther. It's the old UN Protocol on First Contact. I sympathize, of course."

"There's a solution to this, an easy one."

"Go on," he said, facing her.

"Take me with you."

"No," he snorted.

"Make this a joint Titanius-TSA rescue mission."

"Not a chance."

She wouldn't quit that easily. "Clayton, it makes sense. Reason it out. What better way to test our negotiations? If we're considering teaming up, this is the perfect opportunity to demonstrate just how effective the partnership can be."

He stood, arms folded across his chest in a stoic pose, eyeing her with deep suspicion.

The worst he could say is no.

Esther continued. "It's not like you'd be taking a rookie either. I've worked in space, I know the protocols. I bring a valuable scientific and diplomatic presence to your team." She remained seated, straight back, legs neatly crossed. She studied the lines on his face and detected a subtle shift. She let a couple moments pass.

"I don't like it, but I'll take a few minutes to think it through."

She lifted herself up to give him privacy, but he flashed up a hand. "Please sit down, I won't be long." Then he turned his back on her again and renewed his gaze out the window.

That's where he reflects.

Esther kept quiet, monitoring her breathing, giving him the time and space he needed to decide. He would appreciate the political benefits of bringing her along even if it meant a change to his initial plan. It was the right decision, the correct one. For all his engineering prowess, his understanding of politics was better than most.

Several minutes elapsed before he slowly turned back to her and said, "You must understand, Esther, space travel is as dangerous today as it ever was. Oh, undoubtedly the safety record shows a vast improvement from those early pioneer days, but the risks are nevertheless there. You can't simply pull over to the side of the road if you're sick. I wouldn't want you to think this is like a routine hypersonic jet flight or something."

She nodded, but smelled a hint of condescension. She let that slide.

"As well, if the survivors are still alive, we will find them and rescue them, no question. But if an alien encounter presents itself that leads to those two perishing, or any of my crew, I'll choose the aliens over them."

"How could—"

"Even you." He began pacing. "Look, it's simple. I'm a strong believer that what's best for the majority should inform all of our decision-making. The discovery of other sentient life-forms and superior technology benefits all humankind. Think of the potential for exploration, and yes, resource extraction too if we can secure FTL capability. In my world, that's worth the sacrifice of a life or two, and history demands it."

Esther shuddered and fought the urge to vomit. Choosing anything over a human life was unfathomable.

Clayton grinned and continued. "But, I'm not a monster. If there's any way to bring them home safely, we will do it. I want you to understand my position before we travel together."

She stuttered. "You—you mean I can come with you on the mission?"

"Yes. I see how your presence can be helpful and, in fact, I'm surprised I missed it earlier. It's fortunate that fate would keep you in New York." He sat down beside her again and took her hand. She didn't resist. "Besides, as you say, this will prove how well we work together."

Esther nodded and smiled, realizing that bringing up echoes of last night could wait.

"There's one more person I should invite," he said.

"Who's that? Ed Mitchell? Dr. Patel?"

He chuckled, "No, no. Oh my God, no, not Ed! He'd have a heart attack. Not Patel either."

"Who then?"

"The girl, Mary Atteberry ... her father was the man who discovered the signal in '85, wasn't he?"

She nodded. *Surely he already knew that.*

"Now I'm no parent, but I understand how precious kids are to their folks. And, I can imagine her dad would want to see her first, no matter what."

Esther couldn't believe he wanted Jim on the mission. She'd remained mum about his demand and planned to tell him later that she tried, but joining the rescue team was out. "But, he's on the west coast. There's no way—"

"Sullivan will contact him, and one of your people can charter a hyper-flight. He could arrive at our launch pad in Nova Scotia in a couple hours. It's a tight window, but not impossible."

"Let me call Jim first, Clay. I know he'd do anything to save Mary."

Well done, Esther, score points with Jim too.

"Very well. You'll need to get kitted up. Sullivan will take you down to the Prep Station as soon as you've spoken with Atteberry. After that, we'll board the heli-jet to Nova Scotia in thirty minutes."

They stood up together. Esther's heart pounded with nervous excitement. The moment was almost upon her: an encounter with new life!

Kate

"THERE'S GOT TO BE ANOTHER WAY INTO THE damn galley," Kate said. "Let's look at the structure again."

One step at a time, she thought. The next priority was communications but the only mode they had was their suit-to-suit radios. Her indie-comm was toast and there was nothing in the master control room they could use to contact passing ships. If no one knew they were here and alive, a rescue wouldn't be forthcoming.

I hope like hell a satellite picked up our trail.

"I'm ready, Kate."

They exited through the main access hatchway and bounded to their right, past the power cable port they'd installed earlier, and on toward another extended room, the galley. Like the rest of the habitat, this area was 3-D print-built using raw materials from the moon itself, giving the complex a natural, camouflaged effect. However, this extension was shorter and squatter, and no obvious entrance point presented itself.

"Perhaps it's not a galley at all," Mary said, gazing around.

"This room contained something the bosses didn't want to share with the workers. Why else would they keep it secure like this?"

Kate hopped back from the habitat about ten meters for a broader view. With the dust, rocks and other debris, she found it impossible to distinguish anything in the domed structure.

"Start infrared scanning."

Her suit's computer chimed and panned through the frequency spectrum in her visor. Kate shifted her head back and forth to ensure full coverage. It was during the second pass that something on the building caught her eye.

"I found a reading a couple meters to your left, ground level. Can you check it out?"

Mary took two long strides and knelt down in front of the outer wall. She brushed away the dust that had accumulated like tufts of snow where the habitat met the surface, then worked her way up, her palm outstretched.

"See anything?"

"Hang on a sec."

At a point about a meter off the ground, Mary brushed furiously then stood back, frozen.

"There's a handle here, embedded in the concrete."

Kate bounded over and joined her. Mary had pulled a screwdriver from her belt and started prying the tab away from its recessed pocket. It finally yielded, and the pull-ring popped up.

"Things are getting curiouser and curiouser," Kate muttered. "Shall we see what this opens?"

The hole in the ring only accommodated one thick-gloved finger's width, and despite several attempts, neither Kate nor Mary could generate sufficient force to yank it open.

Frustration blanketed Kate's mind. "Screw this," she muttered, and jumped away.

"Where are you going? Kate?"

"Stay there and keep trying to open it. I'll be back in a minute."

She pulled up to the scooters, still paired, a few meters from the main access hatchway. Kate released the holds on the second scooter—the one Mary usually rode—and fired it up, raising it off the surface, and flew to where Mary knelt wrestling with the latch.

"There's a cable and winch at the front . . . you see it?"

Mary leapt over to the hovering machine and poked around its nose. "Got it."

"Attach the hook to that pull-ring. I'll pull on it like a Christmas cracker, even if it brings down the entire wall."

Adrenaline poured through Kate's veins as the stew of fear and frustration bubbled up inside her, causing a sense of déjà vu.

This is no different than an old Spacer assignment when I was Mary's age.

"It's all hooked up."

"Okay, move away and stand by."

Kate punched the button on the dashboard for the winch and, as it strained to pull the access port open, the scooter's antigrav thrusters revved up.

"The damn thing doesn't . . . want to . . . budge," she grunted. She applied more force to the cable and stood up on the foot plates as she worked the machine. In the back of her mind, the echoes of her Spacer days crept in, but instead of haunting her, the opposite happened. Kate suddenly lost the feelings of shame, of being victimized by the program. What she felt . . . was . . . *alive.*

This is who I am.

She locked the winch, manipulated the machine to add some slack to the cable, then revved it up in full reverse, grinding hard on the access port. The scooter bucked in protest but nothing more happened, so she did it again. And again. And . . .

The LunaScoota flew aft this time, twisting momentarily until Kate wrestled it under control and lowered it on the Moon's surface. She looked up to find Mary rushing over to a large rectangular hole in the concrete wall. She and the machine had yanked the access port open, but in so doing, she also pulled the latch out of its housing completely.

Mary's helmet light shone, and she knelt down in front of the gaping void, pulling fistfuls of rubble away. Kate switched off the scooter and joined her.

"What do you see, Mares?"

Mary was half-way through the small access port. Only her legs from thighs down remained visible.

"This is a galley." She paused and added, "And a lot more, too. I'm taking a look." Mary wriggled through the crack and disappeared into the pitch black inside.

A minute passed, and Kate asked, "What's in there?" She crouched to peer in, saw nothing but Mary's helmet light flashing on various dust-covered bits and pieces of storage containers.

"Definitely the galley," she said. "There's an industrial cooktop and work space and, like, cupboards everywhere."

"What else, Mares?"

"Hang on."

Her strained breathing, punctuated by running commentary and flashes of her suit light, allowed Kate to mentally map the layout. Near the far access hatchway to the main control room where they got locked out, a series of empty storage closets stood rigid ... food pantries, she figured. To the right sat the cooktop and an open area where shelving used to be. Throughout the space, debris and dust was scattered about, reminding her of dryer lint back home in San Francisco.

"Nova City!"

"Whatcha find?"

"More oxygen canisters!" Then, after a short pause, "Oh, hang on. I think they're all empty."

"That's okay, we can still use them."

"There's two boxes here ... looks like ... yeah, ten in each box."

Kate lay down in the dust and leopard crawled part way into the access hole. In a corner to her right, she spied a small workspace, apparently abandoned. She pointed to it and flashed her own helmet light. "What's that over there?"

Mary jumped over to investigate. In the brightness, Kate saw a tiny workstation with a desk bookended by two closets. A couple of overturned chairs and metal boxes littered the area. She continued her search.

"I don't believe it."

"What is it, Mares?" Kate peered over, back toward her, rummaging through a storage bin on the desk.

"Mary?"

After a moment's pause, Mary *whooped* and scrambled to the access port where she knelt down in front of Kate. "It's a survival kit! There's a large lantern ..."

"An emergency beacon, you mean?"

"I guess so. And some circuit boards I'll inspect, and protein bars." She continued poking through a toolbox sized container. "Oh my god, Kate, there's a portable UHF transceiver in here. Nothing like we used at the lunar lab, and not much in the way of power, but I might be able to fire it up and send a message home."

"Or maybe to a nearby transport."

"Yes, why not?"

"Bring the whole box with you back to the control room."

"Sure, I'll gather the equipment and be there in a minute."

Kate smiled and wriggled through the access port. With two-way radio, they'd be able to contact any number of ships and be rescued. While she didn't want to over-simplify the remaining challenges, this raised her spirits.

Mary pushed the boxes of empty air canisters through the opening, then returned to collect the emergency comms kit from the galley. Kate disconnected the winch cable hook from the latch ring, bounded back to the scooter, and wound it tight to the machine again.

As she secured the winch in its locked position, she scanned the Moon's horizon and noticed that same, now-familiar blue light hovering in the distance over the strip-mined battlefield, watching her.

STORIES EXISTED SINCE THE BEGINNING OF TIME about this phenomenon. Ancient terran civilizations recorded numerous encounters with odd lights in the skies, prophetical signs or UFOs, but historians and conspiracy-busters determinedly chalked them up as hallucinations or fairy tales or too much alcohol in the blood. Without question, Kate's lack of sleep over the past days caused her imagination to play tricks on her, even to see things she knew weren't there. But this mysterious blue light was not confined to her alone: it was a shared experience with Mary.

What are the chances we're hallucinating the same thing at the same time? None.

Mary, helmet off, sifted through the box of electronics on the main console bench inside the habitat's control room. Kate studied her face, saw the excitement in her eyes, the clear disregard for the dangerous state they were in. Despite her age, she understood so much more about the fundamental truth of life than she ever did.

She secured the battery cover on the emergency beacon and placed it on the console and hesitated a moment. "I saw it again."

Mary threw her a cursory glance. "Saw what?"

"That damned light . . . that blue one. It keeps following us around."

She stopped pulling circuit boards out of the comms container and eyed Kate with a quizzical look. "When?"

"Just as we finished up out there, floating above the minefields."

"I guess the aliens are curious, hm?"

Kate refused to consider that. She'd seen all kinds of wonders and strange undertakings in space, especially since the onset of the cold war, but shrugged them off as military artifacts—probes or other sensory devices used by the spies. But this . . . *this* phenomenon was *other*.

"Is that what you think it is? Some probe from the alien ship?"

Mary giggled in that goofy teenage way of hers and returned her attention to the box of radio parts. "What else could it be?"

"And that doesn't bother you?"

"Not at all."

Calm filled the main control room; a sense of peace washed over her. She bit her inside lip until it bled. "Why not?"

Mary studied the board for a moment, then responded. "I suppose I look at it this way. Like, if it's real—and that's a big if—and it somehow comes from the alien vessel, then I ask myself *what could they be watching us for?* I mean, there's no question their technology is better than what we have, right? So, if they meant harm, they would have done something a long time ago."

"But they haven't."

"Exactly. So maybe they're studying us, learning from what we do. I don't know, but if we found alien life, we'd do the same thing: study it. Find out its intentions; whether it's a threat." She arranged the boards on the console. "Either way, the blue light people appear to be happy just watching from a distance, and we've got a more important goal to reach. Like being rescued." She motioned to the collection of boards and other electronics in front of her.

If Kate's theory about the destruction of the lunar lab being caused by the aliens was true, then they *were* a threat, and perhaps she and Mary were being naïve, toyed with, the mouse to the alien's cat.

"I'm heading out to install the beacon on the comms tower. Keep your helmet close just in case, eh?" She secured her envirosuit, then exited through the main access airlock.

THE TOWER WASN'T MUCH OF A TOWER AT ALL. It stood about 10 meters high with several connection hubs for antennas and dishes running up its side. Rather than fight with the telescoping mechanism to bring the mast down, Kate hopped on the LunaScoota and floated to a spot about three-quarters of the way up. The emergency beacon, built for universal applications, affixed itself smoothly to the hub. Before turning it on, Kate scanned the horizon again for any strange lights: nothing but the emptiness of space and grey-white lunar landscape sparkling in sunlight.

Why would they be watching us?

That question had embedded itself in her thoughts and haunted her. When Jim first heard the cry from the Ross 128 system, he felt the aliens were looking for water. Sure, they could extract it from the Moon's surface—there was plenty of ice at the poles—but why do it the hard way when Earth was so close? Perhaps the naysayers were right in 2085. Maybe the Rossian cry for help *was* a ruse.

She hit the power button and turned her head away. The beacon—a rotating strobe like the one on the lunar lab—flashed to life. Kate eased down to the surface and nestled the scooter beside the other, then returned to the main control room.

Mary had the radio open and was poking around with a remote probe from her suit. She read measurements on her helmet's visor, angled so she could see it properly. When Kate joined her at the console, she smiled.

"Good news. This little transceiver appears functional, but we'll need an antenna for it.

Kate unsealed her helmet and removed it. "What's that frequency range . . . UHF?"

"Yeah, so I can build an antenna. But there's another problem too." She picked up the radio and inspected it. "This unit is strictly low power. Probably runs only a couple watts. It must have had an amplifier with it, but I didn't find one. Transmitting a signal is one thing, but getting them to receive it will be a real trick." She focused again on her measurements. "Is the beacon working?"

"Like a big, bright charm." She leaned against the console beside Mary. "The radio's a long shot, isn't it." More of a conclusion than a question.

Mary holstered the probe. "I got so much to fix or modify it's like, I could trim the Yagi we brought in the scooter, but I don't have the right tools for it. Then there's the whole power thing. If we can't juice the transmitter somehow, it'll still be useless. And, there's no connecting cables or feedlines or—"

"Whoa, hold up there, Mares. One step at a time, remember? What's the most important task, the action you absolutely must take before any other?"

Mary slumped her shoulders and thought for a second. "I guess it's figuring out if the radio still works. If it doesn't, then nothing else matters."

"Okay then, so how do you check it's working?"

"I can run a current to it, see if it works and then, if it does, I'll test for transmitter power with the suit probe."

Kate squeezed her shoulder and smiled. "Sounds like you know what you're doing."

Mary nodded, brushed a strand of hair from her face, then pushed half of the boards and electronics away. "First things first."

"While you do that, I'll fill these empty canisters from the oxygenator's take off port for back up. How many so far?"

"Twenty-seven including the ones we brought from the old lab."

Kate examined the intake hub where the oxygenator lines fed into the main control room. Filling the tanks was a simple enough task, but with the limited power running off the scooter battery to the oxygenator, it would take a considerable amount of time to load each one. She pulled a canister Mary found in the galley out of the box, opened its connector, and screwed it into the intake. She punched the button to start replenishing it, and immediately, the hum of the oxygenator inside the habitat changed pitch as it siphoned off oxygen into the tank. The readout on the console hub showed filling time to be just under twenty minutes. Not great, Kate thought, but better than nothing.

She ran through the other environmental readouts on the console's main screen. Air pressure in the control room remained strong. Battery power from the scooter was sufficient although the drain rate was faster than the ability of the machine's portable solar panel to recharge it. At some point, they'd have to switch over to the second battery. Temperature hovered around 12 C.

Still, the oxygenator groaned under the additional load of filling the canister, and the increased draw on their power source was enough to dampen Kate's optimism. After running through some quick computations in her head, she grimaced.

It's a coin toss whether we run out of power first, or oxygen. Either way, the result is the same.

NINETEEN

Atteberry

SOMETIME BETWEEN THE FITFUL HALF-SLEEP after lunch and the ping from the TSA announcing he'd be picked up shortly to fly to Nova Scotia, Atteberry felt older than he'd ever imagined. His knees complained as he hauled himself up from the sofa, and the twinge in his lower back reminded him of the disrepair his body had fallen into. Failing to eat much didn't do him any favors either. Notwithstanding the subtle onset of increasing age, one task remained transfixed in his mind: *save Mary.*

The message from the TSA was simple. Within forty-five minutes, a logistics person would arrive and take him to an awaiting hypersonic copter that would shuttle him across the continent to meet up with Esther at the launch site of a fancy new Moon-bound ship. Along with it came a short list of things to bring with him, surprisingly little he thought but then, he wasn't going on some sightseeing cruise, like she said. He padded into his bedroom and threw some toiletries, socks and underwear into a small travel bag

While he was there, he noticed the framed bed-side photograph of him, Mary and Janet, taken years ago at the beach with the Golden Gate Bridge in the background. His daughter was eight years old, and Janet was beautiful and happy. His stomach knotted. Al-though he'd given up ever reuniting with his ex-wife, Esther had been right all along: somewhere in his heart he still loved her. Deeply. And it was partly because of his inability to let her go completely that his relationship with Esther atrophied in the weeks and months following the Mount Sutro disaster. That, and the fact she insisted on covering up the initial Ross 128 signal he'd heard.

The business of keeping secrets from the people might be status quo for spies and politicians, but how could that possibly benefit the rest of us?

He brushed a finger across the photo, as if wiping a strand of hair from Janet's face, then grabbed his kit and marched down the hall to the living room. As he was about to sit down again, he peered out the window to see a long, black late model hovercar glide into his driveway, settle on the ground, and a young, lone figure emerge. Atteberry met him at the door.

"Mr. Atteberry? I'm Kenley Smith, TSA Logistics. Esther Tyrone sent me to take you to the heliport."

They shook hands and he invited him in. "I've got everything you asked me to bring on the list."

"Good. Any questions then?"

He cleared his throat. "It doesn't seem like much. What about clothing?"

Smith smiled ruefully. "You'll be fitted at the launch site with workskins and any other personal effects you need." He checked the time on his indie-comm. "If there's nothing else, we must leave."

"Yes, of course." He tucked the travel bag under his arm and looked around his empty home, imagining Mary back in it.

"First time?"

"Sorry?"

"First time in space, Mr. Atteberry?"

He faked a smile. "I guess I'm more nervous than I thought I'd be."

"That's normal, but you can relax; the *Echo* is a state-of-the-art scout ship, and by all accounts, a real treat to fly in. You'll be in good hands and before you know it, seeing your daughter again."

They exited the home and jumped into the hovercar.

"TSA heliport," Smith commanded, and the vehicle purred out of the driveway and down the street.

As they merged with traffic on 19th Avenue, Atteberry asked, "Where is this heliport, anyway?"

"At the international airport itself, just off the North Access road."

City College had a campus there, but Atteberry had never spent much time at it since he taught at Ocean.

Smith's indie-comm pinged. "It's a message from Dr. Tyrone. She's about to leave New York for Nova Scotia . . . wonders if we're on our way."

Atteberry gazed out the window at the afternoon sun, his nerves twitching more and more as the hovercar approached its destination.

"If it's any help, sir, my dad did a lot of low orbit flying and such in the civil war. I remember him telling me before my first space flight that once you get going, the beauty of Earth and the stars makes you forget all about your nerves. Then you can really enjoy the ride."

"Thanks, but I think I'm more anxious about what we'll find on Luna than the flight itself."

"Here. Want one of these?" Smith pulled a bottle from his jacket pocket. "They'll help take the edge off."

Atteberry recognized the Calmease pills. He'd taken them before but found they dulled his senses as much as they smothered his anxiety. "No thanks, I'll manage."

They rode the next fifteen minutes in silence until the hovercar turned onto the North Access Road at the airport and weaved its way through narrow laneways to one of the many industrial lots that surrounded the runways. They stopped in front of a tired, low-rise building, absent of any signage except for a small blue and white square at the main door with *TSA* painted on it. Smith entered a code at the access box, placed his face at the scanner, and pulled the door open inviting Atteberry to enter first.

The structure itself was one large dimly lit great room. Directly ahead was a wall-length video screen displaying the TSA logo. A couple of technical operators working computers sat in front. To the right, a set of couches and leather chairs with several auto-servers stationed against the wall. On the left, a group of flight mechanics in overalls and other engineering types were studying maps.

"This way, sir."

Smith led him over to join the aviation crew. He introduced him to the chief engineer, a stocky man in grease-covered clothes and TSA ball cap, then to the flight coordinator. She looked like she recently graduated high school, except for the faint crow's feet around her eyes.

"Are you the pilot?"

She laughed and said, "No, no, I'm strictly on the ground, but you'll hear my voice a lot during the initial stages of flight."

Another woman entered from the main door, tall with reddish-brown hair, and joined them.

"Here's your pilot," the coordinator said.

Atteberry shook hands with Captain Amanda Dumas, and she wasted no time getting the flight details from the crew. Within minutes, he followed her through a secondary door to the apron where a 6-seat hypersonic copter waited for them, looking like something out of the future he'd only read about in his astronomy journals.

"Have you ever flown in one of these birds?" she shouted over the roar of a jet aircraft taking off from the adjacent airport.

"I'm afraid I've done little flying in anything."

She raised her eyebrows. "Then you're in for an awesome ride, Mr. Atteberry."

Captain Dumas helped strap him in to the seat beside her and handed him a set of headphones. The first thing he heard after putting them on was the cheerful voice of the flight coordinator singing out various instructions, weather data and other technical information he didn't understand. The captain responded, running through a holographic checklist displayed on the windscreen, and fired up the engines.

The copter roared, and white-knuckle fear replaced Atteberry's initial anxiety. He held onto the armrests for his life. Dumas must have noticed his face. She smiled, patted his arm, and exuded confidence he only wished he could muster.

Within moments, the copter's thrusters powered up another level and the craft shot vertically a couple hundred meters, hovered for a moment before the hypersonics kicked in and thrust Atteberry deep into his seat as they blasted into the sky.

Mary

AFTER PONDERING THE QUESTION OF WHY one of the mining habitat builders would have a UHF radio, Mary concluded it must have been for the love of the hobby and nothing more. There wouldn't have been any operational reason for it: the evidence of corporate comms devices only around here was clear, and they all worked on different frequencies. So, it was reasonable that a builder—or manager—brought the radio for their own pleasure.

She understood a little about Earth-Moon-Earth communications in the amateur radio world because her dad had spoken of it from time to time. An operator on Earth would beam a signal to the Moon, and bounce it off the lunar surface back to Earth, to contact someone. For many years, it was the challenge of bouncing a signal off Luna that intrigued these hams ... nothing else. Perhaps the owner of this gear bounced signals off passing ships or one of the satellites. It didn't really matter: powering the radio suggested a way to communicate with Earth.

So now what? She'd watched Kate work methodically on various problems: filling several oxygen canisters, determining the integrity of the habitat, surveying the destroyed lunar lab site for answers ... and that kind of systematic approach was what she needed to incorporate into her own operational experience. The scientific method could only teach her so much in a classroom. Only by living the experience would she understand the importance of resourcefulness, of making something from nothing, like Kate.

Kate brought the Yagi in from the scooter. This antenna functioned well when they first contacted her dad through the modified indie-comm, but its dimensions were all wrong for the UHF band. Mary studied the lengths of each element and worked out in her head what the new measurements needed to be to make the transmitter operational. Seven elements in the antenna: the directors, the reflector, and everything in between. Still, there were no task-specific tools around to cut the metal to the required lengths, and she wasn't completely comfortable trimming them too much lest she overshoot the most efficient lengths all together.

I wish Dad was here to help.

Kate kept reminding her to focus on first things first, the most important steps, one at a time. With that in mind, Mary discovered that the small UHF radio worked. She'd hooked it into a miniature power port and briefly fired up the rig. Using the suit probe, she measured the output voltages and currents from the various signal stages and judged the UHF transceiver functional. That was the first thing.

Following that, she needed to confirm whether the unit could transmit a signal into the universe, and determine if someone might receive it. Her dad told her this was the greatest thrill in radio: to send a general CQ call into the darkness and hope a station came back. It was a lot like fishing. You throw your line into the water and see if anything bites.

The Yagi sat in front of her at the main console. It was built to resonate at 222 MHz, but the radio she had operated at 430 MHz. Useless, unless she trimmed the antenna to operate in that new frequency range.

In her suit belt, various tools and probes were available, but the only thing capable of cutting the aluminum elements on the antenna was a three inch pocket saw—no heavy-duty cutter at all. This could take some time.

"You didn't come across any wire cutters in your travels through this place, did you?"

Kate leaned against the console, studying the readings from the main console viewscreen. "Nothing that could handle those."

"Then I'll to have to saw these elements individually."

"Anything I can do to help?"

Mary studied the antenna in front of her. "Yes, if you hold it down while I cut, that would really help."

Kate scuttled over along the console until she sat beside Mary.

"We'll start with the director element first."

She jammed the smaller end of the antenna under Kate's thighs and, using the tiny belt saw, she hacked away at the rod with her good arm, cutting it to the required length. After several minutes of heavy strokes, the element yielded, and a three inch piece of aluminum dropped off. She did the same to the other side of the director.

Then the thought that had nestled in her head arose, and now was as good a time to pursue it as any.

"Kate, could you ever see yourself getting together with my dad?"

Kate sputtered and croaked, "Jesus, Mary, what are you talking about?"

She continued cutting the element. "I'm asking because, like, he trusts you so much and we all get along great, and there's a huge gap in his life right now. So . . ."

Kate's hand reached out and covered the saw. "Mares, I told you this already. I can't feel the same way about him or anyone else that you do. I'm not built like that, remember? It's not that I'm completely unfeeling . . . I just . . . don't share what you have. Besides," she said, releasing her hand, "I have nothing to offer him."

Mary held her thoughts inside for a moment, so Kate continued. "Look, I've thought about it before, okay? Oddly, I do have feelings for him—I like him a lot—but love? I wish I knew what that meant."

After trimming two more elements, Mary straightened up and stretched her back. "Sorry. Half the time I don't know what I'm talking about. Your private life is none of my business." A few awkward moments passed between them.

"Have you ever had a real boyfriend, Mares?"

She chuckled. "I've kissed a couple of boys, you know, fooled around a bit, but nothing serious. No sex, if that's what you mean."

"Huh. You're a smart, science type. Explain physiologically what it was like."

Mary dropped the saw and considered the question. "It's like something heightened all my senses. The world around me came alive, as if I'd been given this amazing insight into how life worked, if that makes any sense. Colors were brighter. Um, I was, I don't know . . . connected."

"Wow."

"But that's not love, not in the way I'm talking about with you and Dad. That was just instinctual, hormonal activity. Physical and emotional lust rather than love."

Kate eyed her ruefully. "You learn all that from books too?"

"Yup, and real life, such as I've lived it so far. My dad always told me *why put your faith in something as fleeting as instinct when there's a richer, deeper love available*? I learned more about *that* kind of love from reading and my dad than I have with any person."

She resumed cutting the antenna elements, and grinned.

Katie

TWO YEARS OF INTENSE TRAINING HAD COME to this: scrabbling over a rogue satellite orbiting the Earth with a mission to repair a faulty communications panel. Hardly what she had in mind to celebrate her twelfth birthday, but the work itself thrilled her.

Her dad would be so proud if he only knew; if he only cared. Screw him. Both of them.

"Katie, there's an access latch to your right. You need to reach that one."

She wriggled around the satellite, the bulky worksuit constraining her movements like thick, oversized clothing. "I see it now."

"Perfect. You remember what to do from here?"

"Yes, Juan," she grumbled with a hint of sarcasm. "I put this thingie in that doodad and run." She smiled as she tugged on the access latch keys.

"You're a big bag of laughs. Just keep moving fast. We need the new panel in there pronto."

She focused on the task. She trained for two weeks on this mission, everything from basic movements and tools in the worksuit, to replacing the comms panel in this particular military satellite. Survival actions, contingencies if the flight pack failed, the detailed visuals on the helmet visor—all information she'd have to understand in case anything went awry.

The protocol for replacing the board was simple: she learned that the first time the trainer went through it. The survival and contingency protocols fascinated her. They considered all possible scenarios, and the bulk of her mission training centered on those, learning what to do, how to respond without hesitation. The delicate balance between intriguing work and extreme danger filled her with excitement, despite her reduced adrenal secretion.

"I'm opening the access panel now."

"Roger."

Katie lifted the latches and yanked the board up.

Curious . . . all the operating lights showed green.

"Juan, are you seeing this? The comms unit seems to work fine." She zoomed in on the various boards and plug-ins with her helmet cam. "All green."

"Roger, nevertheless the mission is to replace the board. Please proceed."

Katie shrugged and thought whatever to herself, then released the clamps holding the comms panel in place. One of the amber system lights flickered, then flashed red. She wrestled a bit with the board before it yielded to her fingers. After securing it in her carryall, she installed the replacement and pushed it in. The system light returned to amber.

"Hang on, I don't think the panel's in properly. I got this alert light going."

"Yeah, Katie, I see it, but everything's showing here as fully operational. It's working perfectly. Well done."

She shook her head inside the helmet. This made no sense. The old board worked fine, and the replacement didn't, but Juan said all's good?

"The light's still amber. Maybe I need to test—"

"Never mind that, all systems are green here. Probably a bum light. Re-latch the access panel and return to the orbiter."

"But—"

"Return to the orbiter now, Kate." His voice became darker with a hint of impatience and something she couldn't quite place.

No one calls me Kate.

It didn't add up, but she'd find out why.

Kate

KATE REFLECTED ON MARY'S WORDS. It was a curious, perhaps naïve take on things: *instinct versus intention* applied to many human activities, not only love. Still, where she was concerned, for as long as she could remember, Kate felt cut off from those around her—Mary, included—by emotions and experiences she simply did not share with them. Some of her old Spacer colleagues who'd kept a semblance of health followed sports or politics, and their passions took them far into those schemes, but she held nothing but ambivalence toward most matters.

Do I lack the capacity for passion in anything other than science?

When she was chosen for the original Spacer Program as a 10-year-old, she thought she'd be trained in computer science and programming to support humanity's push to the inner planets and beyond—a fast-tracked, personal curriculum based on her scores in the Aptitudes. Instead, she never saw her parents again and worked for ambiguous, toxic leaders involved in the development of underhanded political espionage and God knows what else. That, and the surgery that removed her reproductive organs.

She studied Mary working diligently on reconfiguring the antenna for use with the radio, with feelings comprising admiration, jealousy, and . . . what was it? Despair. She first buried the trauma of losing her parents by throwing herself into the work. Then, punted from the Spacer Program after the civil war, she busied herself with teaching at City College, and now with mind-numbing geophysical surveys on Luna.

It's come to this.

Mary challenged her. She recognized that. Forced her to stop running around and to look at—actually *observe*—the world and open up to those emotions she vowed subconsciously never to allow into her thoughts.

Damn you, Mary.

And where had it taken her? Kate fiddled with her suit, feigning busy-ness, monitoring the environmental parameters on the console's main screen, wondering whether someone would rescue them—but more importantly, wondering if she actually *wanted* to be rescued. If so, for what purpose? To return to Earth and some moronic research position or ridiculous classroom? Why continue doing what she'd been doing for the past how many years, running away from all those painful feelings that continued to gouge her? What was the point of it all?

Perhaps something more, something larger, hid behind this experience. Kate had never been a spiritual or religious person: she eschewed reliance on ideas as nebulous as belief in a higher power—believed those who did were ignorant and passive, allowing life to happen *to* them instead of going out and taking charge of their own destinies. Yet, Mary had insight into nature that she did not have, and it fueled her with insatiable optimism and drive. Is that what she wanted?

"When Marshall Whitt and his cronies detained us—before Esther and the California soldiers arrived when the whole Ross 128 signal was going down—he and I shared something."

Mary looked up from her work, her eyes wide.

"Before we escaped and ran up to Mount Sutro where your mom and her team blew the thing up, we were in holding cells, both covered in dirt from stealing around the transmitter site, and for a few moments, we held each other's hands."

"Oh?"

"Yeah, it was odd. I figured he really liked Esther and wanted to pursue a relationship with her, but at the same time, I wondered about . . . I don't know what you'd call it . . . if there was an understanding between us."

Mary peered into her eyes, and Kate held her gaze for longer than she thought was normal.

"What happened?"

"Well, you know the rest, I'm sure. Esther and the soldiers got us out of there and back up to the transmitter site at Mount Sutro where we tried to contact the alien ship. Anyway, I'm sharing this because I didn't experience the physiological things you talked about. That kind of emotion you describe is nothing more than what I get from a poached egg. But I sensed that I was, er, what's the word I'm looking for . . ." Kate turned away, searching desperately to attach the right word, the correct word to what she knew then. "*Safe*, Mary. For the first time since I was a kid." She eyed her cautiously. "Is that love?"

Mary smiled, nodded and said, "If I had to guess, I can't imagine it being anything else."

TWENTY

Carter

THE SUN BLUSHED LAZILY IN THE SOUTHWEST SKY as the Titanius corporate heli-jet screamed over the Atlantic seaboard at an altitude of 2,500 meters, en route to the private spaceport at the Royal Canadian Air Force facilities in Shearwater, near Halifax. Clayton Carter checked his watch every few minutes, mentally coaxing the aircraft faster. It was his style to squeeze more, a little extra not only from his machines but from his people too. He sat directly behind the pilot in the second row of seats, his long legs struggling with inadequate space, Esther beside him. They both wore the standard issue flight suits, breathable Kevlar skins that his astronauts depended on all the time, and looser jackets over top. He couldn't help eyeing Esther's curves, and he glanced at his own flat stomach, wondering if she'd noticed him as she stared out the small, side window at the green and blue landscape below. Last night with her seemed a distant, almost forgotten memory, but still a sweet one.

Esther turned to him and pressed the mic button pinned to her collar. "Why did you build your space port in Nova Scotia, Clayton? You could have chosen anywhere along here, somewhere in Maine, for example." Her voice sounded machine-like through the headphones.

"Well, you're right. Lots of places on the coast were more than happy to accommodate us. But being in Canada—a nonparty to the civil war—offered an extra level of distance and security, and sharing space with the RCAF was a bonus. Any action taken against us would seem like an attack on Canadians." He checked his watch again. "There aren't any guarantees about safety, but they share many of our Northern Democratic values, don't you think? It was a logical choice, and more affordable than anything else."

Esther nodded and returned her gaze to the landscape.

Carter's indie-comm vibrated, and he checked the message coming in from Ed. The *Malevolent* had altered its course, en route to the Moon, with an extra burn. Arrival in about eight hours . . . faster than he thought. There was more.

We're monitoring an increase in traffic from our Asian and Prussian friends. Lots of interest in Malevolent's *new heading, and some chatter about satellite pix from Luna. We may have company at some point.*

Carter grimaced. His deep desire to withhold information from others was a challenging hand to play with all this watching going on. He wouldn't be able to keep his movements quiet for much longer.

He messaged back: *Understood.*

She seemed preoccupied with the coastal scenery, so Clayton checked the *Echo*'s manifest on his device. It refreshed as items changed. Captain Powell's top-notch crew headed the list. They had added him and Esther, along with that egghead Atteberry who should arrive at port around the same time as them. A full complement of salvage equipment had been itemized including a pair of massive excavators, most of it on board at this point. Envirosuits, food and water supplies, comms material, extra skins, repair tools . . . all the standard materials were there.

It doesn't feel right.

He reviewed the stores through another page and found what he looked for: the weapons cache. Not labeled as such for security reasons, but there nonetheless. Carter scanned across the items, recalling what each code referred to, and reconsidered the technical parameters of the *Echo* herself. She was already equipped with standard issue defensive rail guns, like all ships that traveled beyond Earth's orbit, but could also handle heavier apparatus.

He messaged Captain Powell: *Let's increase onboard weapons capability.* He added several of the reference codes and sent it.

Moments later, Powell responded. *R. It'll add another few minutes to prep time.*

Back on the manifest page, Carter followed the various coded items being brought on, checked off, and confirmed as someone loaded them onto the ship's weapons bay. The *Echo* hadn't been designed for combat, but with her vastly improved new engines, the combination of speed and aggression made her a formidable machine against the sluggish behemoths out there. He grinned.

You curious assholes want to tag along? Good luck.

He returned his indie-comm to the holder on his sleeve, peered over Esther's shoulder and pointed out the Nova Scotian coastline. He keyed his mic switch. "A few more minutes, Esther, and we'll be landing."

She smiled groggily as if he'd awakened her. The last twenty-four hours had been a whirlwind, and fatigue had set in on her face. Carter squeezed her hand and said, "Long day, huh? For all of us. We can nap on the *Echo* once we're en route. There aren't cabins per se, but there are sleeping quarters."

Esther nodded. "I'd love a stiff drink and a sleep, to be honest."

The pilot's voice crackled in their headphones. "Sir, incoming flight from San Francisco, about ten minutes away and approaching from the northwest. That'll be Mr. Atteberry arriving on schedule."

"Perfect, thank you!"

"I also have a message from Captain Powell of the *Echo*. He informs me they have loaded all cargo, and she's standing by for takeoff as soon as you're all on board. Prepare for landing in a few minutes."

Esther bolted up and stretched in her seat, squeezing her shoulder blades back. The heli-jet dropped altitude like a stone and flew in low over the Atlantic Ocean toward Dartmouth. Carter leaned forward between the pilot and co-pilot seats, studying the instrument panel and glancing up at the horizon. He picked up Atteberry's flight on the orange radar screen, a recurring blip sweeping in on its own approach to the spaceport.

They flew over half a dozen trawlers and ocean-bound vessels as they neared the coast. The aircraft's speed reduced dramatically, and the vehicle completed its voyage, blades chopping, their sound transforming as the heli-jet passed over land.

Other than a large, block-lettered "T" painted on the flat roof of a drab and inconsequential building, the Titanius hangar was unmarked. The grounds crew awaited their landing and guided the machine to ground. As the craft lowered itself out of the sky, Carter scanned the horizon, overlooking the small cities of Dartmouth and Halifax to the vast, forested areas of the province.

The long shadows of growing dusk crept over the tarmac as the heli-jet touched down and Captain Dumas cut power to the rotors. Carter unbuckled his seat harness and helped Esther out of hers. She reached for her personal bag and placed it on her lap, leaning forward. The captain twisted her body around, facing Esther. "As soon as the engines stop, you're safe to go. The grounds crew will take it from here." Then she nodded and returned to her instruments.

Two men in hunter green overalls rolled a small boarding ladder toward them, holding their distance as the blades slowed down. He paid them no attention. His mind was already on board the *Echo*, pursuing what he believed to be the most significant evolutionary step in humankind's quest for wealth.

Esther

EXCITEMENT TINGLED THROUGH HER ENTIRE BODY as she scrambled across the tarmac toward the Titanius hangar, trying to keep up with Clayton's long strides. They entered the building; it was darker than she'd expected. A row of computers and video screens, u-shaped work tables, and large portable white boards ran along one wall. Half a dozen technicians and other workers busied themselves in front of the boss. Strangely, she saw no evidence of the *Echo* being there.

Atteberry's hypersonic craft descended onto the tarmac within a few minutes, and much to Esther's surprise and concern, her heart skipped a beat when Jim lowered himself out of the vehicle and stepped down. One of the grounds crew greeted him, shook his hand, and motioned toward the hangar. Esther fiddled with a clasp on her travel bag.

"How well do you know him?" Carter said, watching the professor approach the building.

"Not intimately, if that's what you mean." The words tumbled out of her mouth before she caught herself. Heat rose in her cheeks. "But when he shared the Ross 128 signal and Kate Braddock's subspace filter with us, we grew to enjoy each other's company."

Carter turned to her, and a brief, almost imperceptible flash of insecurity crossed over his face, then vanished.

Esther mulled over his words, then decided to own her feelings. "Nothing ever happened beyond coffee and an occasional meal, not that I hadn't wanted it to. Some significant differences of opinion kept getting in the way."

Carter nodded, and marched to the hangar door where he welcomed Atteberry with a *hail fellow, well met* grip and grin. Esther hung back, watching the two men posturing. When Jim caught her eye, her gaze lingered on him.

Damn it, Es, what is the matter with you?

"Ready to go, Doctor? We've got people to rescue and every minute counts."

"Lead on," she said, joining Carter and Jim in front of the main viewing screen. "But am I missing something, Clayton? Where's the *Echo*?"

"Here she is." He nodded at a technician who punched a key on the console. An image of the ship appeared, like she was inside the hangar, yet—

"Oh, sweet Jesus . . . she's beautiful."

Atteberry stepped forward. Blue and green light from the massive screen reflected on his face. "Holy shit." His bag dropped to the floor. "Let's go."

Esther had expected a normal, almost pedestrian scout ship, perhaps with a souped-up engine array. She did not expect laying eyes on a machine as perfect and graceful as this. She swallowed hard, taking it all in.

The *Echo*, dressed in grey with black highlights, rested on squat, efficient landing pads. She must have been 35 or 40 meters long, streamlined in a delta wing arrow for travel through the atmosphere, but cut square at the back where the main engines were housed. Smaller, paired antigrav thrusters ran along the side nacelles. The cockpit sat on top of the ship near the nose, where the pilot ran through various pre-flight activities. Standard complements of rail guns completed the look, a necessary albeit unnerving requirement.

An access hatch beside the main engines had a short ramp leading up to it, and a tech stood in the frame, tablet in hand, waving at others on the ground. Around the hangar was an assortment of storage bins, hallways running away, workstations and antigrav sleds.

"Clayton, she's magnificent, but *where* is she?"

Carter flashed his smile, clearly enjoying his big reveal. "Watch this." He nodded to the tech at the controls, who then barked instructions through a headset before he gave Carter a thumbs up. A low, heavy rumble shivered up through her boots. Then, a section of tarmac opened, and the *Echo* emerged from her underground home, riding a massive hydraulic platform until she was flush with the ground.

"Voila!"

In the early evening light, the *Echo*'s metallic grey shone like gold against a backdrop of deep greens and blue-orange skies. Jim peered at Esther with a pained, anxious look.

"Ready?" Carter didn't wait for a response, but instead grabbed his kit, thanked the surrounding techs, and marched to the door.

"Come on, Jim, let's go find Mary."

Atteberry rubbed his red eyes. A worker handed him two Kevlar skins on the way, then he and Esther raced to catch up with Carter. Once they'd entered the ship through the port side ramp, the tech with the tablet stepped off, nodded, and closed the hatchway.

Carter marched ahead of them through the fuselage, pulling on a headset from a storage compartment. He motioned for them to hurry and follow. "Here, this one's for you, Esther. Mr. Atteberry, there's yours," he said, pointing to an open storage shelf. "I'll give you the grand tour once we leave orbit."

He had already made his way to the bridge and was talking to the pilot. Some thin, muscular woman, who introduced herself as Ishani, escorted her and Jim forward where the thick padded flight seats were, strapped them in for launch, and secured their harnesses. Carter joined them in a moment, grinning like a possessed man as he took his seat and buckled up.

Esther barely contained her amazement at the flashing images on the various viewscreens around her. On one, her own vital signs appeared through sensors in the flight chair, along with numerous impressions of the ship's deck and different camera shots down the length of the ship. Carter's voice boomed through her earphones. He described where the cameras were and what they monitored.

"Once we leave orbit, the ship's simulated gravity will kick in and we can move around."

Esther turned her head and shoulders to her left and saw Jim's tired face, eyes stretched wide. A mix of nervous anxiety and excitement coursed through her body as she leaned back into the seat and gripped the armrests.

In a moment, Captain Powell ran through a pre-launch checklist. From what she could tell, there was a modest crew of five: the captain and pilot, a co-pilot named Elin Jenson, Ishani, a smiley fellow— Fowler Quigg—who'd buckled in on the bridge . . . a comms guy perhaps . . . and another heavyset man called Dub, dressed like Ishani.

The *Echo*'s maneuvering thrusters kicked in, and the ship rose so smoothly she barely noticed the motion. On the screens, through a camera in the ship's belly, she watched the *Echo* pulled away from the tarmac. In an instant, the craft was several thousand meters above ground and rising.

"Here it comes," Carter said, and braced himself in the cushioned seat.

"Engage main engine thrusters."

What happened next, she could only describe as the most powerful, full-body crush she'd ever experienced. Esther was no neophyte when it came to space travel, but it had been a while since she'd flown, and back then, the boats were nothing like this creature. The engines roared to life and in a flash, the ship screamed forward through the atmosphere, burning hard to escape the Earth's gravitational pull, stealing the wind from her lungs.

Atteberry's voice panted over the earphones, a series of *oh my god* and *oh shit*. Gravitational forces ripped through Esther's body, preventing her from looking over at him. She closed her eyes and concentrated on breathing.

After several minutes, the flight became smoother. Esther relaxed and looked around. On the main screen, stars appeared from a nose camera as the vehicle banked upwards. Thin, residual terran atmosphere softened the view like an impressionist painting, and suddenly through it all shone Luna, brilliant against the dark expanse of space.

TWENTY-ONE

Kate

"How's the antenna?"

"Almost done, I gotta finish cleaning the dust out of the feed-line connector." Mary frowned and sighed. "But I'm not sure about power output. It's not responding like it should."

"Let's take a look."

Mary placed the Yagi on an empty spot on the console and showed Kate the guts of the transceiver she'd been working on. When they tested the radio's stages, everything measured normal. Test current flowed undisturbed through each circuit, but something suppressed the transmitter power output as it registered barely half a watt.

"That's not enough to throw a signal across the room, let alone anywhere near Earth," Mary grumbled.

They stared at the growing pile of equipment. The temperature in the habitat now hovered around eight degrees Celsius, and Kate blew into her hands to warm them up. *The excess drain on the power supply must have affected the environment.*

"There's nothing I can do to fix this. We just don't have the right tools or any spare parts. We'll do what we can and hope there's a ship close enough to pick up our signal."

Kate recalled her last discussion with Stan Petrovic from Titanius headquarters about any ships being nearby. There wasn't much traffic, but perhaps they've redirected one now, assuming they're aware of the crisis. Then, out of nowhere, a nervous thought occurred to her. She immediately dismissed it as nonsense, but it kept rattling around in her head and wouldn't disappear.

Would the alien ship pick up a signal this weak?

"I wonder if we can somehow amplify it," Kate suggested. "The Yagi's already capable of transmitting in a tight, coherent beam, but what if there's an external amplifier to boost the output power itself?"

Mary scrunched her eyes in that way of hers when she recalled information, as if she was mentally flipped through pages of data. Kate figured she must have an eidetic memory, and this was how she reconstructed images of she'd seen. One Spacer she worked with on a radioactive waste dump years ago did the same thing, without any noticeable facial changes. His recall wasn't perfect, but more accurate than anything she'd ever experienced. She smiled, thinking about that boy, as Mary sat there.

Finally, she said, "Let's check that box of spare parts again."

Kate lifted the equipment bin onto the console and Mary fished through it deliberately, inspecting each item she pulled out.

"I thought I saw a piece with large fins on it. Anything generating that kind of heat must handle big power." She dove through various measuring devices: a wattmeter, SWR indicator, some random patching cables. "There it is."

What Mary grabbed looked like a clay brick with cooling blades sticking out the back. She turned it over several times, running one of her long fingers over the heat sink, and blowing dust out of the input and output connectors.

"What do you think?"

Mary grimaced and brushed the hair out of her face. "It's definitely a power amplifier, but I've no idea what frequency range it'll operate in. Maybe it's a custom-built job for the habitat comms or something." She grabbed the screwdriver from her belt and applied it to the screws on the bottom of the unit. "I'll pop this off and take a look."

Kate studied her as she tore into the amplifier and wondered what it must have been like for Mary to grow up with an English prof and radio astronomy enthusiast as a dad. One of the lucky ones, for sure. Her own father—at least what she remembered of him—carried himself quieter than Jim Atteberry. He was a gentle, loving man, and read to her in front of the fireplace on cold nights even when she was old enough to read by herself. Not stories from any kind of literary megatext or technical journals though. His were from her own family history, part fact, part fiction, full of deep insights and connections. A flood of ancient emotions rose in her chest.

"There's nothing on this gear to show operating frequency, and I've got no way to measure it. I'm sure the amplifier's built for the UHF spectrum, and that's what we want, but without knowing its bandwidth, it could be useless or worse."

Kate refocused on Mary's words. "How so?"

"Well, if the frequencies are off, it simply won't work. But there's a chance the higher output power will feed back into the radio circuits. If that happens, it could fry the transceiver completely. Anyway," she added, "the amp seems to be intact if you want to fire it up."

Kate stood up and stretched, not knowing what to do and desperately hiding her uncertainty from Mary. Not long ago, she'd never had an issue with decision-making. When did that change? Mount Sutro? First coming to Luna? Or did it begin with the Rossian ship emitting a shock wave so powerful it took down the entire lab?

Before she could reason it through, Mary's head snapped up from her equipment, her eyes scanning the control room. "What's that noise?"

Kate listened and heard it, too. She glanced at the main screen displaying all the environmental parameters, but nothing adverse appeared. All green lights. Even so, Mary was right. An odd sound emerged from the side of the habitat where the oxygenator feed entered. The machine *felt* different; the pitch of its operating frequency altered slightly. Then, the connecting spigot where the empty air canisters were being filled coughed and cracked. Kate's heart plummeted deep into her gut.

"Shit."

She jumped over to the canister and closed the tap on the outport, but the oxygenator continued hacking and sputtering. Kate adjusted the power flowing into the unit to stabilize the apparatus. At first, there was no change but, over the course of several seconds, the machine returned to its normal operating parameters. All environmental lights remained green on the viewscreen. It *sounded* right again.

Mary dropped her work on the radio and joined Kate at the oxygenator outport.

"We'd better not get too comfortable here, Mares," she said. "I forget this machinery hasn't been used in a while."

Mary leaned on her elbows in front of the main viewer, studying the array of green lights and flickering measurements. "But we're okay, aren't we?"

"For now, yeah, but I don't think we can keep filling those air tanks. It's putting that much more strain on the system."

Half a dozen filled canisters lay in a row on the dusty floor like bodies in a makeshift morgue, holding 15 to 20 minutes of oxygen each. Barely enough time to do anything but wait.

"We've gotta get that radio working and get the hell out of here."

Katie

THEY RARELY HAD PERMISSION TO LEAVE the Training Center campus unescorted, but Katie hacked into the panopticon security program and dropped in a few lines of creeper code, leaving the impression with their overseers that all was normal.

She and Martin squeezed under a low point in the wire fence by the kitchen prep building and flitted off into the woods. Twenty minutes later, they sat across from each other at a food joint, stuffing burgers down their throats.

"Happy birthday, Katie. Thirteen already, hm?"

She wiped her mouth and shrugged. They finished their meals in silence, ignoring the stares and odd smiles of the normies around them.

"C'mon, we'd better get outta here."

She pushed her plate aside and stood up, then waited for Martin to finish his drink and join her. He'd grown taller these last few months, but hadn't lost that frail appearance, or the distance in his eyes. Katie noticed a bearded man sitting on a stool at the counter, staring at him and grinning. He winked as the two darted outside.

"What was that about?" she asked.

"That slob? Never mind, I've seen that look before. Most normies ignore us Spacers, but some of them are weird. My trainer said they're curious about us because, well, we have no real parts, no real sexuality."

Katie sniffed. "That is neural."

"Yeah, so like no puberty, no real gender I suppose. Some freaks are attracted to that."

They strolled down a side road toward the park, sticking to the shadows, caught up in their own thoughts. Katie had had the dreams, strange ones where sometimes she was a boy and sometimes a girl. Since she'd cut her hair a year ago to prevent it from interfering with her space work, she looked more like some boys she remembered from the higher grades at her old school. Bony, and angular. Nondescript.

"Katie?"

"Hm?"

"What are you?"

"What do you mean?"

"Boy or girl, you know. Are you a boy or a girl?"

Katie stood like a statue under a large maple and faced him. Wind rustled through the leaves and swirled around them, tousling his beautiful hair. She looked up into his eyes. They were puffy and red.

"I guess I'm still a girl, mostly. Why?"

He gulped and inhaled. "I think I might be too."

They continued wandering through the park. She held his hand for a while as they shuffled back toward campus. No other words passed between them.

The next morning, Martin wasn't at breakfast. Katie over-heard a group of trainers say when they cut him down from the window, one of his eyes had popped out.

Kate

FOR SEVERAL MINUTES, KATE SCANNED THE environmental parameters on the console's main screen, looking for any kind of trend, any evidence of a pattern. Finding coherent signs or signals in apparently random data was her forte. In fact, it was her filter designed around pattern recognition that allowed Jim to isolate those first transmissions from Ross 128.

She regretted ever helping him out. That small decision to use Spacer technology, contravening the agreement she signed when they finally turfed her out, took her down the path to this point right here, right now: marooned on Luna with little hope of surviving. Not that she honestly cared about her own life much anymore, but to think Mary could die under her watch filled her with heavy guilt and remorse, reminding her of the girl-boy Martin.

"What's on your mind, Kate?"

"Hm? Oh, yeah . . ." She drew a deep breath and refocused on the display. "I'm looking for possible patterns in the data here. Actually, it's the deviations I'm really interested in."

"Anything out of the ordinary?" Mary had returned to work on the radio and amplifier, matching cables and connectors, and removing all useless parts from the workspace.

"No, at least nothing I can see. Perhaps it was one of those hiccups in the machinery." The oxygenator had been running quietly since the odd thumping sound a few minutes ago.

"On the other hand, I don't want to hang around here any longer than we absolutely must. The place is giving me the creeps."

Mary smiled and said, "I know what you mean. Walking through the dark sleeping quarters when we first arrived here weirded me out. Like, not that long ago men and women lived and worked at this mine site, hm?"

"A few years now, I suppose. Anyway, it all looks good again here." She adjusted the external heat control on her envirosuit. "How much time before we can transmit?"

"Not long. I have to make sure the connections fit tightly, then mount the antenna on the comms mast."

"And your elbow? Still good?"

Mary flexed it back and forth, rotating her shoulder. "Yeah, just really stiff. I'm keeping the medi-patch on."

Kate marveled at the speed of her recovery. There was a time when she could heal that quickly too, in the early Spacer days. Not so much anymore. The daily anti-rad pills she took had the unfortunate side-effect of thinning her marrow blood, making her bones significantly more brittle than when she was Mary's age. Having been off them now for two days—maybe longer—the withdrawal symptoms had flared up, especially the pain that kept chewing away at her gut. Like a smoldering fire finding oxygen, and coming back to life.

She considered Mary again, enlivened by this experience, happily working on the radio project. The fear existed, she'd seen it, but Mary could somehow keep it compartmentalized, distancing it from the work she undertook. Some of her Spacer colleagues had done that—some still did—and, curious, Kate wanted to understand. Was this ability born to them or learned? If the latter, then how could she learn it, too? She asked her about it.

Mary glanced up from her equipment and answered, "To be honest, I don't even think about being afraid. I mean, sure, I don't want to die up here and I miss my dad a ton, but that doesn't stop me from doing things." She snapped the heat sink back on the amplifier. "If I dwell too much about the danger we're in, I suppose I'd become paralyzed with fear of dying." She shrugged her shoulders.

"So, you're able to consciously block out the fear? Is that it?"

"I don't know, I just don't see the point of worrying about things that haven't happened yet." She paused. "Why all these questions?"

Kate hopped on the console and swung her legs over the edge. She could watch Mary working and keep an eye of the main monitor. "I'm curious. I mean, overcoming fear is a major accomplishment—something I haven't been able to do all that successfully. Yet, here you are, 17 years old, talking and behaving like some ancient, wise mystic."

Mary's laughter filled the control room. She rubbed her fingers, and shook her head. "I read a lot of books. You know that. I must have picked it up somewhere along the way, 'cause I never really think about."

"Most of us have to make conscious decisions to be brave."

Mary threw the remaining unused radio gear into the storage box and shoved it aside. In front of her on the console lay the transceiver, the small amplifier, the Yagi antenna, and a random collection of patch cables. She looked over at Kate. "So, remember the farty old existentialists had a saying about consciousness and finding their own meaning?"

"Sure. 'I think therefore I am'. Descartes, wasn't it?"

"Yeah, he proved his existence only because he could think. But you want to know something?"

"What?"

"He and the others got it wrong."

"What do you mean, Mares?"

"All the ancient texts show this." She stood up and eyed Kate with a curious, almost whimsical smile. "For me, it's the other way around."

TEN MINUTES LATER, KATE'S SCOOTER HOVERED in front of the telescopic comms tower. As she'd done before with the emergency beacon, she lifted the LunaScoota up, and secured the antenna at the highest point possible, close to the tip of the 10 meter mast. Earth floated over the horizon and she pointed the beam toward it. Then, she ran the coaxial feedline down the tower, and along the dusty compound until she came to the input junction connectors on the far side of the habitat. She dismounted and took several more minutes to secure the uncooperative outer feedline connection before she contacted Mary.

"All set?"

"Stand by. Let me check it."

As Mary verified the connection inside the main control room, Kate again experienced that anxiety of being watched. She stole cursory glances around the habitat, looking for anything different, any deviation from what she expected.

What could possibly make her so paranoid?

They were the only souls on the surface of Luna, except for whoever or whatever was skulking about in an alien spacecraft half-buried in the dust on the eastern limb. Still, the hairs on the back of her neck fluttered. She turned away from the habitat, gazing past the parked scooter toward the horizon. There was nothing there. No bogey-man, no bug-eyed monster, no strange blue light hovering overhead. Only the cold, grey monotonous landscape of this planetary abortion against the stark backdrop of endless space.

"It all checks out, Kate. We're in business."

"We can test the radio?"

"Roger."

"I'll double-check the power from the other battery and be right in."

Kate floated around to the main access hatchway, dismounted, and brushed new dust away from the secondary scooter's battery. She confirmed power levels remained solid, and the portable solar array they'd set up functioned well, even if it couldn't keep up entirely with the drain on the battery's reserves. Hopefully, they wouldn't need it much longer.

"Systems are a go out here, Mares," she said. "Let's do this."

Kate

THE FREQUENCY READOUT FROM THE LOW-POWER transceiver glowed orange in the dim light of the control room. Mary sat cross-legged beside it on the console and tuned the receiver to 435.800 MHz in the UHF band. Static from the small internal speaker crackled against the backdrop of the oxygenator pumping fresh air into the habitat.

"Hear anything?"

She turned a couple knobs and listened intently. "Nothing. I wonder if the receiver's sensitive enough to pick up any signals." She adjusted the VFO to investigate other frequencies in the band, with no change in the low-level static. "You're sure the antenna's pointing to Earth?"

Kate placed her helmet on the console. "Yes, as far as I can tell from eyeballing it."

Mary returned the VFO to 430.800 MHz and leaned back.

"Anything special about that frequency?"

She rubbed her eyes with the palms of her hands, exhaled, and said, "Dad used to hang out on it when he listened to his radio astronomy cronies around town. I don't know if there's something unique about it or not, but it's familiar."

Both remained silent for a moment. Kate thought she heard a voice in the muddy static, but more than likely fatigue played tricks on her.

"You're sure the antenna is—"

"Mares, I'm sure."

Mary flashed a look she hadn't seen before, a sweep of frustration and defiance. The circles under her eyes grew darker and for a moment, she'd aged ten years in a matter of minutes. Her face also had a familiarity to it. She'd seen it in herself and others during those brutal all-night training sessions the Spacer overseers put them through. Personalities changed in seconds. One eleven-year-old even sliced her wrists with a utility knife outside Kate's dorm. Made a hell of a mess.

"Come on, let's check the connections, okay?"

Mary didn't move.

"Now!" She preferred not to use that tone of voice but knew from experience that over-tired soldiers and Spacers responded best to direct, firm commands, and this was no time for either of them to vacillate.

"Sure, okay."

"Let's start with the feedline coming in." They bounded over to the large input junction and followed the cable to the connector. Kate unscrewed it a half-turn, inspected the pins for dust or damage, and handed it to Mary who also checked it. Then she reinserted the connector to the junction box and secured it with another twist.

"We'll check everything in here before I go back out."

Next, they traced the feedline up to the antenna input connector on the transceiver. Mary unscrewed it, and they both inspected the holes and pins before she put it back. Still no change in the audio; it remained full of static. Meanwhile, the activity seemed to help Mary regain her composure.

"It's more than odd, Kate, that plugging and unplugging the antenna makes no difference to the audio. Like, we should hear something, even static crashes from solar flares. But we're not." She closed her eyes, head down. "I wonder if I cut the elements wrong."

"Or there's a problem with the connection at the antenna itself?"

"I can go check," she said, reaching to pick up her helmet.

Kate shook her head. "I'd rather have you stay here. You know what you're looking for and how to operate that equipment, so I'll go."

She fastened her gloves and secured her helmet seal, then vanished through the airlock. She radioed, "I'll confirm the connection point on the outside of the junction box first. If there's any change, tell me."

"Roger."

Kate maneuvered the scooter to the back of the habitat where the junction was located. She unplugged the feedline and inspected it. Some dust infiltrated around the pins, but nothing significant, so she plugged it back in. "Any change?"

"Negative."

"Okay, I'm off to the antenna."

The scooter hovered around the top of the comms tower. Kate floated to the reflector side of the Yagi and confirmed visually that it pointed toward Earth. She pulled on the mounting clamp and noted it was solid; it appeared to be fully secure. Finally, she removed the feedline connector from the antenna itself. That's when she noticed one of the coupling pins had bent over.

That little bastard.

She continued hovering in place at the top of the tower and balanced herself on the machine to repair the connector. She had a pair of pliers on her utility belt and, although not quite the right tool for the job, she bent the pin to its original position. After manipulating the connector back and forth in its socket, the pins finally fell into their respective holes, and she jammed the feedline in and screwed it securely.

"Kate, it's working!"

"Great. I'm heading in."

THE RADIO SANG WITH ACTIVITY. NUMEROUS SIGNALS filled the control room, some weak, others strong, from operators on the near side of Earth.

"Jesus, Mares, you did it." A rush of tears welled up. Mary jumped up and down.

"I need to test that amplifier first, then we can break in on a conversation." She gazed at Kate with those large, blue eyes. "We're almost there."

The power booster Mary dissected earlier sat in line between the transmitter output and the antenna. She flipped the toggle switch on its facing and the unit's light glowed.

"At least we know it's operational."

Kate stood behind her, holding her helmet. "So, if it doesn't work, we're stuck with low power, right?"

"Correct."

"Even that might work, given all the active stations."

Mary tuned to an open frequency and picked up the microphone. "I'm going to key the mic first to test it. The output will show on this meter." She pointed to a measuring device the size of an indie-comm that also patched into the radio.

"Got it. Let's give it a shot."

She flashed Kate a thumbs up, held the microphone in both hands, and closed her eyes and squeezed the push-to-talk button.

The screech coming out of the radio's speaker pierced the air, causing Mary to throw the mic down as if it bit her. The odious smell of burned circuits and plastic filled the room, and still the radio blared like an urgent klaxon.

"Mary, what's going on!"

"I—I don't know. That amplifier . . . the voltage is cascading!"

Kate hopped to the main screen. The environmental parameters all shone orange and red. The power level indicator measuring output from the scooter battery had dipped to extreme lows. Control room lights flickered out one by one. Worse, the rhythmic thrum of the oxygenator had morphed into an ever-increasing pounding like a machine gun spitting out bullets.

Kate reacted quickly. "Pull the plug on that thing! Now!"

Mary yanked the power supply leads from the radio, killing the screeching noise. A puff of smoke erupted from the unit, and its operating lights faded to black. The oxygenator, however, continued hammering away, overloaded with surging current, until finally, it coughed and sputtered, and with an ear-splitting metallic bang, the machine stopped.

No sound emanated from the control room, now completely bathed in darkness. For a brief, suspended moment, Kate dared not breathe. She couldn't see Mary in the black shadows, but her short panicked breaths told her she was there. As the echo of that shattering screech faded, she picked up another sound, a faint one that sent a shiver of terror down her spine.

A slow, high-pitched hiss crept into the room.

Then her ears popped as the pressure fell.

TWENTY-TWO

Kate

THE ACRID SMELL OF MELTED ELECTRONICS CONTINUED to swirl around the control room. Kate drew shallow breaths; the toxic air burned her throat and nostrils.

We're not going to make it.

The primitive part of her brain screamed as panic set in. It was the same ugly fear that teased her back at Mount Sutro when some thugs threatened her life. She couldn't predict when or where it would raise its head—she'd never truly felt this threatened as a Spacer. Perhaps more happened to her at the Tower than simply discovering the Rossian ship heading toward Earth.

The escaping oxygen wheezed louder now as it found a hairline crack where the oxygenator portal entered the habitat. She closed her eyes and focused on controlling her breathing, her emotions.

This is no time to lose it. You've managed these things before.

But her brain didn't work like it had in the old days, and Kate shook her head, struggling to find her voice. "Mary, get your helmet on," she said calmly. Nothing but a haunting whimper and the clack of shivering teeth floated from Mary's direction. Her breathing worsened. "Damn it, Mary, get your helmet on!"

"Yes . . . yes . . . okay."

Kate snapped hers in place and fumbled for the light switch on its side. When it clicked on, she scanned the room and found Mary, helmeted, slouching over the console beside the destroyed transceiver. She pulled her gloves on. Through the suit-to-suit audio channel, Kate called her. "Let it go, Mares. Nothing we can do about it now and we've gotta refocus."

"I don't understand what happened," she whispered, her voice weak and distant, all the confidence of youth shattered.

Kate jumped over and checked the clasps and seals on Mary's envirosuit. She felt the fear and frustration too but wouldn't dare let Mary see it. "The damn thing blew up, that's what happened. Whatever that amp was, it screwed everything up, drawing way too much power from the scooter battery and overloading the system."

Mary found her helmet light and flicked it on. She inspected the damage. "Maybe I can clean this up and try again . . ."

Kate grabbed her arm. "Look at me, Mares. We're done with the radio, understand?"

She cried softly.

"Refocus, now, come on. Our new problem is oxygen, okay? We've gotta move on."

Mary's face, lit up by environmental data scrolling across her visor, appeared spotted and deflated.

"Control your fear . . . don't let it dictate who you are or what needs to be done next. Take hold of it just like you told me." Kate surprised herself with the words Mary had said to her a few short hours ago. The old Spacer overseers taught the same thing; panic had no place in those toxic work environments . . . no place in the frigid vacuum of the cosmos. "It's simple," they used to tell her. "You freak out, you die."

She needed to find something for Mary to do, to get her refocused.

"Here, see those canisters we filled? Gather them up, put them on the console, then bring all the others we have from the scooter and wherever else. Got it?"

Mary nodded, sniffed, headed toward the row of cylinders.

"How much oxygen is in your tank right now?"

"Just under two hours."

"Good. That's good, Mares. I also have a couple."

Kate hated pretending they were anything but doomed, but what could she do? Each canister held around 15 minutes' worth of oxygen. They were never intended for use other than emergencies. She'd filled seven with the oxygenator, and they'd collected another dozen from the destroyed Titanius lab. The math looked harsh: about one-and-a-half hours each on top of whatever remained in their main tanks. Addition and subtraction, like all formulae, didn't care about context: numbers were numbers, and these were as cold as the deadly vacuum outside, the same vacuum that now swallowed up the control room of this abandoned mining habitat.

Three and a half hours each. We're not going to make it.

"Will you come outside with me?" Mary's voice had strengthened, and Kate detected her confidence returning. Taking action—any action—pushed her back to the now.

"Sure. I've gotta check the scooters, anyway."

With power no longer available in the habitat, Kate had to manually open the inner airlock door. When the seal broke around the hatchway, trapped, pressurized air jettisoned the door, smashed into her chest and slammed her against the adjacent wall. Mary kept her footing and helped her up. Then, they walked through the airlock. Kate pulled down hard on the second manual latch and pushed the exterior door open.

As Mary collected the canisters from the LunaScoota, Kate knelt beside her and examined the on-board battery and solar array. Whatever happened to the oxygenator didn't appear to affect the scooter, other than drain the battery's power. Nevertheless, the portable array still functioned and recharged the spent cells at a much higher rate now that no current was being siphoned off. A few hours would yield a full charge.

Moot, perhaps, if they couldn't locate more oxygen.

"There are 12 canisters here, Kate. That doesn't leave us enough."

"Sure doesn't. We'd better find more."

"We've been through this dump more than once. Is there any place we haven't looked?"

Kate's fear rose again and she fought to keep her eyes focused on one problem at a time. "I don't know if we'll stumble across any more canisters, but our biggest issue right now is doing whatever we can to stay alive until someone rescues us."

"If they're even aware we're marooned."

She stood up, and scowled at her. "Hey, that's enough negativity. Get your shit together, Mares, and help me look for more tanks. I'll go through the sleeping quarters again, and you check out that galley area, okay?"

They separated. Kate returned to the habitat and opened the hatchway to the workers' quarters. After degassing the airlock, she methodically worked her way through the storage bins and closets again.

"Kate?" Mary's voice in her helmet speaker interrupted the search.

"Yes?"

"I'm sorry for destroying the radio, and I'm sorry for being a completely neural ass just now."

Kate grinned. "Hey, Mares, thanks."

Twenty minutes later, they met up again in the control room. With the main hatchway open, a slice of sunlight cut geometric shapes through the room, reducing the gloom. There were no more O_2 tanks.

"What now?" Mary asked, gazing around the dark room.

Suddenly, a warmth of clarity flooded over Kate. She folded her arms across her chest and leaned against the console, then cast a furtive glance at the monitor and frowned when it showed nothing but a black screen.

"Now, we wait . . . and pray."

TWENTY-THREE

Mary

"I FEEL SO USELESS JUST SITTING AROUND HERE."

Mary paced through the shadow-filled main control room. They'd already supplemented the oxygen tanks on their envirosuits with emergency canisters, and each had under an hour left. For most of that time, they had spoken little, each lost in their thoughts. Now that the end crept closer, Mary's primitive brain was on high alert.

Kate, sitting on top of the console with her legs stretched out, appeared philosophical and resigned to her fate. "Your words make sense, Mares."

"Which ones?"

"About the inevitable end. None of us lives forever. The only questions about death are how and when. Most never know, but we do." She looked at her. "And look at us, bored, hanging around this old dump, waiting to suffocate. I suppose I'd always imagined dying while working on something."

Mary kicked the dust with each footstep she took. "Not much different from what folks in nursing homes do." She stopped and nodded at Kate. "You ever think about what it's like to be old?"

"Nah. Not at all."

"Why not?"

"Oh, I guess deep down I expected to die way before hitting old age." Her voice grew softer in Mary's helmet. "When I first realized they'd recruited me for the Spacer Program, I was far too young to understand what it meant, but none of us expected to be around long with the work they had us doing. When I went into teaching, and the cancers bloomed all over my body, I took those god-awful anti-rad pills and figured I'd have a few years left."

"Yet, here you are."

"Uh-huh."

After a minute or two of silence, Kate chuckled and said, "I'm like a cat. I should have died ages ago but I'm still here, like I got multiple lives or something."

Mary smiled and joined her on the console. A renewed connection appeared to this survivor with the lost childhood and serious emotional problems. "If by some miracle someone saves us, Kate, like if you have a new chance at life, what will you do differently? Anything?"

Another minute passed. Kate's measured breathing filled her helmet's audio and fell into the same rhythm as her own. She squeezed her recovering elbow and shoulder, surprised to find they'd almost completely healed.

Whatever Kate did, it worked.

Then, as if reading her mind, Kate said, "Your wing's better, eh?"

"Like it never got dislocated in the first place."

Kate nodded. "I'm not sure how to answer your question, Mares. I mean, what *could* I do differently? I'm a curious scientist and computer programmer. It's all I know how to do."

Mary frowned. "That's what you've done, but if you're given another chance, are you saying you wouldn't change a thing? That you'd still be doing this kind of work somewhere?" She waved her arm around the habitat.

"Maybe . . . Seems like we're all born to do certain things. Some are teachers or pilots or garbage recyclers. I'm a computer scientist."

Mary fell silent. A gentle warning chime pinged in her helmet showing the oxygen level was diminishing. Half an hour left to kill.

"Okay, suppose you could go way back to a time before you were a Spacer. Like, suppose that whole program didn't exist. Then what would you have done?"

Kate chuckled again and commented about her thousands of questions. Then she said, "I had this dream of living in the woods when I was a kid. I pictured myself building a home with a tall, handsome man and a couple of kids running around. I'd do some kind of science 'cause as long as I remember, I've been interested in how the world works. But, yeah, that's what I wanted. Something simple. . . physical."

"So why not do it again? If we're rescued, I mean."

"Big *if*, Mares," she said, "and even if by some miracle we're found in the next twenty minutes or so, I doubt I could ever pursue that old dream."

"Why not?"

Kate harrumphed. "I'm sick. And not just the cancer blooms or the shit in my head. Do you get that?"

Mary puzzled over why she didn't want to get better, as if she'd given up. That seemed unlike her.

"Messed up, isn't it? I suppose, now that I think about it, the reason I seek no help for these things is because I fear what I might become. See, for the past twenty years, I've defined myself a certain way: a diseased, sick, ugly, androgenous Spacer. An outsider." She paused. "One of those thugs at Mount Sutro called me the 'runt of the litter'. That hurt."

"Oh, my god."

"Yeah, but here's the thing. He was right, Mary. He was right. No matter what I do that's what I'll always be."

A few minutes of silence rolled by. At the 15 minute mark, the oxygen depletion warning chimed louder and a small amber O_2 symbol flashed on her visor. Mary ignored it.

"Yeah, so, this is me."

Mary realized she understood little; that simply reading about things was a sorry, incomplete substitute for actually experiencing life. Studying books and lectures on emotional health could in no way prepare anyone for the visceral hate of yourself and the world so much that you had to carve random patterns on your chest and stomach in a twisted attempt to bury that pain. Yet, somehow, Mary's love of books had given her insights and knowledge of the human condition that prepared her for her own journey. Perhaps the answer to all this depended on finding a balance between the two.

She suddenly heard Kate breathing in a stuttered, ragged rhythm through the helmet audio.

"Kate?"

A pause.

"Yeah, crazy, isn't it?"

Mary reached for her gloved hand and squeezed it.

Carter

"WHAT'S OUR ETA TO LUNA, CAPTAIN?"

Powell turned to face Carter who leaned over his shoulder. "Three hours, forty-five minutes, sir."

He smiled and shook his head in wonder.

What a machine!

"Any other ship movements detected?"

"Have a look, sir."

Captain Powell toggled a viewscreen to a three-dimensional display peppered with a rainbow of colored icons along with their velocities, trajectories, and spacecraft identification data. Although Carter had some familiarity with this graphic, it still took him a moment to get the *Echo*'s bearings in relation to Earth and the Moon, and then understand what the symbols represented.

"Are you serious, John?"

"Well, sir, we figured we'd have company once we broke Earth's standard orbit, but this is something other." Eight icons—ships of various nationalities, corporations and alliances—fluttered across the screen. The only commonality between them was their course trajectories; they all targeted Luna. "Still, none of those boats can match our speed. It'll take at least a day for the fastest one—the *Xing-Xing*—to approach lunar orbit."

"What about those, Captain?" Carter pointed to two separate blue icons approaching the Moon from deep space. "I recognize our cruiser *Malevolent*, but the other . . . what's going on there?"

Powell zoomed in on the symbols. The *Malevolent* had several hundred thousand kilometers on the second cruiser, the

Volmar, but the distance between them appeared to shorten. The captain adjusted the touch-screen display controls to highlight trajectories and intercepts. He said, "We didn't expect the *Volmar*'s improved velocity. The data show she's more or less running equidistant from *Malevolent*. See?" He displayed a time versus distance graphic for the two vessels. "*Volmar* pulls up, then eases back here . . . and here."

Carter frowned. "What do we know about the Prussian cruiser?"

"She's a typical PR-three heavy, sir. Same dimensions as we've seen on the ships in the Martian mining runs, but capable of carrying a larger crew and mid-range weapons. Built for speed, no doubt, but limited."

Carter stood erect and pulled his shoulders back. He anticipated some interest in the *Echo*'s voyage, but not to this extent. Still, it made sense for the *Volmar* to be suspicious of *Malevolent*'s course change to Luna. By keeping her distance, she signaled curiosity rather than aggression.

"Keep me apprised, Captain, of any deviations. I don't want a conflict with the Prussians or the Chinese or anyone else if we can help it." He pivoted, then stopped, leaned back down and whispered. "But make no mistake, John, if we have to unleash firepower to keep those bastards away from Luna, we will."

"Understood."

JIM ATTEBERRY HAD RECOVERED FROM THE shock of leaving Earth and sat transfixed in front of a viewer displaying Luna. A running line of data in the screen's corner measured distance to the moon, the *Echo*'s velocity, ETA, and other parameters. Carter eyed him carefully and sat beside Esther. He patted her thigh and smiled, but she tensed up and shifted her weight.

"How's he doing?"

Esther peered over at Atteberry. "Much better now, I think. You know," she said after a moment, "he feels his daughter and Kate Braddock are still alive up there."

"His faith in miracles is strong."

"Be honest with me, Clayton. What are the chances we'll find them alive?"

Carter shrugged and made a sour face. "Minimal to non-existent. I mean, the entire lab went dark. Lunarsat images show nothing left. How anyone could survive that level of destruction is beyond me." He stared into her grey eyes and leaned in. "But we know they did because they contacted your friend here. What we don't know is whether they're injured or what kind of oxygen they have. Notwithstanding the odds, we'll do everything we can to bring them home. You have my word."

Their tête-à-tête was interrupted by shouts and orders ringing out from the bridge. Atteberry leapt up from the viewer and shifted his gaze to where Captain Powell and Communications Officer Quigg scrambled over the comms panel. "Mr. Carter? What's going on? Have they found something?"

He pulled himself out of his flight seat. "Stay there, Mr. Atteberry," he said with quiet confidence, and marched toward the bridge. Esther followed close behind. He didn't stop her.

"Sir," Quigg drawled, "it's—it's an encrypted message from the HQ." He pointed at the comms screen. "Not sure if'n it means anything, but—"

"Play it, Officer."

Quigg punched a button on the monitor and the video message rolled. Ed Mitchell's head shot appeared from the Titanius Operations Center. He looked abnormally haggard and confused standing in front of Stan Petrovic and a couple other comms specialists.

"At 0330 UTC, we detected a brief EM pulse from the *Aristoteles* Mine Site. Duration was 16.8 seconds. Frequency . . . *what was it again, Stan? (garbled) Right, thanks . . . 430.800 MHz.* Not a recognized transmission frequency to us. It was a single, unmodulated pulse. Then it disappeared again. We can't tell yet whether it's natural, or . . . I've ordered the lunarsat folks to swing the bird over that area ASAP, but it'll take a while. No immediate danger to any ship. Will keep you apprised. Titanius out."

Carter stroked his chin. "What in the hell?"

By this time, Esther had moved to his side. He glanced at her. Atteberry now also hovered behind.

"Any ideas?"

Esther shrugged her shoulders. "That old dump hasn't been used in years, not since the strip mine infrastructure was built about, oh, a decade ago now." She turned to Quigg. "Are you sure it's not an echo from something? A ghost signal? We see those a lot in our SETI work."

Quigg glanced at Carter, then back at Esther. "The data Titanius sent us suggests it's real, ma'am."

Atteberry, lurking in the background, raised his hand like a shy schoolboy.

"I recognize that frequency. It's in the UHF amateur radio band."

Carter glared at him. "What does that even mean?"

"Well, the UN allocates the frequency spectrum for different users, and—"

Captain Powell interrupted. "Sure, of course." He punched up an image of the old mining site on the main viewer, back when it was operating. "Our crew must be there. We can't be certain yet, but it definitely looks like a radio transmission."

"The hell?"

Atteberry whispered, "Oh my god, it's them." He grabbed Esther by the shoulder. "It's them, Es."

Carter felt smothered and guided the two civilians off the bridge. "Stand back for a moment." He huddled with Powell and

Quigg, and in a low voice said, "Do you think that's our people? That they're somehow still alive?"

Captain Powell's eyes lit up. "It's one possibility, sir."

"What, or who could it be if it's not Braddock and the kid?"

Powell and Quigg exchanged glances.

"Well?"

The captain cleared his throat. "I suppose it's possible someone else beat us to Luna." He added, "I don't know how that could happen. We've been monitoring the Moon since the lab went dark, and there have been no ship signatures around it at all. So, sure, it's possible there's someone else there, but unlikely. . . " his voice trailed off.

Carter took a deep breath and clenched his teeth.

Could the Rossians have anything to do with this?

Atteberry slipped around to the bridge again.

"I thought I asked you to stay back?" Carter's voice sounded a little too authoritative for his intention.

"It's them, Mr. Carter. It's Mary. My girl. She knows radio, and she knows the UHF band I operate on at home. She's trying to contact me . . . I mean us, from that strip mine. It's the only explanation that makes any sense."

Carter worked his jaw for a moment and stared at the graphic of the mine site.

Is it possible?

"Captain Powell," he said with deliberate emphasis, "how fast can the *Echo* fly?"

Powell glanced at the ship's data flashing on the dashboard. "I—I have no idea, sir. We've never pushed her beyond our current velocity."

"Well, Captain, let's find out." He raised his voiced. "Give me everything this boat has. Squeeze those engines until they squeal, you understand me?"

"Aye, sir."

He turned to Atteberry and smiled thinly. "If you're right and that's your daughter at the mine site, we'll find her." Atteberry nodded and drew away again. When he had returned to his seat, Carter whispered to Captain Powell, "Could we hail them on that frequency, John?"

"Yes. The *Echo*'s comms cover all available bands. I can send out an automated CQ and see what happens, but . . ." he shrugged his shoulders.

"What is it?"

"If we beam a CQ to *Aristoteles*, those other ships may take action. They're curiosity now is primarily focused on us and this ship, not Luna. You might want to maintain silence until we achieve lunar orbit. Another hour or two won't make a difference, sir, since we're limited by our own velocity."

Carter narrowed his eyes and sighed heavily. Even though the internal conflict pulled him in every direction, he'd known John Powell many years and trusted his judgment. "All right, let's maintain radio silence but I want you to monitor that frequency and if you so much as hear a static crash, you tell me."

TWENTY-FOUR

Kate

"WARNING. O_2 DEPLETION IN TEN MINUTES."

Kate checked her levels, then resumed staring at the main access hatchway where sunlight carved distinct geometric shapes into the dusty floor. And, where a blue shadow also appeared.

"See? Our little friend must be back."

Mary lifted her head and peered around. "What the hell is that, Kate? Some EM probe from the Rossian ship? It doesn't seem to be a natural phenomenon."

"No idea. I've been so focused on getting our asses rescued I've had no time to speculate about it." She hated this waiting. "Ten, fifteen minutes, eh? Well, I'd like to spend my last moments checking it out rather than just waiting around to die, if it's all the same to you." She stood and moved toward the access hatchway. "You wanna come, Mares?"

Mary shrugged and joined her.

They exited the mining habitat and studied the dark sky, but the blue light had vanished.

"So much for that," Mary said. "If it's linked to the alien ship, they sure seem shy."

Kate snorted. "Agreed. Elusive and skittish little buggers. I'm going back in." She kicked the surface around in front of her, but didn't move.

"Wait a sec, is that it over there?"

Kate followed Mary's arm. She pointed toward the grey horizon where the original strip mining operations took place.

"I can't see anything."

"You're looking up too much. Go right down to the horizon."

She squinted, but still nothing jumped out at her. She cycled through the infrared spectrum on her visor, but all she detected were some shadows where a few outbuildings remained from the operations.

Outbuildings?

"Do you not see the light, Kate?"

"Never mind that. Get on the scooter."

"But—"

"Right now, Mares! There's something else out there."

Kate scrambled on the LunaScoota, unplugged the solar charging cables and fired it up. Mary slipped on behind her, grabbed her waist, and the machine immediately pulled away from the ground and circled out toward the mining fields.

"*Warning. O$_2$ depletion in six minutes.*"

"Do you see those buildings? They could be maintenance sheds or warehouses leftover from the mine operations. I should've known to check there."

"You think there's air inside?"

"We'll know soon enough." The scooter screamed over the mining fields in seconds. Machines had dredged long tracts of the moon's surface into deep trenches. Excess, useless material was piled beside them, like levees.

Two outbuildings appeared directly ahead, and Kate throttled down and landed in front of the first. She hopped off and bounded toward it. The structure must have been 20 meters tall and at least another 30 meters long. A large roll-up door was smashed in, where at some point, Kate figured the massive extraction machines had been housed.

"*Warning. O$_2$ depletion in five minutes.*"

Inside, their helmet lights surveyed the gloom. A concrete platform off on one side was the only discernible object. Kate bounded over to inspect it, but other than a dusty pair of broken tractor treads, nothing remained.

"Come on, let's check out the other one."

"*Warning. O$_2$ depletion in four minutes.*"

The second building, not 5 meters away, squatted eerily in the dust. Waves of debris had washed up alongside it, kicked up from all the activity once upon a time, and this made the structure appear as if it had bubbled up from the lunar crust like magma. Kate figured it to be about a quarter the size of the first hangar, but unlike that structure, it had no equipment-sized door. Instead, an access hatchway like the one on the habitat appeared half-buried in rock and soil.

"*Warning. O$_2$ depletion in three minutes.*"

"Kate? My oxygen's running out and … and … I think I should, I don't know, pray or something."

"We're not done yet, Mares. Help me get this hatchway open."

They scraped and dug around the access door, pushing debris away until she motioned for Mary to stop. A mangled external lever remained in the locked position. Kate pushed down on it with all her weight, but it didn't budge.

"Warning. O₂ depletion in two minutes."

"It's backwards. It pulls up. Try the other way."

Kate yanked on the handle, but it was completely jammed and refused to yield. Then, lying on her back in the dust, she pressed upward on it with both legs while Mary pulled.

"Damn it!"

She paused, then pushed again.

"Warning. O₂ depletion imminent."

The latch didn't budge.

In a final, desperate act, Kate kicked up on the lever with everything she could muster, and the handle shifted a fraction. Again and again, she kicked at it until, in a sudden release, the mechanism popped up and the hatchway sprung partly open.

"Quick Mares, get in and check for canisters. This is it. This is all we got."

Mary squeezed through and Kate picked herself up and followed.

Inside, their helmet lights crisscrossed the floor and walls in a frantic attempt to find what Kate hoped might be there.

"Warning. O₂ depletion imminent."

Like the hangar, nothing remained.

"Kate?" Mary's voice sounded hollow.

"Over there!"

On the left, a long line of storage containers leaned against the wall. Mary bounded over and pulled hard on several of them. Empty.

Kate joined her and together they ripped the doors open. Some bins spilled machine parts and other mining components, but no oxygen canisters.

"*Warning. O_2 depletion imminent.*"

"Last two, Mary."

She hesitated in front of one and glanced at Kate who stood aside the other. "It's been an adventure, Kate. Thank you for being here."

Kate nodded, choking back the lump rising in her throat. Then they threw open the container doors.

Heavy-duty bins tumbled out of each. The first one Mary opened held a pair of boots and an envirosuit. But the second fell on its side, and several dozen oxygen canisters—not the emergency kind they'd found in the habitat, but full envirosuit capacity—splayed out into the dust.

Kate's visor flashed a multitude of warnings now, her breathing failing.

"Mary, eject my O_2 case and replace it."

"But what if—"

"It won't matter, right?"

Kate fell on her knees, hands on thighs, and relied on her Spacer survival training to regulate her breathing and maintain her oxygen just long enough to keep going a few more seconds.

"Ready?"

Kate nodded. When her tank ejected, her visor turned solid red and warnings screamed at her, but she blocked the noise and concentrated on holding her breath and not allowing panic to creep in. She closed her eyes . . .

In a moment, fresh O$_2$ filled her suit. She inhaled deeply and checked her vitals. All visor warnings had vanished and the oxygen level indicator on the bottom right shone a beautiful green.

She turned around. Mary had collapsed in a dusty heap beside her. Kate rolled her over onto her stomach, unlatched the empty tank and slammed a new one in.

It didn't work.

Christ!

Mary's visor flashed red, and she'd blacked out. Kate scrambled through the storage bins and found one last set of tanks. She grabbed the set and knocked it hard into the holder on Mary's back. Nothing happened. She scanned the area frantically, saw only dust and empty bins around her, fell on her knees and closed her eyes.

No . . .

She unlatched the tank, reset the connector in Mary's back, and slammed it in again. In an instant, all the warnings in her visor ceased. A few seconds later, Kate heard her breathing grow stronger and a moment after that, she came to.

Mary eased herself up into a squatting position, hands on thighs, head down, inhaling deeply, exhaling slowly. She lifted her eyes.

"You . . . are . . . a goddamn . . . cat, Kate."

They pulled each other out of the dust. Kate inspected Mary's tank, to make sure all safety latches and seals fit properly. Then Mary did the same for her. They'd bought themselves eight hours of life and, with it, another chance to be saved. If only someone, or something, could save them in time.

Then she had an idea.

"IT'S A SHORT REPRIEVE, MARES, NOTHING MORE. Why I didn't think of these outbuildings before, I don't know, but thank god the workers who came before us were sloppy and left their kit behind."

The LunaScoota hovered outside the mining habitat before Kate nestled it down into the soft dust again. Sunlight bathed this area of the Moon, and that allowed her to maximize the solar charging of the scooter's battery.

Mary hemmed and hawed, before asking, "Kate, did you see the blue light out there or not?"

"I didn't, but when I looked out on the horizon where you pointed, the buildings showed up on the infrared display." She paused. "You saw something though, right?"

"Yeah, no mistaking that light for some other phenomenon. Once we got close to the buildings, I forgot about it and lost track. The blue, Kate... that blue ... like no color I've seen before." Mary wandered a few steps beyond the habitat's main access hatchway and surveyed the grey and white moonscape, the pitch black sky. "Something weird is happening here, don't you think?"

Kate joined her. "I do. It'd be great to solve the mystery of the blue light and how it's related to the Rossian ship, but fate gave us a second chance to live, Mares. Let's figure out our next moves." They rummaged through the scooter's cargo bay where they'd salvaged another tool kit from the mining outbuilding.

Just under 8 hours each.

Kate poked around the cargo area. "Options?"

Mary picked up a piece of wire cable they'd brought from the Titanius lunar lab, thought for a moment, and shrugged her shoulders. "Stay here and hope someone rescues us, or I could have another poke at the radio?" She tossed the cable back in the bay.

"Sure, but there's something else we could do rather than hang around this dump, waiting for some savior to miraculously find us."

"What's that?"

Kate adjusted a tie holding back some of their tools. "Fly to the *Mare Marginis*. Perhaps the Rossians can help." She lashed the new kit to the front end of the bay.

Mary hopped around the scooter, sighing. Finally, she stopped in front of Kate and said, "Well my curiosity is overloaded with the alien ship, so from that perspective, yeah, like I want to go see. Who wouldn't? But there's practical considerations, Kate, like, we'd pretty much use all our oxygen just getting there. And if we arrive okay, then we've got the same problem we had before: trying to get into that stupid thing."

"Good points. So," she secured some of the other loose cables, "would you prefer staying here and waiting?"

"Dammit, Kate, you're putting this on me."

"Not at all. If you want to stay here and wait for a ship, I'm with you." She studied the cargo hold for any other loose bits. "But if none arrives by the time our tanks run dry, how would you feel?"

"What do you mean?"

"Mares, we've been lucky so far, but I don't want to push it. If this is the end of the road, I need to know what the hell that ship is doing here, and what's going on with that blue light. I have to understand even if I die a minute later. Do you get that?" She pointed toward the horizon. The light had returned, floating above the moon's surface about a kilometer away.

Mary gazed at it for a moment, then shook her head. "It looks like you're already planning to go." She motioned at the preparations going on in the cargo bay and muttered, "I'll grab the other tools from the control room."

"Does this mean you're good to travel?"

"No, I think we should stay here," she whispered.

Mary bounded away and disappeared into the gloom of the habitat. It was the odd change of heart that confused her. Mary

254

had seemed fearless, curious, passionate about the world and its people. She'd cajoled her out of her own funk.

Something's not right.

Dark shadows filled the space in the habitat when Kate entered moments later. Mary slumped on the console, her shoulders bent forward and legs dangling off the edge. Bits of destroyed radio gear lay strewn about.

"What's up, Mares?"

Her breathing quickened in short fits. Kate remained silent, allowing her as much time as she needed to open up. A couple minutes passed.

"Two things. First, like, it would make sense that Titanius knows about the lab explosion, so they'd do whatever they could to investigate. They'd send a ship and a day or two later, it would arrive. Second, they'd find a vessel already out here to search for us, like the *Aristobulus* or something." She turned to face her. "Think about it. A boat could be orbiting up there right now, preparing to land or send a shuttle down any minute. If we keep playing catch the moving target, our chances of being saved could actually be worse."

Kate chewed the inside of her lip, opening the sore already there, tasting blood. It's not as if she hadn't thought of these points before. One truism the Spacer Program taught her was: if in doubt, stay put and wait for help. But the passivity, the resignation of not *doing* something, anything, ate away at her. They had trained her to *do*, to constantly be in action, and sitting around waiting for others to act didn't appeal to her at all. Not then, and not now.

She closed her eyes, clashing with feelings of remorse, guilt, and that entrenched desire for the cold burn of a knife digging into her skin.

"Does that make sense, Kate? It kills me to sit on the sidelines, and my brain is screaming at me to shut my mouth, hop on the damn scooter, and see what those Rossians are up to. You know that, don't you?"

Kate nodded.

"But I honestly feel we should stay here this time. Perhaps after we're rescued, we can investigate that ship." She paused. "What do you think?"

Kate sucked hard on the inside of her lip and waited until an alternative presented itself. Do the safe thing—nothing—and hope someone else saves you. Or, do something, with no guarantee of anything, and more risks it could fail. "You may be right, Mares. The best action could very well be to do nothing. However," she shifted her weight on the console, "let's approach our situation thoroughly. What if we consider the travel option as if it's the only one available? We take a few minutes, map out a course to the *Mare Marginis*, calculate O_2 reserves, battery power and so on. We look at all needed actions as if we were going."

Mary considered this, and asked, "Then what?"

"Then we look at the pros and cons of each one. Mary," she said, "We should decide what to do based on the cold equations of logic, right?"

"I suppose."

"Okay, so let's map out how we could do it first. We've got eight hours of oxygen, plus or minus. It'll take us five hours to get back to the destroyed lunar lab site, and another hour from there to the alien ship site, right?"

Mary stood up and paced. "Yes, but that assumes we retrace our path. You said we didn't come here in a straight line."

"True."

"So, if we plotted a more direct course from here to the *Mare Marginis*, how long would it take?"

Kate hopped off the console and returned to the scooter. Mary followed. She punched in the coordinates on the nav screen for the *Mare Marginis* where the Rossian ship had been. The first recommended route took them back to the *Mare Crisium* along the same path, more or less, by which they came to the mining site. Approximate travel time: 6 hours, 28 minutes.

Barely enough time to do anything.

Two other alternative routes appeared. One took them along the Moon's northern limb, then east to the ship site. Approximate travel time: 9 hours, 10 minutes.

"That one's out of the question," Kate said.

The second alternative route displayed a direct path; rather, most of it was a straight line with some notable exceptions. Kate selected it and reviewed the route parameters. Lunar mares and associated flat terrain covered most of the route. The challenge appeared just west of the *Mare Marginis*. Almost 500 kilometers of cratered, broken and rocky moonscape presented a major obstacle for them, and the scooter's navigation algorithm showed a bird's nest of paths zig-zagging through it.

"Can't we just fly above it all?" Mary asked.

Kate studied the elevation data, zooming in and out on it, following the proposed route. "Parts of it, yes, but the scooters aren't designed for flying over ten meters above surface, or else their grav engines lose their connective traction, remember? Still, look at this." She pointed out a couple travel time approximations. "If we followed the suggested route, it would take us about 7 hours. Not bad. But check this out." Kate varied the recommended scooter parameters such that the route across the terrain became fully straight. No negotiating around craters or volcanic cones.

"Four and a half hours?" Mary asked.

"Yes, but there's a reason the algorithm recommends against doing this. Flying up and over rocky hills and down into craters is dangerous. We can increase velocity and make the trip faster, but the risks of an accident are significantly greater." She looked at Mary. "Still, we could squeeze about three hours of quality alien time in there."

Mary grunted and perched herself on the edge of the cargo bay, silent.

Kate peered southeast over the horizon in the general direction of the *Mare Marginis* and this time, when the blue light reappeared like a candle in the window, she was not surprised at all.

TWENTY-FIVE

Atteberry

THE ANXIETY OF NOT KNOWING TORE INTO his thoughts like a recurring nightmare. Atteberry believed the brief EM pulse had to be Mary's doing; she'd seen him operate on that frequency numerous times back home. But would she still be alive when they arrived? And there was Kate to think about, too. He'd taken her friendship for granted over the years, but now with the pressure on, Atteberry recognized that she'd grown to be more than his best friend. Something between a lover and family, yet neither. He grew itchy with anticipation, as if spiders explored his flesh, and couldn't stop moving, pacing.

Esther reclined in her flight seat across from him, catching a nap while the *Echo* screamed toward Luna. He studied the history in her face and wondered what might have happened to them if the Ross 128 signal hadn't been discovered? Moot point, to be sure, since the alien craft had brought them together in the first place. He still liked her *that way* despite their problematic differences, and held her in deep regard, but the opportunity for anything more than a tenuous romantic possibility had come and gone. To try reigniting those old feelings now would be awkward and forced.

Carter marched around the bridge like the big boss he was, leaning over the pilots, studying viewscreens. Atteberry caught glimpses of their conversations, figuring they'd be reviewing rescue protocols and such. Instead, the CEO seemed more interested, almost in a joyful way, in the other ship traffic being generated. Un-able to relax, he heaved himself out of his flight seat and wandered up to join the crew.

Carter's right hand grasped the captain's chair from behind. They both studied a graphic of icons floating in a three-dimensional grid. "How many vessels now?"

"A dozen so far. All originating from Earth."

"Fascinating . . ."

"Excuse me, Captain," Atteberry interjected, "but why all this interest in a simple rescue mission? I mean, I get that ships have an obligation to help, but is this normal?"

Carter flashed him a brief, surprised look, and answered, "Oh, they're mostly curious, like children when they see a new toy. It's clear to them all that the *Echo* is the fastest vessel out here and they simply want to have a peek." He paused, motioned to the vacant comms station and added, "Take a seat, Mr. Atteberry, and join us. Quigg's off for the moment, so sit."

Atteberry's eyes widened, and he slipped in behind the smooth, ergonomic console, brushing his fingers over the clean workspace in front of him. He welcomed the distraction.

A series of messages scrolled over the primary comms screen, catching his eye. He read a few and said, "Looks like some of those ships don't know what we're doing, judging by the inquiries."

"They probably don't." Carter took up a position beside him and skimmed over the incoming traffic. "Understand that whenever a new ship goes into service, we all want to learn as much as we can about it."

Atteberry grimaced. "But these notes, I mean, they're asking why we're en route to Luna. It's as if they don't even realize we're on a rescue mission."

Carter's eyes narrowed, and he scrutinized the comms screen again. "Perhaps they honestly aren't aware, and genuinely want to help if we need them. Difficult to tell. There's not much honor left among the space-faring nations and corporations."

The cycle of messages continued scrolling over the viewer.

"Would you like to send a transmission to them all, Mr. Atteberry?"

"I don't understand."

Carter stood up tall, looked around, and said, "Apparently, I've lost Mr. Quigg to a meal. You seem to know a fair bit about this sort of thing, so would you step in for a while?"

Atteberry glanced hard at the equipment in front of him. He quickly identified two types of radio transceivers, one short range, the other deep space. A data reader, a full suite of viewers displaying various operating parameters, and backup systems completed the bulk of the station's core. Above the dashboard, the primary comms viewer pumped out written messages from other ships and a handful of terran outfits. Everything about the setup had been designed for simplicity and ease of operation. And, it pleased him to contribute more directly to the mission.

"I'll give it a try, Clayton—I mean, Mr. Carter."

"Please, let's dispense with the formality, shall we? Call me Clayton."

"Call me Jim."

Captain Powell smiled at him and winked. Co-pilot Jenson nodded.

"All right, then, let's send a message to all ships and interested terran observers." Carter cleared his throat. "Comms Officer?"

"Oh, that's me. Um . . . yes, sir."

"Open all interspace hailing frequencies and transmit the following."

Atteberry scrambled. He put in an earpiece, surveyed the frequency tabs on the short range transceiver, found the commands on a small screen above with Carter's help, and punched the button that read "INTERSPACE FREQ".

"Ah, frequencies open . . . you're good to transmit."

Carter paced, head down, his hands clasped together behind him in a theatrical pose. Then he stopped beside Atteberry and bellowed, "Attention all ships and terran observers in this sector. This is Clayton Carter of the *Echo*. We are currently en route to Luna where two of our people there require help." He paused. "While we appreciate your interest and offers to assist, you undoubtedly have noted the *Echo* is the fastest vessel in space, and we expect to arrive shortly. So, no need to follow. *Echo* out." He nodded at Atteberry, and he ended the transmission.

"That'll give 'em something to fuss about."

He choked back the desperate lump forming in his throat and ignored the fatigue in his body after a couple days of no sleep.

Hang on, Mares. I'm coming.

Captain Powell interrupted his thoughts. "Sir, two more ships have entered the sector, bearing three-three-zero mark 15 . . . heading to Luna."

"Three-three-zero? Where are they from?"

"Point of origin is the Martian system. Stand by . . . ship signature data is coming in."

Atteberry wondered why Carter suddenly looked concerned. He didn't know all that much about Mars and its colonies, or Eros, other than that moon held significant resource interests.

"Two similar vessels, sir . . . heavy security cruisers."

"Registration?"

"Prussian Consortium." Powell looked up from his viewscreen and caught Carter's eyes. "Brandenburg class, sir."

"Is one of them the *Volmar*?"

"Negative. *Volmar* continues to follow the *Malevolent*."

"Shit."

A wave of panic rose. "What—what does that mean, Captain? Clayton?"

Carter pulled on his chin and sighed. "I don't think it's anything we need to worry about. The PC does a lot of excavation on Eros and they also support a community on Mars."

"What are 'heavy cruisers'?"

"Security ships, Jim. We have several, like the *Malevolent*, as do the Chinese, the Indians, and a bunch of resource outfits. They're escorts, basically. Keep all our freighters safe and snug."

Atteberry shook his head. Something didn't add up. What would compel these craft to abandon their posts on the Martian run and head to Luna? More was going on than a mere interest in the *Echo* and her ability to fly fast, more than offering to assist in the rescue of his daughter and his closest friend.

Esther had awakened and now joined them on the bridge.

"Look at you," she said, smiling at Atteberry.

He noticed she'd sidled up to Carter a little too closely, a little too quickly. Carter pulled away a fraction of a centimeter. She cocked her head to the side, eyes sparkling.

Captain Powell said, "Sir, is there anything you'd like to do about the cruisers?"

Carter scrunched his eyebrows together and thought for a moment. Then he smiled coldly. "No, John, not yet. We've got a mission to accomplish first."

Atteberry stared at the primary comms screen. Various messages continued pouring in from all over the sector. Offers to help, offers to support, random comments about the *Echo*'s flight capabilities, criticisms of Carter's leadership and so on. But Atteberry had a nagging doubt there was more, something *other* going on below the whispers. His gut screamed: *this is not a mission to save Mary*. His head replied: *not at all.*

Esther

"ESTHER, DO YOU HAVE A MINUTE?"

Jim Atteberry threw her a furtive, inquisitive look. A sudden change had washed over him, and his eyes shone wide with fright.

"Sure, I was about to get some juice from the galley. Wanna come?"

She led him off the bridge, and they walked without speaking to the narrow galley in the back third of the craft. On their way, they passed Quigg returning to his post, and nodded. Inside the kitchen area, Jim slumped down at a small metal table while Esther pulled two juices from the dispenser.

She watched him with curiosity. The boyish enthusiasm from a few minutes ago at the comms station had been replaced with worry and restlessness. Dark circles expanded around his ragged eyes and his greasy hair flew off in all directions. He thanked her for the drink, took a sip, and stared into a corner of the room.

"There's something going on here, Es."

"What do you mean?"

He drew a deep breath, clearly frustrated. "Can you just tell me?"

"Tell you what, Jim? What are you talking about?" Her voice betrayed a hint of annoyance.

"This rescue mission isn't a rescue mission at all." Those soft blue eyes met hers and plumbed her soul.

Esther sat upright, shifting her weight awkwardly on the metal stool, drawing circles with the juice container on the tabletop. Jim was no idiot. Surely, he recognized how slim the chances of finding Mary and Kate alive were, even if they had transmitted that spurious pulse.

"It *is* a rescue mission. No one knows if—I'm sorry but I've got to be blunt—if Mary is alive, and indeed if she is, we have no idea what kind of shape she's in." She paused, took a sip. "Is this about Clayton?"

He remained silent.

"Clayton Carter is many things: ambitious, resourceful, used to getting his way. I have no illusions about what he's capable of doing, but he's no heartless monster. Look around you for a moment."

Atteberry glanced through the galley and back out into the ship's main quarters.

"He's pushing these new engines harder than they've ever been stressed. They haven't even gone through a full range of testing yet. So, sure, he'll salvage anything he can from the Titanius lab up there, puff out his chest for his competitors, and maybe see what that alien ship is all about—"

He flashed daggers at her.

"—but first, he's going to save your daughter and your colleague because above all else, I think—I hope—Clayton's a humanist. That's what drives him."

Atteberry's face tightened, and he stared at his drink.

She couldn't fathom the gut-wrenching patience he needed while they raced to the Moon. He wrestled with the anxiety of not knowing what they'd find. He already lost his wife to some espionage racket years ago, and now he may have lost Mary too, and there was nothing in her lifetime of experience that ever came close to that kind of pain. She placed her hand over his.

"Jim, you know he asked for you specifically to be on this flight, against my better judgment. He cares, you see?"

Atteberry sighed. He hadn't thought of that. "You're right. It makes sense to recover what's left of the lab, I get that. But did I hear you correctly?" He lowered his voice. "Does he know about the alien ship, too?"

Regret suddenly flooded her mind as she struggled with not being up front with this man—the one she still had some residual feelings for despite their insurmountable philosophical differences. She fidgeted with her juice container.

What have you become now, Esther?

He hadn't caused her renewed career focus after Mount Sutro. She didn't blame him at all for apparently putting his own interests ahead of her welfare or the integrity of the TSA when the tower came down. They both had jobs to do, lives to lead. Now, with a Titanius partnership imminent, she felt the rush of being in command of all aspects of her life. What did it matter that she'd pawned her ethics for power and control?

"He's heard the rumors too about the ship and its FTL tech. Spies still ply their trade and I suppose the word about that Rossian ship on Luna got out."

He eyed her suspiciously. "From you?"

"No," she held his gaze, "but regardless, if they're there, I want the TSA to make first contact."

"Thank God he didn't learn it from you, Es. Thanks." He finished his drink and ran his fingers over his hair. "I suppose that explains why so many other ships are interested in what we're doing."

"It's not unusual to attract a crowd up here." She paused. "Did you happen to notice where they came from?"

"Mostly Earth. Two Berlin class cruisers or something coming in from Mars."

She stopped twirling her drink. "You mean Brandenburg? Prussian ships? So that's what they were talking about when I joined you."

"Yeah, the captain seemed nervous about it, but Clayton dismissed them."

Esther closed her eyes, thinking this through. If the Consortium and others also knew about the alien ship why had they waited until now before investigating? The rumor mill operated 24/7 and no one could chase down everything the grapevine offered, so maybe they only paid attention to it when the *Echo* lifted off. She needed to speak with Clayton about this.

"Now you're looking nervous, Es. There is something else going on." His voice rose. "These aren't ships offering to help with the rescue mission, are they? Are they?"

At that moment, Clayton appeared in the galley doorway, mock concern on his face. Atteberry stood up. She noticed his fists clenched.

"Jim . . ."

"So," he said, "What's the truth about those cruisers?"

Clayton glanced at Esther, then beamed. "Well, that's the big mystery, isn't it?"

"Not to me. Tell me, what do you know about the vessel from Ross 128?"

His smile vanished, and his eyes narrowed, but he wouldn't back down or pretend. "Honestly, not much other than hearsay. I recall you were the first to recognize an unknown signal years ago, and that you and Esther and several others investigated it. But the last I heard, the code turned out to be a ghost."

"Is that all?"

Again, he glanced between them. "Other than rumors, yes."

"What about the one that goes like this: the alien ship is already here and for some reason planted itself on the Moon . . . and that it's likely been there for some time."

Carter cocked his head. His face remained unchanged. "Why all these questions, Jim? Is there something I'm not aware of?"

Jenson appeared in the hallway. "All weapons systems are online, sir."

"Thank you, Jenson."

Esther's jaw dropped. "Weapons! Clayton, what the hell is going on? I didn't think the *Echo* was a gunship."

Clayton entered the galley. "Let me explain."

Atteberry sat down and Carter swung his leg over a stool between the two. "First, the *Echo* is a corvette class scout ship, but we both appreciate, Esther, that every boat out here needs some kind of defensive capability. Space is far too dangerous for an unprotected craft."

She nodded silently.

"Second, once we rescue Kate and Mary, I need to protect my lunar lab assets from the magpies . . . assuming there's anything left to salvage."

He folded his hands together on the table in front of him and looked squarely at Atteberry. "I've got billions of dollars' worth of assets up there, much of it containing technology years ahead of anybody else. So, I make no apologies for making the salvage a priority and protecting those assets from curious onlookers, no matter who they are or what motives they pretend to have."

Esther crossed her arms. "But these ships, except for the cruisers, are nothing more than science vessels and runabouts, yes? Hardly worth warming up weapons for."

"Come now," he smiled, "don't be so naïve. There could easily be a Trojan horse in the mix, just waiting to snag my tech. Either way, we must prepare for any eventuality." He leaned back. "What's with that face, Esther. There's nothing you wouldn't do to protect the integrity and assets of the TSA either, including hiding evidence of the existence of some mysterious alien vessel." He glared at her. "Is there?"

She didn't respond. She recalled the half-truths, the file and data purges, her conscious decision in 2085 to distance herself from all of those Ross 128 stories circulating back then. Carter understood what she had done, but blew it off as the price of leadership. Atteberry simply stared off into the corner.

After he excused himself and left the galley, the two exchanged silent glances.

Cover-ups were one thing, but no alien vessel or first contact was worth this kind of armed confrontation. He had to be stopped.

TWENTY-SIX

Kate

MARY GATHERED ALL THE DISPARATE RADIO parts from the top of the console and dumped them in one of the storage bins. She grabbed a handful of connector cables. "What do you think about these? Worth taking?"

Kate's eyes widened under her visor. "If we decide to go, then yes. As long as something's not destroyed, let's bring it." Mary tossed the cables into a second bin and hopped up on the console.

"Do you still want to stay here and wait for a possible rescue ship?"

"Something tells me not to."

"Oh?" Kate could only see part of Mary's face through the reflections on her visor as she stared at her palms and flexed her fingers open and closed. "It's that light. I can't get over it."

"Like we're being watched, right?"

Mary studied her hands. "Not only that, I think the Rossians are behind this, and not because they're simply curious creatures."

She didn't want to consider it, but since Mary raised the question of the light and how it somehow connected with the alien ship, ignoring the fact they weren't alone couldn't continue. "What are you getting at?"

"I'm not sure. I just find it strange that we saw the blue light in the sky on our way here and also hovering around the habitat." She faced Kate. "But what got me was its appearance on the horizon, showing the way to these oxygen tanks."

Kate chewed her lip. Her own biases prevented her from considering all possibilities, like this light being a ball of energy or sentience, or perhaps a probe. Maybe Mary had touched on something. If it came from the Rossian ship and in fact was observing them, it reinforced her idea that creatures were hiding in that vessel buried in the dust. However, without knowing their purpose here, speculating on their actions was risky.

"Do you think the Rossians somehow prevented our deaths by guiding us to the mining outbuildings?"

"On its own, no. But when I line up these sightings, it's clear there's something more going on."

Kate drew circles on the dusty console and considered what the alien light could mean. Too many questions popped into her head, like *what are they looking for?* and *why would they guide us along?* She still couldn't be certain whether that ship was the Rossian one, but either way, it obviously had superior technology. So, what was it up to?

She thought back to when the Titanius lunar lab was destroyed and how she suspected the alien craft was behind it. "Recall, Mares, that we both believed the Rossians blew up the lab."

"I remember."

"So perhaps they're responsible for this light too, and there's some purpose for watching or guiding us across the moonscape." Kate paused. "But without knowing more, we have no clue what they're doing. I'm confident, though, that if they wanted to destroy us, they would have done it already."

Mary spun around and stood up. "That's true. If we're still here, they must have a reason for keeping us this way. Like, if that light is a guide, again, the question is why? For what purpose?" She hopped over to the access hatchway and wandered through the airlock until she was outside. "Come and look at this, Kate."

She slid off the console and walked out. Off on the horizon, the blue mystery hovered in the black sky.

"What do you think now?"

Kate grimaced. "Let's take a bearing on it." She opened the wrist pad on her left arm and punched up the nav locator. On her visor screen, the moonscape appeared with various cross hatches, azimuthal readings and distances to geographic objects. The blue light remained eerie and motionless on the horizon, the only bright object in the sky other than Earth. Once she lined it up in the finder, she zoomed in and the measurement grew more precise.

"Extrapolate to a thousand kilometers."

"Acknowledged."

A second window appeared on the visor displaying the moon's surface and a bright yellow trajectory bisecting it, showing the route from the habitat, through the blue light, and off into the distance.

"Share screen with Mary."

"Acknowledged."

"Oh, my god. Do you believe it now?"

Kate continued aligning the light in the nav locater's object finder. "Let's see where it ends up." A pause. "Extrapolate another 2500 kilometers."

"Acknowledged."

The display zoomed out from the moon's surface. Additional crater zones and mares appeared on it, including the *Mare Crisium* and the *Mare Marginis* where they'd discovered the alien ship. Cutting across the screen was the thin, yellow trajectory line.

"Kate?" Mary's voice was barely audible.

She focused with a renewed intensity on the nav data. "Zoom in on the trajectory around the *Mare Marginis*."

"Acknowledged."

The display shifted and the region in the northeast quadrant appeared larger, covering a 100 km by 100 km area.

"Target the following coordinates: 33.1 North, 86.1 East. Zoom in to an area that's one square kilometer around those coordinates."

"Acknowledged."

"Overlay all current geophysical data."

"Processing."

Mary gasped. On their visors, they both saw the yellow trajectory carve a straight line from left to right, through dust and debris and volcanic hills. Across the screen, mag and VLF data, along with known geologicals, all appeared. In the center of the graphic, a grainy image of the Rossian vessel rose out of the gloom, bisected by the yellow line.

"That can't be a coincidence, Kate."

"Agreed." She minimized the image on her visor and stared at Mary. She already knew the answer to her question, but asked it anyway. "Still want to hang around here and wait?"

"Not a chance."

Mary

IT WAS LIBERATING TO FLY HER OWN SCOOTER again now that her elbow and shoulder had healed, and with the course plotted into their machines for the *Mare Marginis*—a direct route straight across the crater impact and volcanic zones near the target— Mary conceded the extra time at the alien site trumped the risk of flying over that area. Despite the nagging misgivings, she understood that waiting for someone else to come by and *possibly* rescue them paled against the allure of first contact and whatever that may bring. Like Kate, she preferred doing things. More importantly, she wanted to meet the elusive Rossians.

"Hey Mares, if you want to catch some sleep, now's the time to do it. Nothing but flats for hours." Kate flew about 50 meters off her right at two o'clock. What she admired about her the most was her decisiveness and resourcefulness. Spacer training perhaps, or simply the way her DNA was built. Didn't matter. She made a mental note to ask about her parents when they returned to Earth.

When?

Definitely. She had an intuition someone would save them. Where it came from, she didn't understand, but putting the pieces together, she argued that strange blue light over the mining outbuildings was no accident, no random act of nature. This entire adventure, ever since the Titanius lab imploded, was being orchestrated by external forces.

"Kate, you think they want to make contact when we arrive?"

Kate's scooter zig-zagged in broad arcs in the distance. "I don't know, Mares. Anything's possible." A momentary burst of static filled her audio. "You?"

"Yeah, I do." She paused, looked straight toward the horizon, then down at the dashboard and said, "See? That blue light ahead is like Saint Elmo's fire. It's an omen."

"Mary, seriously, put the autopilot on and get some sleep."

Two years ago, she'd hallucinated when the Alaskan flu hit. That bug knocked her flat for three weeks, and she was convinced the Earth had fallen prey to crab-like aliens. Despite running a nasty fever, she insisted on wearing a coat, hat and mitts to bed. She and her dad laughed about it later, but at the time, it was real, frightening, unknown. This felt the same.

"Maybe you're right. I'm not thinking straight." She toggled the autopilot throw switch, engaged the alarms, and the machine beneath her settled into a rhythmic hum, five meters above the loose, dusty sediment. Within a minute, she slouched in a sleeper position and drifted into the black.

KATIE

A YEAR HAD PASSED SINCE MARTIN'S DEATH. The overseers and their full training schedules prevented her from processing the emotional fallout of his hanging. Martin wasn't the only one. Another girl-boy stepped in front of a speeding hovercar while on a weekend leave in Memphis. The trainers claimed it was an accident, but she and the other Spacers knew better. They'd all experienced those feelings of isolation, of otherness, of ambiguous identity shrouded in silence . . .

The projects kept her moving, focused. Twelve to sixteen-hour days left little time for Katie to wonder about anything else. Early cancer blooms happened to be the small price to pay for the fascinating work, and the anti-rad pills helped manage those. She'd often spend several months in and around the Martian colonies, or weeks in low Earth orbit sabotaging NDU satellites. She'd long since passed the point of caring about the morality of such work: it was the science and, yes, the danger that sustained her. Besides, what else could she do? Prostitute herself to the freaks who followed her?

That all changed when she'd flown to Amsterdam with a few friends on a two-day pass and melted into a club.

"I wish those creeps would quit staring."

Pat swallowed a mouthful of beer and smiled. "They're harmless, Katie. Ignore them."

She shrugged, popped a greener and washed it down with a shot of vodka. "Harmless, eh? Sure, until they pester us for favors. You watch," she said, eyeing a chunky woman with blue hair, transparent top and tattoos on her arms. "That follower over there? She'll swing by in a minute or two."

Pat smirked and spat on the ground beside the patio table. Tracy laughed. "Well, I for one don't mind being propositioned. It's easy money, kids. Try it sometime."

"You're mad, Trace," Pat sighed.

Katie lit up a smokie and said, "You guys wanna get out of here? Head to the river and max out or something?"

"Are you serious? No way! We just got here, and the night's hardly begun. Tracy's barely warmed up."

"True," he said.

"And I've only got a few hours to enjoy the scenery before heading back to Eros. In fact," Pat added, checking her indie-comm, "time is wasting, my grunts." She stood, swayed for a moment, then disappeared into the night.

Without a warning, Tracy rose and stumbled off, leaving Katie alone at the table. She checked messages and finished the smokie, its effects tickling her spine, then noticed a shadow over her. She peered up to see a follower, the one with the blue hair and tattoos who'd been watching them.

"You a Spacer?"

276

"What's it to you?"

"Makes no never mind to me. Spacer or not, you're cute."

Katie ignored her.

"You wanna split and take a walk along the Amstel?"

She dropped her indie-comm and stared coldly at the normie. She had a thick, pretty face, no makeup, and a full body under the transparent blouse. The decision to leave with her happened in a flash.

"I'm Penny," she said once they'd found the shadows of the side-road leading to the river. "I'll be honest, okay? I'm a follower."

"I gathered." Katie ambled along, head down, smelling the nearby water. The greener took hold, causing her vision to narrow at the edges.

"But I've never talked to a . . ."

"A Spacer?"

"Yeah. I just like to watch, mostly. But there's something about you and, well, I told myself years ago to follow my instincts and something cosmic told me you'd be okay with a bit of company—you know, just to spend an hour or so with. I hope you don't mind."

Katie's shoulder brushed against her. She stopped, catching her balance. "Penny is it?"

She nodded.

"Listen, Penny, I don't know what you're expecting from me. Is it sex? Money? Bragging rights? All I want is to waste a few hours with someone, without being ogled by freaks." She paused. "You okay with that?"

The follower smiled warmly, and her eyes sparkled. "Totally. My flat's nearby where we can hang."

"Noves. I'm Katie."

They walked a few more minutes until the Amstel river came into view, pitch black with speckles of light dancing off its surface. A couple cruisers chugged along, laughter and soft music drifting over the water.

Penny reached out and took Katie's hand, interlacing her fingers. What shocked her wasn't so much this stranger's touch as her own acceptance of it. The last person to hold her hand was her father. She wasn't blind: she understood what Penny did and why. Still, though she felt nothing that way *toward* her, Katie loved the idea of being normal that came with it.

"Penny, I—you understand I can't do anything, right? It's not just that they cut me up: the feelings aren't there either, no matter how much I want them to be. It's like I never grew older than ten." She hung her head, staring absently at the ground rolling under her.

"Listen, here's the truth," Penny said, stopping and holding both Katie's hands to her chest. "Look at me, hm? Within that body, you're still a human being like anyone else, and we all need touch and companionship. So, perhaps you want some honest company for a few hours. No strings attached. No bullshit."

She wrapped her arms around Katie's bony waist and pressed hard against her. Katie tensed at the sensation of another person this close, and Penny conjured memories of her mother's embrace.

"Sh."

She kissed her lips gently. Katie held her breath. Her legs went numb, either from the drugs or . . . she shook her head, pushing Penny away. Her hands trembled.

"I want none of that, not a damn thing. Do you get it?" she whispered.

Penny stroked her cheek, her chopped hair, then caressed her arms. "This isn't about sex, don't you see? I can get that any time with any normie girl or boy or mixed I want. This is more."

"Don't say that. It means nothing." But she knew deep down, it did mean something.

Penny clasped her arms around her, tightening the hold. "Let me show you, Katie, how gentle and perfect we can be."

"I'd better get back to my friends."

"Kiss me. Just pretend, and—"

"Please. . ."

"But I've never really had a—a Spacer like you before. Don't you want to spend a few hours with me, Katie? Say you want me."

Katie sighed and relaxed, allowing Penny to draw her into an embrace, but couldn't bear to look in her eyes. She felt the warmth of her full chest; the fingers clutching her back, the scent of exotic perfume, and couldn't deny her new-found feelings. There was something dark about this; ugly and vaguely familiar, yet foreign. An image of young Martin struggling with his own sexual aware-ness crept into her mind. She wondered what it must have been like living as a boy-girl.

Katie smiled, then leaned up and kissed her tentatively on the cheek, wincing at the stab of shame in her neck. Then she searched Penny's eyes and found comfort there.

TWENTY-SEVEN

Carter

"Incoming transmission from *Malevolent*, secure channel, sir." Quigg, having retaken his post at the comms station, nodded at the red-lettered message header from Captain Russo.

"Put it on the main screen."

Quigg punched a tab on the dash and *Malevolent*'s gloomy, confined bridge appeared. Carter smiled when Laura came into view, took her seat in the captain's chair and faced him. He hadn't seen her in person for almost two years. The only officer in his fleet tall enough to look him straight in the eye.

"Laura, you seem well. What's up?"

ECHOES IN THE GREY

Captain Russo tugged on her flight suit and glanced at the data pad on the chair's arm. "I'm afraid it's not great news, Clayton. We're still a ways from Luna, and the *Volmar* continues to maintain her distance, but there's a new development you should be aware of if your own sensors haven't picked it up yet."

"What's that?"

"We've got two more Prussian heavy cruisers en route from the Martian sector at full burn, heading your way."

Carter glanced at Jenson with a questioning look and said, "We're not picking up those birds, Laura. Full burn you say?" He eyed the co-pilot again, who opened her palms and shook her head.

"That's not all, Clayton. They're running dark. No response to any hails. Transponder data is suppressed, which is why you don't see them."

Carter furrowed his brow. He'd prepped the *Echo* for a possible conflict and felt confident she'd hold her own in a confrontation with a cruiser just through speed and maneuverability. But two? "How are you tracking their movements?"

Captain Russo twisted her lips. She was all business, and Carter couldn't think of anyone he'd rather have out there watching his back.

"We have countermeasures for this situation. Prussian cruisers leave signatures in their burns, but you have to look for them specifically. Here," she paused and pointed to one of her crew, "I'll get Lopez to send the filter coordinates."

"Much appreciated."

Jenson and Captain Powell turned to a panel on the dash. She toggled a switch and the tracking viewer blinked. Two cruisers appeared.

"Can you confirm heading, Jenson?"

"Yes, sir. Luna."

"ETA?"

"An hour, give or take."

"And ours?"

Jenson checked the view finder. "Another thirty minutes, sir."

Carter worked his jaw and seethed, muttering under his breath. Then he turned to the *Malevolent*'s captain again.

"How far away from Luna are you, Laura?"

"Still another seventy-five minutes. If the Prussians are bent on conflict, we won't be much help."

"I guess we'll have to take our chances."

Russo leaned in closer to the viewer, concern straining her face. "Those ships are built for combat, Clayton. Not only do they possess formidable defensive weapons, including conventional nukes, but they also train their crews for this sort of conflict." She lowered her voice. "I've seen them in action, Clay. One, the *Henrik*, ripped a Brazilian freighter apart in seconds . . . *seconds!*"

Carter remembered the incident on the Saturn run several years ago. Many resource companies, including Titanius, suspected the *Bolivar* did more than haul ore and ice from Saturn's moons. Free-floating calypso mines scattered along the route and around Rhea and Dione attacked and disabled numerous freighters. Diplomatic efforts proved useless, and threats of taking complaints to the United Nations rang hollow with no concrete evidence. Then, a Prussian cruiser—the *Henrik*—opened fire on the *Bolivar* without warning, annihilating it, and after that, the calypsos mysteriously vanished.

"Laura, is the *Malevolent* in any danger against one of these cruisers?"

She smiled that frosty smile again. "We can hold our own against any boat out here. My concern is what they could do to the *Echo* before we rendezvous at Luna."

Captain Powell stared at him grimly.

Carter sniffed. "We've got speed and size on our side, and I'm not looking to beat my chest with the Prussians. It's possible our stranded crew up there is still alive, so once we arrive at Luna in a half an hour, we'll rescue them and salvage the remains of the lab before those cruisers know what the hell's going on."

"Understood. We'll continue on course for Luna."

Then he had a thought. "Stand by one, *Malevolent.*"

He motioned to Quigg to cut the audio. Jenson's eyes widened, and she gazed sheepishly at Captain Powell.

Time for a diversion.

Carter took charge. "Jenson, stay focused. Are any of those terran ships following us of Prussian registration?"

She swallowed hard, paused a moment, then scanned her monitors, checking ship transponder data from the tracking icons. "Yes, sir, three of them. A science vessel, a mining shuttle, and a decades' old corvette."

Carter flexed his fingers. "Which is the most important to the Consortium, Jenson? The science craft?"

"Negative, sir. I'd say the corvette. Even though she's old, she's likely got weapons and military spy capability."

"Captain Powell, your thoughts?"

"I agree. There's a reason she's still in service."

"All right, then." He turned to Quigg and nodded. "Open the channel again."

Quigg toggled the audio and Captain Russo looked up in anticipation.

Carter stroked his chin and grinned. "Laura, I've got a slight change of plan."

She raised an eyebrow.

"I'd like you to lay in an intercept course for one of the Prussian ships following us from Earth. She's a corvette called—"

He glanced at Jenson, who answered, "The *Nachtfalke,* sir."

"Get that, Laura?"

283

"Plotting an intercept course now."

"Good. Target that sewage bucket and bring weapons to bear on her as soon as you're in range, but don't fire. Just make sure every living creature in the solar system knows you've got that ship in your sites. Let's give those cruisers something else to think about."

"Acknowledged. Intercept course plotted and," she nodded to Lopez, "engaged. *Malevolent* out."

Jenson exhaled and leaned back in the co-pilot chair, clearly shaken and nervous. Captain Powell stood and motioned to Carter to meet off the bridge. When they'd found a quiet spot out of earshot, he placed his hand on Carter's shoulder. "You don't have to worry about Elin Jenson. She's a solid pilot and quick on her feet, just a little skittish in the face of those cruisers."

"I'm not concerned in the least, John. You're the best crew ever assembled and I'm confident we'll emerge from this un-scathed. Remember, that little corvette out there will soon real-ize she's got a galactic cruiser bearing down on her, weapons drawn, like a high-speed truck on a collision course with a single-seat hovercar."

Powell's face suddenly flinched.

"Come, John, let's see what those cruisers do now."

Kate

THE BLUR OF GREY, WHITE AND BLACK MOONSCAPE merged with the gentle thrum of the LunaScoota, creating a hypnotic effect that lulled Kate into that half-state of consciousness. She fought des-perately against the powerful urge to sleep. Her mind replayed images of the Spacer Training Center, young Martin, the drugs and alcohol on pass days once she'd shipped out to the danger zones with her unit, the intense loneliness that pierced not only her heart but the skin of her soul.

Tracy was right, or maybe he simply parroted the trainers when he said, "Survival was a sequence of small steps." Either way, slogan or truth, those words had kept her going during this nightmare.

She cycled through their bio-signs on her visor and noted Mary had entered beta sleep. Soon, she'd have to wake her. The crater zone loomed ahead, and they'd have to reduce speed—at least to 75%—to pass over it safely.

Above the horizon, like a warning, a beacon, perhaps even an omen as Mary had quipped, the eerie blue light glowed, guiding the way to the alien ship on the outskirts of the *Mare Marginis*.

Twenty minutes before we hit the crater zone.

Kate set an on-dash timer, rose to eight meters, checked Mary's position behind her one last time, and yielded to the thick shadow of fatigue that penetrated the marrow of her bones and gripped her in a vice-like hold.

I need to speak with Jim . . .

She surrendered to the black.

WHEN THE BONE-JARRING SHUDDER CAME, Kate was in the depths of a dream where she'd been dumped into the passenger hold of a republican shuttlecraft orbiting Eros, dazed from lack of oxygen, thankful for being rescued from NDU pod-thrusters. She squeezed her eyes into focus as a man approached from above. When she resolved the face, Dr. Marshall Whitt kneeled beside her and whispered, "Welcome home, Katie," his voice trailing off in an infinite echo. . .

Emergency alarms filled her helmet and Kate's eyes fluttered open. For a moment, she had no idea where she was, the image of that asshole Whitt burned into her visor and his arrogant voice resonating through her brain. Then, the familiar surroundings hit her. *Luna.* Fully conscious, she realized the scooter flew at an awkward angle. She grabbed the controls to correct the roll, but the craft wouldn't respond.

"Mary."

A vast field of rock, volcanic cones and craters surrounded her as the craft screamed at a horrifying list toward a massive outcrop. Her altitude leveled out at a meter and a half, and Kate pulled on the throttle to climb higher, but the controls were dead in her hands. Velocity registered 320 km/h. The scooter had lost a stabilizing thruster, hitting something along the way, and vibrated under the strain. A huge boulder slashed by on her right, but part of the cargo hold clipped it and sent the machine spinning like a top.

"Mares, wake up, damn it!"

She shifted her weight as far back in the flight seat as she could to pull the scooter up, but the craft continued twisting on its course through the rock and debris field. Kate considered releasing the safety harness and taking her chances by jumping off the stern. Given the lunar gravity, she might get lucky and not be completely eviscerated on contact.

Her helmet comms crackled. "Kate, where are you?"

The G forces crushed her into the harness and flung her around. She pulled her eyes open but saw nothing but a kaleidoscope of black, grey and white, and washed out rocks and impact zones, against a flashing veil of red warning visor lights.

Her lower left rib caved first under the violent crush of the scooter's malfunction. She struggled to reach the harness release pad on her chest, but the thrust of forces snapped her brittle arm at the wrist, and she screamed in pain.

Another jolt shook the craft and its nose lurched up, leveled out, and regained the horizon. Kate's head felt like it would explode as blood sloshed through her body. Her dangling right hand looked surreal, adrenaline masking the pain so far. That strange sound she kept hearing in her helmet was her own desperate moan.

Her reprieve ended just as abruptly. The scooter rolled on its side again and had lost its course. Kate shook her head to maintain consciousness and pounded the harness release. It remained fixed. She hit it again, and again, losing her breath each time. Nothing happened.

Mary's scratchy transmission broke through in a rush of static.

"Kate?"

"Mary, I need help!"

No reply came.

The scooter's nose dipped under the horizon again and the craft lost altitude. She monitored elevation as sparks and blue lightning spilled from the undercarriage.

The alert in her helmet sounded. *Three meters.*

She rocketed over a small impact crater. Directly ahead, a wall of rock and debris rose out of the ground.

Two meters.

The scooter wouldn't come close to clearing that. Her only hope of survival depended on whether the craft nosed down into the soft dust before smashing into the rock wall. Either way, it would be over in seconds.

"60 CCs of pseudophine."

The powerful painkiller hissed into her helmet.

One meter.

If the nose touched down first, she'd be squeezed through her harness like spuds in a potato masher, or sent tumbling into the rock. Kate hammered at the release pad again, sending a fresh wave of pain and nausea from her ribcage.

Milliseconds before the scooter slammed into the dust, the restraint snapped open and she instinctively pushed up and away from the machine. Her momentum carried her toward the wall but somehow, she cleared it enough to avoid a deadly collision. In her peripheral vision, she saw the LunaScoota disintegrate on contact with the lunar surface.

Kate tumbled through the space toward the debris field. Despite her broken wrist and crushed ribs, she pulled herself tightly together and braced for impact. When she hit the rock-strewn moonscape, she careened into the void again, fell, then bounced for several hundred meters before coming to rest on her back.

She gulped, catching shallow breaths. The integrity of her envirosuit remained intact although her visor display had grown dark. Waves of nausea rose, and black spots filled her vision. She coughed once, choking down vomit, then just before drifting into unconsciousness, the image of Jim Atteberry holding young Mary in her rubber boots on his lap appeared, that night when the Mount Sutro Tower crashed to the ground.

TWENTY-EIGHT

Mary

"KATE, COME IN!"

Her last garbled message disappeared in a crash of static, then the link died. After she'd roused from a nap and realized Kate was in trouble, Mary slammed her scooter to a full stop and immediately scanned the area. Sharp rocks and impact craters surrounded her; the bleak moonscape stretching beyond the horizon. When Kate no longer transmitted, she circled back, and retraced her path.

She nosed the scooter up until it whined at 12 meters above surface and cruised at an agonizing 20 km/h over the jet trail carved in the patchy dust. The limited scanning function on the scooter's dash revealed nothing. No other vessel in the area. No debris. Too much interference from the rough terrain, perhaps? On her visor, she cycled through the infrared filter but that, too, proved futile, so her only reasonable course of action depended on following a slow, methodical search protocol: retrace her path until Kate's trail appeared, then track that.

Twenty minutes passed before Mary spied the missing scooter's pattern off her port side. She nudged the throttle and powered away, following the rough line over the rocky field. After several kilometers of steady flying, the trail suddenly veered to the southeast. She slowed and surveyed the area. Still no sign of Kate or the other craft.

Her scooter must have malfunctioned and flown off-course. But why didn't she adjust?

If Kate had been dozing, she may not have noticed the change in direction. The lack of sleep from the past few days now affected her mind, so perhaps she hallucinated too. Mary lowered her altitude to five meters and followed the trail over rocks and through the craters. In a few moments, she saw evidence of the scooter hitting a massive outcrop, altering its course again. One of the machine's rear stabilizers jutted out of the surface dust, surrounded by fresh rock debris and puffs of suspended particles.

"Kate, can you hear me?"

The trail became harder to follow as the rocky zone grew more dense, and more dangerous. In those short patches of smooth surface that appeared, the missing scooter's path looked like a series of overcast stitches sewn in the surface with their distinctive on-off pattern.

How the hell did her machine manage that?

Mary reasoned the engine must have been sputtering at that point, but the regular scar pattern suggested they weren't caused by a malfunctioning nacelle; rather, the scooter was spinning on its roll-axis.

She followed this new trail through the zone, losing it sometimes where the rocks and outcrops dominated the surface, picking it up again over dust-filled craters and pockets. Judging by the distance between the stitches, Mary concluded Kate's machine had been running almost full throttle, but she dared not attempt covering the area too quickly for fear of missing something.

Several more precious minutes passed, each one spent looking for Kate meant one less searching for safety in the Rossian vessel. The whisper of an idea breathed into her thoughts: she should abandon this search and save herself. But she shook her head and dismissed it.

When Mary looked up, her jaw dropped at the sight of a massive outcrop stretching from the horizon into the black sky. The wounded scooter's trail headed directly for it. Icy panic crept up her spine and buried itself in her head. She gained altitude and pushed her own machine toward the looming rock wall.

As she approached the huge outcrop, the path revealed that Kate had somehow wrested control over the craft's roll as the jet trail on the surface straightened out.

The dash scanner blinked as mangled bits and pieces of the destroyed scooter rose out of the dust and rock at the base of the wall. When she arrived there, nothing remained of the machine except slivers. More importantly, no one could have survived that impact. Mary's heart sank.

After reining in her emotions, she discovered the pilot's seat nestled against an outcrop, and searched for Kate's body. That's when she noticed the harness had released, possibly jarred loose from the crash itself, or perhaps because she freed herself from the craft before it crashed.

She could be anywhere . . . and alive.

"Kate, are you there?"

She flew in a pattern of ever-expanding circles, beginning from the empty pilot's seat. Soon, she bumped up against the rock wall and, rather than continuing with her search path, she explored the base of the massive outcrop. A small vee-shaped opening cut across a chunk of the wall and Mary followed, reasoning that if Kate had been thrown from the machine, her momentum would have taken her into the wall, and possibly over it or through this cut.

The space between the jagged rocks squeezed the LunaScoota, and Mary had to maneuver the machine delicately around the opening, being careful not to damage any of it. When she cleared the wall and drifted down the other side into an adjoining rock-filled crater, she again cycled through her infrared filter.

In the distance, less than a thousand meters away, a grey shadow appeared in her visor unlike the density of the surrounding rocks.

Kate?

She pushed on the throttle and flew toward the object.

Kate lay sprawled on her back in the dust beside a smattering of boulders. Mary ditched the scooter and leapt toward her. The green bio-light blinked on Kate's visor, showing the integrity of the envirosuit was intact and that oxygen circulated. Still, when she attempted a bio-link, the connection remained elusive.

Way too much damage.

Kate's arm bent awkwardly just above the wrist, but other than that, she saw no other apparent breaks. She had to establish a link to assess her injuries and life signs, but the remote access and direct line port weren't functioning at all.

"Kate, can you hear me?"

No response. The impact must have knocked out comms.

She didn't want to move her without more information about her physical condition, but with limited oxygen and time melting away, Mary needed to get her to the Rossian ship and find a way inside, into the void they'd imaged. Tackle the crisis in small steps.

First, I have to find that ship.

Then, through the amber visor, Kate's eyelids fluttered.

"Kate?"

She heard nothing with the comms down, so she motioned for her to lie still, but Kate tried rolling onto her side, failed, and slouched back down. Then she mouthed something and chinned the controls. Suddenly, her visor lit up and static from her radio filled Mary's helmet.

"Kate?"

Her breathing rasped through her helmet audio, ragged and labored. She finally established a bio-link and her vital signs scrolled across Mary's visor. She studied them and grimaced.

"Tell me what you need."

Kate grunted and mumbled in a slurred voice. "My ribs. . . are broken. Wrist. . ."

"I see it. You've got a clean break right through the radius and ulna if I were to guess. On a scale of one to ten, how much pain do you feel?"

"I'm drugged up, Mares. . . so a two."

Mary placed her hand on the side of Kate's helmet, and she instinctively turned her head toward it, despite the distance between them. "I've got to get you to the Rossian ship. Can you move your legs?"

"Yes, but. . ."

"Quiet now, just rest."

Mary bounded to the scooter and ripped the restraints securing their equipment in the cargo hold.

"Mares. . . what are you doing?"

"Making room for you."

She hauled out the useless radio cables, tools, extra solar panels, and the portable excavator.

Kate lifted her head. "Not the... the excavator. You'll need that. For the ship."

"I can't get you in there with it, so I'm leaving it behind and I'll just have to dig with my hands and whatever else I can find."

"No, don't do that. Leave me here. Save yourself."

She finished her prep of the cargo hold and returned to Kate. She knelt down beside her. "Let's be clear. I'm not leaving you."

Kate winced and struggled to prop herself up on her side. "You must. Look, I'm useless now... I'm done. But you still have a chance. Go... go without me."

Maybe this could work. If I can access that ship, find help somehow, then return for Kate.

She reasoned it out, but the option didn't sit well.

"Sorry, I'm taking you with me."

"Don't, please. Go... now. Come back for me... later ... if you must."

Mary stood up and hesitated.

"Go!"

Atteberry

LUNA'S MONOCHROME SURFACE PROVIDED A STARK contrast against the pitch black sky as *Echo* assumed a standard orbit. It reminded him of the old historical film he'd seen at one of the Astronomical Society's presentations back home, showing grainy images of brownish-yellow craters as mapping satellites passed overhead. The Moon looked far more beautiful over the Pacific on a clear night than up close, but nothing compared to the artistry of Earth.

"We'll be above the *Aristoteles* mine site in a few minutes, sir." Captain Powell stood on the bridge, hands folded behind him, studying the main viewscreen. Carter, Atteberry and Esther joined him from their stations. "There's been no further EM signals from here."

Atteberry asked, "Aren't we landing?"

Carter hesitated. "Let's take a fly-by first and see if Kate and Mary are there. Captain Powell, standard procedures."

"Understood." He turned to Quigg. "Initiate automated hails on all known *Aristoteles* frequencies. Jenson, maintain present altitude and commence scanning patterns. Life signs will be too difficult to detect from here, but keep looking for any kind of fresh debris, scooter tracks, or other evidence that Kate and Mary are there."

"Aye, Captain."

Atteberry fidgeted, his hands pulling on his cheeks as he watched the main viewer. Esther placed a hand on his arm. "It'll be okay, Jim. We'll find them." Her warm eyes comforted his dark thoughts though he knew damn well the chances of them still being alive were slim. But, he smiled and admitted to himself that being with her on this ship with him as he searched for his daughter and friend, felt right.

"*Aristoteles* coming into view, Captain," Jenson announced. "Adjusting for geostationary orbit."

The abandoned mine complex blended in to the lunar landscape so well that it took Atteberry a few moments to distinguish the lines of the outbuildings and the curves of the main habitat. A beacon and damaged solar array drew his eye and revealed the habitat.

Powell moved closer to the main viewer. "Zoom in on that, Mr. Jenson. Magnification 10." The screen flickered, and the habitat was unmistakable now. "Clear up that focus, please."

"Aye, Captain, working on it."

The *Echo*'s high-powered scanning cameras shifted, and the images resolved to such a clarity that Atteberry felt he could reach out and touch them.

Evidence of human activity abounded. Numerous scooter tracks scarred the area, and someone had cleaned at least a couple of the large solar arrays of dust.

Carter, arms folded across his chest, asked, "Captain Powell, are these trails and such recent? I understood that footprints could last millions of years on the moon's surface."

"I'd say it's a mix of old and new, sir." He pointed to an area in the mine fields. "See all these tractor prints? They look new, but these are already several years old. However. . ." He circled the front section of the habitat. "The scooter trails here are definitely fresh."

Atteberry broke in. "How do you know, Captain?"

"The mine operations didn't use LunaScootas. They relied on rovers since their lower speeds and greater hauling capacities made them far more practical for this kind of in situ operation." He turned to face Atteberry and raised his eyebrows. "But someone's been shuttling around. See how they crisscross the whole area? How they take off toward the outbuildings here. . . and here?"

"We've got to land!" Atteberry grabbed Carter by the arms. "They're still down there!"

Carter pushed him back. "Stand down. They may have moved on."

"What are you talking about?"

"Do you see the scooters anywhere? Unless they're parked in the buildings, it appears they've gone somewhere else." He nodded at Powell. "Am I right, Captain?"

Powell hesitated and studied the images from Luna. "It's a mystery. I suppose they could have taken the machines inside an outbuilding, but why they'd do that makes no sense."

Esther, standing beside Atteberry with hands on hips, said, "If they needed electrical or computational power, they may have rigged something up inside." She moved closer to the screen and studied an area that jutted out from the habitat's core. "Something's happened over here. See the damage? Perhaps they brought the scooters in here, but I'd bet they're at an outbuilding."

She turned to Carter. "There's only one way to know for sure, Clayton. We need to land."

He scowled. "No."

Atteberry panicked. "We've got to go see. They could be in there on their last breath. Please, for the love of God, Clayton, take the ship down and let's check it out."

"Can't do that."

"What the hell is the matter with you?"

"Stand down, Mr. Atteberry!" Carter's voice boomed over the hum and white noise of the *Echo*. "I don't want to waste my time chasing ghosts."

Atteberry's eyes widened and his jaw dropped, mouthing silent words. Powell and Jenson averted their attention back to their stations. Automated hails and telemetry data whispered in the background.

"Clayton!" Esther grabbed him by the arm and pulled him aside. Then she wrapped an arm around Atteberry's shoulder. He lowered his head, stunned.

Carter said, "I'm—I'm sorry, Jim." He paused a moment, then regained command. "Still, we're going to have some seriously nasty cruisers on us any time and my priorities are salvaging my tech and finding that alien ship."

Atteberry stared at him. He grabbed the back of Quigg's seat and leaned into it. "I thought this was a rescue mission."

"The needs of the many. . ."

"Don't give me that crap. I get it. Sometimes sacrifices must be made for the greater good. But the people involved make their own sacrificial decisions, not some mine boss or ship's captain or anyone else. You have no right to play God." Atteberry fought hard to keep his emotions in check, but they leaked out all around him.

Carter stared him down, clearly not interested in changing his mind, and the ensuing tension filled the bridge. Ishani and Dub had joined them at this point and assumed positions behind their CEO. Atteberry knew Dub's only role on this ship was security and hauling heavy crap. He clenched his fists and watched the big man.

Esther moved forward. "Clayton?" Her voice, though warm, carried an authority that he had not noticed before. "If Kate and Mary are in that habitat, we have to get them." She turned to the co-pilot. "How long would it take to land this craft?"

Jenson looked at Captain Powell, who nodded at her to proceed. "Only a few minutes."

Esther returned her gaze to Carter who fumed stoically in the center of the bridge. "Please, Clayton, let's go see. We'll know immediately if they're there, or if. . . they're still alive."

"No, Esther. We don't have time."

She threw Atteberry a glance and pursed her lips. "This isn't the kind of relationship or partnership I can support, Mr. Carter. You're the boss here, and no one questions that. But we have a moral obligation to find those women before anything else." She moved closer to him. "Please, Clayton, let's go see, then we'll take care of the salvage and look for the alien ship."

"In a godless world, Esther, morality is fluid. It means nothing more than a bowl of soup." He grunted. "But I hear you. That said," he chewed his lip, then shifted his gaze to Atteberry. "I won't tolerate this talk-back on my ship again, understand?"

Atteberry sighed, burying his outrage, and nodded.

"Do you, Esther?"

"Yes. Thank you."

Carter stared at the *Aristoteles* mine site on the main viewer. "Captain Powell. . . take us in."

Mary

PLUMES OF DUST KICKED UP FROM THE LUNASCOOTA as Mary rose and guided the machine away from the crash site en route to the alien vessel. Kate remained behind, propped up on the rocky surface. She kept telling herself that Kate's reasoning was sound: she'd stay so Mary could get to the Rossian ship, find a way in, then return for her. It would save time, but the primary benefit was maintaining space in the cargo hold for the portable excavator to clear the area around the hull.

One small step.

Her helmet audio crackled to life. "Keep in touch, Mares. Let me know what you're doing." Kate's voice faltered and was barely readable.

"Roger."

Mary didn't plot the new course in to the scooter's guidance system until she'd cleared the major rock wall. No sooner had she done this than the mysterious blue light appeared again on the horizon, aligning itself with the coordinates of the alien vessel.

The scooter vibrated underneath her as she flew it around the craters and debris field, but despite the progress, Mary felt sick.

You can't leave her behind.

She eased up on the throttle and hovered over an open, patchy area between several large boulders. Logic didn't help.

Reason didn't work. No matter how she teased out various scenarios, the over-riding fear of what would happen if she failed to enter the ship crushed her.

"Kate, I'm coming back." She nudged the throttle, retracing her path through the danger zone to the crash site.

"No . . . don't. Save yourself."

Mary ignored her, and within a few minutes, she grounded the scooter near Kate and immediately hopped out and unlashed the excavator from the hold.

"You'll need that. Don't. . ."

She knelt beside her. "How much pain are you in now?"

"My whole arm throbs from the broken wrist. My. . . my ribs hurt like hell if I try sitting up. Definitely an eight even with the pseudophine."

Mary paused for a moment. Traveling in the back of the cargo hold on the portable seat lacked the cushioning and security of the pilot chair—she knew from having done it earlier. No other options presented themselves.

"You'll have to juice up for the ride to the ship."

"No. . ."

"Don't argue. It'll be tricky clearing the debris field and the hold isn't designed to carry people, let alone injured ones. Hit the juice and let's go."

Kate ordered up another blast of air-borne narcotic then sank into the dust.

Getting her into the cargo hold challenged everything she'd learned during her training about rescue protocols. With the extra dose of painkiller, Kate's body relaxed into dead weight, and al-though she was thin and wiry and in a 1/6th gravity environment, moving her arms and legs so as not to exacerbate her injuries took time and considerable effort.

Finally, she lay Kate down in the hold and strapped her in with makeshift tethers.

"Sorry to leave you on your back, but I don't want any more pressure on your ribs. You'll just have to stare into the black abyss until we reach the Rossian ship."

"Mm." The extra shot of painkiller had reduced Kate's voice to a series of grunts and wheezes. Mary figured she must be so out of it she likely didn't know where she was at this point.

She fired up the scooter, pulled out of the dust, and hovered for a moment over the crash site. "We're heading out now, Kate, you and me."

"No. . . leave me here. . ."

Mary ignored her and shuttled her way through the debris field, buffeted by massive rock walls and boulders, following the glow of blue light shining like a bauble in the dark. She focused all her attention on manipulating the craft through the danger zone, speeding up where possible, but mostly keeping it slow until she could open the throttle again on clear moonscape.

"Mary. . . I have to help Martin."

"Hm? Who's Martin?"

"I have to help him. . . before he. . ."

She drifted in and out of consciousness. Mary remained silent and concentrated instead on exiting the danger zone and arriving safely at the Rossian ship. As she approached the vestiges of the rock field, she hovered in place a meter off the ground for a moment, and wriggled around to check on Kate. She still lay in the hold in the same position as Mary had left her earlier, biosigns functioning almost normally except for the lower heart rate and presence of heavy narcotic in her blood.

How much of that juice did she take?

"Mares?"

"Yes."

"Leave me here, sweetheart. I'm so ugly. . . so broken. Say. . . say hi to your dad. I always . . . loved him." She wept freely now.

"I'm not leaving you." She couldn't tell if Kate was hallucinating, but with that much juice, no one could remain lucid for long.

"Let me go, let me go. . ."

"I won't ever leave you."

Mary faced forward again, nudged the throttle and cruised over the edge of rocks and out of the danger zone. The only features standing between her and the Rossian ship now were ancient basalt flows, the odd outcrop, and fields of dust.

"Let me. . . sleep."

She pulled back hard on the throttle and the scooter lunged into motion.

". . . what I am now. . ."

Fifteen minutes to the site. Then half an hour's worth of oxygen to dig.

". . . don't forget me. . ."

TWENTY-NINE

Esther

THE ONLY OTHER SHIP SHE'D FLOWN CAPABLE of space flight and land-ing on planets or asteroids was the *Gordon Bennett*. That hap-pened years ago shortly after she joined the TSA, and that boat wouldn't measure up to half of the *Echo*'s capability.

It's amazing how far we've come in two decades, despite the political upheavals.

She often wondered what the world could have accom-plished if the United States circa 2070 had remained intact, but Esther understood history: no nation, no movement, no empire lasted forever. The breakup of the USA was inevitable, and even the founding fathers understood the fragility of dreams, so the only question facing them was: when?

The *Echo* touched down about 50 meters from the main *Aristoteles* mining habitat. She, Jim Atteberry, Ishani, and the heavy-lifter Dub had suited up on descent and now prepared to walk on Luna's surface. Jim looked nervous as hell, no doubt overwrought with concern for Mary and equally overwhelmed with the reality of landing on the moon.

"Everyone ready in there?" Carter's voice boomed from the other side of the airlock door.

Ishani checked each one in turn, making eye contact, verifying helmet comms worked, then gave the thumbs up.

The external pressure in the airlock changed, oxygen vented out, and the doors between them and the space vacuum opened. Ishani pulled a switch and a ramp unfolded from the open door to the Moon's surface.

"Let's go!"

She led the way down the slope, followed by Dub, Esther, and Jim pulling up the rear. Half way down, she turned to check on him. He looked all around, taking a step here and there, stopping, gazing at the space. She waited for him, then wrapped her arm around his elbow, and guided him down to the surface. "Jim," she said, "you can gush about it after. We've got a job to do. Are you still okay, because if not, now's the time to go back."

"Thanks, but I'm good."

"Even if they're not alive?"

"Yeah, even that." He looked ahead to the habitat. "Let's go."

Ishani hopped to the *Echo*'s supply access door. It stood about a meter from the surface. She unlatched it, and pulled the flap open. Then she leaned inside and returned a few moments later with a couple of flight packs.

"Dub and I are gonna check the outbuildings. You and Jim reconnoiter the main habitat."

"Will do," Esther said.

She and Atteberry bounded toward the main building. As they hopped along, they both noticed Ishani and Dub floating above the surface of the mine fields.

Atteberry couldn't contain himself. "Those flight packs are pretty amazing. Why didn't they give any to us?"

Esther continued jump-walking. "They're difficult to control. I don't know about you, but I've had no training on them, and sure as hell don't want to learn how to fly with one now."

Within a few minutes, they arrived at the habitat's access hatchway. Esther noticed the dust had been brushed away from the door, from the solar arrays, and saw the telltale tracks of a scooter's landing pads close by.

"They were definitely here, Jim."

He hung back, paralyzed in surface material up to his shins.

"Come on. This is no time to lose it. You want to find Mary's whereabouts, right, one way or another?"

"Yeah."

"So, let's find her."

He took a few steps forward, and Esther grabbed his arm and pulled him the rest of the way to the open airlock. She squeezed through the main access portal and saw that the corridor into it was clear as well. They had both been here, no doubt about it. Several footprints all around the habitat told her that. Before pushing the door to the control room fully open, she glanced at Jim. He stood right behind her. She saw his eyes and tight mouth through the visor. "Take my hand," she said. "Turn your helmet light on."

They pushed through the door and entered what looked like a command center to Esther. A horseshoe-shaped console table greeted her, with all kinds of equipment strewn about on top of it and off to the side. On the right was a junction for power and cable hookups. Further up on the left was a closed door, and then another access hatchway—opened—that led god knows where. She noticed him studying a box of radio gear.

"My girl was here, Es."

"Kate, too. These prints weren't made by just one person." She dragged him toward the console covered in electronic parts and bits of antenna. "I'll bet this is where they tried contacting you on that ham radio frequency of yours."

Atteberry pulled away from her and knelt down in the dust, picking up and examining various pieces of gear, cables, and a circuit board. He kept dropping them.

"You okay there, Jim?"

"Yeah, just not used to these gloves I suppose."

"They're obviously not here now. Let's check out that area on the right."

She had already hopped over to the access hatchway, following the footprints that abruptly stopped. The portal was partially open, and she pulled on it until she could slip through. "Come on, Jim."

He bounced awkwardly toward her.

"Let's see what's in here."

As her helmet light illuminated the dark recesses of this part of the habitat, the first thing she noticed was the damage along one side of it where some machine had ripped it open. She recalled seeing this from orbit. Sunlight found its way in through that hole, but the corners of the area remained in deep shadows.

"This looks like the sleeping quarters for the builders. See all the lockers and cot frames?"

"Yeah."

"Jim, you go up that way." She pointed to the right-hand side. "If you find anything, shout. I want to go through here."

Jim walked along the side of the quarters that remained intact.

"There's lots of footprints here, Es, but no other sign of Mary. Or Kate."

Esther poked around the opened lockers, speculating on what they'd been looking for. "They were here, too, exploring. Maybe searching for radio gear, or tools, or emergency oxygen canisters. Hard to tell from this mess."

"So, where are they now?"

He still poked around the far wall of the habitat, picking up and dropping small boxes and the odd chair.

"Great question. Unless they're in one of those outbuildings, they've moved on."

At that moment, Ishani's voice broke into her helmet. "Esther, Ishani. Come in."

"Go ahead."

"Dub and I have checked both sheds here in the mine fields. Looks like they ransacked the storage lockers and exchanged their oxygen packs for others. We found two empty Titanius tanks in one of the buildings."

"Are they there now?"

"Negative. We got footprints and scooter tracks, but no bodies."

Esther glanced at Atteberry. He seemed indifferent to the term Ishani used.

Just as well.

"Okay, there's evidence they were here too... some radio parts and a couple of tools. A bunch of cables all about." She paused. "You getting all this, *Echo*?"

"Affirmative." It was Carter's voice. "Are you ready to come back and move on?"

She looked at Jim and shrugged her shoulders. He nodded.

"We're done here, *Echo*. Jim and I are returning to the ship now."

"Dub and I are gonna meet you there. Ishani Out."

Atteberry led the way through the access hatchway, across the main console room, and out the portal. Standing on the lunar surface, he then turned to her. "They didn't die here, Es." He smiled through the visor, his soft eyes full of hope. Esther nodded, but despite the growing possibility of finding Mary and Kate alive, the prospect of contacting an alien life form was at least as important. Perhaps even more. And the Rossian ship was the only other place left to go.

Katie

SHE STUDIED THE SHORT, BEARDED MAN WITH *derision as he sipped a glass of ice-water across from her. Katie pushed the empty coffee mug aside and leaned forward, fingers clasped together on the table.*

"Why should I listen to you?"

Dr. Marshall Whitt returned her gaze and patted his lips dry with a napkin. "Because I'm offering you a chance to work on far more interesting projects than what you're doing now." He also moved in and lowered his voice. "Katie, your true skills lie in programming. Everyone involved in the Spacers knows that, yet here you are still tinkering around with malfunctioning satellites or, if you're particularly lucky, your overseers might assign you to some mining operation on the Martian run."

Despite his smarmy, self-important demeanor, the little asshole was right. Five years ago, at the Aptitudes, she scored highest in logic, sequencing, pattern recognition. Even though the Program had given her opportunities to work on amazing projects—at great physical and personal cost, she reminded herself—she believed they overlooked her true skills.

"That may be, Dr. Whitt, but I heard an expression in Singapore once about 'the devil you know', so what do you really want?"

He narrowed his eyes and peered around the cozy coffee bar. They both noticed a group of followers gathering at one of the side tables, glancing their way.

"Do you want to leave?"

Katie grinned and waved at the worshippers. "Nah. I'm used to this now."

"Very well." He took another sip and wiped his lips again. "You remember I rescued you in orbit one time when your flight pack malfunctioned?"

"Uh-huh. So?"

"If you missed it, I'm on the republican side."

"United Confederate States? Big deal, I have no interest in politics."

He smirked and shook his head. "What are you, Katie, 16?"

"Fifteen."

"And you've done more living in the last five years than most space engineers and scientists accomplish in a lifetime. Look, you were recruited into the Program back when the US was unified, more or less. That's all changed now."

"The work is the work, Doctor."

"Yes, but to what end? You can fix satellites, sabotage others, infiltrate various manufacturing operations and plant spyware, but have you ever considered the reasons why the Program came to be in the first place? And what's become of it with the civil war?"

Katie had seen many of her colleagues recruited to one side or the other. It would unfold like this: he'd talk political gains, the greater good for all humankind, offer her exciting new challenges. Ultimately, the work kept her going, along with an imperfect loyalty to Pat and Tracy. She saw no reason to pick either camp now that the Program itself got squeezed.

"I told you I'm not interested in the shifting politics. Just the work. So, if we get hired to sabotage NDU or UCS satellites, or to *bugger up one of the new republics, I could not care less as long as there's a challenge for me in it."*

Whitt leaned back and stroked his greying beard, but continued studying her face. "My two boys were both recruited years before you came along."

She cocked her head, feigning indifference.

"I dropped them off at the Testing Center and haven't seen or heard from them since." He winced. "The hardest thing for a parent to do is lose a child."

Katie thought about her own mom and dad and how they'd abandoned her. She felt a twinge of emotion rise in her chest. "Yeah, I suppose that's tough, but not my business."

"I'm telling you this, because I want you to understand that I'm sincere. You probably recognize I'm not a professional recruiter, and I've never approached a Spacer before, so please believe me when I say that I'd like to give you something more meaningful, more challenging."

"Why me?"

"Perhaps you caught my attention when my ship picked you up? No matter. I need someone with your programming skills on my team. I need you."

The crowd of followers continued staring—a mix of young and old, various genders—talking among themselves. She'd seen this before, too—egging one of them on to approach and ask her for a date, *then offer her money. That was Tracy's thing, not hers.*

"What is it you do again?"

Whitt smiled and placed his hands palm down on the table. "I'm with a space science research and operations team in the South UCS. Our focus is on cracking faster-than-light communications and related travel problems. The war gets in the way, I'll admit, and sometimes we take a contract for necessary funds, but it's FTL that keeps us going."

Could be interesting, but something about him didn't sit right. She studied the new tattoos on her forearms, then said. "Tell you what, Doctor, if my situation changes at all, I'll keep your offer in mind."

"That's all I can ask."

"Great." The followers grew noisier. "I'm gonna take off out the back. If you could stay here and pretend I've gone to the restroom, buy me a few minutes, I'd appreciate that."

"Consider it done."

She stood, glanced at the freaks, and pushed in her chair.

"Oh, there's one more thing, Katie."

"Hm?"

"I know people who can keep those followers away from you, if they ever bother you too much." He raised his eyebrows, took another sip of water, then added, "Just say the word."

Mary

THE MAGNETIC DECLINATION READINGS ON THE scooter's dash fluctuated as Mary approached the *Mare Marginis* en route to the Rossian ship site. These wild variances, thought to be caused by metallic ore deposits, were the primary reason for investigating this area in the first place, but what if the alien vessel was behind them instead? What if the Rossians had been up here longer than anyone realized?

Mary decelerated and swung around the site in a wide sweep, performing an initial survey of the area. Logically, she understood that only a few days had passed since she and Kate had undertaken a spate of geophysical tests here, before the Titanius lab implosion, but it felt more like weeks. Her body ached with fatigue.

311

"You still with me, Kate?"

"Hm? Yeah," she whispered, "I'm feeling a little more with it, but I hurt like hell. Are we close to the site?"

"Yup, we made it. I'm taking a quick look around before landing."

She scanned the area through her infrared visor filter, located the submerged vessel, and nestled into the soft dust a few meters from the ship's bow. The amber light out here on the edge cast a surreal, rusty color across the drifts and craters.

"How much oxygen is left?"

Mary glanced at her bio-signs. "About half an hour. No time to lose." She unlatched the tailgate to the cargo hold. "Can you move?"

"I don't think so. Prop me up so I can see?" Kate's voice slurred in guttural tones.

She's so whacked up on the juice, it's like totally neural.

Mary lifted her back and secured her against the hold facings. She placed a folded tarp and a bag of tools around her for support.

"Thanks, I don't want to miss a thing."

The area surrounding the Rossian ship resembled a battle zone. Rock and dust pock-marked the surface, apparently from the sonic wave that also knocked out the Titanius lab. Some of the measuring instruments Kate used lay crumbled here and there. Mary knelt and brushed a thin layer of dust from the ship's hull, then ran her palms over it. In the rusty sunlight, the vessel's dark skin glistened like tiger's eye chalcedony. She cleared a patch about a meter long. The metal—if that's what it was—contained no tiling, no rivets, no imperfections whatsoever.

Twenty-six minutes.

"Talk to me, Mary. What are you looking at?"

"The ship's hull. . . it's so smooth. I'm going to clean as much of this crap off as I can and look for an opening. By the way," she pointed overhead, "the blue glow is back and directly above us."

Kate shifted her weight in the hold and grunted. "Is it. . . a probe or sensor? A drone, perhaps?"

"Too high for that."

"Scan it."

Mary stood on the hull and stared at the hovering blue light. She cycled through a general sensory diagnostic, but the analysis came up empty, nothing but INSUFFICIENT DATA and UN-KNOWN QUALITIES. However, sensors showed this *thing*, this *watcher*, comprised a central core. Something solid. Just because the qualities of it were a mystery didn't make it any less real.

She shut down the scan. The light remained above the site, unmoving, like an old, distant star.

I'm wasting time.

"Kate, if you're able, keep an eye on that visitor. If it moves or anything else happens, let me know."

"Will do."

For a full five minutes, Mary brushed and kicked the debris from the Rossian hull until the clear patch grew several square meters. Despite the cooling system in her envirosuit, her own exertion and stress caused her to sweat and wheeze.

Twenty minutes.

She crawled over the ship's surface, scanning with her visor filters for any anomaly that could show an access port or passageway in. Nothing.

"I don't know, I can't see a thing." The elevated panic in her own voice surprised her. She inhaled deeply and closed her eyes, calming herself down.

"Try the tap code."

Mary knelt and drew the heavy wrench from her tool belt and hammered out the familiar code her dad heard years ago, a sequence of atomic numbers for hydrogen and oxygen: one, one, eight. Then repeated it.

After tapping the signal several times, Mary paused and waited for a response. A thought struck her that perhaps the Russians had attempted making contact, but the sounds of a return code were lost in the vacuum of space. The likelihood of that happening must be slim, she reasoned, given the level of technological advancement. If these beings could travel faster than light, communicate on a subspace level, and turn into blue stars, then they could certainly make contact if they wanted to.

Why are they silent?

"Any change in that light, Kate?"

"No, it's still way up there, and hasn't moved as far as I can tell."

Fifteen minutes.

"I'm thinking this isn't going to work. There's nobody here."

"Keep trying. You can't give up."

Mary turned to Kate, her palms down on her thighs as she knelt on the hull. Kate had listed to one side in the cargo hold, but her head still faced the sky. "Listen, we've made it this long, but I'm done. I'd like to spend my last few minutes thinking about things, know what I mean? Maybe drift away on pseudophine."

Kate's voice gained strength. "I do, I honestly do." She shifted to a different angle. "Look. Do you see it?"

Mary stood and headed over to the scooter. Her gaze followed Kate's arm. Beyond the horizon, the only bright object in the void was the planet Earth. Mary's jaw dropped. The entire European continent and Northern Africa sat under a cloudless sky. She watched the shadowy day-night line carve the Atlantic Ocean in half from north to south. Solar flares had charged up the magnetic field, and dim, green shifting sheets of auroras bathed the poles.

314

"Earth is beautiful, don't you think?" Kate's voice, although strained, filled her helmet audio.

"It's like the most glorious thing I've ever seen."

"Keep trying, Mary, don't give up yet. There's some kind of. . . of intelligence in there, or around us. . . keep trying."

She hopped back to the hull, investigated the structure one more time with her diagnostic filters and, registering no changes, she knelt again and pulled out the wrench.

Help us, please.

Mary gazed at the blue light, immobile, mocking her from the safety of the sky.

What more do you want?

THIRTY

Carter

"PLOT A COURSE FOR THE TITANIUS LAB, CAPTAIN POWELL, and take us there as soon as you're ready."

"Aye, sir."

Carter marched back toward the flight seats where Esther, Jim, Ishani and Dub had removed their gloves and helmets and waited for him. They took turns detailing what they'd found, and all agreed Kate and Mary had likely returned to the lab site, despite numerous scooter trail signatures crisscrossing the area in all directions. Atteberry expressed some hesitation, thinking out loud that perhaps they had gone elsewhere, but there was no logical reason for that.

Carter listened in silence, arms folded across his chest, as Ishani finished her report from the mining outbuildings. Beneath him, the *Echo*'s vertical thrusters engaged, and the ship rose into the dark sky.

He punched the transmit tab on the comms panel beside the seats. "Captain, maintain low altitude and keep scanning for survivors."

"Aye, sir."

Esther peered at the viewscreen as the ship cruised over the moonscape. "How long to get to the lab?"

"Fifteen, twenty minutes at this velocity."

"Can't we go any faster?" Atteberry sounded tired but no less defiant.

Carter eased into his seat. "Of course, but we might miss them. Our sensors are efficient, Jim, but not limitless, so we rely a lot on visual investigations."

Atteberry nodded but maintained a puzzled, angry look on his face. He turned to the viewscreen and kept standing while the others took their flight seats.

CARTER'S ESTIMATE OF THE TRAVEL TIME TO THE LAB site proved accurate: they arrived in just under sixteen minutes. Captain Powell flew in a large elliptical path around the imploded structure and debris field, allowing Carter and the crew to survey the extent of the damage.

"Sweet Jesus. . ." Atteberry muttered to himself, leaning in to the viewscreen. Esther gasped when she saw the remains of the lunar habitat.

Carter's face tightened. "Bridge, any signs of other ships in the area?"

"Stand by."

Esther asked, "Did a ship do this?"

He shook his head. "It seems unlikely, but I don't want to take any chances. If the Rossians are here, we must be prepared to engage them."

Jenson's voice came through the intercom. "Mr. Carter, no ships other than the ones we've been tracking."

"Good. What about life signs?"

"Negative, but there aren't any . . . carbon signatures either."

Atteberry looked at him and was about to speak when Carter cut him off. "Is it possible we missed them en route?"

"Mr. Carter? Powell here. That is a possibility. There's an inordinate amount of interference and it's affecting our scanners more than I thought."

"How can that be?"

"Well, we're still testing out various systems on board and bio-readers are one of those we haven't completed yet. Plus, the solar flare activity is strong right now, which impacts data integrity and reliability. Nothing we can do about that."

Atteberry smiled.

"Something funny, Jim?"

"Oh, no, it's just that Kate would know how to filter out that noise."

"Well, perhaps she'll be able to one of these days." Then turning back to the comms, he said, "Bring us in for a landing, Captain."

"Aye, sir."

The *Echo* slowed and hovered over a clear area to the north of the lab site, then immediately descended, kicking up dust in its path.

"You four head out and look for any indications of what happened to our lost crew."

Ishani took charge of the group and they hurried to the airlock, their heavy boots clacking on the floor grates as the *Echo* settled on the surface.

Carter returned to the bridge. "Where are those Prussian cruisers, Captain?"

Powell cycled through to the tracking screen and pulled it up on the main viewer. Various terran ships continued on their journey to Luna, except for the aging corvette, the *Nachtfalke*, which had come to a full stop in the face of the *Malevolent* that was now staring her down.

"Sir, Captain Russo has been apprising us of *Malevolent*'s actions. She says the *Nachtfalke* has backed down, which you can see on the screen here," he pointed to the ship's icon, "and it's having the desired effect."

"How so?"

"The *Volmar* has diverted from its course to Luna and is heading toward the standoff, as is the *Edelgard* from the Martian run."

Carter stroked his chin, then leaned on the back of the captain's chair. "The timing is critical here, John. How long before *Volmar* is in weapons range with *Malevolent*?"

"Approximately an hour at current speed."

"And the *Edelgard*?"

"Couple hours, minimum."

"Good, now what about the other cruiser, the second Brandenburg class?"

"It's over here." Captain Powell pointed to another icon on the right-hand side of the screen. "She's maintaining her course to Luna and continues to run dark."

"Time?"

"Twenty minutes or less until she achieves high lunar orbit."

He frowned. "That doesn't give us much time to salvage the area or find the other two."

"No, sir, and little time to hunt that alien ship."

Carter turned to a secondary monitor displaying the ruined lab site. The four crew from the *Echo* had fanned out to cover the ruins. Their names and critical suit data followed them on the screen. Ishani and Dub focused on the habitat where the scientific computers would have been. She knew what to search for. Esther and Jim appeared to be following tracks through the debris field, stopping frequently to inspect various pieces of equipment and saving what they could on the antigrav sled.

"Quigg, open a channel to the group."

The comms officer toggled a switch and pressed a button on his dash. "Channel open, sir."

"Esther, Jim, what have you found?" He watched them stop moving and then Esther turned to face the ship.

"Some odd clues here, Clayton. Lots of footprints that must have been made by Kate and Mary. When the habitat blew, a fresh layer of dust fell. Over here," she pointed to her right, "they pulled something from the debris, and scooter trails are everywhere. Not sure you can see from there, but one of them conducted a search pattern."

Carter had noted the geometric patterns in the area when the ship performed its reconnoitering fly-by. "Any idea where they went from here?"

Esther and Atteberry conferred and waved at several areas in the zone.

"It's hard to tell. Jim believes they must have gone northeast, but there are also lots of other trails heading that way, too.

Captain Powell turned and said, "Their last surveys were on the limb, near the *Mare Marginis*, sir. Could be from that."

Carter worked his jaw, considering the information. "All right, keep looking for anything interesting." Then, "Ishani, you there?"

"Yes, sir."

He drew a deep breath. "I'd like you to focus on retrieving our computers and any data pods that may have survived. Any proprietary tech must be retrieved as well even if it's destroyed. We can't let any of it fall into the wrong hands."

"Understood."

"*Echo* out."

Carter leaned against one of the metal support beams. The whereabouts of the two women remained unknown. They should have been at the abandoned mining habitat, but weren't. Or they should have been here, but aren't. The only other place Kate and Mary could be was with the aliens. That being the case, if he could find them, he would undoubtedly discover what he truly coveted.

The most curious riddle had nothing to do with the survivors' location. What kind of destructive power had blasted the lab to bits leaving no scorch marks? The implosion could have been caused by a malfunction in the oxygenator, but that likelihood was slim. These proven pieces of equipment simply did not contain that much energy to create a blast radius this size. No, something else was at play here, something never seen before.

If the Rossians were responsible for this destruction, why did they destroy it and where are they now?

He turned to Captain Powell.

"Are the weapons still online?"

"Aye, sir, nice and warm."

"Good. Keep a sharp eye out, John. We're not alone up here."

Kate

THE CHIME RINGING IN HER EARS WAS THE 10 minute O_2 depletion alarm, but in Kate's mind, polluted with heavy narcotics to dull the throbbing of her injuries, it reminded her of the confused, haunted tolling of the Saint Paschal carillon in Villareal.

Ten minutes. . . the pain will. . . end.

"Disable. . . all further oxygen warnings." They were redundant now.

A voice, too, somewhat familiar, rattled around in her mind. Her mother? Her eyes fluttered open and struggled to focus on the shape standing before her.

"Kate, you awake?"

"Hm? Um. . ." She shook her head and inhaled.

Mary knelt down beside her. "Listen, it's no use. My oxygen's just about spent with all the exertion, and I'm spent."

"You must keep trying. . ."

"No. No, I'm done."

"Let me see."

Mary shifted Kate's body to a new angle, propping her again. In her line of vision, the dark hull of the alien craft shone like amber gunmetal. Directly overhead, the blue light maintained its silent vigil, and just over the horizon, the Earth glowed like a jewel against the black sky. She caught her breath at the site.

"Can you move me onto the hull?"

"Why?"

"I can't give up. . . I . . . need to find a way in . . . to save us."

Mary sighed and lowered her head, but otherwise remained motionless, so she dug her heels into the dust and, using her good arm for support, pulled herself along the surface toward the ship.

"Kate, please. . ."

A moment later, Mary's arms wrapped around her, jostling her onto the hull. "Lay me on my back."

"Sure." She eased her down, so she again faced the sky.

"Give me the wrench."

"Whatever for, Kate?"

"Please. . . the wrench." She opened her hand and within moments, she felt the weight of the tool in it.

The first strikes were weak, but she gathered her strength, raised her forearm at the elbow, and swung hard. She repeated the blow, then tapped out the H$_2$O code.

"Knock, knock."

She turned her head and saw Mary sitting beside her

"Don't be sad. Look. . . what we found buried in the grey dust. In a few. . . minutes. . . we'll be off on a new. . . adventure." Kate's voice sounded hoarse and dry to her, but as she continued tapping out the code, losing track of the pattern and falling into a series of rhythmic thumps, a warm peace settled over her.

This is. . . only the beginning.

"My oxygen's done, Kate."

Mary's arm reached over and dropped on her chest. She released the wrench by her leg and put her hand over Mary's. Between the narcotics and the thickness of the envirosuit and gloves, she felt nothing but an unbearable heaviness, a sense of being or presence around her. This wasn't like a human touch. It was almost better, safer, more complete.

Mary blacked out first. In a few minutes, her brain would cease functioning and she'd die in her sleep. Kate shifted her weight on to her good side and gazed over the moonscape at Earth. She smiled, then darkness writhed around her, and she fell down supine again. She passed in and out of consciousness, staring now at the blue light as it danced and flickered across the sky. When the aroma of baking bread wafted through her mind so real she could taste it, the last vestiges of logic and memory made her realize the end had come.

Kate closed her eyes; the beautiful Earth's perfect isolation filled her remaining lucid thoughts. As she drifted into the shimmering black, she sensed her body suddenly afloat, as if being carried away.

THIRTY-ONE

Kate

VOICES AND IMAGES REVERBERATED TOGETHER in the black hollow of Kate's consciousness until that moment when, between the dream state and a tenuous foothold in reality, she understood without a doubt and as impossible as it seemed, that she was still breathing.

The dull ache in her side hit her first, causing her heavy eyelids to grind open, and she realized the envirosuit had disappeared. The searing pain of her broken wrist stabbed at her brain. Her terrifying scream, sounding distant and detached, pierced the last vestiges of sleep, and the wisps of dreams faded into the darkness.

Where the hell am I?

Kate knew where. She saw no farther than a meter in front of her. Everything fell under a cloak of thick gloom. The cold floor below her sent shivers through her body, but fresh air filled her lungs, and in a moment, she regained strength and soothed her pain.

"He—hello?"

Her throat stung, and she did not recognize her own voice as it croaked into the surrounding black.

"Mary?"

She held her breath and listened for any sounds, but the only noise was a weak, low-level hum consistent with the background thrum of a ship, or some kind of machine. Kate had no doubt she was inside the alien vessel. How she got in remained a mystery, but the last thing she recalled was blacking out on the ship's hull, followed by a sensation of being carried.

Could the aliens have picked me up and brought me in? If so, what did they do with Mary?

In a few moments, her eyes adjusted slightly to the darkness, and she made out a few rudimentary shapes, but nothing familiar. Behind her, less than a meter away, stood a wall extending upward into the black—the ship's side, perhaps. She dragged herself over to it and, fighting against the agony penetrating her body, inched her way up against it and dropped her head back.

"Hello? Mary, are you there?"

No sign of anyone or anything else presented itself in that space. Despite years of working in life-threatening situations followed by intense isolation on Luna, Kate felt a deep fear the likes of which she hadn't experienced before. Previously, a human element ran through the work: either people around her or technology built by them. This ship, however, was something other, and whether or not she liked it, being on board an alien craft filled her with a strong desire to go home—to be back on Earth teaching, or programming, or helping Jim discover oddball signals in space.

If only he was here. I'd tell him so much.

A scrabbling sound pulled her out of her thoughts. A movement—or was it her imagination—in the dark.

"Is someone there? Mary, is that you?"

The pain in her shattered wrist shot up through her shoulder with an intensity that almost caused her to pass out, and despite the cool air around her, beads of sweat peppered her face.

I've got to find her. Work the problem, Kate.

She leaned back and stared at the nothingness surrounding her. First, she needed to establish her bearings, and that meant moving, mapping the area with her good hand to create a mental image of the place. With luck, she'd find Mary in the gloom, too. Every breath she gathered put more strain on her ribcage. Even shallow panting held no promise of comfort. Worse, without the pressure of her envirosuit, her wrist swelled up like a balloon.

She began mentally imaging the space with the smooth wall behind her. It curved into the floor—no corners or hard angles—as if the room had been hollowed out of some thicker material. Then, she dragged herself along the wall's base, estimating the distance she covered and searching for any kind of reference on the structure. If this was, indeed, the Rossian vessel, the technology to run it remained a mystery. The only sound she heard was that uniform hum in the background.

The elapsed time since she blacked out on the hull and woke up here was unknown. If the point of living in this inky darkness was to disorient, then mission accomplished. She continued mapping with her finger tips moving, then resting, and noticed a few more blurred shapes ahead.

That's where I'll go.

She caught her breath, wiped the sweat from her forehead, then prepared to move again. As she placed her weight on her good hand to pull herself along, a new sound hit her, a *click-click* noise, faint, coming from the blurred shapes. She strained her eyes to see better, but her pupils only dilated so much. A moment passed. No other noise came.

The wall swept inward, and Kate followed it along, noting it remained completely smooth, like the floor, and the hull. No rivets, switches, handles. . . nothing you'd find on a terran vessel. As she inched her way closer to the objects, she called out for Mary again with no response.

Could she still be on the surface?

Then a set of amber lights appeared, dimly glowing in the shadows. Two of them, in a horizontal line. Finally, something different, a sign of life, a reference point. . . perhaps a way out. With renewed vigor, she pulled herself along the wall toward the pair of lights, wondering if they formed part of a command panel or sensor array.

When she'd dragged herself to within a couple meters of the dim source, she suddenly stopped cold. Her breath froze, and her mouth fell open. She lost all awareness of the pain in her body. All she could do was stare.

The amber lights blinked at her.

THIRTY-TWO

Esther

ESTHER AND JIM COLLECTED ANYTHING THAT LOOKED even remotely important and placed it all on the antigrav sled they hauled around behind them. The debris field spanned several hundred meters in diameter, with an elliptical pattern where the leading edge faced east. In her zeal to find Clayton's precious gear, she almost missed the frequent rupture scars on the Moon's surface, as if a massive quake had rumbled through the area.

But that's impossible. Luna's inert or, at most, only micro-seismic activity has ever been detected.

Atteberry had been quiet for the past several minutes. As he picked through the debris, he frequently stopped and gazed around the forsaken moonscape, as if by looking over the grey, Mary might suddenly appear.

Esther dumped a mangled viewscreen on the sled and moved closer to him. She checked in with him on a private channel. "How're you holding up, Jim?"

He turned awkwardly to face her, still getting used to the envirosuit's bulk and how to work its helmet functions. "I'm trying not to worry too much, but one minute in this place and I—well, it's hard to believe anyone survived whatever malfunction happened here."

"You think it was an accident?"

"Sure, I mean, what else could it be?"

Esther strained to see his eyes through the glare in his visor.

"Come on," she said, "let's collect what we can and talk on the way."

They bounced over to an outcrop that had backstopped several projectiles, including what remained of the habitat cots and some storage bins. Jim searched through the material, picking up bits of clothing, a pair of moon boots, and a dust-filled book. He stared at her.

"Mary's stuff?"

"She preferred. . . *prefers* books over e-files." He placed the bin on the sled, paused a moment and gathered himself. "So, what's up, Es?"

"Yeah that. I didn't want to broadcast, but I don't think this was an accident. Check out the blast pattern." She pointed east toward the leading edge where the habitat and oxygenators had once been, and waved around the area in an arc.

"Notice it?"

"What am I looking for?"

"If you look toward the limb—that way—there's a series of patterned undulations in the Moon's surface." She stood close to him. "If this had happened on Earth, we'd all say an earthquake hit this habitat, but on the Moon there's nothing we know of that could produce P and S waves like back home."

His eyes widened with fear and excitement. "So, something else, something outside, must have destroyed the lab."

"It's a possibility, and I'd say it was some kind of shock wave that did it. Have you noticed the absence of any scorching?"

He paused a moment before answering. "Well, yes, I wondered why the stuff we're salvaging shows no melting or burn marks at all. It doesn't look like an explosion, but I figured it was because of the vacuum."

She took a few steps away and poked around a pile of thick conduits and other wires, stooping over to pick some up and toss them in the sled. "I can't think of any natural phenomenon capable of doing this. Not up here, anyway."

"Are you saying the Rossians were responsible? That they have a weapon powerful enough to flatten the entire lab site?"

Esther's thoughts drifted to the time the Ross 128 alien ship almost got her and a lot of other people killed back in 2085. Destroying the evidence surrounding that event assuaged her fears and effectively repressed her own emotional fallout from it. Now, she picked at that old scar, unleashing a flood of feelings she hadn't thought about for years. Yet, here she stood on Luna, with the possibility of first contact within her grasp. Her heart raced.

"It appears the Rossians and their FTL technology brought them here, possibly years ago. So, yeah, I've no doubt they're behind the destruction of the lab. The question for me is: why?"

Atteberry said, "Maybe they've got Mary and Kate, too. I know those two: both curious sponges for knowledge, so I'm sure they're at this ship, wherever that may be."

Esther pulled a desktop power supply out of the dust, turned it over in her hands, and placed it on the sled. She breathed deeply. "I agree, and judging by the upheaval in the surface, I'd bet they traveled east." She pivoted. "There's another problem, too. Clayton Carter wants that FTL tech—we all know that. But if he figures out the Rossians may have weapons capable of this kind of destruction, he'll want those too. And you've already seen how eager he is to start a fight with the other ships."

Atteberry's shoulders slumped.

"It's imperative we find the Rossians, Jim, and if Kate and Mary are on that vessel, rescue them before this situation turns ugly. Let's not forget there's at least another dozen boats up there, all targeting Luna."

"We can't just piss around here collecting scrap metal for his highness, then. Let's find that ship." The unfettered desperation had returned to Jim's voice.

"Right, but now we're looking for more clues to their where-abouts. They were working to the east, but they've been all over the past couple weeks."

Atteberry pulled the antigrav sled to a fresh pile of broken parts while Esther scanned the area. She cycled through the EM filters on her visor, searching for anything to help them deter-mine the location of the survivors and the alien ship. She leaned toward the eastern limb. Apparently, that's where the most re-cent surveys were conducted, but scooter trails radiated out from the lab site like spokes from a wheel hub, so Kate and Mary could have gone anywhere.

"Es, what are these things?"

She bounded over to the debris pile where Atteberry, kneel-ing, scraped around in the dust. She knelt beside him, moved a couple of enormous rocks aside, and helped extract the items from the mess. He'd uncovered three data tubes, two of which contained large dents and deep scratches. The other one appeared to be relatively unscathed.

"Do you know what these are, Jim?"

"Not a clue."

"Data tubes, capable of storing massive amounts of information. The kind used in massive data collection projects, like geophysical exploration."

"So, they might show where Kate and Mary were working on the day the lab blew up. Those events could be related."

"Assuming they contain the latest information, yes. More importantly, there may be intel on that ship, too." This was exactly the type of clue they needed. "Switch comms back to the main channel."

He moved his head in the helmet, then gave a thumbs up. Esther did the same, then called out, "Hey Ishani, you copy?"

"Go ahead, Doctor."

She clicked her helmet cam on and lifted the containers in front of her. "You see these? Titanius data tubes, right?"

"Yep, definitely. I've got you on visual. Me and Dub will be there shortly to help search for more."

"Roger. Copy that, *Echo*?"

"Captain Powell here, Doctor, and we acknowledge. As soon as you've completed a thorough investigation of the area for more, bring everything you have back to the ship post-haste."

"Will do, Captain."

"Oh, and one more thing, Doctor. Just a heads up that we're under a serious time crunch here and with so many other ships incoming, we'll all need to move fast. Understand?"

"Copy."

She put her arm on Atteberry's shoulder. "Let's scour the area for any more of these. Keep an eye out for other conventional memory devices, too." Through the visor glare, she saw him smile. Their next steps now depended on the integrity of the information in these tubes. Given their condition, and the amount of dust that likely penetrated the casings, recovering useful data remained a massive challenge. Still, his smile released those buried memories of their blossoming romance, and a new rush of emotions filled her.

Esther nodded and smiled back, then continued digging in the grey.

THIRTY-THREE

Kate

IN HER CHEST, HER HEART THUNDERED, hammering against her ribs and climbing her throat, catching her breath, and paralyzing her entire body.

Amber-colored eyes, barely visible in the thick, dark void, watched her. Now that Kate understood what they were, she stared right back, unable to process the churn of emotions, the significance of the first encounter, the heavy fear that suffocated her, the joy and shock that tumbled in her mind.

I can't breathe.

Kate shut her eyes, squeezing every thought away, and focused on taking one short breath . . . just one . . . only one.

Inhale . . . exhale . . .

A measure of calm quelled her shaking body, and by redirecting her thoughts to the pain in her ribs and wrist, Kate tightened control over the visceral terror that threatened her ability to function. She groaned, and her eyelids fluttered open.

The shadowed scene in front of her remained the same: alien eyes, thick darkness, and a low level hum permeating whatever this place was. She stared at the unmoving glow and wondered if her mind was playing tricks.

Are those blinking eyes or flickering lights?

She shifted her weight on the floor, relieving the pressure on her ribs, and continued staring at whatever those things were. For several minutes, nothing changed: no movement, blinking or anything else.

Kate's rational mind took over from the frightened prehistoric amygdala and reasoned that these lights were inanimate. She gathered her strength and hoped her voice wouldn't be lost.

"Mary, are you out there?"

No response came. Kate took several shallow breaths, comforted by her body's return to normal operating parameters to the extent it could, given the injuries. She reached out with her good arm and resumed inching along the smooth wall toward the shadows.

This time, there was no mistake.

They moved.

Kate suddenly felt nauseous and fought to control her physical reaction to what she experienced. But it was clear: something else hid in the gloom, watching as she crawled, keeping a respectful distance.

If this other being was a Rossian alien, it didn't square with her idea of what a technologically superior creature should look like. Perhaps she, like so many other humans raised on science fiction movies and other over-the-top shows, had been culturally brainwashed into believing aliens must be larger than life, reptilian, crab-like warmongers who spoke English. As Kate wriggled along the wall, pausing after each shift of her body, the size and shape of the Rossian became clearer even though she only caught glimpses of its rough silhouette and features. It made no threatening moves.

She approached an obtrusion, a type of pedestal, and moved her hand around it in the dark. Like the other physical objects of this ship she'd already sensed, this small dais was smooth at the edges, half a meter or so square, and another half meter high and flat on top. A stand? Command platform?

The amber eyes continued staring from across the gloom, and as the minutes passed, Kate's curiosity supplanted her initial fear of first contact with an alien life form. She estimated the distance separating her from the creature to be about five meters though it was impossible to be certain given the darkness.

She leaned against the pedestal, easing her weight on it for support while keeping eyes fixed on the Rossian. After another few minutes during which Kate listened for any anomalous sounds in the space, she grunted, pushing the pain aside, and whispered, "Welcome to Luna."

Her voice quivered more than she wanted it to, and her mouth had dried out completely. She tried to salivate by moving her tongue around and faux-yawning to stretch her jaw muscles with limited success.

The alien remained frozen in its place.

"My—my name is Kate. Do you have one? A—a name, I mean?"

Silence.

She gulped. "Have you seen my friend Mary?" She waved her arm desperately, pretending to outline Mary's form.

Nothing.

Kate winced as pain spiked up to her shoulder like a gunshot. She readjusted her position against the pedestal. "I need to find . . . her. My friend Mary that is." The absence of any recognition from the alien filled her prehistoric brain with new life, and a fresh wave of fear spread across her thoughts. Cold sweat broke out anew on her forehead. Before she caught herself, Kate already began speaking. "Did you take my suit? That keeps the . . . pressure on my injuries. Painkillers would help, too." She narrowed her gaze and grunted. "Any of this making sense?"

It blinked.

Perhaps talking to this creature had an effect. Perhaps this being, living in the dark, was as curious about her as she was about it. She spoke just above a whisper.

"Can you tell me where you're from? I'm assuming Ross 128, but that's—that's a name we call it." She surveyed the gloomy space again, shifted her weight, and said, "It's really dim in here, don't you think? Hm?"

An old tune popped into her head, one her mother used to sing when she needed cheering up, when the darkness filled her brain like a black mist. She forced herself to inhale and hummed out loud.

You are my sunshine, my only sunshine. You make me happy when skies are grey . . .

Perhaps it was the absence of words or the raspy sweetness of her humming, but when the alien heard Kate make this sound, it *scuttled* in its place. That's the only way she could describe the sound, like dog nails on a marble floor, a clicking, scratching sound, the sound of claws on metal. Then, she realized the Rossian wasn't making random noises. She stopped humming and listened. The pattern made her blood run cold.

Click.

Click.

Click Click Click Click Click Click Click Click

Jim's tap code, the atomic numbers for H_2O. If any doubts remained hiding in the recesses of Kate's subconscious mind regarding the truth of this creature, the familiar code that symbolized the discovery of alien life forms chased them away.

She dared not move. The Rossian tapped several more times before stopping. Kate wasn't sure given the hyper-sensitive state of her mind, but she thought it had made a noise, something guttural and ancient, lasting a fraction of a second. Her desire to find Mary remained at the forefront of her thoughts, but maybe the creature needed to establish her motives before helping out. First things first.

The eyes blinked again.

Kate curled her hand into a fist and with her knuckles, rapped the same code out on top of the pedestal. The taps against this hard surface sounded dull and muted compared to the high frequency clicks the creature made, but she mimicked the rhythm of the pattern as best she could, repeating it the same number of times (five or six?), then pausing.

More scuttling.

She sensed the alien's movement more than seeing it, faint wafts of grey and black shadows against the dark background, the eyes turning away, turning back. Then a harsh light flashed, catching her off-guard and causing her eyes to shut and her head to turn. After a moment, when she reopened them, the creature had moved closer. She instinctively pressed against the rounded wall behind the pedestal and drew in her legs, despite the pain ripping through her chest.

The creature stopped. It stood a couple meters away. Kate saw a much clearer image of it now. The Rossian appeared to be about a meter tall with a head and torso, and spindly, jointed legs, tapering down to points on the end.

Four limbs? Six?

The creature held an object close to its torso, then placed it on the floor and scrabbled back into the shadows where it grew silent again.

"Something for me, eh?"

Kate groaned as she stretched out her legs and wriggled toward the object, pausing frequently so as not to startle this skittish being. When she'd moved close enough, she reached out. It felt like a cup, tiny in her hand, and filled with warm liquid. She raised it to her nose and sniffed. It smelled of. . . lavender? A flower? It could very well be water, but just as easily something deadly.

Her parched throat ached for whatever this was, poison be damned, so Kate sipped the contents of the cup once, twice, then downed the remains in one gulp and waited.

THIRTY-FOUR

Atteberry

THEY FOUND SIX MORE DATA MEMORY TUBES scattered in the dust, all in dubious condition. Ishani retrieved a few other items too, pieces of equipment Atteberry would have missed, but held importance to her and Titanius.

They entered the ship through the supply airlock and, once inside the *Echo*, helped each other remove their helmets and gloves. Carter met them near the stores, and Ishani debriefed him on the salvage operation. They spoke in low whispers, but he caught the odd word from them, like "memory" and "disaster."

Carter suddenly beckoned him over. "Jim, I want you to work with Quigg and get these tubes analyzed right away." He didn't wait for Atteberry to reply; instead, he marched toward the bridge, barking more orders to Ishani and Dub along the way.

He stumbled after them in his moon boots. Carter yelled back at him, without missing a step. "For crissakes, lose the goddamn suit!"

Esther joined him and released the clasps on the side of his envirosuit, then unbuckled the boots and heaved them off.

"Thanks."

"Jim, keep your suit at the ready just in case. I'll join you guys in a few minutes."

He slipped into his flight shoes and jogged up to the bridge where Quigg and Jenson inspected the memory tubes. Neither looked pleased as they turned the cylinders over in their hands.

"How can I help?"

"Take these two," Quigg said, "and get 'em cleaned up in the workshop."

"That's beside the kitchen, right?"

The comms officer threw him an odd look. "Beside the galley, yeah. You'll find an air compressor in there. See all this here shit?" He pointed to the connection pins. Dust covered them completely. "You're gonna have to pressure blow the crap out of these. Every piece has to sparkle, understand?"

"Got it."

"Any problem, just holler at one of us."

Atteberry cradled the memory tubes and carried them off to the workshop. There was a small wooden bench and a standard set of tools: drill, saw, multiple screwdrivers, a couple of soldering guns, and other supplies like wire, strips of metal, PC boards. In the corner, he found the tabletop air compressor used in fine electronics. It sat beside an onboard 3-D printer.

He studied the switches and nozzle, flipped the machine on, and waited for the pressure to build. Esther popped in behind him. "Quigg's checking out the other tubes, but they don't look to be in any kind of usable shape."

"We'd better hope they can access these two, then."

"Yeah." She stood beside him at the bench, and inspected the cannisters under a magnification light. She paused, placed her hands down and sighed.

"Something on your mind?"

"I'm nervous about all this. I overheard the captain talking with Clayton. There's a stand-off out there between one of his ships and a foreign spy vessel, and it's creating all kinds of diplomatic problems."

Atteberry frowned. "That's the least of my concerns right now."

"I know, Jim, I understand, but the last thing anyone needs is an interplanetary skirmish. Tensions are already at the boiling point, and it won't take much to set one of these maverick captains off."

He moved the tubes aside. "What are you saying? That we may have to abandon the search for Kate and Mary?"

She hesitated before answering. "What I'm saying is, Carter's first priority is finding the Rossian ship and taking its tech, not rescuing your daughter." She returned her gaze to the bench. "It wouldn't surprise me if he takes off the minute he finds the alien technology, whether or not the women are there."

He worked his jaw, desperately hoping the anger that now seethed in his blood would dissipate. Esther rubbed his shoulder. "I'll do everything I can to stop him from abandoning the search if it comes to that, Jim. You know that, don't you?"

He felt the fear and rage displaced by a new sensation of comfort. "I do." The compressor pinged; it had reached the desired pressure. "You wanna help?"

She smiled and, after finding a couple pairs of safety goggles and handing a set to him, she secured the first tube on the bench.

Several minutes passed before they both were satisfied the connection points on the tubes would not get any cleaner. They each carried one back to the bridge. Jenson leaned over a tiny workspace to the left of the comms station while Quigg played with different controls and kept looking up at a small viewscreen.

The display showed nothing but white noise.

"Are y'all sure the data's intact, Jenz?"

"Affirmative. It's in there, but we simply don't have the right equipment to extract it."

"Okay, screw it. Let's try one of them there clean ones."

Jenson disconnected the damaged tube and set it aside. Esther handed her the one she carried. The moment Jenson hooked it up to the input cable, Quigg's display came to life. File after file scrolled down the viewscreen.

"Beautiful, ain't it Jenzie?"

"Affirmative."

Atteberry stepped forward. "How can you tell what's on it?"

"Give 'er a sec." Quigg tweaked one of his controls and the scrolling of filenames slowed to a crawl. "The directory's almost loaded, and then we'll check the dates for what kinda data is in there."

Atteberry peered around the bridge while they all waited for the memory header to load. Carter lingered on the other side in deep discussion with the captain. One of the main viewscreens overhead panned across the lunar horizon, capturing most of the lab ruins as it moved. Ishani and Dub had made their way aft.

"Well, that ain't a-gonna help us."

Atteberry turned to see Quigg and Jenson staring up at the header information. "What's wrong?"

"These are from a few months back. We're looking for something more recent."

343

Esther chimed in. "You may yet find this useful, though."

"I doubt it, Doc. All this info was sent to headquarters a while ago. See here?" He pointed to lines of code in the header. "It's been analyzed to hell and back." He looked at Atteberry. "Well, time's a-wastin'! Let's get that there other tube hooked up, yeah?"

"On it," Jenson said, and she disconnected the first one like a pro. Atteberry handed her the last cylinder that could help them, and she plugged in the suite of cables.

As with the previous tube, the files scrolled down on Quigg's viewscreen. The header information stopped in half the time.

"Well, lookee here, folks." Quigg pulled the filenames down the screen and slowly read off a few of the codes.

"What do those mean?" Atteberry asked.

Jenson and Quigg both grinned, and the co-pilot brushed her hair back and said, "Mr. Atteberry, it means we've found the last memory tube Kate Braddock worked on. It's not necessarily the last location they worked at, but this is the information that could tell us the area where they might have gone, and what we're up against."

Atteberry swallowed hard. "How soon will you know?"

"Minutes. We just need to find the most recent date of entry, download the geophysical data associated with it, and—"

A double-chime, signaling an incoming message from Titanius headquarters, cut Jenson off. Carter strode over to the comms panel and Captain Powell took his seat in the chair. Quigg checked his dash and said, "It's from Ed Mitchell. Do you wanna take it privately, Mr. Carter?"

"No, put it on the main screen."

"Aye, sir."

The Titanius logo flashed in front of them, followed by a slight delay. Mitchell faded in, surrounded by several workers in blue company uniforms and large banks of computers. Behind him, panels of viewscreens displayed various images of ships,

Luna, and strings of numerical data. Atteberry, along with the others, instinctively moved closer to Carter.

"*Echo* . . . New York. Come in."

Quigg nodded to the CEO. "Secure channel's open, sir."

He faced the viewscreen. "New York, this is *Echo*. Good to see you, Ed. What's the latest?"

"Uncertain, Clayton. We expected blow back from the international community the moment you left for Luna, and we got it in spades. I assume you're tracking the convoy of ships en route to your location?"

"Affirmative."

"You'd best prepare for another group, too. Security cruisers have been redeployed to intercept the *Echo* on your return. The Brazilians, Russians, Indians . . . all the major powers. Plus, we've got other resource conglomerates threatening to launch legal action and impose blockades along the mineral runs. Our own NDU government's knickers are all twisted over the diplomatic conflict, and they're pressuring us to come clean with our intentions."

"That's not entirely unexpected, Ed."

"True, but what worries me is the number of security cruisers heading your way at full burn, on top of what's already there."

Carter frowned and folded his arms across his chest. "How many are we talking about?"

"Intel shows a dozen cruisers have altered their courses. Half that group is en route to Luna; the others are on an intercept course with *Malevolent*. She's standing off with the *Nachtfalke*." Ed paused a moment, looked off-screen and nodded, then returned to face the viewscreen again. "How much longer will you be up there?"

Carter shrugged his shoulders, peered around the bridge at the crew, then met Atteberry's gaze. "As long as it takes to complete the mission. Now, is there anything else?"

"No, sir. We'll continue monitoring terran comms and keep you apprised of any changes. New York out."

Quigg closed the channel. They all waited for Carter to speak. He stroked his chin, lowered his head, then looked at Atteberry, Esther and Quigg. "Let's get that data analyzed, folks." Then, he turned to the captain. "Mr. Powell, as soon as Ishani's finished securing the salvaged equipment in the stores, make sure this bird is ready to fly on my mark."

"Aye, sir."

"Jenson, I want you with me at the nav station. We'll need various routes plotted and standing by to get us the hell out of here."

"On it, sir."

The crew sprang into action. Atteberry joined Esther and Quigg at the data screen showing all the files on the memory tube. They identified the last few entries Kate made and downloaded their contents into the *Echo*'s computers. Within seconds, the massive files had transferred successfully.

Esther had more experience in data analysis and planetary imaging than Quigg, so she took charge of converting the mountain of numbers into maps. The first image she resolved showed near-surface structures in the vicinity of the *Mare Marginis*. She also produced several others of the area, including radar and high-resolution tomographic scans.

"What exactly are we looking for, Es?" Atteberry toggled through the images.

"Anything that seems out of place, artificial, perhaps even a ship."

He flipped back to the radar image. "You mean like this?"

Esther peered up from the panel where she'd been filtering the data and stared at the viewscreen. A shadowy section of the terrain appeared.

"What do you make of it?"

She adjusted the filter parameters and the contrast between the target and the surrounding material improved. "See these things, Jim? Those are survey markers on each side of the anomaly. Kate must have felt there was something odd. Here, I'll improve the resolution." She refined the adjustments until the shadow stood out clearly.

Atteberry gaped at the object. Its shape and dimension suggested the thing was, first, artificial, and second, built for speed. He'd wondered what the Rossian vessel looked like, and figured it must have been a large, powerful craft—perhaps the size of one of Titanius's cruisers. To generate faster than light speeds would require massive amounts of energy, at least that's what conventional physics taught him. The dimensions of this compact ship confused his sense of logic.

Esther touched his arm. "This is what Kate found . . . what she didn't want others to know. It's the Ross 128 ship, Jim. I'll bet my life on it."

Quigg locked the image in on the bridge's main screen. "Captain? We found it!"

Carter jumped from the nav station toward the viewscreen and ran his fingers along the ship's perimeter on the viewer. "Is it underground?"

"It is, Clayton," Esther said. "A meter or two below the surface."

"Where is she?"

"*Mare Marginis*. Quigg has the precise coordinates."

"I'm sending them your way, Jenzie."

Carter returned to navigation, followed by Esther and Atteberry.

Jenson plotted the coordinates into the ship's drive computer. "The area is about 600 kilometers from here, Mr. Carter. We can be there in less than ten minutes."

Carter smiled and slammed a fist into an open palm. "First class work! Captain Powell, you have the course laid in for the *Mare Marginis*?"

"Aye, sir."

"Stores secured?"

Powell checked his dashboard. "They are, sir."

"Then get us the hell out of here!"

Carter looked straight at Atteberry and nodded. Then he winked at Esther. She lowered her head, averting her gaze.

THIRTY-FIVE

Kate

THE WARM LIQUID TASTED SWEET AND FAMILIAR compared to the re-cycled habitat swill she'd been drinking at the Titanius lab for the past five years, and she recognized exactly what it was: water.

Kate returned the cup to the floor, and tapped out the H_2O code with her knuckles, then waited silently in the thick dark-ness. Within a minute, the alien tapped the 1—1—8 signal back to her. She smiled. "Thank you." Kate slid back to the pedestal and leaned against it, keeping the curious creature with the wide golden eyes in her sight at all times. The pain from her injuries intensified again, and Mary's disappearance screamed in every thought.

"I'm afraid . . . I have nothing . . . to give you, but can you tell me where . . . where my friend Mary is?"

She struggled to breathe—the misery and swelling in her ribs constricting her lungs—and closed her eyes. The warmth of the water coursed through her now and, perhaps because she was so thirsty and beaten up, she felt it flow throughout her body, into her torso and arms, down her legs, pooling in the crevices of her nerve endings. It had a soothing quality, and Kate finally relaxed again.

"I wish you . . . you understood my language. I must find Mary . . . the other one like me. Is she here, or . . . still outside?" She paused, hoping for some movement from the Rossian. None came.

This creature isn't in any rush to act . . . and I'm in no shape to force the issue. Perhaps that's its way. If it's already been hiding here . . . a while . . . it may not understand my impatience.

She hummed the *tune* again, more to comfort herself than any-thing else, and moved her good hand up to her chest, slipping it under her Kevlar skin.

You are my sunshine . . .

Her flesh was clammy as she passed her fingertips over the scar field. She hated herself for doing this, for being so weak, so incredibly ugly, but couldn't stop. Her thumbnail traced one of the fresher cuts that had crusted over but easily opened under her pressure.

. . . my only sunshine . . .

With each successive pass, she dug the nail deeper into her pain, and winced with relief.

. . . you make me happy . . .

After several minutes of scraping, Kate pulled her hand out and licked the tips of her fingers. She patted her top down on her chest and closed her eyes, savoring the sensation of her moist, sticky shirt on skin. The inevitable wave of shame broke over her, but no matter: the comfort allowed her to breathe easier, to process the encounter with an alien life form, to assuage the fear over Mary's whereabouts.

When she peered around a moment later, the creature had inched nearer and froze when she made eye contact.

"Hey, it's all right if you come closer. I can't move . . . I . . . my wrist, you see?" She pointed to the broken arm, now swollen to the size of her calf. The alien clicked its limbs on the floor and approached another pace, then stopped.

. . . the other night dear . . .

. . . as I lay sleeping . .

It took a step closer. She quit humming and whispered, "I won't bite . . ." A ferocious cough seized her and she immediately groaned as fresh pain exploded in her chest. The alien scuttled away into the shadows and blinked.

"Yeah, I've lived in fear the same way . . . most of . . . my life, too." She clenched her teeth, fighting the urge to scream. "God, I need help. Mary!"

Minutes passed before the Rossian clicked back toward her, inching even closer, and froze. Kate again saw its general form. Its height reminded her of a child about seven or eight years old, and she smiled and snorted at her own preconceptions regarding extra-terrestrial life. This child-sized creature was no bug-eyed behemoth: just the opposite. Its small stature and thin limbs gave it an air of fragility.

"I'm going to . . . shift my position here, little one. No need to freak out . . . okay?"

The alien stood perfectly still.

"So . . . here I go." Kate pulled herself over on her side and wriggled into a new spot against the pedestal. As she did so, she kept an eye on the creature, anticipating it would dance back into the deeper shadows. Instead, it remained fixed in place in front of her.

"Good . . . that's better. So maybe we're not as frightened of each other." She reached out a hand, palm up, as if to say *I have no weapon; this is all I am.* "Can you . . . tell me where Mary is? Hm? I've got to know." It moved again, scratching up to within a meter.

Despite the gloomy surroundings, the alien's shape grew more defined as the distance between them diminished. She heard it breathing—much slower and longer than a human—and noticed a faint, musty odor coming off it. Nothing offensive; rather, an animal scent, like a wet dog. Its head had a face of sorts, though unrecognizable as that of a person, and was elongated front to back. The darkness prevented her from discerning the details of the torso, but its limbs reminded her of crustacean legs: jointed, hard, and tapering to knobby points at the end. In fact, this creature appeared more crablike than anything else, except possessing a vertical stance instead of a squat one.

The thing scrabbled closer again and this time, the golden eyes looked up, its gaze darting across her face, her chest, over to her injured arm, and back to her chest again.

"Pretty ugly, eh?" She kept her palm out, and whispered even softer now, as if sharing a secret. "Tell you what . . . little one . . . if you can find me my suit, or . . . or bring me a magic pain-killer, I'll be . . . your friend for life." She winced again and groaned. "I wish you . . . understood me."

The alien's breathing rate suddenly increased, and she thought it opened a mouth. A deep, guttural purr-like sound emerged from its body, slow and steady, similar to the noise animals made after eating.

Kate gulped and wondered what she'd gotten herself into now, but realized the only way to find Mary and get off this ship was to befriend this creature. She smiled shyly, pointed at her chest, and said, "*I am Kate* . . . Kate." Then she waved a finger at the alien and raised her hand, palm up, as if asking a question.

The raspy moan came again, lasting several seconds, as the golden eyes blinked in rapid succession.

"Kate . . ." she said, pointing to herself again.

The next sound it uttered was like a person speaking, except slowed down so much it was unintelligible. Kate studied it for any kind of pattern, something she could mimic, perhaps, but the *words* sounded completely random. She shook her head and smiled.

The creature tried again. This time, it had made an adjustment. The vocal frequency increased and the sound it produced now reminded her of an Australian didgeridoo. Whatever message the alien conveyed, it remained a mystery, but Kate's belief that the alien meant her no harm solidified.

She groaned and said, "This is good. Will you tell me where . . . where my friend Mary is?"

The Rossian took another step closer. It stood within a breath of her legs. She dared not move.

"Okay . . . this is getting to me . . . for real now." She pressed her back against the pedestal in an unsuccessful bid to melt into the background.

When the alien *spoke* again, the frequency of its sounds fell in the range of a normal human voice. She thought it must have adapted the way it communicates so she could hear, and that possibly this thing had been trying to speak with her all along. The noises also contained patterns, as if the creature formed proper words now, but they remained unrecognizable.

She mimicked the long, drawn out utterances of the alien, and said, "I . . . am . . . Kate . . ."

The alien clacked on the floor and blinked rapidly. It increased the speed of sounds it made, cycling through several frequency ranges. Then, in a soft voice identical to Kate's pitch, the creature spoke these words: *"I . . . am . . . Kate . . ."*

Kate held her breath. She stared in disbelief, unsure whether to vomit or cry, her body incapable of managing, of categorizing the rising swarm of emotions. She tried swallowing, but her throat refused to function. Before she processed the words, the creature continued. "I . . . am . . . Kate . . . mm . . . is . . . broken . . ."

Her paralysis was complete, mouth agape, trying desperately to speak, to find a scream.

The creature sidled up next to her face, its warm breath on her cheek. Then it raised two of its knobby limbs and leaned in toward her chest.

THIRTY-SIX

Esther

"TAKE US WITHIN 50 METERS OF THE TARGET, JOHN."

"Aye, sir."

Captain Powell circled over the coordinates of the alien ship. Given the lack of sunlight on the eastern limb, the *Echo* bathed the area with a combination of landing and search lights, giving birth to eerie, yawning shadows across the moonscape. Evidence of Kate and Mary's work was everywhere. Several pieces of equipment had been scattered about, and they had excavated part of the Rossian vessel, as shown by a small patch of black contrasting with the surrounding brownish-grey. Esther stood in awe, fighting hard to keep her emotions quelled and to focus on the task at hand: find Kate and Mary, make first contact, and prevent Carter from starting a goddamn war.

"There, sir, by that outcrop, three o'clock!" Jenson spotted it—a LunaScoota nestled in the dust.

Atteberry pointed at the viewscreen. "Just the one? I thought there were two." Silence. "Anyone see the other?" Esther put her hand on his arm and squeezed it.

"Setting her down over there, port-side, sir." The Captain targeted a flat, open area. The viewer showed a yellow landing grid superimposed on the surface, and within moments, the *Echo* landed, kicking up dust from its thrusters.

Atteberry broke from Esther's hand and raced toward the back of the ship.

"Jim?"

"Mr. Atteberry!" Carter stared after him, hands on hips. "Where do you think you're going?"

Atteberry stopped near the flight seats and turned around. "I'm getting my suit on. I'm going out to find my daughter!"

"You'll do no such thing unless I permit it. Get back here . . . now!"

He hesitated, looked at Esther, then aft where the airlock was.

"Don't be foolish, Jim."

His shoulders slumped, and he lowered his head, seething as he returned to the bridge.

Esther met him half-way. "Let the crew handle this. If Mary's inside that thing, we can only assume she's okay. Reason it through." She studied his eyes. Fear covered his face and the corners of his mouth twitched as he struggled to keep from exploding, and how he stood there, vulnerable, helpless, overwhelmed her with a deep need to hold him and tell him everything's going to be fine. Instead, she glanced down and patted the small of his back.

Carter surveyed the area, ordering Jenson to zoom in here and there. Nothing suggested any activity, but they pieced together what must have happened. Esther realized one, or both had searched for an entrance into the ship. Multiple sets of footprints covered the site, but it was impossible to tell when they were made. She also recognized the same crustal ruptures here as she'd seen at the destroyed lab site.

"Mr. Jenson, could you do a 360 scan?" Esther followed the upheavals.

Carter, stroking his chin, turned from the main viewscreen. "What is it, Doctor?"

To hide it from him or the crew any longer made no sense. "See those breaches, Clayton? They head west from here."

"What about them? They look like meteorite impacts."

"I saw the same ruptures at the lab site."

Jenson panned the camera around the area, applying night filters to the images so the structures were more visible.

Esther continued. "I doubt they're natural. Luna's basically inert, and if meteorites did cause these, where are the craters? They'd have to be massive to create this kind of upheaval."

Carter turned to face her and narrowed his eyes. "What are you saying? Come, out with it."

"Well, it's only a theory at this stage, and I don't want to jump to conclusions—"

"Dammit, Esther, tell me!"

The hairs on her neck bristled. She hesitated a moment, then said matter-of-factly, "I believe this ship caused those ruptures by emitting a . . . a kind of shock wave that targeted the lab intentionally, propagating over the surface. That's what destroyed it."

"A sonic weapon?"

Esther remained silent.

"Son of a bitch."

Carter paced around the bridge. She glanced over at Atteberry, but he was lost in his own thoughts.

"Very well. Ishani . . . Dub, suit up. Take the excavator and clean the rest of the crap off that ship. Jenson?"

"Sir?"

"Target all forward weapons on that thing and plot an escape course in case we have to bail."

"Aye, sir."

Captain Powell stood up. "Clayton, we're awfully close to a firefight with a vessel we know nothing about. Perhaps we should run diagnostic scans of that ship first . . . learn as much as we can about it."

Atteberry interrupted him. "Don't forget there may be lives in there, too. We have to rescue them, not blow them up!"

"Stand down, Mr. Atteberry."

"The hell I'll stand down!" He followed Ishani and Dub off the bridge.

"Atteberry!"

Esther raised her hand. She spoke in a low voice so only he could hear. "Let me talk to him, Clayton, but please, listen to the captain. If this ship's capable of destroying a lab 600 kilometers away with a seriously tight shock wave, we may be in over our heads. Let's gather some basic data first before doing anything."

Carter fumed at her, but he was no idiot. He thought a moment, then relaxed. "All right. You rein in the professor and we'll scan that thing. But to be clear, I won't hesitate to do everything I can to protect the *Echo*."

"I understand. Thank you."

Esther marched down the ship's fuselage, rolling her eyes. She found Atteberry struggling with clasps on the envirosuit.

He threw her a hopeless look, and slumped on the prep bench next to Ishani, who had already suited up and was running the safety checklist with Dub. "I feel so useless."

She sat beside him and stared at the bulkhead across the aisle. "We're almost there, Jim. Understand, everyone's nervous, on edge. Not just because of this unknown ship out there or finding Kate and Mary, but also because of the situation above us."

He looked at her, confused.

"We haven't seen this many ships converge on the Earth-Moon system for decades. The trip home, no matter what happens here, could get messy."

He shook his head. "I just want to hold my daughter again and see Kate. I don't care about anything else, and I sure as hell don't give a rat's ass about that bossy prick you seem to like."

Esther sighed and remembered what she found so frustrating about this man . . . how single-minded and selfish he could be. She toughened her tone. "Okay, then stay out of the way and let the crew handle this. You're not helping when you go off half-cocked like an immature teenager."

When he turned to face her, a cold fire burned in his eyes. He said nothing; only glared at her.

"Relax, Jim. Between me and Captain Powell, we'll make sure Carter fully understands the significance of his actions. I've been dealing with him a lot longer than you, remember."

"Okay." He said the word, but she doubted he agreed.

"Good." She stood up. "Let's return to the bridge and learn more about this ship."

They strode off toward the bow, Esther leading the way. She turned around to throw him a reassuring smile and noticed out of the corner of her eye Ishani and Dub in the background, suited up, ready to enter the airlock, arming themselves with laser rifles.

THIRTY-SEVEN

Kate

SHE COULD NOT MOVE.

All she managed to do was squeeze her eyes shut and wait for this creature to strike. She heard it clacking around, its rapid breathing, and caught the odd, faint smell it gave off. When it touched her torso, she turned her head away, recoiling, and every muscle in her body tightened in anticipation of more pain. Instead, warmth pulsated through her from two pressure points, one on the side of her chest, and the other near the bottom of her rib cage.

Kate slowly opened her eyes, first one, then the other. Soft blue light glowed from the tips of the alien's limbs touching her, illuminating its body, reflecting off its smooth face—the same hue she'd seen in the sky that brought her and Mary here. After several seconds, it released her and gently pulled away, grunted, and scrabbled off into the shadows. The blue disappeared.

She trembled with a strange assortment of terror and comfort. The warmth from the creature's touch continued to work through her, swirling around her chest and arms, but also covering her entire body. Kate gasped and struggled to push herself up on the pedestal.

The stabbing in her wrist subsided first and within a few minutes, had dissipated completely. Her ribs took a moment longer, but the dull pain that had racked her side melted away, leaving her speechless and, for the first time since the accident, capable of drawing a full breath.

The creature continued staring at her from the black shadows across the void, its amber eyes glowing steadily, blinking sporadically. Kate watched it now with renewed curiosity. She tested her pain-free wrist, turning it slowly from side to side, astonished how the swelling drained from the area so quickly. Then she brushed her rib cage, applying pressure to the bones and muscles, and never winced.

"What did you do?"

The alien voice floated out from the dark shadows. "*I am Kate* is broken . . . little one Keechik helps . . ."

Kate wiped cold sweat from her brow and ran her fingers over her chest. Warmth continued to radiate from her in a soothing way. "Is . . . is that your name? *Keechik*?"

"The little one Keechik."

"You understand me now."

She heard the creature shifting in the dark, grunting. "The little one Keechik watch . . . mm . . . study all the *I am Kate* beings . . . many of you . . . learn units . . . sounds . . . mm. . ."

Kate felt her ribs and chest again where the creature's limbs touched her, then stroked her healed wrist and forearm.

This is a miracle.

"Keechik, do you know where my friend is? She is taller than me, with longer hair." Kate brushed her hand over her head. "Mary was with me outside, on the surface." The eyes blinked.

"The *friend Mary* is here, *I am Kate.* Safe."

Thank God.

"Where is she? I have to see her."

The creature did not answer. Instead, it scuttled around in the shadows, making various guttural noises. Finally, Keechik's voice ruptured out of the dark. "*Friend Mary* . . . must remain . . . alone now."

Kate leaned forward from her sitting position on the pedestal, elbows on her legs, her head hanging down. If the creature spoke the truth that Mary was safe why couldn't she see her? She sighed with frustration, then sat up straight and tried a different line of questioning.

"How many of you are in this ship?

"The one Keechik is . . . confused, *I am Kate.*"

She considered another way to ask. "Keechik is alone here? Or are there others?"

Clacking sounds and grunts floated out from the shadows on the other side of the void, followed by an eerie, woeful cry like that of the mourning doves she remembered from the Spacer Training Center.

"Keechik?"

The howl-song continued for several minutes, evoking in her deep fear and sadness. Not the dread associated with danger though. Something deeper, ancient, and timeless.

When the moaning finally ceased, Kate remained silent, listening to the low-level thrum of the vessel, and watching the wide golden eyes.

"Only little one . . . Keechik . . . remains. No more."

Kate relaxed her shoulders and her entire body softened. She whispered, "What about your home? Any others there?"

"No, *I am Kate* . . . only little one Keechik remains."

Could this shy creature be the last of its kind?

"The little one Keechik is . . . mm . . . too alone."

A new flood of warmth washed over her. This Rossian had not come to invade the Earth; it came because it was lonely. That H_2O code wasn't just about finding water. Keechik searched for other sentient life forms, capable of contact and communication. Perhaps most important, someone to keep this creature company.

"How long have you been here, on Luna?"

"Mm . . . over four of your Earth's solar rotations, little one arrives. Followed your signal here. Stopped on . . . on this Luna."

"Why did you bury your ship in moon dust? My home, the Earth, has lots of people who would love to meet you. Why not—"

The creature scuttled about wildly in the dark, its eyes widening and blinking rapidly. "No, no, no, *I am Kate*, no, no . . . too much . . . too much."

She brought her hand to her chest and rubbed it. Something had changed there, too. Slipping her fingers under her shirt, she manually inspected herself. The cuts and scars had gone. The darkness prevented her from seeing anything other than dim shapes, but her fingertips didn't lie.

"You . . . you healed my cuts too?"

"*I am Kate* was broken . . . little one Keechik helps."

"Keechik," she said, "can you make it lighter in here? I'm blind here in the dark."

The creature moved about and, in a moment, the light in the void increased . . . nothing close to daylight, but Kate now saw the surrounding room, the low, smooth ceiling, various consoles—like the computer stations she knew from the lab—across from her where Keechik huddled, and a control station with small holes throughout.

Perhaps that's how this thing runs the ship, by placing its limbs in these slots.

The creature also appeared in its complete form for the first time. Six spindly legs used for motion and, presumably, running the vessel. A thin, small torso, and a horizontally elongated head. The amber eyes dominated its face, but it had a small mouth. There were no discernible ears or a nose . . . no hair of any kind, no uniform.

Keechik shifted. "Others, like *I am Kate*, come now . . . many arriving."

"I don't understand."

"Come . . . and see . . ."

Keechik turned toward a console and inserted a pair of its limbs into different holes. Images flickered on the ship's wall showing the *Echo* on Luna's surface and two figures rolling an excavator off the supply portal.

Kate stood, testing her balance. Her head almost touched the ceiling. She now had a way home and smiled with disbelief. Then, something odd occurred in her . . . a different warmth pulsing inside her. She had to sit down.

No!

She brought her hand to her chest again and gasped.

No, no, no . . .

She stared at Keechik as confusion and horror enveloped her. "What did you do to me?" She brushed her hand over the two growing lumps of flesh protruding from her chest.

"*I am Kate* was broken."

Mary

HER FIRST THOUGHT WHEN SHE REGAINED consciousness was of being strapped into the flight seat of the shuttle that transported her to Luna when she began her internship with Titanius. Then, as the veil of confusion lifted, Mary realized she was somewhere else, immobilized, and lying supine in almost pitch darkness. Her head was under pressure, restrained, warm. Her eyes slowly adjusted to her surroundings, and the only logical explanation was that she'd been rescued and brought into the alien ship.

Where's Kate? Where am I? Why am I pinned down on this . . . platform?

Her fingers moved, but her arms were buckled down beside her, as were her legs. A restraint also held her chest and she couldn't move her head. The envirosuit had disappeared, but she didn't need it in this oxygen-rich, pressurized atmosphere.

"Hello?"

Her own voice sounded foreign to her, and deadened immediately in the black. Mary looked around but saw nothing. Her dad used to tell her, when she struggled with chemistry and the concept of atomic particles, that *just because we can't see something, doesn't make it any less real.* Perhaps her helmet had been removed to prevent her from scanning this area in different EM ranges and discovering . . . *what?* That she's imprisoned on an alien ship?

She shouted louder this time. "Hello!"

In the stillness of this place, Mary sensed two key things. First, something pinched into her skull, like the teeth of a comb, but all over her head. Nothing had penetrated the skin, but the pressure points were uncomfortable. Second, a faint sound, a hum of machinery, a power source *out there.*

"Kate?"

Every nerve ending in her scalp fired and danced. Instinctively, Mary lay perfectly still, her breathing becoming erratic and short. She waited for more to happen.

"Kate..."

The tips of those pressure points on her skull grew warmer and suddenly, a blue light—*that* blue light—shone above. Something happened to her mind... *in* her mind. Images, sensations, impressions overloaded her thoughts, invading her own memories like a virus, supplanting them with—

Oh shit!

—foreign experiences that didn't belong to her. At least, she hadn't thought they were her recollections, but now they were as real as everything that had taken place over the past few months, from working with Kate on surveys, to screaming over the moonscape, to seeing her home, the Earth, from her deathbed on the ship's hull.

Except this time, she understood. Mary had gained access to the alien's thoughts, its history, journeys, experiences. They overwhelmed her with a flood of information. Her neurons couldn't keep up.

Horrific images of a peaceful race being wiped out by a mysterious disease, ripped her heart in two.

Stop it...

The loneliness of a solitary survivor, marooned in space, homeless, with no one for company.

No... no more...

The curiosity and hope with the discovery of these carbon and water bi-pedal creatures, studying them from a safe distance, afraid of being seen, yet desperately wanting to be around them but not knowing how. Guilt over destroying their habitat by accident, misunderstanding how fragile they were. Learning cultures, languages, conflict, space travel. Overcoming intense fear to guide them to the ship, bring them inside when they posed no threat.

I can't . . . please . . .

Unlocked secrets of the universe, of new scientific discoveries, energy, space-time, the origin of life, an underlying, overshadowing creative force giving birth to it all.

I . . . no, I . . .

Mary's mind no longer functioned as it once had. She tried parsing the incoming alien information as it rushed at her—*into* her—at breakneck speed, but her brain refused to absorb so much in so little time. She shivered involuntarily, incapable of processing anything, feeling wave after wave of intense suffering and isolation swamp her.

Somewhere, her own experiences had been washed away. There were diluted glimpses of whatever remained, images of her dad, of Kate; bits and pieces from the last twenty-four hours. In her mind, she reached for them, desperately grabbing at any remnants she could find, but her personal memories kept drifting further and further out of reach, disappearing in the crush of overwhelming alien history.

In a final attempt to stop what was happening to her, Mary opened her mouth wide to scream, but nothing came out. She convulsed sporadically on the flat surface, held securely by restraints, and watched the images in her mind drain into complete black.

THIRTY-EIGHT

Katie

SO, IT'S COME TO THIS.

Katie stared at her bare chest in the bathroom mirror while he waited in the other room. The cutting field didn't seem that bad, she rationalized, and perhaps in the dark he would mistake them for surgical scars. Then again, chances are he'd see that as a bonus, an extra thrill. Anti-rad pills had cleared up most of the cancerous blooms that dotted her torso, so no issues there. Tracy's voice kept echoing in her mind, don't take it all so seriously, Katie, but she couldn't help it: she was built this way.

She buttoned up her blouse again, confirmed the credit transfer had taken place on her indie-comm, and stared in the mirror. Dark circles were permanently etched under her eyes now, and her jawline had become more pronounced and angular, more like that of a man. The way she chopped at her short hair, leaving it asymmetrical and butchered, gave her a feral look, except for one thing: the down-turned mouth exuded a defiant sadness that made her wonder what the hell happened?

Nineteen years old. There were no prizes, no rewards, nothing intangible either. Tracy would say, "You remove your clothes, then his or hers, and embrace them. Some don't even want you to do that—they prefer watching. Others go for a bit more, you know, contact. That's your call. I charge extra for that."

"Trace, what if I can't . . . pretend?"

"Hey, they're paying so they can brag about seducing a Spacer. They get off on it. Just go along, play it coy. Oh, and it wouldn't hurt to smile once or twice."

In the mirror, Katie practiced smiling, struck different poses. She frowned and shook her head.

Who are you trying to fool?

The flat was a one-room affair that smelled of cabbage, as did the man. He couldn't have been much older than her, mid-20s perhaps, and looked shifty and nervous. He sat on a loveseat watching as she drifted in, smiled nervously, and undid her buttons.

"You don't have to do that," he said in a soft, melodic voice.

Katie stopped, fingers trembling. "I thought . . . ? Isn't this what you wanted?"

"No. Well, not now anyway."

She narrowed her eyes. "Are you screwing with me?"

"No."

"So what am I doing here?" She reached for the indie-comm in her back pocket. "I'll refund your money, okay?"

"Carrie, I—"

"It's Katie. My name's Katie, for crissake."

The man stood up and approached her. He towered above her head, with well-trimmed hair, and a disarming, pleasant face. She caught the glint in his eyes from ocular implants, the kind that still cost a fortune.

"Katie, do you ever get lonely?"

She squirmed and continued looking at him with deep suspicion. "What are you doing?"

"I'm asking a question. I've paid for your time, and I'm asking a question."

She had to think about this, not about his query—being miserable was evident—but about how much to disclose. She still wasn't convinced that all he wanted was to chat. That's not how the script went, but he had seemed genuine when he approached her at the coffee shop, unlike any of the other followers, and didn't push. She exhaled, feigning boredom, and said in a clinical voice, "All right, to be honest, I'm pretty much lonely all the time. I have no real friends . . . tried that once, and they either died or disappeared." She thought of young Martin dangling from the window.

"So, being alone is your choice?"

She averted her gaze and scanned the room. Nobody asked her these questions before, or cared to probe into her feelings. But there was something about the fellow that put her at ease. Perhaps it was a ruse. He may even be one of those Spacer murderers who drift around from time to time, but her instincts wouldn't buy that.

Out of habit, Katie rubbed her chest up and down with her fingertips. "No, this was not a choice. One minute I'm taking the Aptitudes, the next, getting butchered. Me and all the others."

"Come, sit down."

She joined him on the loveseat, her thigh brushing against his. "Why do you stick with the Program?"

"Why? It's all I know. I don't think I could leave now. At least when I'm working, I'm by myself and don't have to deal with ass-hole followers and. . . sorry."

"That's okay."

"At some point they'll turf me I suppose, and then I'll have to figure out what to do."

He folded his hands together in his lap. "Have you ever been in love, Katie?"

She burst out laughing in a nervous, defensive way, and ran her fingers through her cropped hair. "Me? You've got to be kid-ding."

He looked straight into her eyes.

"Not kidding, eh? Well you are an odd duck. Let me guess: graduate student? Doing research?"

He smiled sheepishly. "Busted."

"Right, okay, maybe I should just be going." She stood and straightened her blouse.

"If that's what you want, but answer one more thing before you go."

"What is it?"

He rose up and faced her, staring at her chest and the entrails of cutting scars that peeked out around the Vee. "Those . . . do you cut?"

Katie looked away and pursed her lips. Her cheeks flushed with shame. When she spoke, the words came out in whispers. "Yes, I do. I can't help it, can't stop."

"May I see?"

"No."

"Please, Katie. I'm not here to judge."

She fought back the lump gripping her throat and dropped her arms. They were abnormally thin and bony compared to his.

"Have a look, then."

The man slowly undid the buttons on her blouse and pushed the panels aside. Katie's eyes welled up, but she vowed not to let him see one tear drop, and choked them back.

"Katie, I . . ."

"There's nothing there if you want to touch. I mean, it's your time."

He traced various scars across her chest and upper abdomen with his middle finger. She'd seldom allowed anyone to see these, let alone feel them, and after a moment of tracing, she inhaled through her teeth at this new sensation, and closed her eyes.

The man stopped and buttoned her up again, then studied her with fear and sympathy on his face.

"Like I said. I can't stop. Besides," she added, tucking in her blouse, "it's all I know. I couldn't wear those other replacement tops and pretend to be a normie. These scars, my shit . . . these are me." She turned to leave and whispered, "I can never be more than this . . . than what I am."

She left him, mouth agape, and disappeared into the warm night.

THIRTY-NINE

Atteberry

ATTEBERRY FIDGETED BESIDE QUIGG ON THE BRIDGE, desperate to be out there looking for Mary instead of watching Ishani and Dub haul the massive excavator across the Moon's surface toward the alien ship's hull. Esther huddled with co-pilot Jenson at the nav station, conducting high-level scans of the area and reviewing geophysical data they found in the memory tube. She was right: whatever fate had befallen his girl and Kate, they needed to learn more about this craft and its inhabitants. Still, it tore away at him.

Carter, meanwhile, fumed beside Captain Powell in front of the main viewscreen. "It's not that big a vessel, John. We can have the damn thing unearthed in a matter of minutes."

"True, but we're dealing with a completely unknown entity. Think about it. For the first time in Earth's history we know there are other sentient creatures out here. Let's take a minute or two like Dr. Tyrone says, learn as much as possible about them and establish contact. Perhaps even get inside that ship."

Carter worked his jaw and sighed, resignation spreading over his face. "Very well." He turned to the comms station and scowled. "What have you two found?"

Atteberry let Quigg do the talking. "No apparent EM signatures at all, no heat or radiation I can detect. She's like no boat we've encountered before, sir."

"Have you determined the hull's composition?"

"Not completely. It appears to be an aluminum-titanium composite, but there's some other compound in there as well that don't register in our info systems."

Carter paced again and frowned. "So how the hell do we communicate with them? Walk up to the front door and knock?"

Atteberry swallowed hard, and when no one else answered, said, "Actually, Mr. Carter, that's exactly what we do."

He stared at him in disbelief. "What are you talking about?"

"Well, years ago when I first heard the Rossians, they used a tap code based on the atomic numbers of chemical elements."

"Yes, yes, the whole water story. What of it?"

Atteberry ran his palm over his forehead. "It's a long shot, maybe, but why not do it again? Have one of them tap it out on the hull." He pointed to Ishani and Dub wrestling with the excavator. "Or let me try."

Carter glanced at Esther, who now stood watching the conversation while Jenson continued scanning the area. She said, "It's worth considering. Look, Kate and Mary are here, right? That scooter didn't fly itself. In the absence of any evidence to the contrary, they must be inside that ship."

"I'm not sure I buy that."

"Regardless," Esther added, in measured tones, "that tap code is the only thing we have that worked."

Atteberry swallowed hard. He wasn't about to allow this opportunity to rescue Mary pass him by. "Let me help. I know the rhythm, the pattern. I can reproduce the signal they sent."

Before Carter could respond, the *Echo* was being hailed. Quigg opened the channel, listened, then turned to Captain Powell. "Urgent message from the *Malevolent*, Skip."

Powell glanced at Carter. "Put it through."

Captain Russo appeared on the main viewscreen, standing beside one of her officers.

Powell motioned to Jenson to return to her position in the co-pilot seat. "Captain Russo? *Echo* here. What's the situation?"

"It's heating up, John. The *Volmar* fired a warning shot over us moments ago. We're holding steady with the *Nachtfalke*, but the situation's tense." She approached her own comms screen. "How much more time do you need?"

"Laura, Clayton here. Are you in immediate danger now?"

"No, sir. We can hold our own in a firefight with *Volmar* if it comes to that, but sensors show there are more cruisers on the way. We'll be pinned down shortly and we're woefully outgunned, so I have to know how far to take this standoff."

Captain Powell and the rest of the crew turned to face Carter. Atteberry felt the tension on the bridge, figuring their fearless leader talked big, but did he truly desire open conflict?

Esther was the first to speak up. "Clayton, this isn't what you want. Think it through."

He glared at her. When Esther glanced Atteberry's way, her look reminded him of the fear they both lived years ago at Mount Sutro when Marshall Whitt wanted them dead. He couldn't let this situation impede Mary's rescue. "Tell that ship to stand down, Carter!"

Captain Powell spoke with calm and conviction in his voice. "Mind your place, Mr. Atteberry." Then, turning his attention to the *Malevolent*, he said, "Laura, what's the status of your weapons systems?"

"All online and fully operational."

"Defenses?"

"Full hardshields available, but we're keeping them down for the moment. Don't want to needlessly provoke the Prussians."

Powell maintained that smooth, calm tone. "Good. Keep sending a message to the *Volmar* and all others that you're simply protecting the Titanius mission on Luna and have no desire to engage. Our salvage operation is complete here, but we're still looking for the missing techs. Not sure when we'll be finished."

Captain Russo smiled curtly. "Understood . . . thanks John. *Mal-evolent* out."

"Yes, thank you, Captain." Carter regained his voice and posture. Atteberry eyed him with deep suspicion, wondering how much longer Powell would allow him to call the shots. In the growing silence, he addressed the captain. "Sir, if I may, I'd like to join the others on the surface and attempt communicating with the alien ship."

Powell raised his eyebrows and glanced at Carter. His expression remained stoic and defiant. The captain turned to Esther. "Dr. Tyrone, please help Mr. Atteberry get suited up."

"Will do."

He stared hard at Atteberry. "I want you to stay in contact with the *Echo* at all times, do you understand?"

"Yes, of course."

"Don't give me the 'of course' business. Lives are at stake here beyond those of your daughter and friend. This is a damned harsh environment, got it?"

Atteberry straightened up. "Yes, Captain."

"If the shit blows and I call you in, immediately drop whatever you're doing and return to the ship. If you hesitate at all, for any reason, I will leave you behind to protect this ship and crew. Understand?"

He pulled himself away from the comms station. "Yes, Captain."

Esther piped up. "Do you want me to accompany him?"

"No. I need your analytical skills here, Doctor."

She pursed her lips and frowned, unable to hide her disappointment. Then, she nudged Atteberry on the shoulder. "Come on, let's go." As they marched to the prep area, he glanced back at the bridge. Carter, arms folded across his chest, watched them leave.

FORTY

Kate

NOTHING REMAINED IN HER STOMACH—NOT THAT there was much to begin with—but Kate continued to wretch, leaving her exhausted and kneeling beside the pedestal. When the heaving mercifully stopped, she spat, dragged the sleeve of her skin across her mouth, and palmed her eyes. Then she hauled herself up and slumped on the dais, staring in front of her in a daze, feeling the stretch of breasts forming on her chest.

After several minutes of silence, save the faint, low-level hum of the ship, Kate peered up and found the creature frozen beside a console. "What did you do to me?" Her voice sounded raw and unnatural.

Keechik raised and lowered its limbs slowly, groaned that familiar guttural sound, and mimicked Kate's strained voice. "*I am Kate . . . is broken . . . one Keechik helps . . . no more broken now.*"

She closed her eyes, at once frightened by the apparent power this being wielded—unlike any molecular manipulation she had ever encountered—and overwhelmed with a heavy and final sense of a full-system ego shut down.

But I am not Kate anymore, you damn thing.

"*I am Kate* is . . . whole now . . . not broken."

She couldn't bear to look at or touch herself *there*. Instead, she drew on her mental Spacer training and forced her mind to concentrate on finding Mary and getting to the *Echo*, no matter what. Still, the screaming in her brain wouldn't quit, and poked through the veneer of self-control, driving her to shout, "Where's my friend, damn you!"

The Rossian scuttled into a dark corner, pushing itself against the smooth wall underneath the projection of the Moon's surface where a third figure had now joined the other two by the excavator.

"The *friend Mary* . . . is safe and . . . helping little one Keechik . . . mm . . . remember."

Kate shook her head, half out of her mind. She desperately fought to control the rage that boiled inside, but to her surprise, had no desire to cut at all, which only enraged her more. "What are you talking about? Where is she?"

"Mm . . . the one, the *friend Mary* is here, I am Kate."

"I'm not Kate," she whispered coldly.

"*I am Kate* . . . mm . . . is repaired. The *friend Mary* helps the one Keechik . . . remember . . . you will come and see . . . soon."

The syntax grated on her, but at least she understood most of what the alien communicated. It appeared Mary was okay and located somewhere on this ship. Who knew what hell this creature had her doing, but she would find out.

Movement in the wall projection caught her eye and caused her to double-take. There was something familiar in that third astronaut's build. His height and broad shoulders compared to the other two suggested it was a man, and the way he moved reminded her of—

"Jim?"

She parked her defiance for a moment and approached the projection, not trusting what or who she perceived there. The angle of the image told her there must be a sensor directly above the ship. *That blue light, perhaps?* The bare hull where Mary scraped dust away, protruded from the bottom of the image. Three figures and one of the industrial excavators stood within a few meters of the craft. At 11 o'clock, the *Echo* rested on a dusty, flat area about 50 meters away. Above the ugly, brownish surface of the *Mare Marginis*, where the sky shone in permanent, pre-dawn light, the Earth glowed above the horizon like a variegated turquoise iris.

Kate turned to Keechik. "Is that Jim Atteberry out there?" The alien clicked its limbs, then grunted. She returned her attention to the projection and asked, "Who's out there?" The creature did not respond. Kate pointed to the images, her eyes widening. "Keechik, let me speak to them."

"No. . . no . . . no."

"Damn it, why not?"

"No . . . not ready . . . the *friend Mary* is . . . not finished . . . come and see." The alien slipped one of its limbs into a hole in the console—an input sensor of some sort—and various images flashed by on the ship's wall. Kate thought the creature might show her Mary's location, and prove she was safe, but instead, the pictures came to rest on a group of ships facing each other in space.

"What—where is that?"

"So close . . . *I am Kate*, ships are here . . ."

She slowly recognized the *Malevolent*, one of Titanius's cruisers, looming in front of a tiny service vessel—a shuttle or cargo carrier. Two other vessels of unknown registration surrounded *Malevolent,* and several other corvette class fliers, some of them Chinese and Russian.

"Keechik, what are they doing up there?"

"Come . . . and see."

One of the cruisers fired a salvo of missiles narrowly missing the *Malevolent*.

"Good God . . ."

"Mm . . . the other ones, like you, *I am Kate* . . . they fight. They come to Luna . . . they . . . mm . . . wish to find me . . . that is why the *friend Mary* is . . . helping the one Keechik . . . to remember."

She turned toward Keechik and knelt down. "Listen, you must stop them. If you have technology to come here and to do this," she pointed to her chest, "then you're capable of stopping them."

Keechik clacked his limbs again, removed the one toggling the images, and crept out from the shadows. Its amber eyes appeared even larger than before, and the creature struggled to keep still, at once watching her, then turning to the projection.

"No . . . cannot stop the others. Too many are . . . broken."

"Broken? How do you mean?"

"Worse than *I am Kate* . . . much worse . . . too broken."

She gathered in a deep breath, threw a cursory look at her chest, and immediately averted her eyes as her stomach pitched anew. She fought to keep the surge of bile down, then refocused on Keechik.

"If they're all after you and your ship, you must leave. Go somewhere else. Leave this place, and let me and Mary return to the *Echo*, the ship on the surface."

"*I am Kate* . . . does not understand . . . the *friend Mary* must go . . . with little one Keechik . . . only *I am Kate* returns."

A shiver raised the hairs on the back of Kate's neck as a new fear entered her thoughts. "No, I thought Mary was safe, that she was helping. She can't leave with you. She belongs here, with her dad, with me, her friends. You must not take her."

Keechik groaned and scuttled about before saying, "The *friend Mary* . . . will come with . . . little one Keechik . . . and see." The creature returned to the console and sunk two limbs into the input holes. The images projected on the wall flashed again, finally stopping on a dark room where a figure lay on a long bed-like platform. As it manipulated its legs, the light in the image increased, revealing Mary on her back, strapped down and twitching, with fine, glowing wires protruding from her head.

"Sweet Jesus."

"The *friend Mary* is safe, *I am Kate* . . . but must leave with the one Keechik . . . when she remembers all."

Kate swallowed hard. "What are you doing to her? Let me see Mary!"

Keechik's golden eyes widened, and he placed the two limbs in different sockets. "Come and see."

A brilliant blue light flashed through Kate's vision and, sensing no motion, she and the creature *dissolved* into the room where Mary lay. At first, her confusion and loss of bearings caused her to freeze in bewilderment. Then she remembered why she was there, and ran to the bed where Mary twitched, unsure of what to do. Hundreds, if not thousands, of tiny filaments were lodged in Mary's skull. Some were marginally thicker than others, and all of them pulsated with a blue and turquoise glow. They reminded her of old-school fiber-optics, still used in some freighters today. She shook her head and panicked, then grabbed at one of the restraining belts and wrestled to loosen it.

Mary's gaze shifted. Panic and confusion crossed her face, and then she frowned. "No, it's okay. I understand now."

"What—what's happening to you?" She kept tugging at the restraints, but they refused to yield. Kate swung around to find Keechik huddled in a shadow by another command console. "What are these wires? What are you doing to her!"

Mary smiled warmly, and tears formed. One trickled down the side of her face toward her ear. Her hands and feet continued twitching, but she didn't appear to be in any pain. Mary whispered, "I understand . . . all of it now, all of it."

"What do you mean? All of what?"

"Everything . . . everything . . . *everything*." Her eyelids fluttered but the calm smile on her face gave Kate pause. She ceased struggling with the restraints and stepped back from the bed. Suddenly, an immense sadness engulfed her, powerful and intense. The time had come to look again, she knew, and Kate glanced at her chest, forcing herself to stare for several seconds before breaking away.

Who am I?

Not only was her body being restored, it was also being healed. The rush of untold emotions swirling through her now felt different, more real and incapable of being buried much longer.

She nodded at Keechik, and in a quivering voice, said, "You have helped me because I was broken."

"Yes, *I am Kate*."

She looked at the creature. "Is Mary broken too?"

Keechik clicked about the floor. "No. The *friend Mary* is helping . . . mm."

"Helping you remember."

"Mm . . . yes."

Kate rubbed her face. Her skin was smoother, more taut than before. Whatever this creature did when it touched her, somehow it repaired all the injured physical elements in her body. Her joint pain disappeared, and her eyesight improved. She felt strong again; even her lungs had cleared. Then another thought struck her.

"Keechik, I've had cancer blooms for many years. Those are cells that keep growing out of control. It's a disease that kills."

"Little one Keechik knows . . . mm . . . but *I am Kate* is no longer broken." A deep guttural sound came from his dark corner. "No more . . . mm . . . blooms. All gone."

Another emotional tumult pounded her and weakened her knees, but she fought to maintain control. "Am I sick—broken—any-where?"

Keechik drifted out of the shadows and scrabbled to within a meter of her. It peered up with wide eyes. "No, no . . . *I am Kate* is whole now. No more broken."

Kate collapsed, at once fighting an overpowering urge to give in and release all the years of frustration and pain and nightmares that crawled into a lump in her throat. She gulped at the air as silent sobs racked her body, until finally, reluctantly, she surrendered to her emotions and allowed ancient, primal moans to surface. They came softly at first, tentatively, but quickly grew until they exploded in a torrent of jagged breaths and tears.

She had no idea how much time had elapsed when the last of the pent-up feelings escaped, and Kate lay spent on her side, eyes closed, curled up on the smooth floor and thinking about Jim's smile.

Thunk.

Thunk.

Thunk Thunk Thunk Thunk Thunk Thunk Thunk Thunk.

Kate lifted her head. The familiar tapping reverberated throughout the ship. Tears covered the side of her face and her wet bangs stuck to her forehead. She wiped them away. "It's *him*, Keechik! Jim Atteberry!"

The creature darted about the shadows, faster than before, and several images reappeared on the ship's wall. One astronaut—it must have been Jim—knelt at the hull. He hammered at the vessel with a small tool while the other two stood nearby.

In the momentary silence, Mary's voice emerged. "Dad? But I'm not ready yet."

Kate rose from the floor and settled beside her. She grabbed onto the bed to steady herself. "I don't care what this creature is doing to you, Mares, we're getting off this ship now."

Scuttling noises erupted as Keechik danced around, but Mary spoke first. "No, Kate, not yet. This isn't finished. There's more to come. The entire history of Keechik's race is being transferred into my memory: evolutionary, social, intellectual, technological . . . everything, and the process isn't complete." Her eyelids fluttered. "I understand now."

Kate turned to the creature. "You must let me talk to Jim and tell him we're here and safe, Keechik. You must."

"No . . . no . . . much danger. The friend Mary is helping."

"For how long?"

"Mm . . . until she remembers all . . . she must remember all."

Kate slammed her fist on the table beside Mary's hand. "Damn it, how much time before we can talk to them!"

Keechik poked its limbs into other sockets, grunted and said, "Seven . . . of your minutes, *I am Kate*."

She stared at the image on the wall. Atteberry continued hitting the hull and pausing. The taps propagated through the walls and floors of the ship, unlike anything she had experienced. The sounds didn't reverberate like knocks traveling through metal; instead, she could almost *see* them rippling through the vessel and its atmosphere like acoustic waves.

Kate scrutinized the creature anew. "What kind of vessel is this, Keechik, I mean its composition?"

"The friend Mary remembers."

Kate looked down on her. Fingers continued to twitch sporadically, and Mary's eyes moved rapidly behind her lids. Her face remained serene.

She strode over to the wall, surveyed it, then rapped her knuckles against it, tapping back to Atteberry. After the first sequence, she glanced at Keechik, but the creature stayed at its command console. It did not try to stop her. She knuckled it out again.

In the images from the Moon's surface, Kate watched the three figures looking at each other. Atteberry tapped the code again.

He thinks it's the alien responding.

Buried in the recesses of her mind was an ancient terran code she'd learned at the Spacer Training Center—one that few ever used now, but they were taught it anyway for its logic and sequential benefits. One Mary recognized and, therefore, one that Jim knew as well.

How does that Morse code go again?

Kate thought hard, turning over old memories like stones from her past, uncovering early teachings and reviewing notes. She wasn't eidetic like Mary, but close.

She positioned herself in front of the wall, took a deep breath, and knocked out a CQ in Morse code, the long-standing lyrical general call to invite contact with anyone who may be listening.

dahdidahdit dahdahdidah . . .

After repeating the pattern several times, she looked at the image again. Atteberry knelt on the hull motionless. She tapped it out again, and this time, he responded with his own CQ that the ship grabbed and propagated through its core.

One of the other astronauts raced back toward the *Echo*.

FORTY-ONE

Carter

Captain John Powell, co-pilot Jenson, and the comms officer Quigg stared at the main viewscreen on the bridge of the *Echo*. Esther remained at navigation, scanning the alien ship, but kept glancing up at the viewer with a horrified look on her face. A hundred thousand kilometers distant, the *Malevolent* and *Volmar* exchanged missile fire as smaller ships in the area scattered like cockroaches in the light.

The *Nachtfalke* had been destroyed.

What remained of her hull floated away, gently spinning like a feather in the breeze.

Carter frowned. He'd stepped in the thick of it now and couldn't talk his way out. "How many lives on that ship, John?"

The captain ran through background data on the *Nachtfalke*. "Eighteen, assuming a full crew complement."

The bridge grew silent again. The only sounds he registered came from *Malevolent*'s battle comms. Captain Russo hadn't been in a firefight since the days of the second Civil War, but her touch for combat had not faded. Her ship and crew dodged fire and man-euvered through the debris field with confidence.

Something caught his eye on a secondary screen: Ishani had returned to the *Echo* and was hauling another piece of equipment from its belly: the Jennings laser cutter.

"Ishani, what's happening on the surface?"

Her radio crackled. "Atteberry's made contact with someone using a tap code on the hull. He says his daughter and Kate are definitely inside the ship. Dub's gonna clear the dust with the blaster and I wanna get the Jennings in position ASAP."

"Inside that alien ship? Remarkable. What else can you tell us?"

Ishani grunted as she hauled the laser cutter down *Echo*'s ramp to the Moon's surface. "The composition of that ship's hull is a mystery, sir. Never seen anything like it."

He raised his eyebrows at Esther working at the nav station. She turned and shook her head. "Esther says the same here. Now listen, Ishani." He returned his gaze to the firefight in space. "We don't have a lot of time to get in that ship, rescue our workers and grab the alien tech, understand? Tell Atteberry to return to the *Echo* posthaste, then Dub needs to excavate the hell out of that thing on the double."

"Understood."

The comms officer aboard the *Malevolent* posted updates on the message feed. Other than the destruction of the *Nachtfalke*, the battle between the two heavy cruisers caused minimal damage. Russo matched the *Volmar's* salvos with similar weapons. She clearly wanted to avoid a full-out attack.

Jenson jumped from her seat. "Sir, Captain, we've lost track of one of the other cruisers."

"The *Edelgard*?"

"Ah, no sir."

Captain Powell, sitting beside her, maintained his cool, calm demeanor. "Explain, Mr. Jenson."

"Even though she was running dark, we've been tracking engine signatures. She was there earlier, coming in from the Martian run, and now . . . nothing."

"What was her last known position and course?"

Jenson tweaked the dashboard controls. "Can't be too precise from her signatures, but relative coordinates are 226 mark 8 and her trajectory was . . . oh Christ." She looked at Captain Powell with wide eyes. "She was en route to Luna."

"Are you sure?"

Jenson tweaked her adjustments again and nodded.

Carter narrowed his gaze. "What is it, John?"

Powell exhaled long and hard. "Remember those two Prussian ships? The *Edelgard* was one, and she's heading to the stand off. If our assumptions are correct, that second heavy cruiser is the *Sara Waltz*, and she may very well have arrived in the Moon's orbit."

"The hell? Where is she, then?"

"Likely on the far side, sir. It would explain the loss of signature."

Esther abandoned her surface scanning and joined Carter in the center of the bridge. The *Echo*, despite her advanced tech and speed, was a sitting duck for a weaponized cruiser as long as she remained immobile. As soon as the *Sara Waltz* swung around, she'd see them in the limb zone and could secure not only the *Echo*, but the alien vessel as well.

"We've got to get off this rock, John."

"Aye, sir. Mr. Jenson, initiate lift off sequence. Fire up thrusters."

Esther stood in shock, her mouth agape. "No! We can't abandon the people out there, Clayton. Call them back in!"

Carter's rage boiled inside his chest. "It won't be for long, but we can't stay here and get picked off by the *Sara Waltz*. In space, at least we have a fighting chance to immobilize them."

"Clayton, no."

"We'll draw them away from Luna, make them think we've got what we came for, and do whatever we can to shut them down. Engines, weapons systems, anything else. Then we'll return and pick up the crew."

"But what if they get to the *Echo* first? She isn't some spy vessel like the *Nachtfalke*, for god's sake! You're gambling with the lives of human beings out there, never mind everyone here. Talk to them first. See if there's a diplomatic way around this."

Jenson interrupted them. "Thrusters ready and standing by, Captain."

Powell turned to face Carter. "Sir?"

He stroked his chin and shook his head. This situation escalated far quicker than he'd ever imagined, but little choice remained. The moment the firefight in space began, all talk became useless. He hated abandoning Ishani and Dub on the surface. The others, he could not care less about.

"Awaiting your orders, sir."

Carter grabbed Esther by the arms. "I'll come back for the crew, Doctor, and Kate Braddock too.

"The *Sara Waltz*'s signatures have been detected," Jenson said, "bearing 101 mark 2."

Powell turned in his seat and looked hard at Carter. "Orders, sir?" he emphasized.

"Don't do it, please. Talk to them."

"20,000 kilometers and closing. They see us, Captain."

"Sir?"

Carter stared at the ship on the screen. She still ran dark but now that she appeared in visual range, the outline of her hull bearing down on his position became clear. In his mind, there was no doubting the *Waltz*'s ability to inflict serious damage. He understood what she was capable of doing from previous skirmishes along the Martian mineral runs. One direct hit of her rail guns could finish the *Echo*. That wouldn't happen.

He set his jaw and raised his chin. "Captain Powell, get us the hell out of here. Now!"

When the thrusters engaged, both Carter and Esther scrambled to remain upright as the artificial gravity system strained under the quick movement. She grabbed on to a flight hook above the nav station. Carter held the back of Powell's seat. At fifty meters elevation, the Echo's full engines engaged.

Powell said calmly, "Increase forward engine thrusters on my mark, Mr. Jenson . . . *mark*." The ship screamed away from the gloom of the *Mare Marginis* on a course over the sun-filled *Mare Crisium*, maintaining low altitude. The *Sara Waltz* arced around, hard in pursuit.

On one of the side viewscreens, Ishani's suit cam showed Dub looking off into space, followed by Atteberry entering the shot, jumping up, waving his arms.

Carter turned away.

Mary

THE ONLY WAY MARY COULD DESCRIBE THE blizzard of information swirling into her brain was like this: a limitless expanse of knowledge comprising the essence of everything. Her hands and fingers continued twitching, but she sensed the data transfer nearing completion and better managed the parsing of it all into categories and layers of memory. Still, it didn't curtail the over-whelming explosion of history in her thoughts.

The room had fallen silent. The last thing she remembered hearing was her dad tapping out a CQ and Kate wanting to leave. Now, the only sound in the ship was that ubiquitous low-level hum pulsing through the platform.

Mary moved her tongue and jaw, trying to find her voice. "Kate, are you still there?"

"Yes."

"What's happening? Is my dad near?"

Silence.

The scratchy clicks of the alien arose somewhere behind her head, and she sensed Kate's presence.

"There's an ugly situation going on out there, Mares. The *Echo* took off in a panic. They abandoned three people on the sur-face, right outside this ship. One of them's your dad."

Mary *saw* the image of the crew in her mind, standing and waving in Luna's dust. *How?* Something terrifying, yet curiously intriguing was happening to her. A clarity she'd never known swiped through her thoughts with a new understanding of how the laws of physics really worked.

We never knew.

The transfer ended. Mary felt the optical wires being re-moved from her skull. Then, the restraints loosened, and she turned sideways to see Kate smiling. Keechik moved around be-hind her at one of the command consoles. Images of the Moon's surface and ships in flight flashed across the wall in a collage of fast-moving, fiery scenes.

"How are you feeling, Mares?"

She closed her eyes and drew a deep breath before answer-ing. "There's so much information, an impossible amount of data,

I . . . I can't process it all yet." She stared at Kate's face. "But I *know* now, Kate. I know everything that happened."

She propped herself up on her elbows and stretched her legs. After regaining her bearings, Mary pivoted her legs over the side of the platform and sat up. She took Kate's hands in hers and studied her body that looked more beautiful than ever.

"Keechik has healed you."

Kate's eyes widened, and she swallowed hard, fighting back tears. "Yes, but now I'm messed up in a different way." She chuckled nervously, then leaned closer, put her forehead against Mary's and whispered, "This isn't me. I mean, I think I'm still the same on the inside, but this," she pointed to her chest, then stroked her lengthened hair, "this is foreign."

Mary smiled. She was overwhelmed by a powerful attraction to Kate and a screaming desire to tell her everything she'd learned from the transfer, but the new pathways weren't completely formed, and she struggled to sort it all out.

Keechik watched them from a corner in the shadows. Short, soft grunting noises punctured the silence in the room.

"It's the last of its kind, Kate. There are no others like it anywhere in the universe, and Ross 128 is not its home. The creature hid there."

The look on Kate's face radiated confusion and trepidation.

How could she understand, poor, sweet thing?

Kate released Mary's hands and stood back. "What happened to you here? I've got to know."

Mary stretched her arms wide and slid off the table, almost losing her balance. She pointed to the mass of optical wires now hanging off the end where her head was and drew in a breath. "Everything this creature knows, everywhere it traveled, its history, all the other life forms it encountered . . . those experiences have been transferred to my brain. It's like I've become not just one of them, but *this one* specifically. The Keechik. Sharing my mind and body."

"But why you?"

"Because of my eidetic memory. I can't forget." Mary shuddered. With a sheepish look, she said, "I guess I'm still adjusting." She leaned against the platform and continued. "The cry for water that Dad first heard reflected how utterly lonesome the Keechik was, floating around the Ross 128 system, not knowing whether other creatures would find it and keep it company. Or kill it." She nodded over Keechik's way. "It only wants what everyone else wants, Kate."

"What do you mean?"

She smiled warmly, reached out and placed a palm on Kate's cheek. She leaned in to the touch. "To be loved, Kate. Simply to be loved."

The alien clacked from the shadows, and then croaked, "The one Keechik . . . is . . . small, *I am Kate.* So small . . ."

Other utterances filled Mary's mind from some newly formed mental connection. She grabbed her head, shook it, and moaned. "Stop, Keechik. It's . . . it's too much. I can't . . ." The pain dissipated, and tears overflowed her eyes.

Kate clutched her shoulder. "What just happened there?"

"I, er, *sensed* it's thoughts. It was . . . terrifying." She met Kate's eyes. "We have no idea how much pain it has. No idea." She fought to process and release the suffering and emptiness the alien impressed on her. Mary's whole body shook with emotion.

Kate opened her arms and embraced her. They hugged long enough for the horrific thoughts of dying alone and full of fear to recede completely. Then she studied Kate. "You are healed now. You understand that?"

She inspected herself. "I don't think I'll ever get used to these. It's like . . . oh God, Mary, it's like I don't know what I am anymore."

"It's more than physical, though. Your mind is changing, too. Have you not noticed yet?"

Kate frowned and pinched her eyebrows together. Finally, she said, "Maybe . . . there's so much I can't figure out."

Keechik scuttled up to them and pointed with a limb to the flashing images on the wall. Kate stood upright and pushed her chin out. "We've got to leave this ship, Little One, and rejoin our friends and family. And you must find a safe place to go. Those humans out there in the ships are looking for you and your technology, and they'll kill you if they need to."

"The one Keechik is not . . . concerned, *I am Kate*."

Mary peered down at the alien. They understood each other without using the words. Suddenly, Mary's eyes widened, and confusion assaulted her emotions. "I can't do that, Keechik."

"The *friend Mary*, you must."

"No, please."

"You are the one to . . . to help remember. You must . . . mm . . ."

Kate spun around. "What's going on? Tell me."

"I can't."

"Tell me now."

Mary slumped back against the table, staring off at the optical wires. Keechik clicked his limbs on the floor again, and she wrapped her arms around her chest."

"Damn it, Mary, speak!"

Mary's lip trembled, and she stared into the shadows. "I'm now the holder of Keechik's entire civilization. It's all been . . . downloaded here." She pointed to her head, then turned to face Kate. "You see, it's not just about Keechik saving itself."

Silence filled the room.

"Mary, out with it. What does being this *holder of knowledge* mean?"

Tears pooled in her eyes and she swallowed the lump in her throat. "Keechik's word for humans is impossible for me to pronounce with my tongue. The closest thing it comes to is *vile*. Humans are *ugly*, Kate."

"We are. That's why this creature needs to hide, and fast. Think about what they'll do to it back on Earth. Stick it in a cage, poke it, cut it open, study its brain. If I understand what you're saying, that would be worse than dying alone."

"But it's not just that. *I* know everything it knows about . . ." she paused, ". . . everything, Kate. Everything. Its thoughts are all duplicated in my mind. Technology, FTL travel, healing . . . love . . . death . . . other alien encounters . . . all inside me." She stared into the darkness, thought about her dad, and wiped back a tear.

"Sweet Jesus, Mares . . ."

"Yes, I know."

FORTY-TWO

Katie

THEY ALWAYS MET IN DINGY HOTEL ROOMS, and everyone knew it, but today something had changed. The hovercab floated through the autumn gloom and light drizzle, then slowed in front of Wills Memorial Building Tower at the University of Bristol. Katie peered out the window at the large, stone architecture that dominated this ancient section of campus, and asked the on-board AI, "Are you sure this is the place?"

"These are the coordinates provided. Please remain seated until the vehicle comes to rest."

The hovercab purred a moment in front of the tower, then lowered onto its parking skids.

"Enjoy your day." Her door swung open.

Katie stepped out and threw her pack over her shoulder. Then she quickly scanned the area to gather her bearings, noting hiding places, trails, the high points, possible kill zones. It had become an important if not a paranoid habit of hers as ingrained in her behavior as the cutting.

She thought this wasn't right. This was unlike any other Program meet-up with Simon.

The indie-comm in her jacket pocket chimed, and she whipped it out and read the message.

Welcome to Bristol, Katie. We're in room 412B.

As she took the steps two at a time, a few students passed on their way down but to her surprise, they paid her no attention. Perhaps because campuses attract people of all stripes, she was just another odd-looker in the crowd. Plus, she could easily pass as a student herself, not being much older than that population.

Katie took the stairs to the fourth floor. It helped bring her legs back to life after two weeks in space, but the exertion burned her chest and throat.

Something's not right there, either.

At her last check-up, one of the Program doctors grimaced when she studied Katie's diagnostics. There were more and more dark shadows appearing on her lungs, and the anti-rad pills had trouble managing them. She upped her dose.

The entrance to Room 412B looked like any other office door: light wood, with black metal numbers glued on. No window. Without thinking further, she knocked.

"Enter."

Katie pushed the door open and stepped inside. The room may have been a professor's office at one point but not anymore. Large, leather couches and two oversized reading chairs dominated a sitting area. A couple of workstations were tucked in to the far corner. Row upon row of books covered one wall, and several floor plants filled the interstices of the place. A small window provided spotty, natural light, but grey skies and dim lighting made her pause a moment so her eyes could adjust.

Two men greeted her. She recognized only the one.

"Katie Braddock, it's good to see you again. Welcome to Bristol." They shook hands. She couldn't tell from looking at him whether Simon Delacroix had once been a Spacer. He never let on either way, but understood the Program and its history so well, she figured he must have done some time in the space trenches. That, and his voice rang oddly high for a fellow of his build.

He nodded to the suited man. "This is Director Sarangan."

"How do you do, Ms. Braddock."

Katie smirked. No one had called her Ms. or Mr. for several years. It sounded foreign to her now that she didn't identify herself by anything but her name.

She dropped the pack at her feet and placed her hands on her bony hips. "This is quite the hang out you have, Simon. What's the special occasion?"

"Have a seat, Katie."

She plopped down on one of the massive couches, and it swallowed up her tiny frame. The two men flanked her in their own large chairs.

Director Delacroix leaned forward. "Katie, I'll get right to the point. We, that is, Dr. Sarangan and I, both agree it's time for you to move on from the Program."

Katie's jaw dropped. She stared at them, confused, but their expressions didn't change.

"I don't understand."

Delacroix cleared his throat. "The career of a Spacer is limited, as you know. The body can only take so much radiation, so much *stress from working in varying gravity environments. Most of your colleagues are finished by the time they're eighteen."*

"I'm not like the others."

"True enough. You're . . . how shall I say it . . . more resilient than most. But the fact remains, Katie, that your latest medical reports suggest your time is up. The, er, infection in your lungs is—"

"The cancer, you mean."

Delacroix paused. "All right, if you wish. The cancer in your lungs is getting more challenging to treat. Unless we pull you from the active roster immediately, you're looking at more surgery. They'd have to remove a lung—the left one is a mess—and part of the right. You'd be hard-pressed to walk up a flight of stairs after that, never mind dismantle satellites in low Earth orbit."

Katie felt as if the couch had squeezed in on her. She listened in deep silence, thoughts racing, as the director recounted in graphic detail all the other health issues facing her. Part way through his dissertation, she filled her thoughts with what she'd do to herself back at the hotel in Paris. It brought her a small measure of sickening, desperate comfort.

"Do you understand why we must pull you out, Katie."

She stared at Delacroix, still unable to process everything he said, then finally resigned and nodded. She scrunched up her face as the implications smacked her.

"What . . . what will I do? This is all I know, Simon. This life is all that I am."

Delacroix leaned back and sighed. "Well, that's where Dr. Sarangan comes in. Walter?"

This man definitely wasn't a Spacer. He acted more like one of those beady-eyed bureaucrats she had to deal with from time to time. Too, the asshole was way too smarmy and smooth to be part of her tribe.

"Katie, we have a placement program for retiring Spacers, and we feel the best thing for you right now is a teaching position."

She burst out laughing. "Me? Teach? That's rich. Me, wrangling a bunch of idiots all hopped up on the brain juice."

"Not exactly. You wouldn't be a grade or high school teacher. No, what we're thinking is a college or university, or perhaps one of the private training centers. Your strength has always been in logic and sequencing, and programming, and there's no reason to quit doing that. In fact, you'd excel in it."

Beady Eyes scratched his head, searching for words.

Katie picked at the front of her shirt. "Simon, must I do any of this? What if I just walk out of here and disappear?"

"Yes, well, you could certainly do that. No one will stop you. But I do hope you take advantage of this placement. We spend an enormous amount of effort building relationships with industry, research circles and so on. I'd hate to see anyone not transition smoothly into a new career."

She thought about hanging out on a campus like Bristol, discussing science and politics with the long-hairs, going for coffee, hopping up in the green pastures with a bag of smokies. "What schools do you have in mind?"

Dr. Sarangan pulled a folded piece of paper from his jacket pocket. He looked at it briefly, then said. "There are three positions available at the moment. The first is at the University of Alberta in the Informatics department. You'd be an associate professor, splitting your time between research and teaching."

"Alberta . . . that's Canada, right? I'd freeze my puny ass off up there. What else?"

The director pursed his lips and his tone shifted. "It's not that cold, actually, but maybe this other one in Taiwan is more to your liking." He cleared his throat. "Same type of work, half research, half teaching, except you'd be in the Physics department and have some responsibilities for managing grad students."

Katie pulled a face. "Babysitting? Yeah, that's a possibility. Bloody hot in Taiwan, isn't it? Politically, I mean, so . . . yeah." She waited for Beady Eyes to continue but he looked away instead. "You said there were three, so what's the other one?"

"It's not as prestigious as the first two, Ms. Braddock. In fact, I'm hesitating now to even mention it given your reaction to the others."

"Oh, go on. Humor me."

"All right. The other position is in San Francisco."

"USF?"

"No, City College. It's a community college. The focus is on teaching only, so there'd be minimal research opportunities for you and, I dare say, you'd likely get bored with it. Still, it's with Computer Sciences and they have a wonderful up-to-date lab. Close to the ocean, too, if that's your kind of thing."

Katie thought about the offers. None of them jumped out at her.

"Simon, are you sure I can't stay a little longer, like perhaps a couple years or even one? Sending me off to some outhouse on Earth is tough, you know?"

The director didn't respond.

Katie sighed. "I see. When do I have to decide?"

Beady Eyes shrugged as if she'd asked the most ridiculous question of all time. "Right now, Ms. Braddock."

She shook her head. The burn in her lungs echoed from walking up the stairs and since the initial shock had waned, she recognized the need to mind her health.

"Send me to that City College, then."

"Are you sure? It's really not—"

"Yes, yes, that's where I'll go."

"Very well." Dr. Sarangan walked over to a workstation and returned with a handful of papers. "You'll have to sign these. Routine things like the job acceptance, confidentiality agreements. And this one," he said, handing her a sheaf of legalese," is the most important."

"What's it about?"

"This is an agreement stating that you won't reveal any of the intelligence or research you've come across in your time with us. It's part of the civil war settlement between all five American republics. They're a skittish bunch, you understand. They fear Spacers will use their specialized knowledge against them."

Katie read through the documents and signed them off.

"Thank you for your service. There's a hovercar waiting downstairs to take you to the airport. Your effects in Paris will be forwarded to you as soon as you've landed." They all stood, then Delacroix guided her to the door. "I know this is tough, Katie, but it's for your own long-term good. Now, is there anything else we can do before you leave?"

"Not a thing, Simon."

"You sure? Colleagues we could tell? Project managers?"

She opened the door and stepped into the hallway, still in disbelief. Then she slowly pivoted. "There is something, Simon."

"Sure, what is it?"

"Call me Kate."

FORTY-THREE

Carter

A SARDONIC SMILE EASED ACROSS CLAYTON CARTER'S FACE. He loved the *Echo* and couldn't wait to build more of them. Sleek, nimble, and fast as hell. With more weapons than a traditional corvette, the *Echo* changed the very essence of short-haul patrolling. As the ship raced over the lunar landscape, drawing the *Sara Waltz* down, he wanted to ensure everyone on board understood that he was in command.

"Captain Powell, can we outrun that bucket?"

"Affirmative. Our strength is acceleration, maneuverability and speed. That said, one salvo from the *Waltz* could destroy us like that." He snapped his fingers.

Carter narrowed his gaze. "But we're not without our own weapons." He turned to Jenson. "Tactically, how do we disable that ship?"

Her hands flew over the command dash. "Sir, she's got rail-guns fore and aft, missile bays all around, protective shielding on her belly and back. There's little we could hit her with that would cause much damage."

"What about engines?"

"They use internal thrusters fueled by isotope-injectors. Extremely difficult to target, and even then, those rods are protected by massive hardshields."

Carter paced, stroking his chin.

"She's still following us, sir," Jenson reported from her station.

"Any sign of aggression?"

"Negative."

Esther Tyrone pulled him aside. "Clayton, they're obviously not interested in a fight. Let's talk to them and explain we're in the middle of a rescue mission."

"What, so they can raid us as soon as we've got that alien's tech on board? No, not a chance. We'll finish what we came for and return to Earth before these idiots know what we've got."

Esther chewed her lip. "I must tell you, this isn't what I expected from a partnership. We need access to your fleet and the TSA can provide you with valuable research, but we can't condone this kind of reckless behavior."

Clayton chuffed. "What are you on about, Doctor?"

She stood tall, striking a defiant pose. "Let me be clear. Either you make peace with the *Sara Waltz* right now and rescue our people on Luna—including Kate Braddock and Jim's daughter—or any potential partnership with the TSA is off."

Her face reddened in the warm, amber light of the bridge as she stared him down. Carter worked his jaw, choosing his words carefully. He wasn't about to be upstaged and challenged on his own ship, especially by some bureaucratic, has-been scientist. "You and I will discuss this later, Esther, but the situation right now calls for a tactical response. If you'd like to have a pleasant chinwag over tea with the Prussians or whoever else, that's your business, but out here on board the *Echo*, I own what happens." He lowered his voice and leaned closer to her ear. "So, if you don't want to go along with that, I suggest you remove yourself from the bridge and buckle into your flight seat. Understand?"

She didn't flinch. Carter realized this woman drew her strength and resolve from a very deep well, but he could go toe to toe with anyone, and he wouldn't be denied.

Esther blinked, and silently fumed as she withdrew to the flight seats and out of sight.

"The *Sara Waltz* is preparing for a pass at us, sir. Gaining altitude to leverage a better shot." Jenson's voice remained firm and professional, but her face showed traces of strain and trepidation. Carter turned his attention to the main viewscreen. He stood sto-ically, unsure of what to do next. He threw a cursory glance at Powell.

The captain eyed him, then said coolly, "Mr. Jenson, don't lose our relative position. Swing around and follow that ship. Maintain a 2,000 kilometer separation."

"Aye, sir." The *Echo* jumped as her thrusters increased their burn.

"I'd rather take my chances with short-range weapons than nukes. They likely won't fire their missiles this close, so don't let them pull away."

"Aye, sir. We're at 2,000 kilometers and holding distance."

"Thank you, Mister Jenson."

Carter broke into more pacing and rubbed his fingers. Despite his desire to be seen as a strong leader and in charge, he felt the bridge crew judged him for his lack of flying and space experience. And rather than worsen their view of him by pretending he knew everything, he deferred to Captain Powell, and assumed a standing position beside his chair.

"Mr. Jenson, let's take a closer look at that ship."

"What do you have in mind, sir?"

"I don't want to engage in a firefight. That wouldn't end well for us. But if we can disable her main engines and force her weapons off-line, that'll buy some time to finish the rescue mission."

Carter fumed inside. His competitive instinct screamed at him to destroy that barge and send a message to anyone else who might think about taking them on, but Powell didn't see it that way.

You may be the captain, but I own this ship, and you work for me.

Powell glanced at him and his eyes said, in that one quick glimpse, everything that Carter despised. It was an act of defiance, not based in philosophical differences or dislike of authority: no. This was borne from competence. Powell knew the *Echo* and her capability better than him. That made the captain the de facto leader and reminded Carter of those self-righteous engineers and know-it-all scientists he'd had to fight at every turn as he built his career and business. Perhaps that's why Esther tasked him so: she was one of *them*.

"Mister Jenson," Captain Powell said in an almost bemused tone, "access my directory and locate the file called 'Powell's Plans'. It's buried in there."

A moment passed as the co-pilot searched the system. "Got it. Do you want me to put it on screen, sir?"

"Affirmative, on the beta monitor. I don't want to lose sight of the cruiser."

Jenson hit her dashboard and the smaller viewscreen flashed bright with a schematic of the *Sara Waltz*'s main systems. Carter approached him. "Is that . . . Where did you get these, John?"

Captain Powell allowed a brief smile, but didn't answer. Instead, he directed Jenson to pull up the weapons tactical data and overlay it with engines.

"If I recall, Jenson, the *Waltz*'s engineers are trained to focus on building efficiencies at every turn. Normally, that's a good thing, but when it comes to ship design systems, I feel they've made a critical mistake. Look there." He pointed to various power nodes running throughout the ship. "Rather than build independent routing for each system, they piggy-back them. This saves energy and space, but the downside is if one system fails, it often takes out others. Not an issue when your role is escorting mineral barges, but it could be in a firefight."

Carter made a mental note to have Ed check his own fleet.

"Do you see a way to immobilize that beast, Mr. Jenson?"

She thought a moment, then shouted. "Aye, sir. Aft access portals! Minimal shielding because there's nothing tactical there, but several power routing nodes all share the space in that section. If we can squeeze a tube in there that should disable her."

"Indeed." He stood up, walked to her station, and took a position beside her. "Mr. Jenson, ready two thermite torpedoes and target the aft access portals. We're only going to get one or two shots away before she returns fire, so lay in an evasion course, too. The second we launch, hit those thrusters, understood?"

Jenson swallowed. "Aye, sir."

The *Sara Waltz* cruised forward, but with the Echo in close proximity, she couldn't make a run. Then, the cruiser veered hard to starboard, exposing her flank as she circled the area.

"On my mark, Mr. Jenson ... wait for it ... steady now ... *mark!*"

Two green flashes filled the main screen as the torpedoes were released, ignited, and locked on to their target.

"Now, Mr. Jenson, get us the—"

Captain Powell hadn't even finished the order when the *Echo* lurched hard to starboard and evasive maneuvers kicked in. The ship hurtled through space on a 3-D zigzag route toward the far side of Luna. As they pulled away, a small burst of light appeared on the screen where the *Sara Waltz* was hit.

"Status of the target, Mister Jenson."

"Stand by, Captain." She adjusted her viewer and confirmed readings. "Direct hit, sir. Indications are that ... main engines are off-line ... hardshields down ... weapons disabled ... and ..." She paused.

"What is it?"

Jenson turned to him with horror on her face. "Life support systems disabled."

Carter felt a wave of excitement and pride.

"Mr. Quigg, inform the *Sara Waltz* we'll help restore her life support and other systems as soon as we've completed our rescue mission."

"Aye, Skip."

Powell turned to Carter and winked, then regained his chair.

"Set a course for that alien ship, Mr. Jenson. Let's finish what we started."

Kate

THE TWO WOMEN HELD HANDS AND WATCHED the events in space unfold before them on the wall projections inside the alien vessel. The *Echo*, having disabled the heavy cruiser, flew straight toward them. Keechik remained in a shadow-filled corner near the console. Over the past several minutes, it had grown noticeably quieter. Having downloaded its memories into Mary's brain, perhaps it truly didn't care what happened next as long as she was safe. But this was problematic. As soon as the TSA, Carter, or anyone else realized that Mary held the secrets of the universe, she would become their target of interest, and Earth's history was littered with human madness in the pursuit of treasure. Mary's solution appeared to be to leave with the Rossian.

Kate had to stop that from happening, and that meant confronting Carter once and for all.

She stared at the images of the ships above; the cruiser floating helplessly in space, and the *Echo* preparing to land. She whispered to Mary, "Can you fly this thing?"

She turned and shook her head. "I've processed most of the knowhow, but I lack the physical capability. The Keechik's limbs are multi-sensory. It manipulates the craft through those thin input ports on the command consoles. My fingers aren't built for that."

"Then we mustn't let the creature pretend there's nothing important going on here." She grabbed her arms and peered into her eyes. "We've gotta find a way to talk to your dad without Spider-legs around."

"He can't help us," she sighed. "I don't want to leave, Kate, but I must. The knowledge I've acquired is far too dangerous in the hands of people like Clayton Carter. Either I go with the alien, or you must kill me before we get to Earth. There's no other option."

Keechik clacked, and Kate grimaced. "Forget that. Listen, you and I must return home together, and Keechik will have to disappear and find someone else to be its walking memory tube."

"No . . ."

411

"It can't just abduct you like this. Jim needs you . . . hell, I need you. Once we're home, we can figure out a way to keep your knowledge from others until your safety is guaranteed, but in the meantime, no one's the wiser."

She turned to face the alien. "You gotta leave right away, Keechik, and find another . . . creature to help you remember. Surely with everything you know . . ." Her voice trailed off as she realized if it had been easy, Keechik would have found someone a long time ago.

The alien had inched closer to them and now stood a meter away. On the screen, the *Echo* had just touched down. One of the abandoned astronauts bounded out toward it while the other two remained at the vessel. Keechik scuttled briefly, then said, "The *friend Mary*, you must come . . . and see, mm . . . out there . . . come and see . . . help remember . . ."

"No, I won't let her," Kate said. Then, she pointed at the projections on the wall. "Oh, my god . . ." The large astronaut rolled the excavator closer to the ship while the others stood back, and after a moment, the image clouded over in a plume of rock and dust. The excavation had begun.

"Keechik, go."

"*I am Kate*, the one Keechik will leave . . . with the *friend Mary*."

She struggled to keep her frustration with the creature at bay, then thought of something and knelt down to Keechik's level. It scrabbled back a pace. "Will you let me speak to them?"

The alien paused. "No . . ."

"You must let me try to stop them and give you a chance to get away."

Again, Keechik paused as if uncertain.

Kate could not hear the excavation underway outside the vessel, but she and Mary both saw what happened. In a matter of minutes, the massive excavator had ripped away the moon dust cover. When the screen cleared, a deep trench had been dug around the perimeter of the ship. She counted five figures on the surface now and recognized Jim bouncing off to the side.

"Let me speak with them, Keechik. Maybe I can convince them to stop. If not, they'll destroy your ship before you get away."

"No, *I am Kate* . . . mm . . . too dangerous . . . the one Keechik and *friend Mary* must leave."

Kate played it out in her mind. If those two left together, what would happen to her? Would Keechik dump her on the surface?

No, Kate, you can't let her go.

She attempted a different tack. "Keechik, do you know the one called Jim Atteberry, Mary's father?"

"Yes, the Atteberry . . . mm, yes . . . he is broken, too . . . all are broken . . . *I am Kate* must not speak with the Atteberry."

"Keechik, please. If you take Mary away, she may never see him again. If you won't allow me to talk to him, please let her speak with her father. Just for a few minutes."

The creature snorted and clacked, then scuttled back to its shadows. "*I am Kate* . . . mm . . . the *friend Mary* may speak with the Atteberry . . . not long . . . mm . . . only minutes . . . then we leave."

Kate spun around to face Mary. "Please get Jim to stop Carter from blasting into this ship. Don't let on what Keechik's entrusted you with because who knows if Carter is monitoring everything, okay?"

She gulped and steadied herself against the transfer platform. Kate nodded to Keechik and said, "Thank you, please open the comms to Mary's dad, the Atteberry."

The room filled with the crackle of helmet radios and messages from across the solar system. The cacophony was deafening. Kate picked out the raised voices of ships' crews in combat;

multiple languages of others en route, what sounded like proto-cols from Eros. Just as quickly, Atteberry's voice had been iso-lated and the other chatter faded out.

Mary took a step forward toward the wall where his pro-jected image flashed. "Dad, can you hear me?"

On the screen images, Atteberry jumped and gazed around.

"Dad, it's me."

He looked at the alien vessel, then grabbed his helmet, fell to his knees and sunk into the moon dust.

FORTY-FOUR

Carter

CARTER AND ISHANI HAULED THE LASER CUTTER across the 30 meters of dust and debris, rumbling toward the alien craft. When he saw Jim Atteberry on his knees, he asked Ishani on a private comms channel, "Any idea what that idiot is up to now?"

She chuckled. "With him, it could be anything, but I'll keep an eye open, and make sure he doesn't interfere." She yanked the Jennings cutter to the left. "Wait a sec . . . Mr. Carter, switch to the main radio channel."

When he accessed main comms, Atteberry's shrill and panicked voice spilled out into his helmet. He prattled on to Esther back at the ship, crying about Mary this and Mary that.

"The hell?" Carter shifted the cutter into position, bounded over to Atteberry kneeling in the dust, and said, "What the Christ is going on here? You'd better return to the *Echo* immediately, Atteberry, and stay out of the way."

"She's in there! For crissakes, Mary talked to me. She is inside that ship, and Kate too. We've got to get in."

Carter loomed over the fallen man, hands on hips. He looked over Atteberry's head toward the *Echo* and said into the radio, "Esther, are you picking up any life signs from that vessel? Any markers at all?"

The comms crackled and after a moment she replied, her voice strained and tired. "Still nothing, Clayton. It's like that ship isn't even there."

Carter chewed his lip.

It would've been so easy to drill through that alien craft and cut her open like a tin can, survivors be damned, and grab the tech. But no . . . no . . . the asshole's daughter had to be alive after all this. If it was only that walking corpse Kate Braddock, I wouldn't think twice. But the girl. . .

"Ishani, did you find any access portals on this thing?"

"None that I saw. How 'bout you, Dub?"

"Negative. I've gone over the vessel real careful like, and as far as I can tell, the entire surface is a one-piece made of the same smooth material. Totally unreadable. No joiners, no ports . . . just one continuous skin."

Carter leaned over and yanked Atteberry up by the shoulders. "Get your shit together, man, will you? We're going to drill into that thing and find your daughter."

"No! They're inside and safe, but you can't do this. She warned me not to try getting in."

416

"Why not?"

Atteberry didn't answer.

"I see." Turning his attention to Ishani, he barked, "Is that cutter ready?"

"Yes, sir."

"Good. Target the closest edge and let 'er rip."

"No, for the love of—"

The laser cutter sprang to life. Ishani stood behind the machine, holding on to the manipulator arms and straddling the foot locks like she was riding a scooter. The tight red beam splayed against the edge nearest to her. Sparks flew, momentarily lighting up the darkness at the moon's limb, then quickly choking in the vacuum.

"No!"

Atteberry pushed Carter away and lumbered awkwardly toward the cutter. Before he reached it, Dub appeared from behind the machine and tackled him, throwing the man back into the dust. Carter arrived a moment later. "Don't let him out of your sight."

Ishani continued torching the vessel. Splashes of light danced up from the surface like a flickering candle, but the beam had no effect. The laser would have cut halfway through a terran ship by now, but this alien material would not yield. She targeted a couple other spots on the hull and fired. Still, it remained impenetrable.

Quigg, back on the *Echo*, interrupted Carter's attention. "Sir, the *Malevolent* is hailing us. Captain Russo standing by."

He nodded at Ishani to keep firing the cutter, then wandered away from her position. "Put her through."

Russo's voice, thick with worry, piped into his helmet. "Clayton, we're having fun playing hopscotch with the *Volmar*, but the game's heating up. More vessels, including the *Edelgard*, are en route to our location and we will need back up sooner rather than later. Any chance the *Echo* can assist?"

A twinge of panic shivered up his spine, but he quickly suppressed it before it had time to take root. "We're almost finished here, Laura, then we'll be on our way. How's your crew?"

"They're the best in your fleet, despite what John Powell might have you believe. We'll sign up for another round and play coy until you arrive." Her tone abruptly changed. "Try not to take too long, Clay. We're the only ones out here."

"Understood. Carter out."

He marched back to the Jennings and told Ishani to kill the power. Then he grabbed Atteberry by the chest handle on his envirosuit and ripped him from Dub's grasp. "Talk to me. Are you still in contact with your daughter?"

"No, not anymore. As soon as you fired up that . . . that *thing*, she went silent."

He stared into Atteberry's visor and saw his eyes wide with rage. *There must be a way into that ship. How did Kate and the girl get in?*

"You better not screw with me, Atteberry."

"And you better not do anything to hurt my daughter, or so help me, I'll rip you apart with my bare hands."

"Let's be clear," he raised his voice, fully recognizing that Ishani, Dub, and everyone back on the *Echo* could hear him. "The tech inside that vessel is more important to humankind's future than a couple of miserable lives. If the wrong people get it, our entire planet could be doomed. So, if we can't get what we came here for, I'll blow that damn thing out of the dust and salvage it for parts before I allow anyone else to take it from me."

"Fuck you."

Carter sneered. "So, we finally understand each other. Good. Now contact Mary and do what it takes to find out how the hell they got in there. Talk to her, tap to her, use goddamn sign language if you have to. Help us all get inside, or so help me God, I'll turn the *Echo*'s weapons on that scow right now. Understood?"

Atteberry's straight, defiant posture held for a moment longer, then, almost unnoticeably, his shoulders dropped. Carter pushed him away.

FORTY-FIVE

Kate

"*I AM KATE* . . . MM . . . MUST RETURN TO THE OTHERS . . ."

Keechik grunted and placed two of its limbs into the command console access ports. "Then . . . the one Keechik and . . . and *friend Mary* . . . will leave."

Without warning, the ship sprung to life with ambient light, and Kate discerned the full dimensions of the room. It appeared to be a combination of a medical bay, engineering, and operations center. Dozens of images filled the surrounding walls from all over the solar system, including the outer planets, ships on mineral runs, and what could only be other alien worlds. Her mouth opened, and she was overwhelmed by the distance of it all, the immensity of existence, and how small she was in it.

Mary approached her and touched her shoulder. "How are you?"

"I—I'm not sure." She closed her eyes, and said, "Something's happening to my mind, like I've been living in a fog my entire life, and now the veil is lifting. Does that make any sense to you?"

She smiled. "Yes, completely. This is what the Keechik does: it heals the broken creatures, but as you can see, it's easily overwhelmed." She looked at her with caution. "Kate, it feels the pain of all sentient beings close to it, but there's too much for the creature to process. Like what's happening out there. It senses all that emotion."

Kate cast her eyes over to the alien. It continued working on the console, bringing various systems online and apparently preparing the ship for flight. She returned her gaze to Mary. "How long has it been on Luna?"

"Several years."

"What was it doing all that time?"

"Studying us from a safe distance, learning our ways, our language. It's an explorer, Kate, not a threat."

She looked at her with a puzzled expression. "Then what about me? I've been up here five years, and it never made itself known?"

"The Keechik avoided you at first, since you were so close, but then saw you were broken and hurting, and . . . waited." Mary's gaze disappeared into the distance and a pained look crossed her face. She stared at Kate with wonder and compassion, then shook it off and continued. "In its timeframe, the creature has only been here a few . . . hours compared to our years. When I arrived, it grew more curious about the two of us together. Then, when our survey work began here in the *Mare Marginis*, Keechik grew increasingly cautious and afraid. That's why it sent a shock wave to the lab when it thought we were a threat. It was meant as a warning, but was far stronger. Keechik did not understand the wave would destroy our habitat." She wrapped her arms around herself again. "I feel—I mean, *it* feels awful."

Mary peered at the floor as if recalling a memory. "The blue light?"

"Yes."

"The creature watched us through that. It's a self-contained scanning design, standard microwave frequencies, powered by . . . well, that's not important. When we were in real distress there at the mining site, the light guided us here, remember? The Keechik overcame its own fear to save us."

Kate worked her jaw muscles and her mouth became hard. "Wait, you know how to build one of these scanners?"

"Yes."

"A ship like this, too?"

Mary thought a moment, searching her mind. "Uh-huh, yes." Then a terrified look clouded her face. "That's why I have to leave. While the knowledge I now hold could benefit humankind immeasurably, it might also destroy us all if it falls into the wrong hands. Like Carter's, or . . . or even Esther's." Her eyes welled. "They can't help themselves."

Then Mary and Keechik said unison, as if they spoke with one voice, "I can't accept . . . that burden . . . *I am Kate.*"

Kate slammed her fist against the wall. Her sudden resolve grew out of countless hours of Spacer training, simulated emergencies, and real-life close encounters with death. She wouldn't let Mary leave with this creature. It would destroy Jim. On the other hand, could he be trusted with keeping her secret if she returned to him? His open-book philosophy would sentence her to a cruel death at the hands of so-called scientists, never mind the warmongers.

There had to be another solution. She peered over at the alien quietly manipulating the console controls. Then, she gazed at the images flashing across the walls and lowered her head. Two *Echo* astronauts hauled the excavator and laser cutter back to their ship. The three others milled about its access ramp.

This can't be good.

"Keechik," she shouted, "Let me speak with them, now! This has to stop."

Mary gaped at the flickering images. The alien clacked and groaned, but otherwise ignored her. Instead, it continued to work the console as if nothing else mattered.

Perhaps it didn't.

Kate's frustration chewed at her gut and she fought the urge to scream. After spending the last 20 years *doing*, she struggled with *not doing*. On the wall, the projections showed the *Echo*'s port side railgun flaps opening. Three of her crew remained on the surface, standing still beside the access ramp. She stared at Mary, imploring her to convince the damned alien to stop the madness, but she simply looked away.

Finally, Keechik grunted, "*I am Kate* . . . must leave now . . . mm . . ."

"Not without Mary. We *both* need to go and you've gotta haul ass out of here, too. The *Echo* means business, Keechik, and Carter always gets what he wants."

The alien vessel was the quietest ship she'd ever been on; only the hum and purr of whatever systems it used to operate continued in the background. She sensed Mary and the creature shared some kind of mental connection although Mary hadn't discussed it. Still, the way she observed Keechik with a mix of kindness and reassurance, suggested the two were *discussing* something.

Mary raised her head. "Comms are open again, Kate. You can contact the *Echo*."

"Thank you." She steeled her eyes and turned to face the wall projections, but before saying a word, she nodded to acknowledge Keechik's and Mary's effort in making it possible.

"*Echo*, alien vessel, come in."

Static and white noise crashed through the room. Keechik toggled one of the input ports.

"Echo, alien vessel, Kate Braddock here. Come in."

After a brief pause, a calm voice responded. "Alien vessel, this is Captain John Powell of the *Echo*. We read you, Kate. Over."

Thank God.

"Captain Powell ... I'm glad to hear your voice. Mary Atteberry and I are alive and well, I repeat, we're both alive and well. There's one alien on board here, frightened as hell, and we're all a little worried that you may be planning to fire on us. I beg you, Captain, please stand down. Three lives are at stake along with the history of an entire civilization. Over." They waited for an answer. None came. She looked at the others. "Copy that, *Echo*?"

Silence hung in the air like the sword of Damocles. Then, "Stand by, alien vessel."

Kate glanced at Mary. "Are you able to hear them telepathically?"

"No. Only the Keechik and I share some thoughts, you know, from the transfer, and those are muddled at best. I didn't pick up any telepathic ability, Kate. What I experience with the alien is more like impressions if that makes any sense."

Kate stared hard at the images. "I wonder what the hell's going on. For sure, your dad's probably shitting kittens by now."

She allowed herself a thin smile at the visual. "But I hope they're not actually debating my request to stand down."

Keechik scuttled about at the command console. "Mm . . . the one Carter . . . is broken . . ."

"That he is."

Mary took up a position beside her in front of the wall screen. "Maybe you should leave now. Explain to my dad about the knowledge transfer when the time's right, and why I can't return. Save yourself."

"Forget it. Either we both go, or we both stay, and our friend here insists you must leave with it."

The air crackled again.

"Kate, this is Captain Powell again. Sorry for the delay. As you can appreciate, everyone has a thousand questions here; a thousand concerns. Mr. Carter, Dr. Tyrone and Jim Atteberry all believe you and Mary should exit the ship immediately and join us in the *Echo*."

She opened her mouth to answer but Mary put a hand on her forearm and shook her head. "If we leave, they're just going to fire on Keechik. Dad and Esther may not think that way, but what about Carter?"

"You're right. I don't trust him. Never have, really, but he's brilliant and powerful and doesn't like backing down from anything, and that makes him dangerous." She paused and thought a moment. "Let me try something." Kate cleared her throat and pulled at her skins. Still not used to those *things*, her hand brushed against one and she blushed. "*Echo*, can you guarantee you won't fire on the alien ship? That you'll give it time and space to leave unharmed?"

Another long pause.

"Negative. We both understand the importance of that vessel's technology. Besides, Esther thinks it may be responsible for the destruction of the Titanius lab, so there are costs that must be borne . . ." Powell let his voice trail. The implication, however bizarre to Kate, was clear: the *Echo* would not allow the ship to leave.

"Mm . . . *I am Kate* . . . the *friend Mary* and the one Keechik must go . . ."

The odds didn't play well in her favor. Mary said the vessel could probably withstand initial railgun blasts, based on what she learned from the creature, but anything sustained would damage it and likely kill them.

There had to be another solution . . .

"Alien ship, *Echo* here." Now, Clayton Carter spoke. "Ms. Braddock, time is not on our side. I want you and the girl to leave immediately and rejoin the crew here."

Kate snapped back. "Stand by, *Echo*. It's not that simple." She pivoted. "Can this bird take off now?" Mary glanced at Keechik.

"We . . . the ones . . . cannot fly yet . . . too soon," Keechik offered in a soft, forlorn voice.

Carter boomed again over the radio, filling the space between them. "This is your last chance, Braddock. The implications of that alien vessel to our species are far too great to allow it to go its own way. That Rossian is trespassing."

"Excuse me, but you'd murder us to prevent this ship from taking off? What kind of monster are you?"

"Not a monster, Braddock, far from it. I'm a savior. And as we all know, the needs of our 12 billion individuals on Earth outweigh the moralistic whims of a couple of souls on Luna. Surely you understand that." The static crashed again as if emphasizing the point. "You have one minute to exit the vessel, then we open fire. You've been warned. *Echo* out."

Damn it.

"Keechik," Kate shouted, "is there anything you can do to stop them? Send a compression wave at 'em or something?"

The creature did not answer, and she recognized a heaviness in her gut she hadn't experienced since one of her lonely Spacer trips to Amsterdam.

Captain Powell's voice came on again, softer now, with a hint of pleading. "Kate, please . . . for Mary's sake . . . come back to the *Echo*."

"Negative. Mary can't return, and I won't leave her." She fought the tremble in her lip. "Listen, thank you anyway. Each of us has to do what is right." She paused a moment. "Is Jim Atteberry nearby?"

"He's here, Kate." There was a smattering of clicks and frequency oscillations, then Jim came on the radio. "Kate, oh my god, is Mary there?"

"Yes, Dad."

"Please come home, Mares. You and Kate. I can't—I mean—I'm lost without you both."

Mary leaned against the transfer platform while Kate stared at her with wide eyes. "Is there any way you can see yourself returning?"

"No, you know it's impossible. They simply can't help themselves."

"You need to tell him."

Mary stared at the image of the *Echo* on the wall screen, her railguns at the ready. "Dad, please understand. I can't come back, Daddy, no matter how much I want to. I—I can't do it."

Then Kate chimed in. "And I won't abandon her here, Jim, you know that."

The pause was deafening. Finally, Atteberry responded. "Kate, please. I'm begging you. Bring my Mares home. What is more important than being together, the three of us? Please..."

Kate choked back the burning lump forming in her throat. It sounded like Jim offered her a chance for them to be a family, however that's defined. And, healed, she'd be able to support him and Mary in all ways. By working and living and, yes, loving together, she knew they could accomplish great things.

She watched Mary stand tall, empowered by conviction that she was doing the right thing, the necessary thing, taking the appropriate logical course of action to save them all from themselves.

Kate smiled at her, and she nodded. "I'm sorry, Jim. As painful as this is to say, we can't leave this ship."

A moment later, the port side battery of railguns glowed red in the horrific grey-orange light of the Moon's limb. Mary gasped. The guns chuffed once, and before the shot even registered in her brain, the alien vessel rocked with the massive impact of that energy burst, sending it hurtling across Luna's surface. Kate lost her balance, and the shock flung her hard against the transfer platform. Her head smashed into a corner of the table, and blood poured out of her nose and ears. Her vision blurred and high-pitched ringing in her ears blocked all other noises. Mary slumped against the far wall, unmoving.

Kate spat blood and bile from her mouth and struggled to maintain consciousness. On the screen, she saw grainy images of the *Echo*'s railguns preparing another salvo.

FORTY-SIX

Kate

KATE STAGGERED BACK UP TO THE WALL SCREEN. A gaping distance
had opened between them and the *Echo* as the railgun blasts had
sent the ship flying. Keechik maintained its post at the command
console, knobby limbs flashing in and out of the control input
ports. She wiped the blood off her face with her sleeve.

The creature's amber eyes met hers. "*I am Kate*... must
leave now... mm... the one Keechik and the *friend Mary*... the
holder.. must go..."

Kate felt a sharp pain in her side and her head pounded from
being concussed. Surprising to her, she had no desire any more

to hide and scar herself. That burden had disappeared. "You know I—I can't abandon her. I won't." She knelt beside Mary and checked her breathing. "You're right, though. Another blast from those rail guns and we're finished." She turned toward the alien. "Let her go, and I'll leave with her. Then you can take off to safety and be done with these assholes."

"No, *I am Kate* . . . the friend must come with . . . mm . . . with me."

Suddenly, a flash of light erupted on the wall screen, pulling Kate's attention from Keechik. In an instant, the ship tumbled and spun across the lunar terrain again, yet despite the *Echo*'s aggression, the alien vessel refused to crumble under the force of all that power. When it finally came to rest in the dust, the gap between the two vessels had widened even more. Kate lay prone on the floor. Something had pierced her leg, and the burn tore through her body. Mary, dazed, sat in a heap behind the platform table. She mouthed words, but none emerged.

Keechik's dark moaning grew from the depths of shadows covering his command station. It was the same lonesome song she heard from the creature earlier, and it carried with it a depth of pain the likes of which Kate could not comprehend.

"Alien vessel, this is the *Echo*." Carter's voice boomed in cheerfully. "Braddock, are you there?"

She raised herself into a sitting position and stared at the wall screen. "I'm here. Stop firing on us, you asshole."

"I will not. But it's your lucky day, because despite my personal wishes, there are some on board who would like to see you live. So, I'll give you another chance—your final one—to abandon that ship and return to the *Echo*, no harm no foul. Those first two shots were near misses, Braddock. The next one won't be."

Kate drew in a deep breath and frowned. She peered over at Keechik who stood quietly at the command station, watching her with wide eyes. Its mouth, drawn tight, held what she could only describe as a kind of defiant dignity engulfed in an overwhelming sense of loneliness. As she stared at the creature, she spoke. "We can't leave this ship, Carter. Our deaths will be on you."

The radio crackled. "Ha, you sound like the mewling professor, all self-righteous and moralistic." He paused. "But I'm a practical man, Braddock. I look at what I can do to benefit all humankind, and I'm prepared to make sacrifices for the greater good. Mineral extraction and processing pay for global infrastructure, education, health care. Now you may not like the idea of carving holes in moons and planets and using what God Himself gave us to use, but I see my work very much as a social good for all. That's why I want what's in that ship. I want that faster than light technology. I want to know the composition of that ship's hull that can withstand a Jennings laser cutter's full beam. And I want whatever else you have in there that will improve our place in the universe."

Kate placed a hand on her stomach, then over her chest. Keechik's ability to heal her physically was material manipulation on an atomic level. History was replete with stories about healers who performed wonders with a touch or a word. Was it possible these creatures had some deeper understanding of physics and nature than the rest of us? A vile image arose in her mind of this fragile alien, caged in a corporate facility, being forced to heal all the broken humans with the means to pay for such a service. Yet, if cancers could be eliminated rather than treated, and mental illness healed instead of bandaged up in platitudes, that truly would benefit all.

Carter continued. "I think the problem with you Spacers, Braddock, is that you're so task-oriented, you never see the big picture. Run a survey here. Fix an algorithm there . . . just task after task after task. No vision at all."

Keechik, as if sensing Kate's evolving thoughts, scrabbled alongside her, peering up at her face with large, soft eyes. "No . . . *I am Kate . . . no . . .*"

"But never mind. If you won't leave that bucket and return to the *Echo*, I'll eliminate the obstacle and simply take what I want."

"Murderer!" Kate yelled.

"Emancipator, actually."

Mary stirred in the corner. Kate rushed to her side and helped her up. The blast had bruised her face, but otherwise she was unhurt and Kate brought her back to the wall screen where Keechik rested on his thin limbs. The creature gazed at Mary, then at Kate. It wore an expression of resignation on its face.

Like a human being.

When Keechik spoke, its voice was raspy and guttural, almost a whisper. "I am Kate . . . the one Keechik feels . . . small . . . but you and . . . the *friend Mary* . . . you must leave . . . return to your kind . . . mm . . ."

Mary shook her head groggily. "No, it's too dangerous. When they discover I'm a holder of your knowledge, they'll rip me apart."

The creature moaned long and soft. "You . . . must . . . hide your knowledge from all, *friend Mary* . . . mm . . . but you and *I am Kate* must go . . . must go now . . ." Keechik stared up at them, blinking its amber eyes repeatedly. "The one Keechik . . . is broken . . . will find . . . another."

"Another what?" Kate asked.

"Mm . . . another companion . . ."

Carter's voice boomed on the radio. "Last chance, Braddock."

"Stand by, *Echo*." She envisioned a suddenly plausible future, on Earth, with Mary and Jim, living free and healthy, teaching other Marys and exploring the night skies together. The idea, the promise of it, tingled throughout her body.

What I want.

She gripped Mary's arms. "What do you think? Could you keep your knowledge away from everyone else?"

Mary slouched and thought it through. "I don't know. If anyone found out or suspected . . ."

"I can help. You, me and Jim . . . let's work together to keep it hidden. We'd make it our . . ." she narrowed her gaze and smiled, " . . . our primary directive."

Mary's eyes welled up, and she hugged Kate tightly. Keechik slunk back to its shadows.

"*Echo*, alien vessel. Braddock here. We're coming out."

KEECHIK POKED ONE OF ITS LIMBS IN AN INPUT PORT, and a section of the wall slid open, revealing their two envirosuits. Kate helped Mary get into hers, then pulled hers on except for the helmet. She looked at the creature, slumped in the shadows.

"Where's the, er, access port?"

"Mm . . . no port, *I am Kate* . . . mm . . . dimensional phase shift. I release you . . . one by one . . ."

The soft moans from the creature's corner worried Kate. "Maybe you'll find a friend Keechik, another companion soon. At least your history is safe."

Keechik averted its gaze. "The one Keechik . . . is . . . broken now . . . *I am Kate* . . . broken . . . small . . ."

"Alien vessel, your time's up."

"Stand by. Mary's coming out first, then I'll follow. Braddock out." She gave Mary's suit a final check, then nodded at her and stepped back. Keechik moved its limb in the command console and Mary *blinked* away. In an instant, she appeared outside the ship's hull. She looked around, then bounded slowly, carefully, toward the *Echo*. A lone figure beside the *Echo*'s access ramp raced across the moonscape to meet her.

Jim.

Kate turned to look at the alien. "Keechik, is your ship able to fly?" The creature raised its head slowly, its face covered in a pain that filled the room, and Kate, empathizing with it, knelt down. "Can you fly?"

"Yes, *I am Kate* . . . mm . . . I can leave now . . . mm . . ."

She understood what it meant to be completely isolated, alone and afraid. The years she spent on Luna before Mary came—hell, even before she arrived—were torture. But she couldn't take Keechik with her to Earth.

Still, abandoning this creature would be . . .

She gazed at the wall screen. Jim and Mary embraced like forsaken echoes in the grey and orange darkness. The remaining two astronauts walked out and joined the reunion, quickly embracing them. Above the *Echo* and over the horizon, Earth glowed a bright blue, calling her home like a sailor's candle in a window.

Kate smiled and knew a deep, resting peace that she'd never experienced before. She set her helmet down on the ship's floor, then unlocked the seals of her envirosuit.

"Let's go see."

ABOUT THE AUTHOR

David Allan Hamilton is a writer, teacher, and publisher living in Ottawa, Ontario. He has edited and published numerous collections of stories from writers attending the Ottawa Writing Workshops since 2017, through DeeBee Books.

David has enjoyed a career with the Federal Public Service and has been a contract instructor at Carleton University. He holds a B.Sc. (Honours) degree in Applied Physics from Laurentian University and a M.Sc. in Geophysics from the University of Western Ontario and has undertaken literary studies at the University of Sheffield. His own stories often combine his love of the natural world and the possibilities of science fiction. His first novel, *The Crying of Ross 128*, was published in 2018. This is his second book in that trilogy.

You may wish to contact or follow David at the following:

Davidallanhamilton00@gmail.com
davidallanhamilton.com
deebeebooks.com
ottawawritingworkshops.com

Twitter: @DAHamilton
Instagram: Davidhamilton1261
Facebook.com/ottawawritingworkshops

Acknowledgments

I would like to thank my family for their ongoing support during the writing process. Your encouragement means the world. Also, I have benefitted greatly during the creation of this novel from the writers in the Ottawa Writing Workshops, in particular: Heather Gray, Debbie Bhangoo, Frank Kitching, Mike Marshall, Glen Packman, and Nick Forster. Your early feedback and suggestions helped me immensely.

Thanks for reading! Please add a short review on Amazon and Goodreads and let me know what you thought!

Don't miss the shocking conclusion to the Ross 128 First Contact Trilogy!

Janet Chamberlain, an aging field operative with the Northern Democratic Union—and Jim Atteberry's ex-wife—is compelled to undertake one last mission: to save their daughter Mary from those who will stop at nothing to scrape her mind for the alien secrets she holds. Chased by the ruthless Benedikt Winter of the Prussian Consortium, and coveted by Titanius CEO Clayton Carter, the Atteberrys search for a way to remove the alien Keechik's knowledge that is destroying Mary's brain.

But time is running out . . .

Against a backdrop of increasing global tension and deteriorating peace in North America, Jim desperately pursues a solution while Janet contemplates the unthinkable: kill their daughter to protect the future of all humanity.

As galactic warfare breaks out, the *Echo* is conscripted to offer Mary one last chance at life, but Winter is determined to seize both her and the ship to promote his own diabolical vision of the future. Can humanity survive these final Three Days Of Darkness?

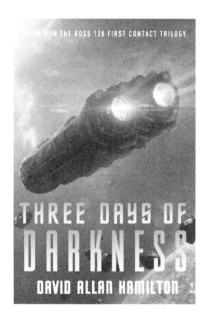

Made in the USA
Monee, IL
23 April 2023

32306053R10256